Growing Old

Growing Old

A HANDBOOK FOR YOU AND YOUR AGING PARENT

David A. Tomb, M.D.

VIKING

VIKING
Viking Penguin Inc., 40 West 23rd Street,
New York, New York 10010, U.S.A.
Penguin Books Ltd, Harmondsworth,
Middlesex, England
Penguin Books Australia Ltd, Ringwood,
Victoria, Australia
Penguin Books Canada Limited, 2801 John Street,
Markham, Ontario, Canada L3R 1B4
Penguin Books (N.Z.) Ltd, 182–190 Wairau Road,
Auckland 10, New Zealand

First published in 1984 by Viking Penguin Inc.
Published simultaneously in Canada

LIBRARY OF CONGRESS CATALOGING IN PUBLICATION DATA
Tomb, David A.
  Growing old.
  1. Parents, Aged—United States.   2. Parents, Aged—
United States—Family relationships.   3. Adult children
—United States—Family relationships.   I. Title.
HQ1064.U5T58   1984   306.8'7   83-47936
ISBN 0-670-11038-8

Grateful acknowledgment is made to Seaver Books for permission to reprint three
lines from E. M. Cioran's *Drawn and Quartered,* translated by Richard Howard.
English-language translation copyright © 1983 by Seaver Books.

Printed in the United States of America
by The Book Press
Set in Electra
Designed by Mary A. Wirth

To My Parents,
Mary Woodring Tomb
and
Alva H. Tomb

Parents, Models, Friends

My mission is to kill time,
and time's is to kill me in its turn.
How comfortable one is among murderers.
                        E. M. Cioran,
                        Drawn and Quartered

Since Penelope Noakes of Duppas Hill is gone,
there is no one who will ever call me Nellie again.
                        An Old Lady,
                        The Viking Book of Aphorisms

PREFACE

This book is written for two groups trapped by circumstance: older people and their adult children. For both, life could be better. The elderly are caught between decreasing abilities and resources on the one hand and continuing potentials and desires on the other. Their grown children are squeezed between the demands of their own children and the expanding needs of their parents.

I think this situation can be improved. Being old will always have difficulties. Adult children will remain partially responsible for their parents, and will be called upon to help them just when other demands are greatest. By overcoming misconceptions and ignorance about old age, however, choices become clearer and decisions more sensible. This book provides essential information about the capabilities, deficiencies, diseases, and other realities of the elderly. It is a reflection of the low status of the elderly and their problems within our culture that some of this information will come as a surprise not just to grown children, but to older people themselves.

This book describes the normal process of aging as well as common medical and emotional problems. It shows how to promote good health and prevent illness, describes family relationships, and outlines the realities of housing, finances, recreation, education, the law, and dying. Additional sources of help are also identified.

Old age can be more than we usually allow it to be. It can be a more satisfying time for both the elderly and their children, if they face its potentials and problems knowledgeably, realistically, and with a determination to extract from the later years the best they have to offer.

This book cannot address all the situations or conditions that can occur in old age; it is meant to be used as a rough guide. When in doubt, consult a professional.

ACKNOWLEDGMENTS

No book is the product of one mind. This book reflects the thoughts and convictions of the many families, older individuals, and professionals I have been privileged to know. I am particularly indebted to those who have shared with me their concerns about and affection for their aged parents.

I also want to thank my wife, Jane, for her support throughout the writing of this book and for her helpful redirection when I began to sound too "academic." And Kathy Council's careful reading and critique of the entire manuscript has been invaluable; the book would have been considerably different without her help.

Professional colleagues read various parts of the manuscript. Thanks are due Dr. Nick Danforth for his careful evaluation of the medical sections of the book, and Dr. Bernard Grosser for his review of the descriptions of several emotional conditions. Moreover, the support provided by Dr. Grosser, as Chairman of the Department of Psychiatry at the University of Utah School of Medicine, was important in allowing this project to proceed on schedule.

Finally, numerous residents at the Bethany Village Retirement Center in Mechanicsburg, Pennsylvania, made valuable suggestions and corrections to selected chapters. Particularly diligent were Mr. and Mrs. Harry E. Crow, Mr. and Mrs. W. Davis Graham, Mrs. Mildred Greer, Mr. and Mrs. Joseph Harbage, Mr. and Mrs. Edmund Tomb, and Mr. and Mrs. A. H. Tomb. Chuck and Esther McGarr of Sun City, Arizona, also carefully reviewed several chapters. I thank them all.

Errors of commission and omission are, of course, mine.

CONTENTS

Old Age

1.

Aging Parents and Adult Children

Your parents are growing old. You wonder what that means for them, and for you. Perhaps your parents continue to be active, self-sufficient, and a pleasure. But for how long? Problems may already be developing: illness, mental lapses, financial setbacks, personality changes. You may have problems of your own (college expenses, health problems, a rocky marriage, too many responsibilities, too little energy). You want to help your parents as best you can. But how?

1. *The Crisis.* During our childhood and early adult years, most of us give little thought to our parents' future; we're too busy concentrating on our own. Finally, however, our parents' situation demands our attention.

It may take years to notice that your parents aren't the persons they once were. They may begin to fail in almost imperceptible ways. He or she may find the family finances harder to manage. Names of friends or football scores from the previous weekend may slip your father's mind. Your mother's hand may shake as she lifts her fork or she may become short of breath during the walk to the store. Eventually, these accumulated failings can no longer be denied—your parents have become old. The day you realize that your parents need support can create a personal crisis for you.

On the other hand, change may come suddenly and produce a sudden crisis. One of your parents may have a stroke or heart attack. One of them may be injured in a fall and never recover. He or she may develop cancer. When such sudden change occurs, the rules which have long governed your relationship with your parents are suddenly abandoned, and new rules must be forged. The lives of both parents and children are changed irreversibly.

Whether this crisis is slow or sudden, and whether it occurs when your parents are 60 or 90, the result is the same: you and your parents switch roles. You begin to look after them, to worry about them, even to supervise them. You lose your protectors, and become one instead. Such a change is often unexpectedly difficult. You may find yourself unready for this and react with anger, anxiety, resentment, or guilt. You will have to come to grips with the crisis that old age often creates in the life of a family.

2. *Coping with the Crisis.* For both you and your parents, the problems and pleasures of old age are best approached with knowledge and a realistic attitude. This book focuses on the former in order to provide you with the latter.

To understand what your parents are experiencing, you should become familiar with the expected changes due to age. Although you may be convinced that old age is a period of decline and dissatisfaction, it's not—at least, it doesn't have to be. Most elderly people enjoy a comfortable, pleasant, and productive old age. They are capable of doing more, and doing it longer, than younger persons usually think. Thus, you should understand normal aging before you relegate your parents, figuratively, to the dustbin.

Although normal aging produces only minimal limitations to former abilities, the diseases of old age can be devastating. Serious physical or mental problems should not be ignored, since any major incapacitation is probably caused by disease. Find out what diseases are likely to occur in your parents and learn to distinguish their symptoms from those of the normal changes due to age. Help your parents to recognize them and to seek treatment early. Although few diseases can be easily cured in later life, many can be controlled, and not interfere with an active and enjoyable life. Work with both your parents and their physician to be certain that treatment is optimum—it can often add to the active years in your parents' life.

However, you can't do everything. You must be realistic about your own strengths and capacity to help. At times your parents will seem a burden. At times you will become angry—at them, at other family members, at yourself. At times you will become resentful or guilty. Expect it. Do not be too hasty to accept sole responsibility for your parents, particularly if that responsibility is likely to be demanding or last a long time. There may be other ways to help provide the necessary care. You must learn to set limits to your duties and obligations. If you don't, you will become exhausted, and no one will benefit.

Part of being realistic is recognizing that you have other priorities.

Your finances may be limited or your health shaky. You may have children at home or, if they're grown up, be in need of that long-awaited break. You may have been putting off going back to school or changing jobs until the children were grown. It is only natural to balk at assuming full responsibility for your parents. Although they may need considerable aid, you must temper your sense of obligation and love with a realistic appraisal of your own goals and limits. To pretend that your parents' care is your first priority when it isn't is the surest route to anger, resentment, guilt, and demoralization for both you and them. .

3. *Living with Old Age.* Most elderly are content, in spite of gradual failures. However, that contentment usually comes only after the elder person evaluates his or her changing abilities and makes a shift in priorities. The elderly come to realize that old age has its own pleasures and rewards, and that previous expectations and desires no longer make sense. They can feel good about themselves, even though past goals are unfulfilled. Moreover, they *must* develop this sense of self-esteem if their later years are to be satisfying.

You can help your parents explore what they want. You can encourage them to remain active and to develop new interests. You can get in touch with their feelings and help them to understand the new life that presents itself in old age. They should understand the myths of old age as well as its realities, so that they can make sound choices. You can help them make a new place for themselves within the family and the community based on these new realities. Although the very old are no longer independent, they are still of value. Help them find ways to contribute and appreciate their own worth, since only then will old age be satisfying.

4. *The Very Old Parent.* A very old and very frail parent may benefit little from all your efforts. Some people, usually during the last year or two of their lives, reach a point where they have no reserves left. They may have to be hospitalized or placed in a nursing home. They may give up trying, no matter what you do to motivate them. If you have done your best—and have determined that there isn't a treatable illness causing their decline—try not to feel guilty. Sometimes they are just worn out.

2.

In Search of the Elderly

The world of the elderly is changing. Their numbers and living conditions have altered during the past several years, and the pace of that change is accelerating. To understand the problems (and advantages) your parents will face, you must understand what it is like to be elderly today.

5. *Young Old versus Old Old*. It takes longer to become old today than ever before. Your parents slip into their 60s and then their 70s and you wonder when they are going to start looking and acting old. Your parents wonder also. They feel good—perhaps they're a little slower or less sure of their footing or slightly hard of hearing—but they feel like themselves rather than like old people. As the talented octogenarian Malcolm Cowley notes, it takes the sight of an eightieth birthday to convince many people that they are no longer middle-aged. Scientists, taking this trend to prolonged middleage into account, have begun to speak of the "young old" (under 75) and the "old old" (over 75). Ignoring even these arbitrary limits, some remarkable individuals continue to act "young old" well into their 80s.

There are many reasons for this change. Older people are healthier today than ever before. Although more than 80 percent of the elderly have a chronic illness, only 5 percent are so incapacitated as to require long-term hospitalization or an institution. Life has become easier. It is easier to get around, easier to prepare food, and easier to obtain help. An infirmity which in the past would have house-bound an older person may now be only a minor irritation. Illnesses previously fatal or incapacitating are now readily controlled. People are also less likely to have impaired their health as a result of prior illness or injury than in the past when the population was more rural, the work more hazardous, pregnancy and childbirth more risky, and good medical care less available. Physically, the elderly *are* younger.

They are also younger psychologically. As the stereotype of the dull, infirm 70-year-old has been gradually replaced by the more accurate picture of older citizens who have considerable capabilities, your parents have become free to "act their age." The result has been an explosion of creativity, activity, and enthusiasm among those elderly persons who are not discouraged by the realization that they can't do quite as much as before. Most elderly are increasingly likely to stay healthy, active, vigorous, and involved well into their 70s and even their 80s.

Where do your parents fit in this changing spectrum of possibilities? What should you expect from your parents and when are you asking too much?

6. *How Many People Will Live to Old Age?* The elderly are the fastest growing segment of the population. The proportion of those over 85 is increasing most rapidly, followed by those 75 and older, with the 65–74-year-olds a close third. In 1900, the 3 million people 65 and older made up 4 percent of the population. By 1980, that figure had climbed to 11.3 percent. Population experts are able to predict with almost eerie accuracy the number of elderly in the future. By the year 2000, there will be 32 million people 65 and older, or over 12 percent of the population. In 2020, when the World War II "baby boom" children are old, approximately one out of every five or six persons will be in his or her retirement years.

The effects of this shift in the age of the population are profound. Public and private services for older citizens are proving to be inadequate, as are some pension funds and Social Security. Poverty is a reality for many people. Mandatory or arbitrary retirement is often a heart-rending practice, as larger numbers of talented 70-year-olds are able to work, want to work, and badly need to work. Health care is frequently unavailable on a regular basis, and there are too few professionals trained in the problems of the elderly. On the other hand, as stereotypes break down, the elderly are increasingly recognized as having greater abilities than they were previously credited with. The political clout of the elderly is growing, and they possess, as never before, an ability to lobby in their own behalf. They have even developed a few sophisticated communities to provide them with a high quality of life. In short, the increase in the number of elderly is forcing significant social and physical changes across the whole of society.

7. *Who Will Live to Old Age?* How long will your parents live? Might they even outlive you? These awkward and frequently painful questions must be considered in order to plan sensibly for the future. Life expectancy can only be estimated; but a review of some of the many factors which influence length of life allows some rough guesses.

Census statistics provide a crude but useful approximation of the average life expectancy. Although life expectancy at birth in the United States has risen from 48 years in 1900 to 73 years in 1976, the difference is primarily due to a decrease in infant mortality and thus has little relevance to your parents. Much more important for our purposes is today's estimate of the life expectancy of a person who is now 65, 75, or 85 years old. A person who has battled to the age of 65 is a survivor. When a man now 65 was born, he had a fifty-fifty chance of living to age 60. Today, he has already outlived more than one half his peers. This hardy individual, who has already proven his mettle, is likely to live many more years. Your parents, just by being old enough to be the parents of an adult child, have already won the battle of "survival of the fittest."

Current data from the United States Census Bureau suggest the following approximate life expectancies:

AVERAGE REMAINING YEARS OF LIFE

Person of age	Male	Female
65	14.5	19
75	9	11.5
85	5.5	7
100	2.5	3

In the information provided by the Census Bureau, the word "average" complicates things. The table given here identifies at least one of those complications—women tend to live several years longer than men. Although men are more likely than women to die from accidents, war, or those diseases which result from smoking or drinking, the major reason for the difference in mortality rate appears to be that women are biologically tougher. They survive infections and illness better. Their system deteriorates more slowly, making them less susceptible to heart attacks, heart failure, and strokes. As a result, men die sooner and in greater numbers. Women make up 60 percent of all persons over 65, and by age 85, outnumber older men by more than two to one. Your mother is likely to outlive your father and to spend many years as a widow with most of her friends also widows. More than one-half of all elderly women are widowed, whereas only 15 percent of elderly men are widowers.

Race plays less of a role in determining life expectancy among the elderly than might be thought. Although blacks and Hispanics are more likely to die from a variety of causes during their younger years, their life expectancy in old age is identical with (or slightly longer than) that of the white population.

Heredity is important—longevity tends to run in families. Your parents are particularly likely to be long-lived if their brothers and sisters, parents, or grandparents lived to advanced age. These lucky ones inherit healthy organs which run down slowly, as well as relative freedom from life-shortening conditions such as atherosclerosis (hardening of the arteries) and heart disease, high blood pressure, and diabetes. Of course, your parents may have spent a lifetime undoing their lucky genetic breaks by eating too much, exercising too little, smoking, or doing any of the many other things which trim years off life. On the other hand, prudent living and careful attention to chronic medical conditions like diabetes and hypertension may compensate for a person's unfortunate genetic inheritance.

Most elderly people don't just grow old and pass away—they die from specific diseases. More than half of all older people die from diseases of the heart and blood vessels and another 20 percent die from cancer. The heart has been considered the weakest link in the aging human body, but in recent years, for the first time, deaths from heart diseases have begun to decrease. Unfortunately, at the same time, cancer deaths have gradually climbed so that these two are still the chief killers. Other common causes of death include lung diseases like pneumonia, complications from diabetes, and accidents. However, your parents' lives may be shortened by any other serious illness.

A host of other factors can shorten (or lengthen) the life of your parents by directly impairing their general health, by contributing to the development of a fatal disease, or by affecting their "spirit." Life expectancy tends to shrink when any of these are chronically present:

    obesity
    poor diet
    a very rich diet
    excessive alcohol (or drug) use
    smoking
    exposure to heavy pollution
    a decrease in brain function (senility)
    poverty
    work which is too exhausting

    excess emotional stress or a high-strung (type "A") personality
    lack of good health care
    feeling lonely and useless

Correcting these conditions or habits can pay benefits in both longer and healthier lives. In contrast, life is normally extended by:

    happiness and a sense of satisfaction
    physical activity and outside interests
    determination—a refusal to give up
    having an accepted place in a community
    a higher level of education
    a higher IQ
    marriage (if happy)
    readily available, good health care

Many of these factors are discussed at greater length in subsequent chapters.

In spite of all precautions, no one lives forever. The oldest person whose life span has been carefully documented was a woman from New York who lived to be 113 years old. The claims of Russians to ages greater than 150 years or of inhabitants of Vilcabamba, Ecuador, to life spans in excess of 120 years appear to be false. Even with the best of inheritance, care, and luck, whether at age 80 or age 110, life ends. Inevitably. The body simply wears out. Kidneys filter the blood less well and the heart beats less strongly. The liver and lungs lose their efficiency. The brain becomes smaller. Even if one of the major diseases does not strike, a minor illness, which would have been tolerated easily in earlier years, proves overpowering and fatal. Thus, some elderly don't die of particular diseases—they simply die of old age.

8. *What Kind of Health Can the Elderly Expect?* Even though good health is more common today and the stereotype of the infirm elderly person is clearly inaccurate, perfect health in old age is the exception. Major diseases are common, as are chronic illnesses, physical problems due to normal wear and tear, and infections of all types. One out of every four people admitted to a hospital in the United States is over 65. Your parents are likely to suffer from one or more common medical problems such as diabetes, asthma, bronchitis and emphysema, arthritis and other joint problems, liver disease, eye and ear problems, high blood pressure, pneumonia, severe depression, and senility. These are in addition to cancer and heart disease. Thus the majority of older persons can expect to have to

wrestle with several different diseases during their 70s and 80s. And they usually do so exceptionally well. Of the 85 percent with a chronic illness, only 40 percent must give up activities, 8 percent must stay at home, 2 percent must stay in bed, and only 5 percent need chronic care in an institution. Most elderly persons spend fewer than eight sick days in bed each year, on the average. In addition, injuries are less frequent—though, if your parent has an accident, expect him or her to spend more than the usual number of days in bed recovering.

It is only by age 80 that the reality gradually approaches the stereotype. By age 85, physical problems have forced almost half of individuals to stay at home. They may not be acutely ill but they have trouble getting around and are thus no longer fully independent.

9. *Where Do the Elderly Live?* Most elderly live where they have spent most of their adult lives—in the same neighborhood, community, and town. They are even less likely to move if they are living in a house that is paid for and have friends nearby. However, in recent years, the warmth and vigor of the sunbelt states have lured many older couples, making the elderly populations of Florida, Arizona, New Mexico, and Nevada the fastest growing in the country. Large retirement communities such as Arizona's Sun City flourish. In spite of the attraction of warm climates, a greater number of older people remain in the northern states. In fact, almost 40 percent of the entire United States' elderly population live in seven northern states: New York, Pennsylvania, Illinois, Ohio, Michigan, New Jersey, and Massachusetts. Like the rest of the population, the elderly gradually collected in the central cities and, recently, in the suburbs. Even those older people who live in rural areas are more likely to be found in towns rather than on farms. This pattern is understandable when you realize that large communities, in spite of problems like crime and poverty, usually have essential resources not found elsewhere, such as ready transportation, access to shopping and medical care, availability of part-time work, and closeness to family.

The last twenty years have seen the growth of retirement communities and low-rent public housing designed primarily for the elderly. In most cases, these special living arrangements, particularly when they form a true community of their own or are comfortably absorbed within the surrounding community, work well and provide pleasant places to live. However, only a few elderly live in such places—most of them live in the general community.

Two out of three older people, whether married or alone, live independently in a home they either own, are buying, or are renting. The majority own their own homes—only one third are renting. This stands in stark contrast to the caricature of the elderly as completely dependent on family and friends for support. In fact, only about 10 percent of the elderly find it necessary to live with their immediate family, and then usually only when they have reached their "old old" years. Another 5 percent live in institutions, predominantly nursing homes. However, that 5 percent is a deceptive figure, since a much higher percentage of the very old spend their last months or a year or two in nursing homes as their physical and mental capabilities fail and they are no longer able to be maintained at home, even by the most loving of families.

10. *With Whom Do the Elderly Live?* As life winds down, changes inevitably occur in the family. The vast majority of 65-year-olds are married. Most live as a couple, while a few still have children at home. Since there are more widows than widowers, fewer than one quarter of elderly men will experience a life alone, while one half of women find themselves living alone by age 75. Of the several alternatives open to a widow or widower, the most commonly chosen is to spend one's remaining years by oneself. Fortunately, living alone is more possible today than ever before, since many elderly have better health and increased economic independence, and find it easier to travel to close relatives. Although the death of a spouse precipitates a rapid failure in a few, occasionally requiring institutionalization, more common responses to the death of a loved one and to the likelihood of a life alone are to move in with family or with a friend. Depending on the people involved and the circumstances, either possibly can work out well or poorly.

As can be expected, there is a variety of living arrangements in people who are very old. Approximately a quarter of individuals over 85 years of age live with one of their children and about the same number live in nursing homes.

11. *How Well Do the Elderly Live?* In many ways, the quality of life can be measured by the level of income—enough and life can be pleasant; too little and life is hard. Most elderly have enough, some are well-to-do; but 20 percent are poor. For that bottom one fifth, many of whom are poor for the first time, Social Security, Supplemental Security Income (SSI), Medicare, food stamps and other supports are not just valuable but essential. For most of the rest of the elderly, finances are of constant concern, but lack of money does not determine whether or not they have lunch, take a bus, or spend a winter's day with the heat off. Widows and other single elderly, particularly if they are very old, are most likely to be poor and in urgent need of financial help. Is your widowed mother's pantry well-

stocked or empty? Does she not go out because she lacks bus or taxi fare? Does pride keep her from asking for help?

Many elderly consider retirement a blessing, but many want to work. Age discrimination is a reality in employment. Even though the older worker has been shown time and again to be productive, relatively accident-free, and reliable, he or she may find it extremely difficult to get a job. About 20 percent of men and 10 percent of women over age 65 are employed, mostly as white-collar or part-time workers; the number working drops off rapidly as they age further.

One of the most significant changes in the status of the elderly in coming decades will be in education. The level of formal education will have risen dramatically by the year 2000, from a median of nine years of school to almost twelve. This should have a profound effect on the quality of life available to the elderly since they should be significantly better able than their predecessors to deal with a complex society.

3.

Growing Old—
Physical Changes

Physical capabilities inevitably wane. Your parents' abilities diminish, their features become coarse, their muscles weaken. You watch them grow old, suffer with them, and anticipate your own decline. How inexorable is this deterioration? What are normal and expected changes and what are signs of illness?

What is most striking is the great variability in physical decline and age of death. Some people maintain good health into their 80s and 90s; others don't. Only some of these individual differences are explained by inherited longevity, good diet, good habits, good health, limited stress, and luck. We neither fully understand why so many people live longer today nor know how long people will eventually be able to live and in what state of health. Better nutrition, control of infectious diseases, and modern medicine provide only partial answers.

It is not always possible to distinguish the deterioration of old age from the deterioration of disease. Many 80-year-olds have blood sugar levels high enough to require treatment for diabetes if they occurred in a younger person, yet the elderly do not appear harmed. Is a painful hip an expected age change in a 75-year-old or a sign of degenerative arthritis? Is hardening of the arteries a disease or is it inevitable? These are questions without ready answers. In spite of this uncertainty, it is essential to recognize the presence of treatable disease in your parent. One way to do that is to become familiar with the normal physical changes of aging and to know when changes are out of the ordinary. In that way you can help your parent remain as active and vital as possible—whether he suffers from a chronic illness or from the ravages of time.

CHANGES IN APPEARANCE

12. *Skeletal Changes.* Physical stature depends predominantly on the shape of the skeleton and the condition of the bones. Both change gradually throughout life but more rapidly during the last decades. Ultimately, the older person is left with changes in his frame which may cause loss of function, chronic pain, and the gnarled look of the very old.

Aging bones gradually lose their calcium, become weakened, and fracture easily. Why this occurs is not completely understood—there are several causes, including hormonal changes, decreased exercise, and limited calcium absorbed from food. This loss is inevitable. It may be slowed by increasing physical activity and eating foods rich in calcium, but it can't be stopped. It is also generally more severe in women, often causing them to look bowed and worn before their husbands do. Along with changes in bone comes thinning and deterioration in cartilage, the tough but smooth gristle which separates bones and allows joints to work smoothly.

Your parents become shorter, perhaps by two or three inches, because the spine has shortened. As the cartilage thins, the discs between vertebrae become narrower. The increasingly fragile vertebrae may compress. The spine may bend forward, producing the shoulder hump so common in older women. The bones in the hips gradually widen, the shoulders narrow, and the joints in the knees, hips, neck, and lower back become rough, stiff, and painful. These changes may become evident first in the late 60s and the 70s, although there is enormous variability. The person who has experienced these changes is not only shorter and more bowed, but also has difficulty walking because of stiff, painful joints. He may fracture weakened back, hip, or leg bones with even minor falls.

13. *Cosmetic Changes.* Our physical appearance is primarily controlled by the shape of our skeleton, the amount and location of fat and muscle, the character of our skin, and our facial features. All these alter significantly during later years, so that our outward appearance may take on an unanticipated form. Your parents may have difficulty reconciling the incurving cheeks, sunken eyes, slender and hairless legs, and narrow shoulders that they see in the mirror with their life-long self-images.

The elderly become leaner and fatter simultaneously. They lose fat from their arms, legs, neck, and face, giving them wrinkled arms, thin legs, and indented cheeks. They gain fat and thicken in the hips and body.

Overall, they gain fat, though their overall weight usually decreases because of muscle and bone loss. Although this shifting around of body fat makes little difference in how well they can function, it makes an enormous difference in how they look and thus how they feel about themselves. For many, the picture of the rounded, elfish old woman or old man is uncomfortably accurate.

Other changes also occur. Hair becomes grayer, finer, and scantier—both on the head and body. This is often more traumatic for women, particularly if they appear to be balding. They may, in embarrassment, wear a wig. Elderly women are also troubled by a sometimes substantial growth of chin hair, requiring shaving. The speed at which hair whitens is an inherited characteristic and is not slowed by a peaceful life or hurried by a stressful one. If the teeth are lost, the jaws may gradually become shorter and smaller—occasionally altering the appearance dramatically and making dentures hard to fit. Ears may become longer, the nose may become flatter, and the eyes may be depressed in their sockets. The skin wrinkles because of the loss of elasticity and the loss of the underlying layer of fat. Wrinkles are more pronounced where the fat loss has been greatest and where there has been long-standing damage by the sun—usually the face, neck, and hands. Oil glands in the skin stop functioning, causing chronically dry skin. Blemishes, in a rainbow of colors, appear: liver spots, moles, bruises, and poorly healed cuts and scrapes.

Muscles not only help create the body's shape—they make it move. Unfortunately, muscle size and strength decrease with age. Arms, legs, and shoulders become slimmer. Our parents look more frail. Physical tasks they could once do easily are now difficult or impossible. This is particularly difficult for someone who took great pride and satisfaction in physical strength and vigor. Happily, these changes are not completely irreversible. A sensible exercise program can help the elderly to remain energetic and spry almost indefinitely. It is vitally important that an older individual remain physically active, since "If you don't use it, you lose it."

INTERNAL CHANGES

14. *Heart and Lungs.* The brain may sleep, the muscles relax, and the intestine lay quiet, but the heart never rests. For 70, 80, 90, or more years it is ceaselessly in motion. Even more remarkable is how well it serves our needs, even in old age. If healthy, a 90-year-old heart beats with nearly the same slow, steady pace that it did fifty years before. It is only with exertion, such as rushing to catch a bus or climbing stairs, that the evidence of aging appears. The aging, less efficient heart must beat much faster than when it

was younger to meet such demands. With the years, the heart becomes thicker, stiffer, and weaker, but it can still meet normal needs. And even an old heart becomes stronger and more efficient with regular exercise.

Unfortunately, the majority of older people in the United States do not have healthy hearts. Most have some hardening of the arteries, particularly the arteries that supply the heart. This atherosclerosis tends to weaken the heart and may cause chest pain and panting on exertion. Marked difficulty exercising, panting with exercise, or pain in the chest, neck, or arms should be considered warnings that something *may* be amiss, and a physician should be consulted.

The lungs, like the heart, are constantly at work—endlessly being blown up and deflated. However, they usually show more effects from this ceaseless wear and tear than does the heart. The tiny air sacs which make up the lung become frayed and less effective; the lungs become stiffer and more difficult to inflate; and the chest wall hardens. It becomes harder to take a deep breath and less air reaches the inner lung with each normal breath. However, these expected age changes usually do not keep an elderly person from being energetic. The problems arise when these normal effects of aging are combined with a life-long history of smoking or of breathing polluted air. This double dose of damage can at times incapacitate an older person and produce lung disorders such as emphysema or chronic bronchitis. Furthermore, although the healthy aging lung continues to meet the demands placed on it, it is extremely susceptible to infections such as pneumonia. Even a mild case of pneumonia can cause a major impairment in your parents' ability to breathe comfortably and meet their needs for oxygen. Any infection in an older person that "goes to the chest" is worrisome and should be looked after carefully.

15. *Kidneys and Bladder*. Kidneys filter the blood to control the amount and concentration of various substances in the body and to remove many of the body's waste products. With age, the kidneys get smaller, filter less blood, and are less able to remove waste material efficiently. Fortunately, because they have ample reserve capacity, this change is seldom a problem. However, when one of your parents becomes ill, the kidneys may have difficulty clearing the extra waste or handling any additional fluid that he or she may be given in the hospital. Also, the aging kidney is less able to keep necessary water in the body, so dehydration can be a major problem—particularly for the elderly person who loses fluid through diarrhea or fever. Finally, many medications are removed from the body by the kidneys. Since the aging kidney does that job poorly, an older individual who continues to take the normal dose of a medication may have it gradually

collect in the body. If one of your parents is taking medication, be aware that some physical complaints may be signs of excessive medication levels in the blood.

The bladder may also present problems. A surprisingly large number of elderly persons sometimes wet themselves. This can be a most exasperating problem and the source of much embarrassment and depression. By the time a person reaches 70, the bladder is less expandable, often contains a puddle of urine because it doesn't empty completely, is less sensitive to being full, and gives less warning before it starts to contract. Women may have more problems because the structures that control urine flow have been stretched and weakened by pregnancy. Men have their own cross to bear—the prostate gland. The prostate, which surrounds the tube that empties the bladder (the urethra), enlarges with age in 90 percent of men. It can gradually squeeze the urethra shut, causing the bladder to empty only with difficulty. In 10 percent of men, this condition must be treated surgically. Treatment of wetting with training, medication, and surgery may be helpful to some individuals of either sex.

16. *Stomach and Intestines.* The gastrointestinal tract extends from the mouth to the anus and includes the esophagus, stomach, small intestine, large intestine, and several other structures such as the liver, pancreas, and gallbladder. Its main job is to digest and absorb food and turn it into energy. It does that surprisingly well, even in very old age, yet there are a few problems which are extremely common.

The task of getting food from the fork to the stomach has several hurdles in old age. (1) Your parents' teeth may be in poor shape, making food hard to chew into a manageable size. (2) The sense of taste in general declines, causing most food to taste similar and bland, thereby taking much of the fun out of eating. (3) The secretion of saliva slows. The mouth and tongue become dry (which may cause halitosis), and food is much more difficult to swallow. (4) The muscles of the esophagus, which automatically and rhythmically squeeze food down the tube through the chest and into the stomach, become less efficient. Food takes longer to get to the stomach and may even get stuck midway. It becomes increasingly difficult to eat while lying down or sitting back—without help from gravity in forcing the food down there is a real risk that something may get stuck at the back of the throat, causing your parent to choke. All these changes make eating more difficult and less pleasurable, creating the danger that your parents may pay less attention to an adequate diet and become slowly malnourished.

Once in the stomach and intestine, food is digested well. There, age causes several changes which don't usually impair digestion but which may give rise to intestinal diseases in the elderly. The stomach cells which produce acid gradually wither away in some people, increasing the risk of stomach cancer. The pancreas produces less useful insulin, and thus many older persons have an elevated blood sugar level, a condition which resembles diabetes mellitus (sugar diabetes). Gallstones collect in the gall-bladder in as many as 30 percent of people over 70 years old and occasionally require surgical removal. The large intestine may develop small outpouches, or diverticulae, which can become painfully infected (diverticulitis).

Perhaps the most common physical complaint among the elderly is chronic constipation. Because the older large intestine is less active, food tends to collect in it and become exceptionally dried out and thus very hard to move along. Unfortunately, constipated elderly individuals may seek relief by trying three methods that usually make things worse: using laxatives regularly; decreasing fluids; increasing consumption of soft foods. Foods rich in fiber often help, but constipation that doesn't improve should be carefully evaluated for more serious and possibly life-threatening medical conditions. An additional and embarrassing problem for people as they reach their 80s and 90s is loss of bowel control. Often the muscular sphincter around the anus is weak and stool is allowed out during "mental lapses." Fortunately, many people can be helped by correcting chronic constipation and by treatments such as biofeedback.

17. *Endocrine Glands.* Endocrine glands, located in different places throughout the body, produce a variety of different hormones which then circulate in the blood to help control bodily conditions such as blood sugar, body temperature, and blood pressure. Surprisingly, as complicated as this system is, it works quite well in the older person. Some of the hormone levels in the blood may decrease with age, but in general the system stays in tune. There are three major exceptions—falling hormone levels allow blood sugar to rise, bones to become fragile, and menopause to occur. (The first two have been discussed above.)

Menopause is the most dramatic failure of the endocrine system. It begins when the ovaries stop producing estrogen and progesterone. As the levels of these hormones in the blood fall markedly, many changes in the female reproductive system occur, including loss of menstrual periods, decrease in the size of the uterus, narrowing and drying of the vagina, and loss of hair. Many women are also bedeviled by hot flashes, which often continue for years. Psychological symptoms such as irritability, sleeplessness, and depression are frequent as well, and may have a partly biological basis.

Older people are less active sexually, but the reasons are usually social rather than physical. The few physical changes that occur should not interfere with an active sex life. Although women who have passed menopause are no longer fertile and have drier membranes, they should still be able to enjoy sexual activity. Likewise, men can still develop an erection, though not as rapidly or frequently as before. (Impotency in a man in his 60s or 70s may have a physical cause, such as diabetes, high blood pressure, prostate trouble, obesity, or the side effect from medication.) However, the major reasons the elderly do not engage in more sexual activity are that they feel ashamed and unsure of themselves, have decreased desire, or have no available partner.

18. *Blood Changes.* A healthy older person should have no abnormal changes in his blood. Anemia is fairly common among elderly persons but is always abnormal. Anyone, regardless of age, who is shown by laboratory tests to have significant anemia should be carefully evaluated medically, since illness, poor nutrition, or some other condition is probably present. On the other hand, the immune system, that collection of specialized cells and antibodies in the blood which fights disease, grows weaker with age. It is not known why this occurs, but older individuals have a more difficult time recovering from common illnesses like pneumonia and influenza. Likewise, cancer may be more common in older persons because the immune system is less capable of recognizing and destroying early cancer cells. Poor resistance to disease makes it important that the elderly receive immunizations during epidemics and that they be treated promptly and thoroughly when ill.

19. *The Nervous System.* Brain cells and nerve cells are not replaced once they have died. Cells in all parts of the brain are being lost throughout life, so that an older person has millions fewer brain cells than he did when young. But the importance of that loss is not clear. The thought of all those cells being lost, in the brain of all places, is probably more frightening than need be. There is no convincing evidence that the loss of a moderate number of cells makes a crucial difference in normal brain functions.

There are no common, serious defects in an older person's nervous system that are clearly due to this inevitable falling away of cells. There are, however, normal changes with age in the function of the nervous system, which appear to be due to slowness and inefficiency in the central processes of the brain. Movements are slower. Balance is not as good and hands aren't as steady as before. Coordination loses its edge also, so it becomes harder to master new tasks or games, although if one of your parents is already skillful at some activity that requires complicated movements that skill may remain. As the complexity of the task and the demand for speed increase, the older person's physical performance worsens markedly. The smooth, rapid, automatic responses of the young are absent. However, if speed is not important and there is time to practice, most elderly people can perform the most complicated movements well. Competing with your father at an unfamiliar video game will probably yield you an easy victory, but beware of challenging him to a game of pool.

The skin may become less sensitive, particularly to touch, and some elderly people may be less conscious of some kinds of pain. Finally, your parents' awareness of and automatic control over internal body temperature may markedly diminish. For example, he or she may develop a life-threatening chill in a cold room without being aware of it—and the older person's body may not readjust the temperature upward. Whenever possible, encourage your parents to be comfortable by adding or removing clothing or adjusting the thermostat.

Though elderly people encounter many changes in their nervous system, most adapt well and only rarely are these alterations incapacitating.

20. *Sleep.* Many older persons become worried that there is something wrong with their sleeping patterns. They notice that they sleep less and sleep less soundly. They awaken briefly but frequently throughout the night. Although they may feel rested in the morning, they find themselves napping for a few minutes during the day. Often the most difficult problem this presents for the family or physician is to convince the older individual that these "symptoms" are normal. The elderly do sleep less and do wake up at night—and that is perfectly normal. It is a problem only if the person is unnecessarily concerned about these changes or if sleep becomes so shortened or broken that it is a true sleep disorder. The important thing to remember is that if your parent feels rested for most of the day, his or her sleep is probably adequate.

CHANGES IN SENSATIONS

21. *Vision.* Very few older persons escape some loss of vision. They may require brighter lighting, have difficulty seeing objects close to them, have trouble with glare, lose much of their peripheral vision, or even be temporarily blinded when going from the dark to the light. Most often they suffer a combination of these problems. The physical changes in the eye that cause these symptoms are usually slow but obvious in their development.

Light passes a series of hurdles as it makes its way to the retina at the back of the eye. It enters the eye through the transparent cornea and then passes through the anterior chamber, the pupil (the dark opening surrounded by the colored iris), the lens, and the transparent vitreous body (which occupies most of the space within the eye) before striking the light-sensitive cells of the retina. Each of these obstacles becomes greater with time. The cornea becomes flatter, thicker, and more irregular. The pupil becomes smaller and more resistant to dilation, even when darkness makes a larger pupil essential for sight. The lens usually undergoes the greatest changes: it becomes less flexible, which makes focusing difficult; it gradually develops a yellow color that lets less light pass; and it is prone to develop cataracts. Finally, the light which does reach the back of the aging eye strikes a retina which is aging itself and is thus less capable of good vision.

All of these predictable physical changes in the eye impair sight and help us understand the following:

1. The elderly have marked difficulty seeing clearly in dim light. Reading with a low-wattage bulb may become nearly impossible. An older person may fall after missing a step in a dark hallway. The label on a pill bottle on the dark shelf of a medicine cabinet may be misread.

2. It can take many seconds for an elderly person's eyes to adjust upon stepping outdoors into the light or upon entering a darkened theater.

3. Not only do objects seen from the corners of the eyes become more indistinct, but the size of the field of peripheral vision shrinks. This makes the elderly parent more likely to bump into projecting pieces of furniture, to be struck by objects from the side, or to fail to notice approaching cars while driving.

4. Most people in their late 40s, 50s, and 60s begin to need glasses for reading. However, as many people pass into their 70s and 80s, their sight becomes less sharp at all distances and glasses are required for most situations.

5. Although several of the vision problems of the elderly can be improved with better lighting, light which is too bright or too direct often produces that nemesis of elderly sight—glare. The older eye develops numerous irregularities and imperfections which scatter entering light to produce glare. Objects become hard to make out in direct sunlight when there is bright reflected light, such as that from a water surface or a mirror, or when there are major light-dark differences, such as those encountered during night driving.

6. Because the structures of the eye are becoming stiffer, the elderly have particular trouble focusing on a moving target and are at a disadvantage when trying to identify something moving rapidly through their field of vision.

7. As the lens of the eye begins to yellow, older individuals have difficulty distinguishing certain colors—first blues, greens, and yellows, but,

by the 90s, even oranges and reds may be lost. Everything may take on a yellowish cast.

8. Most people in their 80s and 90s have some deterioration of the cells of the retina, so that even if the rest of the eye were perfect some loss of vision would occur. In very old age, retinal degeneration may make it difficult to improve vision even with the best of glasses and eye care.

Even though most of these changes gradually occur in the eyes of all older persons, their extent and the degree to which they impair sight vary enormously from one individual to another. People usually have functional eyesight throughout most of their old age. In addition, many sight difficulties can be improved significantly by the use of glasses, magnifiers, and large-print books. Unfortunately, as vision problems increase, it becomes more difficult to find the right combination of lenses and lighting.

Two eye diseases which occur frequently in old age, glaucoma and cataracts, are not normal changes of old age. They need to be recognized and treated promptly (see Sections 213 and 214).

22. *Hearing.* Everyone loses some hearing with age. Starting in the 50s and 60s, or even earlier, it becomes harder to hear high notes in music or high frequencies of any type. Gradually, and almost imperceptibly, the loss extends to the lower registers and begins to interfere with everyday communication. In some older people it never becomes severe enough to cause problems, while in others, particularly men, the loss may be incapacitating. This permanent hearing loss (presbycusis) results from a gradual physical deterioration of structures in the cochlea, or inner ear. However, not all deafness is quite so irrevocable: the unsuspected build-up of ear wax, which is common in the elderly, is a frequent cause of hearing loss. A careful check of the ear canal is always worthwhile.

Presbycusis can drag a host of problems in its wake. Deafness is the great isolator. If you can't hear, communication is difficult; it is hard even to make your own needs known. Talking becomes hard work—it is simpler just to withdraw within yourself. Friends and family may begin to stay away—it is equally hard work to talk to someone with a hearing loss. Life becomes more restricted, less interesting, and less enjoyable. Misperceptions and garbled messages encourage suspicions, and a few hard-of-hearing older people become frankly paranoid. Isolation, loneliness, and depression are much too often the lot of the deaf elderly. Presbycusis can also amplify loud noises. Thus a grandchild's minor violation with the stereo becomes a major offense when heard through aging ears. Finally, ringing in the ears is common.

Hearing aids are usually of significant value only when they are carefully adjusted to the particular hearing deficits. This often means that the aid for each ear must be able to be adjusted separately and that the two aids must be maintained in balance. A poorly selected hearing aid may simply increase the noise. Communication with your hearing-deficient parent is improved by speaking slowly and by trying to eliminate background noise. Lipreading and sign language provide some help, but they are much more easily learned by an elderly person before all hearing is lost. There is a real danger that the parent who is gradually losing his hearing will become depressed and withdrawn. Be alert to this condition and take steps to reverse it. (See Chapter 18 for a more complete discussion of hearing difficulties.)

23. *Taste and Smell.* With age, both taste and smell become less sharp—a mixed blessing. The taste for sweet, sour, and salty all decline, making food seem bland and less interesting. Eating becomes more of a chore and it becomes too easy to neglect good nutrition. Spoiled food may not be detected. On the other hand, poor cooking becomes less objectionable to a spouse whose discrimination has declined, and overly seasoned or salted foods may find a willing taker. The taste for tartness remains; thus fruits are favored by the elderly.

Food not only seems less tasty, but its appealing odors are not as easily noticed. A man's sense of smell is usually more severely affected than his wife's, so the aroma of her freshly baked bread receives fewer compliments. Physical danger may increase as smoke or the odor of a leaking gas line goes unnoticed. Your parents may not be aware of an increase in body odor or the faint smell of urine or feces from a dirty bathroom. It is easy to jump to the conclusion that they no longer care about cleanliness when, actually, they just don't notice the smells. On the other hand, your parents may be spared a number of odors that you must endure every day.

4.

Growing Old—
Psychological Changes

Our stereotype of the psychological changes caused by old age is wrong. Elderly people are supposed to become mentally dull—they don't. They are supposed to lose their memories—they don't. They are expected to become rigid, crabby, self-centered, opinionated, timid, conforming, and dependent—they don't. Nor do they become unimaginative, depressed, withdrawn, indifferent, aloof, or distant. They don't ruminate endlessly about the past. They don't constantly nag and wheedle. They don't ramble; their thoughts don't hopelessly wander. Aging, per se, causes none of these. There are, however, marked differences between the "young old" and the "old old." The young old show some evidence of decreased abilities but, in general, still function very well. The very old show more characteristics we associate with old age but, even then, there are remarkable individuals who continue to perform much as they did twenty years before.

A healthy older parent should be vigorous, alert, active, and happy. Memory should be good, interest high, and he or she should have much to contribute to surroundings and family. Changes in thinking, memory, and personality accompany aging, but none of them is usually severe enough to undermine a rewarding old age. Why, then, do we find all too many elderly who fit the stereotype? The reason usually lies with illness, social impairments, or inadequate living conditions which inhibit the elderly from reaching their potentials.

24. *Sudden Behavior Changes Caused by Poor Health.* Be suspicious if either parent shows memory loss, becomes unusually apathetic, or simply doesn't seem as sharp as before. Be particularly suspicious if these changes occur over weeks or months rather than over many years. The most likely explanation is not aging but poor health.

Always consider psychological deterioration as a warning that something may be going wrong physically. Even a minor physical problem can cause a major psychological impairment in an older person. Unfortunately, often no one is aware that your parent is ill. The individual feels good and has no physical complaints. In fact, the only noticeable change is psychological—in the person's memory, mental quickness, or drive. To complicate matters further, your parent may be oblivious to the psychological changes so apparent to you.

If you are worried that your parent's mind may be slipping, inquire about his health. When questioned closely, does he admit to trouble emptying his bladder but just assumed it was normal and didn't want to mention it? Or is your parent often dizzy on rising from bed or a chair but "it quickly goes away so why worry?" Does his heart flutter occasionally or his chest pound? Are there other symptoms that had previously gone unnoticed? Sit down with your parent and ask.

High blood pressure, high or low blood sugar, changes in blood minerals, a "silent" heart attack or "silent" pneumonia, and many other physical abnormalities can all cause an older person to think or act differently. Heart and blood-vessel problems are typical culprits. But don't leave it all to the doctor. If your older relative is showing recent signs of deterioration, insist that he or she receive a thorough physical evaluation. More may be required, though, than just a visit to the doctor's office. A physical examination can give a false sense of security; often laboratory tests and an X-ray evaluation are also vital. Don't accept "just old age" as an explanation until all likely physical causes have been eliminated.

25. *Other Behavior Changes Caused by Mental Illness or Social Isolation.* Old age is not a satisfactory explanation for psychological decline until psychiatric and social causes are eliminated as well. Nothing compromises an older individual's ability to look competent and alert more than a serious psychiatric illness. Although some psychiatric conditions reflect irreversible physical changes in the brain, many others, if treated, can be rapidly reversed.

Depression, anxiety disorders, emotional losses, and even moderate life stresses can produce serious psychological changes in an older parent. Unless these abnormal conditions are recognized and treated, the person may be left to suffer through premature old age.

Equally devastating to older persons and just as likely to cause them to become dull, slow, and vague are the empty lives so many live. Mental deterioration is to be expected after years spent in lonely apartments and after the poor nutrition and limited stimulation that poverty brings. Older persons who live in active and stimulating environments, maintaining close family and community ties, frequently show little of the decline seen in those less fortunate. That some elderly citizens living in such desolate settings are able to remain interested and alert is nothing short of heroic.

26. *Some Behavior Changes Are Normal.* To decide if your parent is showing unusually early or severe psychological changes, it is essential to know what alterations normally occur with time. As a rule, major changes in intelligence, memory, ability to learn new things, motivation, and personality begin in the mid-70s or early 80s. Even then there are amazing individuals who display no significant decline until their 90s. Change may begin in the 60s and early 70s but should not be great enough to interfere with an active and capable life. If your parents are clearly "going downhill" intellectually or emotionally, assume that something is amiss physically, mentally, or socially until you are proven wrong.

27. *Mild Memory Impairment Is Common.* Memory does slip gradually as a person passes through the 50s, 60s, 70s, and 80s. However, many older individuals and their children are overly alert to what they assume is the telltale sign of aging. Dad's first forgotten dental appointment or Mom's first mistake with the grandchildren's names is considered evidence that a new era has begun—old age. Understandable as that reaction is, it is also inaccurate and unfair.

Mild memory impairment is common in the 70s and 80s but it's a peculiar kind of forgetting. One portion of memory is fine—if you stick a fact in, chances are that it will stay. The trouble is getting the information in and then getting it back out. (Formally, this is referred to as impairment in registration and retrieval.) Fortunately, this kind of memory loss can be improved.

The major reason facts fail to become imbedded in an older person's memory is that the elderly are expected to absorb things as quickly as when they were younger. They can't. With age, the memory slows to a moderate pace—but, at that pace, it works fine. Tips for relaxed learning include:

1. Slow down. Make ample time available. Schedule the whole evening to read something important.

2. Overlearn. Read it today and repeat it tomorrow. Whether it is a

new friend's name or an appointment with the doctor, write it down and look at it several times. Say it out loud so it is both seen *and* heard.

3. Concentrate on one thing at a time. Many elderly people can't tolerate the demands of divided attention and end up remembering little if they're distracted. So arrange for a quiet place to read the paper or to learn new things.

4. Relax. Nothing compromises memory like the fear of failure. It often helps to be reassured that some failure for everyone, young or old, is to be expected.

One's memory does not become "full." New things don't push out older knowledge. Contrary to popular wisdom, younger people are better than the elderly at remembering things from the past. The surprising 70-year-old recollections of some older individuals happen because those memories have occurred to them many times over the years—they have had practice remembering them. Elderly individuals have an enormous amount of information stored away, but frequently it is not available, particularly on the spur of the moment.

Two tricks that can tease buried information out of an aging memory are:

1. Time. Memories emerge slowly, but they do emerge. The young can expect memories on demand, while the elderly may have to wait seconds, minutes, hours, or even days for their appearance.

2. Expectation. A person is much more likely to remember something if it is expected of him and if the person is not worried about these lapses.

In short, a healthy older parent should have a memory that is only slightly less efficient than that of a younger person. To utilize its full potential, however, he should take sufficient time in learning and recalling, should carefully select the time and place for learning, and should be encouraged to view forgetting as only temporary. Most of all, neither you nor your parents should view the appearance of occasional memory lapses as the beginning of senility.

28. *Intelligence and Learning Need Not Diminish.* Perhaps the greatest misconception by elderly parents and their children is that age is inevitably accompanied by mental slowness and senility. With good health and a stimulating environment, intelligence changes little with age. In fact, some aspects of intelligence, such as verbal ability, often increase through the 50s and 60s. Certainly we can find many persons in their 70s and even 80s who are as sharp as most 20-year-olds. These older people think clearly and deeply and can reason as accurately as people half their age. So why do we equate age with dullness?

Once again we mistake a qualitative difference for a quantitative one. The elderly are often highly intelligent, but work at a slower pace. They require more time to mull over and mentally "play" with information before drawing conclusions, but their answers are no less accurate. Unfortunately, many older individuals are severe self-critics. They accept the negative images of old age and give up much too easily. The result is a poorer performance than that of which they are capable. They cease reading serious books, stop involving themselves in complicated political issues, and shrug their shoulders over their taxes. A less satisfying life almost invariably follows this self-denigration and withdrawal from previously important activities.

What's more, not only can the elderly think clearly and creatively, but they can learn new things as well. Persons in their 70s have timidly enrolled in college classes only to discover that they easily kept up with, or outpaced, their classmates. People develop new careers late in life. Elderly people have conquered the complexities of modern photography, triumphed over the home computer, and mastered the intricacies of the internal combustion engine. They can change in completely unpredicted ways—developing interests in art, music, pottery, home construction, science, social problems, politics. Republicans may become Democrats. Democrats may become Republicans. Learning and growth does not stop with retirement, or widowhood, or wrinkled skin, or white hair. However, as with memory, the rules for success change.

Once again, the elderly tend to be their own harshest critics. What they have to realize is that their learning powers are diminished very little, but they must change their approach. You can help your parents interrupt the vicious cycle in which their expectation that they will fail to learn or will not understand or will be confused becomes a self-fulfilling prophecy.

1. Be certain your parents are in good health, mentally and physically.

2. Make them aware of your confidence in them. Encouragement and the expectation of eventual success is the glue that holds the learning effort together. Because they are worried about their declining powers, elderly people become anxious and overcautious when approaching something new. The first couple of mistakes may cause them to back off. Do whatever is necessary to reduce the likelihood of early errors. Encourage them to answer or act when they are ready and not to feel forced or hurried. Although they may become discouraged at first, once they have some skills under their belts, many elderly will proceed with bulldog tenacity.

3. Help them become aware that speed in understanding something new is a poor measure of intelligence. They should plan to take more time

to learn something. Their learning may be slow but complete, so they shouldn't become discouraged if it isn't mastered until the second time through. (Or the third. Or the fourth.)

4. Encourage them to select topics that are interesting or which have direct relevance to their lives—the dull and unessential are learned poorly. Like most of us, the elderly have a limited tolerance for unimportant exercises and generally do better concentrating on something meaningful. They may easily master the complexities of their health insurance coverage but fail miserably at understanding the intricacies of a television game show.

5. Advise them to work on bite-sized pieces. Break a task into its logical parts and master one at a time. A first page of instructions should be mastered before the second is tackled. Many older persons are fond of certainty, and do best if they are sure they understand one step before they move to the next.

The elderly, then, need to be assured that significant intellectual failure is the exception rather than the rule. Although IQ changes become more frequent in the 80s and 90s, the best protection against premature decline lies in remaining engaged—physically, socially, and intellectually.

29. *Activity Is Important.* Most elderly who remain active, interested, and happy find ways to work around whatever declines they experience. They don't submit to old age but consider it a hurdle to be overcome. They should schedule their time carefully and conserve their energy so that they are fresh for important activities. They should plan and anticipate rather than sit and wait. And by approaching tasks vigorously, some are capable of enormous productivity, even very late in life. In fact, selected individuals show essentially no decline in work or creative output, even though they are in their 70s or 80s. These persons are unusual but they are the exceptions that disprove the "rule" of a pointless old age. Even for the majority who prefer to approach their later years at a more relaxed pace, it's encouraging to realize how much potential exists.

30. *The Passion for Living Does Not Dwindle with Age.* Enthusiasm, curiosity, motivation, and the desire to be creative do *not* naturally dwindle with age. Although the passions, drives, and emotions of age are more tempered than those of youth, with good health and the right circumstances most people find their older years interesting and thoroughly satisfying.

With stimulation and appropriate interesting challenges, most older individuals will remain involved in life and will continue to function at a surprisingly high level. However, in our society, old age automatically brings with it fewer opportunities, both social and occupational, and thus we typically see boredom, irritability, frustration, and demoralization. This resignation and withdrawal from life is not an inevitable result of aging. With support and encouragement, most bored elderly people eagerly participate in significant and creative activities. In senior citizen centers and meaningful community groups we see the drive and motivation of which the elderly are capable.

Too much stimulation and too many changes can also cause the elderly to withdraw. They are often overly cautious until they are sure of themselves. They may find excessive novelty or exorbitant challenges too threatening and stressful. This tendency to approach new things slowly needs to be taken into consideration when you help your parents plan activities. Don't force them to change completely overnight—let them warm up to new things gradually.

31. *Perceptions of Time Don't Change.* Both young and old people have the sensation of time flying when they are actively engaged in or preoccupied with a task. On the contrary, bored and frustrated elderly describe the unpleasant feeling of the moments dragging by in endless succession.

However, the way we mark time does vary. When we are young, we calculate our age by the number of years we have lived—the time since our birth. As we age, we make an almost unnoticed shift to calculating by the time we think we have left—the time until our death. We also tend to think of our spouse and friends from the same perspective. (Some of later life's greatest shocks can result from having been far wrong in our figuring.)

32. *There Is No "Older Personality."* People are as different from one another at 80 as they are at 20. Older people do not uniformly become quiet and dependent, or argumentative and complaining, or aggressive and hostile. In fact, personality is amazingly stable and consistent over time. A warm, nurturing young mother is likely to be an affectionate grandmother, while a demanding, inflexible father may become a rigid old curmudgeon. A person who is adaptive when young is more likely to adapt well to the changes of old age. The past is the best predictor of the future.

In spite of the stability of personality, many older persons may change their style and their interests. They frequently become more introverted, more thoughtful, more devoted to their inner world. In addition, some elderly become more cautious and more reluctant to make decisions or to bring things to a conclusion. Often they shift interest from ambition and achievement to humanitarian concerns and the well-being of family members and friends. However, an active and demanding life style may make these changes less likely.

With aging, a fascinating change often takes place—the psychological differences between women and men gradually disappear and even occasionally reverse. Men who throughout their lives have been aggressive and dominant become more nurturing and social, while women become more assertive, domineering, and egocentric. Because they start from opposite poles, the two sexes frequently meet in the psychological middle. Dad, who previously had the deciding say in most important matters, begins to take a back seat to his wife. He plays with the grandchildren and she manages the bank account. And they are both comfortable with the change.

It is possible to adapt to old age in many different ways. One person may isolate himself almost completely and be perfectly happy, although that is unusual and usually occurs in a person who has always preferred his own company. Another individual may need to be frenetically social. Happy older people are usually active, involved with a small group of friends and family, concerned with the problems of others and moderately introspective and thoughtful. On the other hand, there is a royal road to unsatisfactory later years—passivity. The parent who lets decisions be made for him or her, who is socially inactive, and who withdraws from activity runs a serious risk of chronic unhappiness and of "withering on the vine." Although some formerly active persons are anxious to settle back and remove themselves from the rat race, most ultimately find that they are happiest when in the fray.

Life can play cruel tricks. Regardless of how steady and well-adjusted a person has been, a severe stress or life change can occasionally undo his or her stability. In the process, a new and usually less desirable personality pattern may emerge. Frequently the changes are temporary, but occasionally you have a new and unanticipated parent with whom to deal. Before becoming resigned to an unsatisfactory situation for you and your parent, seek help to be certain that a mental illness is not present.

5.

Growing Old—
Social Changes

33. *Your Parents' World Is Changing.* Stretch your imagination. You must, if you are to appreciate how radically altered the world has become for an older person. We live by certain rules and expectations. We expect people to accept us for who we are; to like us if we are likable and avoid us if we aren't. We expect to get ahead if we work hard and presume that better times lie ahead if we are diligent and careful. We take good health for granted. These "truths," however, are not true for the elderly.

The elderly find themselves losing hold on the social structure which has been their support and has defined their actions for many years. Although they may feel the same, the world doesn't treat them the same. They are retired and have thus lost prestige, influence, and power. Their opinions are discounted more quickly than before, if indeed they are considered at all. People on the street look at them and then through them. Their conversation is too easily dismissed as mere chatter. Impressive social skills are now lost behind a wrinkled mask. Their bodies, their health, and their memories are no longer to be trusted. Theirs is a world in decline. But most of that decline is artificial, a product of the way the world treats them. It is essential to recognize how one-sided are our expectations for the elderly, for only then will we sense what they are up against.

The myths and realities of common social situations are discussed below. They include: retirement, marriage in old age, divorce, remarriage, widowhood, grandparenthood.

34. *Retirement*. On the one hand, retirement is supposed to be an enjoyable, satisfying extended vacation—our reward for a lifetime of work. On the other hand, it raises the threat of permanent inactivity and uselessness, and is reputed to plunge a hard-working person into despair. Neither view is accurate, although the picture is generally more positive than negative.

Retirement is a major marker in the lives of most men and many women. Not only does it signal the end of working life, but, in this culture, it often is considered the start of old age. However, most of the problems it brings are not due to retirement itself, but are caused by the discrepancy between the kind of life a person had been living and that which awaits him or her when regular work is given up.

Life changes radically for most people on the day of retirement. Demands on them decrease sharply, as do their responsibility and authority. Income falls, often by more than half. Their time is free—or empty. The accustomed cycle of work and leisure is gone. Although most people look forward to retirement, many are ill prepared for the enormity of the day-to-day changes they encounter. Some people ease into retirement smoothly, while others are at loose ends within days. Still others may have a spree of activity and a sense of freedom, and then later conclude that retirement was not what they had hoped. Reactions during these early weeks or months may include restlessness, irritability, exhaustion, or depression. Usually, however, unpleasant symptoms disappear and older people adjust to their new life style. Give your newly retired parent time to develop a new pattern of life, to find new interests and commitments. However, if he or she still has not settled into a new, acceptable pattern of life after several months, it may be time for a professional to have a closer look at the reasons for this distress.

The leading hurdle to a satisfactory adjustment to retirement is lack of money. Your parent may not be prepared for just how scarce money will be, and may find that many favorite activities, the ones with which he or she had anticipated filling the retirement years, must be skipped because they are too expensive. Other people may be undone by retirement because they have made work and work-related productivity their whole life. Anything else may seem shallow by comparison. They may have constructed their social life entirely around colleagues from work, only to have that world evaporate upon retirement. Still other people discover that the increased time at home elevates minor incompatibilities with their spouse into major battles.

Nonetheless, prolonged difficulties are uncommon and usually have identifiable causes which can be corrected by proper planning. The secret, of course, is for your parents to do that planning well before retirement, so that they have a thorough understanding of what lies ahead. They should free themselves of rosy illusions and unnecessary pessimism.

Nevertheless, most people will find retirement to be a pleasant change. Some individuals enjoy quiet and relaxation, while others immediately begin to cultivate neglected interests. Successful retirement, however, sooner or later requires that a person create a new way of life, one that fits changing interests and abilities. The most satisfied people often are those who regard retirement as a new beginning.

35. *Marriage.* We make the most unreasonable demands of marriages. We want them to be invariably happy and smooth. We expect the partners always to work for the good of the family. And we expect the same relationships to hold between the partners in later years as at the beginning. A close look at marriages that have survived thirty or more years shows us how wrong we can be.

Marriage is the crucial relationship for most older people. It is the center of social life and the point around which most human contact revolves. It provides support and stimulation. Even when a marriage has been dissolved by death or divorce, its shadow lingers and alters the perspective of those who remain. However, the marital relationship is seldom blessed with a storybook calm. It is often turbulent and reflects not only the stresses of old age but also the stresses that accumulate whenever two people live together.

First of all, there is no one right way to run a marriage. A relationship satisfying to one couple may be unendurable to another. Your parents' mutual backbiting may have infuriated and baffled you for years, yet they have stayed together. Perhaps you have been astounded by your mother's toleration of your father's laziness, or by the way he ignores her nagging. Few couples form a perfect fit. Invariably, areas of irritation and disagreement develop. Television's image of the smiling white-haired couple in perpetual placid agreement is myth. Although many older people are extremely devoted to one another, most older couples argue, become angry, make up, laugh, and in general act like any other spouses. Of course, they have had longer to perfect their routines and know their areas of disagreement more thoroughly. And their relationship may be more resistant to change. Don't expect your parents' long-standing marital storminess to mellow with the years. Content yourself with the realization that since they have remained married, the marriage is probably meeting enough of their needs to be beneficial.

However, even a happy marriage has a rocky course in old age. Certain problems common among the elderly can stress, and even destroy, a relationship. Poor health and limited finances lead the list. A chronic illness in one parent can force the other to become wage-earner, homemaker, caretaker, and nurse. Such an overload can strain finances and be so time-consuming as to result in isolation and loneliness. The healthy parent, no matter how well-meaning and devoted, becomes exhausted. Demoralization and resentment follow, and the marital relationship is imperiled. Likewise, financial limitations may force your parents into a style of life never experienced before, leading to self-recrimination and criticism of each other. On the other hand, whatever the stresses, some people are drawn closer by adversity. It is difficult to predict how your parents will respond when times get tough.

Besides these common problems, there is an even more important influence on older marriages—time. Most couples are alone together for years or decades after retirement. This may be their first experience with unbroken contact with each other since before their children were born. Moreover, they are different people than when they were younger. Each has changed through the years, and thus their relationship is necessarily different. Old age often provides the first real test of this new relationship. Without the diversions of work and children, some people draw closer, some become more distant. But, invariably, they must make changes in the ways they deal with one another if the marriage is to be a happy one.

How do you know if your parents are working things out? Marriages that are successful in old age have several common features. Equality is the key. Whatever the relationship between your parents has been, in old age they must share the work and responsibilities. There should be a fair division of labor, although that division may be made along new lines. Perhaps your father now does the housework or the cooking. Perhaps your mother pays the bills. Or perhaps they are both happy with the old division. However, mutual satisfaction dies if one person takes care of the tedious work while the other sits or plays.

Continued activity is also important to a happy marriage. Your parents should develop their own interests, be they similar or different. They should experience new things and grow, and should be encouraged in that growing by their spouse. Only when they are continually bringing something new to the marriage can they prevent sterility from creeping into their relationship. Each must be willing to try new roles. Your father should be willing to relinquish some of the activities of his past role, while your mother must allow him to experiment (if he wishes) with new, more "feminine" activities without criticizing or belittling him. Finally, many of the best marriages need help. If the stresses become insurmountable, they must be relieved. If your mother spends all day, every day, caring for your bedridden father, she must find some time for herself. If your mother is becoming demented, your father will need frequent breaks from her if he is to maintain his own health.

The emotional security of a good marriage cannot be provided by any other relationship. Numerous studies have shown that married elderly people are, on the whole, happier. Although the later years can certainly be satisfying without marriage, the benefits of marriage usually greatly outweigh its disadvantages.

36. *Divorce*. Divorce is on the rise among the elderly, for many of the same reasons it has increased among the general population: people are less willing to tolerate an unsatisfactory relationship; people are seeking self-fulfillment (or self-gratification); the social stigma against divorce has waned; and the increase in everyone's standard of living has made divorce financially possible for many. The increasing rate of divorce among the elderly will probably continue, although it is unlikely to become as common as among younger people.

We know that the results of divorce among younger people are mixed. What about the elderly? Does divorce make sense in old age? Sometimes divorce resolves intractable problems; sometimes it is the only solution to a relationship that has never worked. More often than not, however, divorce is an unsatisfactory solution, one which should be approached carefully. Why?

Some people see divorce as an instant cure for long-standing problems. But often the problems lie within a person, and do not disappear along with the offending spouse. The new life is not always rosy; old problems are replaced with new ones. Most serious of all, however, are the hurdles that complicate the lives of most who divorce in old age. For the majority of older people, particularly women, life becomes meaner after a divorce. (1) Isolation increases. The divorced person must actively seek out social opportunities, since he or she usually no longer fits into an existing social network. Unless a person is naturally gregarious, he or she risks sinking into isolation and inactivity. (2) Income is divided. Often the woman receives the smaller portion, or little at all. Health insurance is a particularly serious concern for divorcing women, since many plans are through the husband's employment, and coverage stops for the woman at the time of divorce. She then needs to find an individual plan which will accept her at her advanced age—not an easy thing to do. (3) The emotional support of a spouse, however unsatisfactory, is lost. A distorted, painful relationship is still a relationship: it provides a person with a role to play and a degree of self-validation. (4) The entire family may take sides and some family relationships may shrivel. The number of family members who remain close usually falls. (5) Health may be affected by divorce. In both partners the rates of serious medical problems, mental illness, and death increase after a divorce. In short, divorce may add to your parents' problems rather than solving them.

However, this does not mean that your parents shouldn't divorce under any circumstances—it only means that they shouldn't approach divorce lightly. It is not a ready-made answer to an uncomfortable relationship. Your involvement should be equally circumspect. Just as it is difficult to predict which troubled couple will ultimately seek divorce, it is almost impossible to be sure who will emerge from a divorce happy and unscarred. Let your parents work out their own solutions. Support them, of course, but try not to enter the fray. You should rarely recommend to one parent that he or she get a divorce, and you should avoid taking sides if at all possible. Although their battles may be as hard on you now as when you were young, they are *their* battles. The roots of your parents' disputes may be unknown to you and the battles may meet needs unsuspected by you. If your parents' distress has become overwhelming to them and to you, encourage them to see a professional therapist. A marriage of decades, however troubled, deserves a careful review.

37. *Remarriage.* One positive effect of recent changes in our social standards is that the elderly feel more comfortable remarrying. The prejudice against late-life marriages is being replaced by a healthy willingness to consider whether or not they will increase happiness.

Whether your parent is single because of divorce or death, you will probably have some soul-searching to do if he or she begins to talk of remarrying. Because you still have loyalties to both parents (even, or especially, if one is dead), you may reject out of hand the notion of your parent's remarriage. Don't—in doing so, you may be spoiling a major source of joy and satisfaction for your parent's later years. Moreover, there is nothing inherently disrespectful to your other parent—living or dead—in such a marriage. It may be viewed as a tribute that your parent wants to repeat such a relationship. And don't conclude that your disapproval is of little consequence to your parent. When it comes to remarriage, the opinions of family members may encourage the marriage or prevent it. Approach remarriage with an open mind and with your parent's best interest at heart.

Why remarry? The reasons, of course, are as varied as the people involved. A desire for companionship is by far the most common. Many people just are not comfortable living by themselves and want to continue the role of husband or wife they have learned so well. The elderly may also remarry for financial or physical security or to have a home of their own.

Some, not surprisingly, marry for love. Although sexual attraction is usually of lesser importance, the desire for physical closeness is often vital, and is poorly met save through a husband-wife relationship. There are also some less respectable, if understandable, reasons for remarriage: desire for a big inheritance, search for a lifetime nurse, or marriage by rebound.

Like any other kind of human arrangement, remarriage may or may not work out well for your parent. When it works, your parent may be noticeably happier, become more active and social, and show improved physical and emotional health. When it doesn't work, he or she will have to contend with a new set of problems. One problem your parent should never have to face is a relative saying "I told you so."

You and your parent should think carefully about remarriage before the decision is made. You both should understand the motives for wanting to marry and your reasons for objecting, if in fact you do object. Are the reasons for remarriage sound? Do they withstand interested (but not antagonistic) questioning? An older person can get married on impulse like anyone else. The possibility of marriage, at any age, deserves a thorough review, and you are a logical participant in that discussion. Do you object to a marriage out of loyalty to a parent no longer present? Are you worried about being responsible for another elderly person? Do you believe that your parent is being taken advantage of, is assuming problems that he can't handle, or is appearing foolish? Or are you worried about losing your inheritance? It is hard for many children to view their parents' prospective spouse as anything but an interloper and, at times, a fortune-hunter. Don't deceive yourself about your less charitable feelings or motives; only when you face your real motives for objecting to remarriage can you help your parent make a good decision.

A late-life remarriage can be a good idea, even a stunning success. Besides the problems found in any remarriage, however, there are two hazards which make such a marriage particularly risky: poor health and little money. These problems must be singled out beforehand for special attention. If your parent or his future spouse is in poor health, he should consider carefully before deciding to get married. Health can change rapidly during the last years of life. A person who is teetering on the edge of a serious illness may become an invalid shortly after vows are taken. In that case, married life may not be what either person expected. This is not to say that such a marriage should not occur, but rather that one must take a realistic look at the future. Financial problems can be just as serious. Does your parent have enough money to get married? Most pensions, Social Security, and health insurance programs reduce benefits after remarriage. Women are frequently so penalized. Often, two can live only more expensively than one. Your parent and his prospective spouse should count where the dollars will come from and where they will go before tying the knot.

Your inheritance can be protected, if your parent wishes. Several useful legal mechanisms include wills, trusts, and prenuptial agreements. Consult an attorney. Such secondary, but important, concerns should not blacken your relationship with your parent, the spouse, or the new spouse's family or interfere with their late-life happiness.

38. *Widowhood.* Becoming a widow or widower may be the most severe blow your parent can suffer. The most common emotional reactions and ways of coping are detailed in Chapter 9. However, several points are worth making here.

1. Death is a consequence of life. One of your parents can expect to be left alone by the death of the spouse. Most commonly, your mother will be widowed.

2. Your parent's response to the loss may be difficult to predict. Don't be surprised if he or she "falls apart," even if your parents' relationship had appeared somewhat cool. Forced independence and the loss of life's predictability can be devastating to someone who has long been sheltered. On the other hand, mourning may be brief. Your parent may be left with a feeling of freedom and release from responsibility, particularly if your mother had spent months or years nursing an invalid husband. Be careful, however, that guilt about feelings of relief doesn't create problems.

3. Widowhood forces your parent to face a new reality and establish a new balance in life. Most widows adjust. Some remarry. Others band together and form a community of single persons. Whatever path your parent chooses, the completeness of that adjustment depends to a large extent upon personal qualities, needs, and energies. If your mother has always been dependent and has viewed herself as inadequate, she may tolerate independence poorly and look to you as a replacement for her lost husband. Be wary of being your parent's solution to the loneliness of life alone.

39. *Grandparenthood.* Forget everything you have heard about grandparents. The gray-haired, rocking-chair granny and the wise old grandpa with a twinkle of fun in his eye are myths. Nowadays grandparents are likely to be in their 40s, 50s, or 60s. They are likely to still be working and to be worrying less about their grandchildren than about their own parents, your children's great-grandparents. (In fact, great-grandparents are more likely to fit the grandparent stereotype.)

Like everyone else, grandparents differ. The only thing they have in common is grandchildren (or great-grandchildren). Some grandparents are in their 40s; others in their 80s. Some live in the home and see their grandchildren every day; others visit only on occasional holidays. Some enjoy their grandchildren; others don't. Some contribute experience and wisdom; others contribute little. Don't do your parent the disservice of judging their performance as grandparents by the stereotype.

What is the reality of grandparenthood? Is it meaningful to your parent? Is it valuable to your children? Two of every three older people enjoy being grandparents. Some find it to be one of life's great experiences, better even than raising their own children. But they enjoy it for different reasons and in different ways. Some visit once or twice a month, play with the children, and leave with a rosy feeling and youthful shouts of pleasure behind them. Others enjoy being the master storyteller (and may be the only one with the time to do it). Others may wish to be a teacher of the old values or a disciplinarian. However, many older people find that the road to becoming a respected and valued grandparent is difficult and requires time and hard work. Still others are interested in their grandchildren, but want to keep in touch at one remove, through your reports and stories. They may find that the charm of a visit wears off after several days and may prefer being a distant presence. A number of other older people have little real interest in their grandchildren and expect to be involved only in case of disaster. Finally, many older people display a mixture of several of these styles. Moreover, the style they are most comfortable with may change with time.

There is no right way to be a grandparent. You must allow your parents to develop their own approach. That individual style may work splendidly and brighten your parents' later years. Think of the gift the grandparent receives: a chance to watch and participate in the growth of a child, a child who is his own flesh and blood. He or she also may receive unconditional acceptance and affection, and have an opportunity to love in return. A grandparent's contribution to the child's well-being can be important, and at times vital. And, all this can occur without the day-to-day responsibilities of raising a child. The grandparent can have the best of both worlds.

However, do not be dismayed if your parents' enthusiasms lie elsewhere. They may prefer the company of people their own age who share their interests. Most older people find their peers to be their greatest source of daily support. They may find toddlers too exuberant and school children tedious. Teenagers may have little time for grandparents and they for teenagers. They may feel too young or too busy to accept the role. Grandparents may appreciate grandchildren only after they have matured.

These likes and dislikes generally reflect your parents' longstanding temperaments and should come as no surprise to you. A person rarely turns into a storybook grandparent upon the birth of a grandchild unless those characteristics were already present. Don't disparage your parent if he or she rejects grandparenthood or finds it awkward. Such a rejection is not a fatal flaw in one's character, but rather reflects a personal style and a time of life. Many people grow to be more willing grandparents in their 70s and 80s. Unfortunately, their grandchildren may be adults before they are ready to be grandparents.

But what value are grandparents to their grandchildren? Again, this varies with the people involved. Young children are generally more accepting and uncritical of their grandparents, while teenagers may see them as dated and out of touch. By the time these children reach their middle 20s, they often conclude that the grandparents have much to offer and listen more respectfully. Of course you determine to a large extent your childrens' attitudes towards their grandparents. If you speak fondly of your parents and treat their opinions with respect, so will your children.

Grandparents can have a major impact on their grandchildren's lives. If your relations with your children are troubled, or if the home is disrupted by divorce or tragedy, grandparents may provide refuge and support and may develop a particularly close relationship with them. Several scientific studies have revealed that, particularly where contact has been frequent and close, grandparents help determine the values, opinions, and ideals of their grandchildren. Often they transmit a sense of family continuity and history better than anyone else, an appreciation of family tradition that serves the grandchild well throughout his life and gives him a feeling of place. In general, contacts between grandparent and grandchild are more supportive and trouble-free than almost any other family relationship. Encourage them.

What are the pitfalls? Predictably, problems can arise from three sources: you, your children, and your parent. (1) You must respect your parent as an independent individual. If he feels taken for granted as a baby-sitter, house-watcher, or gift-buyer, friction will develop. Let your parent select the level of involvement. Nothing will sour enthusiasm faster than a sense that he or she is being taken advantage of. Keep your dealings with your parent on an adult level (see Chapter 7). Don't replay old battles if your parent deals with your children as he or she used to with you. (2) A young, active child may exhaust your parent before you are aware of it, so be alert. An older child (usually a teenager) may have accepted the negative cultural stereotype of the elderly and may refuse to reciprocate affection. Slow speech may try the child's patience and wrinkled skin may put him off, and the child may make these feelings evident. Intercede when appropriate. (3) Your parent may create problems in the effort to be a grandparent. You may feel he or she interferes with your child rearing.

GROWING OLD—SOCIAL CHANGES

Perhaps your parent countermands your instructions, spoils the children, or is too severe with them. If so, discuss it adult to adult. Only rarely is it necessary to lay down the law. However, that should remain your final option. A more serious problem may occur if either of your parents is compromised mentally or physically. Relations with grandchildren can easily become strained if a grandparent is confused, uses poor judgment, is paranoid or profoundly depressed, is frail and in need of constant tending, or is dying. Seek professional advice for complicated situations which involve psychiatric or medical illness.

Grandparenthood can be one of the most delightful and fulfilling of life's experiences. Do what you can to help your parent take advantage of it.

6.

The Elderly Are People Too: Relating to the Aged

40. *Ageism.* We think ourselves enlightened and fair-minded, certain that we long ago exorcised those twin demons of prejudice, racism and sexism. But a third demon afflicts us—ageism. Ageism refers to prejudice against and stereotypes of the elderly solely because of their age. Open or disguised, it is present in almost every person and in most of our institutions. Only the most callous among us admit to not liking older people, but all of us, at one time or another, act as though they are less than acceptable. The irony of this prejudice against old age is that it finally forces us to turn on ourselves—we become the victims of our own scorn. Even as we exercise our biases, we are aging, and the artificial hurdles we place in the paths of the elderly will be there some day for us to overcome.

Few cultures or societies have been free from prejudice toward the old. Ours is no exception. We see it in that cultural weathervane, television, where the elderly are all too often portrayed as bumbling, obtuse clowns or as dull incompetents. In spite of a few recent accurate accounts of old age by the major television networks and such superlative programs for the elderly as "Over Easy," our older people continue to "star" primarily in commercials for hemorrhoids, indigestion, and insomnia. The age for mandatory retirement has been extended to seventy, but that such a limit even exists reveals that we think age more critical than skill to performance. We equate speed with quality in our business life, and demand youthful performers. Airports and bus stations require rapid steps and accurate hearing if we are to avoid being made to feel a nuisance. Only the most courageous elderly are willing to ignore an unwritten social taboo and appear at that temple of the young, the public beach—as though the sun's warmth and sea breezes did not agree with aged skin. In a thousand little ways, the elderly are put in their place.

Our cultural biases rest on a solid base of individual biases. We expect the elderly to be kindly and docile or stubborn and argumentative and are surprised to find someone with a more complex personality. We are taken aback if an idle observation to our elderly companion at a lecture or a play produces a contrasting and, heaven forbid, thoughtful opinion. We expect old people to have old ideas when, in fact, they often think more seriously and originally about important matters than many of us. We expect them to withdraw gradually from active life, and we feel betrayed if they choose to remain involved, particularly if they are in competition with *us*. If we enter a room and find it filled with older people, we are likely to assume that we are in the wrong place—as though their interests couldn't be ours as well. Why do we expect so little of them?

We have an image of the elderly, collectively and individually, and have given them a script to follow. Their lines are few and the play is not particularly good. However, they have been practicing for their part since birth and find that the rest of the cast objects if they change their lines, even if they feel the part is not right for them. Often the elderly have accepted the stereotype of old age throughout their lives and begin to question it only when they don't feel the way they had expected to at that age. By then it is too late and they are resigned to playing their assigned part. We can do better than that for our parents. We can recognize that the elderly are not a breed apart—they are individuals who, with encouragement and the right opportunities, will continue to grow and contribute until death. Ageism robs our parents, and ultimately ourselves, of those opportunities.

41. *Talking Down and Looking Down.* It is all too easy to patronize an older person—to call an old woman "dear" and dismiss her with a pat on the shoulder or to refer jokingly to an elderly neighbor as a "dirty old man" when his eyes light up at the sight of someone one-third his age. Harmless enough, we say; but such casually demeaning comments can be withering to an older person who is instantly reminded that he has been devalued. The solution is to get to know the elderly as mature adults—to recognize that inevitable physical changes like wrinkled skin, trembling hands, poor hearing, or slow responses hide, but do not change, the person underneath.

42. *How to Talk to the Elderly.* Why make a special point about *how* to talk with our parents or any other older person? We've been talking with our parents all our lives and see no reason to change our style now. We talk to an older person with respect. Of course. We talk with them as we would with anyone else, of any age. Not necessarily. In fact, although *what* we want to say may remain unchanged, *how* we communicate most effectively with elderly individuals may have to be modified to fit their changing physical and psychological circumstances.

As people reach their 70s and 80s, they often become deaf to high frequency sounds. Although this initially means not hearing the higher notes on the radio or at a concert, eventually it means losing the ability to hear certain spoken syllables as well—particularly *ch, f, s,* and *th.* A person with a moderate degree of old age hearing loss, presbycusis, hears "plea ange an annel in a ba o of a week tart at ha pa ta evan" instead of "please change the channel since the best show of the week starts at half past seven." Communication is obviously compromised. Until an older person's hearing worsens further, we can partly overcome this deficit by speaking slowly, clearly, and close to the ear, avoiding words with high frequency sounds. Ask them which is their better ear. Even at that, our speech may sound garbled. Hearing such disjointed speech is distressing to most elderly. They frequently turn to hearing aids and lipreading for relief, often to be disappointed. A well-adjusted hearing aid may help, but frequently it simply makes the sounds louder but no less distorted. Lipreading may also be of value, but only if the person's companions speak slowly and with ample lip movement. In either case, the success of a conversation depends on our willingness to change our way of speaking.

Impaired vision can present a similar hardship. Any difficulty in reading, watching television, or determining facial expressions compromises our parents' ability to understand all that is going on around them. They get out of touch, both with the world and with their immediate surroundings. We can improve their lot by insisting on adequate illumination and by assuring the best of eye care. Large-print books, a magnifier, and a large-screen TV will help them remain current with the world around them. Our conversations with our parents can be made smoother by sitting in a well-lighted room, a few feet apart and face to face. The facial gestures that contribute subtlety to speech are then noticeable—and our parents will reward us with richer conversation. (For a fuller discussion of the hearing and vision deficiencies of old age, see Chapter 18.)

In addition to compromised hearing and vision, psychological changes may interfere with smooth conversation and with our parents' comprehension. Time gradually impairs our speed of comprehension, but not its depth. Our parents will have increasing trouble quickly making sense of complicated ideas, but, given time, they can usually understand those ideas well. Many older people also tend to become more cautious in conversation—wanting to get it "just right" before expressing themselves. If you expect and demand a rapid-fire conversation, your parent's speech may become uncertain and hesitant, the answers vague and rambling. The more you press on at your pace, the worse it gets. Your parent's potential for communication is achieved only at his or her own pace. Go slowly. Break complicated sentences into their parts and allow time for reflection on each part. Give explanations and instructions carefully; repeat them. Don't look impatient, as though you were demanding an immediate reply—be comfortable with silences. The result of these efforts should be more profitable time spent talking with your parents rather than a frustrating mutual misunderstanding.

43. *Your Interpersonal Style Makes a Difference.* Old age is a chronic state of mild sensory deprivation. Older parents hunger for information and contact. They want to listen and learn. But they also want to talk and be heard. Thus their ideal companion both gives and receives information. You should actively help them sort through ideas and draw conclusions. Smile, pat them on the back, or give them a hug—these are additional ways of making contact and showing interest. If pleased, laugh openly. Be active, not passive. Other styles may be more appropriate for certain individuals, but, by and large, genuine concern and wholehearted, *noticeable* listening carry the day.

Be equally alert to your parents' nonverbal language—the signals they knowingly or unknowingly send by body movements. Be aware that a tremor in the hands or in the voice may represent anxiety rather than age. Does your father wring his hands or is he unaccountably restless? Does he smile little or with difficulty? Does he sit slump-shouldered with a furrowed brow? These are other ways your parent may communicate with you. Sometimes these unspoken messages are vital, reflecting concerns troubling your parents about which they are reluctant to speak. Don't overlook them.

After a lifetime, do you have nothing more to say to your parents? As you have drifted apart, so have your interests. Are you resigned to chitchat, to cocktail party conversation? A relationship based on such trivialities is bound to be mutually unrewarding. Visits become unpleasant and hard to justify to yourself. You can often reverse this trend by identifying and discussing issues vital to your parents—health, finances, the condition of the house, activities they might enjoy, and much more. Bringing them up to date on the neighborhood and the town is important. Discuss issues vital to you or to friends of yours known to your parents. The list of possibilities is endless.

And don't feel their time spent reminiscing is unprofitable. It may become dull for you, but content yourself by remembering that reminiscing keeps your parents in touch with who they are and who they have been and is a major support to self-esteem. Regular reminiscence also helps them work through the numerous losses which besiege them and gives you a path for introducing current concerns. Also, don't belittle time spent together in silence. Just being together is a form of companionship and communication, assuring your parents that they are still of value. Finally, your parents may offer a window to your own identity. They can often help you, better than anyone else, understand how you became yourself. They can pass on the family oral tradition and give you your roots. Reviewing old photographs or family memories can occupy pleasant hours, providing information lost forever when both parents are gone. Has your parent tried to write (or dictate) a family history?

44. *Communicating with a Stroke Victim.* Different problems arise in communicating with the parent who has had a stroke (Chapter 20). A stroke occurs when blood flow to part of the brain is interrupted long enough to injure brain cells. Some cells may gradually recover; others may die and leave permanent damage. Symptoms vary from paralysis to blindness to loss of speech and depend on which part of the brain is injured. When one or more of the language centers is involved, your parent loses normal speech—develops an aphasia. Communication becomes difficult. Your parent may not understand your words or the words he or she reads. Or your parent may know what he wants to say (or write) but not be able to find the words. Or he may suffer from one of the numerous other peculiar ways language can be deranged.

Trying to continue warm, personal relations with a parent who has suffered such damage is exhausting. Just the effort of passing the simplest of ideas back and forth can leave you drained and frustrated. Your parent may be avoided by former friends or given more rudimentary care by nurses and attendants than a person who can speak easily. Thus the stroke victim is likely to become lonely and isolated. That person is also likely to react with frustration, anger, depression, or withdrawal—the struggle is more difficult for him or her than for you. In addition, it is all too easy to assume that garbled speech indicates senility. Don't! Although some stroke victims suffer a significant decrease in intelligence, many are as bright as before. They appear intellectually compromised because the words don't come. Don't treat them as though they neither know nor care.

There are several ways to facilitate communication with a parent who is language-damaged.

1. Mind your manners. Difficult as it may be to watch your parent struggle and fail, try to remain hopeful and calm. Do not criticize, patronize, or show anger, even when your parent becomes angry or abusive. He or she is already embarrassed and disheartened by failure.

2. If the major trouble is in understanding you, speak slowly, use simple words and short sentences, and allow time to digest what has just been said.

3. If the problem is in verbal expression, get your parent to slow down and take plenty of time to answer. Encourage him to keep trying, even if he fails frequently. Be accepting. Be calm. Take occasional breaks. Encourage short answers. If your parent can't find the words, suggest the use of gestures, facial expressions, touch, and pictures.

4. Never give up in noticeable disgust—be an active participant until the conversation reaches a natural conclusion. However, recognize that some stroke victims have damage so widespread and profound that real communication is almost impossible.

5. Your parent may not understand what has happened. Be certain the physician (or yourself) has explained the physical basis of the problem. Assure your parent that he or she is not "crazy."

45. *Communicating with the Senile Parent.* Elderly people who have lost significant intellectual ability and memory (Chapter 11) are frequently hard to talk with. Not only don't they appreciate the significance of what they say, but they may also be confused—about where they are, what they're doing, or who you are. Although genuine communication is unlikely if a parent is profoundly confused, confusion often waxes and wanes. Pick your time. Try to talk in a quiet room free from distractions. Interrupt if your parent begins to ramble. Try to keep your parent looking at you. Whether lack of understanding or confusion (or both) is the primary difficulty, your parent often knows and can describe how he feels, even though he is unclear about what is going on around him.

The other major hurdle to spending time talking with our senile parent is our own reluctance. "It seems so fruitless." "He doesn't seem to understand anything I say." "He doesn't remember anyway." Our parent may not resemble the father or mother of our memory any longer—he or she has become a stranger. Or, perhaps all of your parent's worst personality characteristics have become more marked. All these reasons for neglecting an unpleasant task may be accurate and may represent some of our deepest feelings. Yet even a markedly senile older person can become anxious, depressed, or lonely, and can be comforted by our efforts to maintain contact. As long as our parents can still recognize us, our efforts have value.

7.

Getting Along: Old Age and the Family

You were raised in a family. Your parents cared for you; perhaps well, perhaps poorly. You profited from their strengths and suffered from their weaknesses. They adjusted to your ups and downs as well. You cradle fond memories and you bear scars—so do your parents.

Now that they are old it is your time to care for them. They have changed, as have you. You now have a new relationship with them. Or do you? Do you deal with them as they are, or as they once were?

You will encounter new problems as your parents age. New demands will be made of you. How can you help your parents? What do you owe them? This chapter will help you sort through the welter of forces influencing your relationship with your parents. It should help you better define how you feel about them, and why.

THE FAMILY LIFE CYCLE

Your family is as unique as its individual members. However, as you and your parents age, your family undergoes predictable changes. To learn what to expect is to avoid misjudging crucial events in the later life of your parents and in your relationship with them.

Your parents' family life began before you were born and continues through regular stages to their deaths. In spite of how it appears to you at the time, your childhood and adolescence are only middle chapters in the life of the family. Your parents' world does not end when you leave home, but only enters a new phase. This has not always been the case. In the last century people married and had children late and died comparatively young. Children frequently were part of the household until the end. Nowadays your parents may have lived little more than half their lives by the time you have left home. What is left for them, and where do you fit in?

46. *The Approach of the Empty Nest.* The first period in your parents' life after children occurs during the years in which you are saying goodbye. Perhaps you have left for college and visit only during vacations, or have a job, live away from home, and visit less frequently. In any case, you have begun a new life in which your parents are no longer central. This is usually a time of excitement and expansion for you. For your parents, it is a time of contraction and of facing the reality of the "empty nest." How your parents weather this change depends upon their flexibility, interests, and values. Many (if not most) people find this to be a time of new freedom from past responsibilities and financial obligations. It can become a period of personal growth. Often it is described as the best time of life: "The kids are grown. We love them but we've done our duty and are glad they're on their own. We're still healthy, we have enough money, and we can do the things we've always wanted."

However, for a few individuals, life closes as the last child leaves home. Their children have been their life and the thought of not having someone to work for and live for is almost unendurable. This is most likely to occur among women who have restricted their lives to the roles of mother and housewife. Overinvested in their children, they may attempt to circumvent the empty nest by frequent telephone calls, uninvited visits, a move to the house next door, and other means that force an artificial, and often unhealthy, closeness. Or they may create situations (for example, "deteriorating" health) or inducements (free rent) which assure that one of the children stays home. Such a need for overinvolvement may spring from an insecure, dependent personality, a failure to develop any interests beyond the family, or an empty marital relationship. Occasionally the situation is reversed and it is the child who can't break free of the nest. However such dependency develops, it typically works to the ultimate dissatisfaction of both parent and child.

Fortunately, this kind of dependency is uncommon and usually lasts for only a short period of time. Both parent and child realize that their relationship is unsatisfying. The parent may develop new interests which allow separation from the children to be tolerable, while the child may leave the home or break off contact temporarily. Sometimes, however, a very turbulent parting of the ways may polarize the relationship between parent and child so much that the wound never heals. This is unfortunate since both parent and child usually change in the months or years which follow; it is then two very different people who are available to make peace.

47. *The Approach of Retirement.* The years after the children have gone are pleasant years. The children are out of the home but they return often enough for visits to be enjoyable. (According to the 1980 census, 6 out of 7 children live within one hour of their parents.) The children's news is of great interest, but distance softens disappointments. Finances are sound; careers should be peaking. Long-neglected interests can now be pursued. There is time, but not too much time, to spend with the spouse. Health is usually good and vigor only slightly reduced.

However, change one or more of these features of late middle age and the "best years" lose their luster. During this time, vague outlines appear of the problems that will come to dominate old age. Now is the time to prevent what is preventable through better financial and health-care planning for the years after retirement.

48. *The Years after Retirement.* Retirement is reputed to mark the end of meaningful work and the beginning of a spiritual decline for working men and women—a decline which drags the spouse in its wake. Not so! For the vast majority of working people, retirement is a relief and a joy. The external rules that have governed their lives for so many years disappear, and most people find that refreshing. They can rise when they wish and follow their own whims during the day without fear that someone is getting the jump on them in the rat race. Many elderly would like to keep occupational interests and skills alive by useful part-time work, though few are interested in working full-time, even if they could.

But there are problems during these years, some of which are directly related to retirement. For some individuals, their work has been their life. Their self-esteem may have stemmed from being a producer: the expert bricklayer, a very competent secretary, the top salesperson. They may have trained for years to master a set of skills or an area of knowledge, and their identity has come from performing those skills: they *are* a doctor, or a mechanical engineer, or a lecturer in European history. Or they truly may enjoy their work, and be unable to find a similar activity after retirement. Moreover, complicating everyone's retirement is the sudden loss of a regular income. If poorly prepared for, such a loss can represent a major hardship.

However, stopping work is of secondary importance to post-retirement happiness for most people. More significant is the transformation retirement causes in a couple's life style, their relations with one another, their interpersonal contact and daily schedules. For the first time husband and wife are thrown together all day long, all week long. They must come to terms with that change early or risk growing gradually disenchanted with having one another around. They *must* carve out new roles for themselves since the old roles no longer exist. The husband is no longer the breadwinner who spends all day at the job—he is the man who is constantly underfoot. The wife is no longer the homemaker pulling her fair share of the family load—she is the woman expected to press on indefinitely with what she has always done, while her husband takes his ease. New responsibilities and expectations must be decided on between husband and wife, or resentment and bitterness will result. There is no single correct division of labor, but most elderly couples are most satisfied with an egalitarian system. Even so, it is useful for a couple to plan time away from each other on a regular basis. Visits with friends, university classes, meeting of church groups, or attending basketball games all serve this purpose. As at any age, those who grow the most have the most to share and are the most interesting to be with.

Equally important to a successful retirement is the ability to use time creatively. These are the years to be active and avoid stagnation. These are also the years that see the appearance of physical and mental limitations, although the real impact of those changes are delayed until the 80s and 90s for many people.

49. *The Appearances of Failing Health.* The next stage in the life cycle is ushered in by a long-dreaded deterioration in health. One partner, often the husband, is usually afflicted first. If the affliction is sudden and fatal (as in a heart attack), life may go on for the other partner without long-lasting changes. If the failing health is slow and severe, it can affect every aspect of the lives of both people, constricting all their activities and forcing one to care for the other indefinitely. Previously sound finances can be compromised and a high quality of life may tumble. Physical and mental disabilities are the most important stressors and agents of change experienced by the majority of old people.

You can expect to be drawn in at this point. Few elderly couples are able to tolerate serious disability without help. Most often this means help in finding a physician, in transportation, or in essential housework, but it can also mean help in finding them a new home or having them move in with you. These are hard years for the whole family, years which test the quality of the relationships of everyone involved.

———

50. *Death of a Spouse*. When one parent dies, the rules are instantly changed for the spouse. Usually the wife survives: four of every five women over 75 are without husbands. After the grieving (see Chapter 9), a new life must begin. If, as is often the case, she is in good health, she can expect to live many years, either alone, with a friend, or with a new husband. This time of life may be filled with uncertainty, but also with pleasant anticipation.

When the surviving spouse's health begins to fail, the family usually becomes involved. An older person, alone and with a serious disability, has great difficulty without help. A few elderly persons who are determined to maintain their independence will confront any hardship in order to stay in charge, and in their own home. However, most older people will be receptive to help from the family with home repairs, housekeeping, meals, transportation, etc. Finally, the time may come when it only makes sense for your surviving parent to move. When and if that happens depends on your parent's need and desires, your resources, and your own desires. Often families elect to have their surviving parent live with them instead of in a nursing home or other medical facility. However, many older persons ultimately do spend some time in a nursing home when family skills and resources prove inadequate to meet their needs.

FAMILIES TODAY

If we are to understand what can be expected of our family relationships and are to appreciate how much our family is like or unlike others, we need some basic knowledge about families. We need to rid ourselves of myths about the family which cause us to anticipate the future inaccurately.

51. *Myths and Realities of the Family*. 1. There has never been a golden age for the elderly. There has never been a time when the elderly have been uniformly valued and revered. In most cultures and throughout most of history, they have been tolerated only to the degree that they had power or could contribute to the larger group. Typically, healthy older women capable of domestic duties had a place whereas infirm elderly men did not. Even the rosy image of elderly parents living with loving and admiring children and grandchildren in rural nineteenth-century America is largely myth—even there, respect depended on whether their knowledge of farming was sounder than their children's and whether they owned the farm. Life today may hold more promise for the elderly than it has in the past, but only if conditions are right.

2. Most elderly want to be independent. They do *not* want to rely on

their children for housing, care, or money. Most want to live near their children, but complain that living with them is too limiting. They may disapprove of their children's life style, feel that the home is too noisy and disrupted, contend that their children become too bossy, or simply feel that others in the home interfere with their own pleasures. Only 15 percent of the elderly live with their families, and they are primarily the very old, the very sick, and the poor. Moreover, many of these older individuals are living with their families only temporarily, until they are able to return to independence in the community or until they enter an institution. The dependent and clinging older person is the exception.

3. The elderly do not "milk" the resources—financial and otherwise—of their adult children. People over 65 give as much in terms of money, labor, and emotional support to their children as they receive from them. This is a change from times past and is due primarily to better planning among the elderly and to programs like Social Security, company retirement plans, and Medicare. This mutual economic autonomy makes for improved family relationships. In fact, numerous surveys have noted that older adults feel the greatest aid their families can provide is emotional support and a sense of continuity.

4. On the other hand, the elderly are not abandoned or neglected by their families. Nine out of ten elderly parents see one of their children at least every month, while 50 percent see a child every day. Even when they become frail and ill, their families are willing to look after them: the majority of elderly who are ultimately placed in a nursing home have been cared for in the family home first, and one half of all bedridden older people live with their families. Most commonly it is an adult daughter who accepts her parent into her home. Though a few elderly have no one to turn to when in difficulty, most who do have families remain independent as long as they can and turn to their families only when they need help.

5. The generation gap has been overrated. Much to the surprise of many older parents, grown children often end up adopting the goals and values of their parents. This is profoundly reassuring to many an older person.

6. Finally, most parents and their adult children like one another.

FAMILY RELATIONSHIPS

The presence of elderly parents may present the greatest challenge a family ever faces. Ironically, parents who brought a family into being may stress it to the breaking point during their later years. Their behavior, like yours, can draw a family closer together, or blow it apart. Known obstacles to good relationships within a family exist, whether they are created by you, your parents, other family members, or harsh reality. To recognize these hindrances is to take the first step toward avoiding them.

52. *Obstacles Created by the Children.* 1. When helping your parents through their final years, above all else you must come to terms with your feelings about both of them. Do you love them? Do you like them? Are they your friends? Are you ashamed of them? Are you indifferent? Do you despise them? Although you may find it hard to admit, you are capable of the same range of feelings about a parent as you are about anyone else. You want to care for—and to be known as someone who cares for—your parents. If you don't care or if you don't even like them, you may be crippled by guilt and self-recrimination. To avoid this you must recognize and accept negative as well as positive emotions and try to identify their origins. That you experience bad feelings towards your parents from time to time does not indicate that you are a bad person. The problems and frustrations that elderly parents present to you make such feelings inevitable. Moreover, no parent is immune to such undesirable qualities as anger, greed, and spitefulness—which can produce equivalent responses in you. If you insist on recognizing your honest feelings about your parents and if you reject the fiction that you are the perfect child of perfect parents, your relationship with them is more likely to be a valuable one.

2. Do you love your parents, or your memory of them? Is it hard to maintain a relationship with your parents because neither of them measures up to the person you once knew? The parent who was important to you in your youth no longer exists. Although most of the qualities that endeared this parent to you and those that you disliked are still present in modified form, you must come to terms with someone else, with an old person. It is all right to admit that you preferred your parent as he or she was. However, it is not all right and is usually destructive to compare an older parent continually to an unrealistic standard from the past. Don't feel cheated and resentful if this individual isn't as capable, vital, or in control as before. It is the parent standing before you today, shortcomings and all, with whom you have a relationship.

3. Perhaps you treat your parent as a memory rather than a person because you are frightened. Perhaps you need to have a strong, capable, and ever-present parent protecting you. If you lose that protection, you will feel abandoned and vulnerable. Thus, you treat them as though they were indestructible. You may refuse to take physical complaints seriously. When you visit, you expect to have meals prepared for you, a room with fresh linen, and attention—as though you were home during a college vacation at 18, rather than as an adult child on a visit at 38 or 58. If your car is running roughly, perhaps you'll ask your father to fix it. He may shovel

snow when he shouldn't. Or cut the grass. Of course, many of these activities may be well within their reach. In addition, your parents may want to appear indestructible and will insist on doing some of these things anyway, or they may enjoy doing them to stay active and vigorous. But if your requests and expectations push either of them beyond what is comfortable, make them too tired, or encourage them to feel as if they were failing you, something is wrong. Reflect on your underlying reasons for making the demands you do on your parents. Do they reflect their best interests or your needs and fears?

4. You may become too invested in your parents: too interested in the details of their lives. You may insist on doing everything for them, even when they can do things for themselves. You may want to assume responsibility for the running of the house, or the supervision of finances. Why would you do this before either parent is ready for such "help"? Perhaps because you are eager to be certain that they finally have the ease and relaxation that they have long deserved, without recognizing that what many elderly people need most is meaningful activity and a sense of still being useful. Perhaps because you have misjudged your parents' abilities and expect too little of them. Perhaps because, without being fully aware of it, you have long wanted to tell your parents what to do, to dominate. And how are your parents likely to respond? Unfortunately, too often elderly parents give in and relinquish control of their lives. Such surrendering of authority frequently results in an inability to manage the various other aspects of life, which is not the consequence that you wanted or expected when you took control. On the other hand, the parent who does not surrender authority may find himself embroiled in interminable battles with his children. If you find yourself volunteering to do more and more for your parents, particularly if they only grudgingly consent, examine your motives. It is always difficult to determine when to intercede in your parents' behalf, so try not to confuse their needs with yours.

5. Perhaps the battles you have with your parents are merely extensions of battles ongoing since your youth. Do the issues between you center around your independence or your competence? Do you find yourself doing things for your parents just to prove a point or to prove yourself? If so, you may never have developed the thorough sense of independence and autonomy that we all seek during our adolescence. The unfortunate consequence is that the wrong points are made and the wrong issues discussed with your now-aged parent.

53. *Obstacles Created by the Parent.* 1. Most of the obstacles to smooth, mutually supportive family relations created by children may be presented in reverse by parents. Thus they may not like you, or they may prefer one of your brothers or sisters. They may be most comfortable thinking of you as the child you once were and may attribute qualities to you that are no longer there. (Be careful that you don't try to live up to their dated expectations of you: the child who always makes silly mistakes, the one who does the work the other kids neglect, or the one who never follows through.) They may act as though they are indestructible and in control, making unwise decisions, endangering their physical safety, and creating interminable squabbles with their "interfering" children. Your parents may be overinvested in you, insisting on knowing every detail of your life and providing unwanted advice at every turn. Their preoccupations and misperceptions, as well as yours, can critically impair your efforts to establish a helpful, adult relationship.

2. Certain diseases to which the elderly are prone interfere with close relationships. Some may make your parent less graceful, charming, or likeable. Parkinson's disease gives an older person a stooped, shuffling gait and a rigid, unsmiling face. Depression takes the hope from the voice and the sparkle from the eyes. Dementia gradually steals away the personality, ultimately leaving you with someone unfamiliar. Other diseases may make communication difficult, if not impossible. Both loss of hearing and loss of sight make any older parent harder to reach. A stroke may damage the language centers of the brain and destroy the ability to speak or to understand your speech. A long illness is likely to strain the family's personal and financial resources. These very real impediments to maintaining your relationship with your parents take concerted effort to overcome.

3. Elderly parents are still people, with all the faults of people. They may create dissension within the family by behaving badly. They may be irascible, belligerent, demanding, bigoted, spiteful, distant, or cruel. They may attempt to manipulate their children or play one against the other. They may exaggerate symptoms to get sympathy. They may display the withdrawal, regression, or overly dependent behavior that is common in older people who feel overwhelmed by life. In addition to this obviously undesirable behavior, some elderly people create waves by their continual efforts at independence or change. Your father may grow a beard and go to poetry readings in coffee houses or may insist on riding a motorcycle in heavy traffic. Your widowed mother may decide to remarry or may give up the family home to "hit the road" in a motor home. Although some of your parents' behavior may be worrisome to you, be cautious. Unnecessary family intrusiveness can be a major impediment to the late-life happiness of an older person who needs a continuing sense of identity and separateness.

54. *Obstacles Created by Others and by Reality.* By and large, the "others" who interrupt smooth relations with your parents are your brothers and sisters and other relatives. Problems may arise over everyday things or from the way you feel about one another, feelings rooted in the past. Frequently a crisis in your parents' lives will precipitate, often unexpectedly, a family crisis fueled by present and past conflicts. The result can be a battle which may rage for years, continuing even after the deaths of both parents.

1. The stress of having aging parents may bring out the worst in everyone, or the best. One of your parents may suddenly become ill and need physical, emotional, and financial support. He or she may be chronically ill or debilitated and require daily help for months or years. In these circumstances, the cracks within the family may begin to show. Innumerable decisions need to be made. Who drives Mom to the store? Who helps with the laundry? Who visits every day to check that Dad is all right and to help with a meal? Who helps keep the house clean? Who picks up the tab for the operation? Who manages the finances? Who makes the important decisions? (Who tells the parent of the decision?) If a parent needs to live with one of the children, with whom? For how long? All are tough decisions. Each requires thoughtful coordination among all the children and other concerned relatives.

Unfortunately, all too often the solutions to these problems are settled on almost by accident. The person who lives closest to Mom takes her to the store, cleans the house, prepares the meal, and visits daily. The most well-to-do child pays the bills. The oldest son (or the person who pays the bills) makes the decisions. The oldest (or youngest) daughter takes Dad into her home. These "automatic" solutions rarely work well. Any inherent injustice or unfairness in them invariably leads to resentment and animosity among family members. It is usually much better for everyone potentially involved with your parents' care to meet as a group and mutually agree on individual responsibilities. Certainly no one should be assigned a duty without participating in the decision.

2. The seriousness of the problem the family faces is not the only factor affecting its solution. Just as important are the relationships among family members. It would be ideal if we could deal with one another as equally responsible adults. Unfortunately, that rarely happens. Our perceptions of individuals with whom we have grown up are often distorted. Our understanding of our siblings, and theirs of us, were crafted in the past and may no longer be relevant. Long-buried family memories, and animosities, surface. You may still see your older brother through adolescent eyes, even though you are nearing retirement. Thus you may defer to his opinion unnecessarily. Or you may be the older brother who expects to be listened to carefully and who expects to make the final decision. You may still be

locked in battle with your younger sister for your parents' affection, and may volunteer to help out beyond what is sensible for you and your own family, in part because you have a need to appear prominent in your parents' eyes. Your past role within the family may determine, sometimes unwisely, what role you are "elected" to play during the current crisis. You may be asked, and feel compelled, to do more than your personal resources allow because you have always been the responsible one, Mom's favorite, or the one with "a heart of gold."

The consequences of adapting present behavior to fit images from the past are almost always undesirable. These images are usually inaccurate. Yet we fall into those old patterns surprisingly easily, and make important decisions based upon such unsatisfactory family assignments. Try to identify your historical role in your family. Is it affecting your behavior today? Is it an irritant, perhaps one of which you are barely aware? Is it interfering with close relations with your parent or with other family members? If things have gone seriously awry in your family's relations, consider getting the help of a professional such as a psychiatrist, psychologist, or social worker. An outsider can often identify patterns of behavior that are remnants from the past.

3. As your parents age, the most serious obstacle to maintaining close relationships is likely to be daily reality. The problems become too serious; the demands too great. You may be forced to choose between spending time with your own family and spending time with your parents. There may not be enough money (or time) to go around. You may become drained. If you try to do too much, you risk the understandable resentment and bitterness of your own family. If you do too little, you risk seeing your parents decline more rapidly and withdraw from you in despair. And if you refuse the role of caretaker, you risk feelings of guilt—feelings that are often most severe after the death of your parents, when it is too late to change things. Perhaps there isn't enough money for both your own family's needs and your parents'. Perhaps your brother should give more (you think), but doesn't. As your parent fails, battles rage over who gets the antique dining room chairs or deed to the house. Families have been torn apart over a pair of prized salt shakers missing from the parent's home since the son's last visit. After your parent's death, do you respect the names of each of you that she has taped to the backs of objects in the house? Who gets "stuck" with most of the responsibility for taking care of an ailing parent during his or her final months or years? Who takes him into her (or his) house? How do you reimburse that person for his time and expense?

These questions demand answers. In most families, relationships and events during the parents' final years go smoothly only if everyone is involved in caring for the aging parents. There is absolutely no substitute for sitting down in a family conference, clearing the air, and making plans. However, even in the best of circumstances, inequities creep in. An elderly parent may criticize the person who looks after him, while speaking glowingly of the one living across the country whom he or she never sees. Much to the dismay of their overburdened daughters, many older women expect less and are satisfied with less from their sons. Your brothers may complain that your attempts to clean your parents' apartment are inadequate, without volunteering to do it themselves. The best protection against letting grievances impair your parents' care or your relationship with them is to maintain an open forum with involved family members and to be certain that important problems and feelings are discussed regularly and openly.

Psychological Problems

8.

Emotional Health and Common Emotional Problems

We want our parents to enjoy a happy and fulfilling old age, of course, but are often surprised when this happens. Unfairly, we expect old age to be a time of boredom, sadness and resignation. We thus overlook its many rewards and satisfactions. Moreover, our pessimism can make us unwilling to intercede in our parents' behalf. We (and our parents) may fail to appreciate that luck is less decisive than determination. Few circumstances, including old age, are so unyielding as to exclude happiness and satisfaction.

Emotional health comes naturally to many elderly. Others can cultivate it. The road to such well-being is clearly marked and surprisingly predictable. But specific mental illnesses form pitfalls along the way. They must be watched for and either avoided or treated, if possible. If your parents' later years seem unfulfilling, begin the search for an explanation by reviewing the normal psychological changes of aging (see Chapter 4). Then, decide if they are promoting their own happiness or unwittingly undermining it (see next section). Finally, become familiar with some of the mental illnesses that can lay waste to anyone's later years, particularly depression (Chapter 10), senility (Chapter 11), and unhealthy responses to loss (Chapter 9).

EMOTIONAL HEALTH

55. *Fostering a Satisfying Old Age.* Unless unusual circumstances supervene, your parents' old age should be a success. They should have accepted their limitations and have few regrets. Both of them should look forward to their days with anticipation and should feel that they are experiencing one of life's good times. Whether or not this happens depends mainly upon basic needs being recognized and met, since old age is not inherently unpleasant.

The basic needs of the elderly are, not surprisingly, similar to ours. We all require self-respect, meaningful activity, friendship and love, health and freedom from pain, and a sense that life has value beyond ourselves. The guidelines given below for attaining happiness in old age are similar to those for people of any age. Of course, specific recommendations may vary with your parents' unique interests and temperament.

1. Involvement. Not even good health contributes as much to emotional well-being in old age as does an active and involved life. With few exceptions, activity breeds happiness, while inactivity breeds discontentment. Your parent *must* stay active. Too many elderly take retirement or the early indications of aging as a sign to withdraw from the action. Freed of the demands of a job or of previous living arrangements, they abandon old habits, interests, and activities. That is a mistake. Instead, they should amplify those interests, or replace them.

Old age is the perfect time to cultivate interests long neglected. It is the time to read, attend plays, join discussion groups, pursue political or philosophical topics. It is a time to learn to swim, bowl, hike, ride a bicycle, or build furniture. Your parents could take classes at a local college or university, or even enter a degree program. Or one of them might master local natural history, become a bird watcher, or attend (or give) lectures at the meetings of local naturalists' groups. Old age is a good time to learn to paint, practice serious photography, become a connoisseur of serious music, write poetry or short stories, compose a family history. Your parents could become contentious (it might be good for them) and participate in a local political or environmental activist group. The list is endless and the variety enormous. There are possibilities to suit every interest and physical ability. Your parents' involvement in activities that they enjoy and value is one of the best safeguards of psychological health. If neither of them is involved or interested in becoming involved, be alert to the presence of depression or some other psychiatric condition.

2. Health. Every effort should be made to promote good health during the later years (see Chapter 13). Although we tend to assume that poor health and incapacitation are the lot of the elderly, most older persons lose

few important physical abilities. Moreover, most illnesses common in old age don't unalterably interrupt happiness and satisfaction.

Unfortunately, some chronic diseases do become so stressful that psychotherapy may be necessary. In addition, unrecognized medical illnesses of many different types (for example, anemia, thyroid disease, diabetes) may cause emotional distress. Any effort to help a dispirited parent should include a medical checkup and assurance that his health is sound.

3. Social relations. Most people require close human contact for continuing emotional health. Some people need only a spouse or a close friend or two; others feel deprived without numerous friends and social engagements. Still others find that their family meets all their needs for socialization. In general, older people are happiest if they have both someone with whom they are intimate and a circle of acquaintances that extends beyond their household. Once again, the needs of the elderly are little different from ours—it is human nature, at any age, to want to be liked, understood, valued, and cared for. It is equally important to care for someone else. Thus the most satisfied elderly individuals are usually those who remain socially active and determinedly replace lost relationships with new ones.

However, old age is the time of lost friends and loved ones. Increased frailty and diminished finances make it harder for your parent to get around and to meet new people. The result is isolation, which can only be prevented by a determination to make new contacts and have new experiences. If you notice your parents slipping into a pattern of fewer friends and fewer outings, intercede. If he or she always has been slow to make friends, help by suggesting possibilities and encouraging him or her to get in touch with social groups. Help arrange transportation to visit old friends. Encourage use of the telephone. Anything that increases activity and involvement in the outside world is also likely to keep your parents socially alive. You can often serve as a crucial catalyst to prevent your elderly parent from withdrawing.

4. Meaningful life. If we have failed our older citizens anywhere, it is by convincing them (and ourselves) that they have little to offer. Like the rest of us, the elderly want to live meaningful lives. They want to contribute. They want to be valued by their children as more than living keepsakes—comforting reminders of days past. What makes a life less meaningful at 70 than at 40? Nowhere else has our culture's depreciation of the elderly taken a greater toll.

If we let them, the elderly can offer a lifetime's worth of experience and knowledge. They are the only ones who are able to view the whole sweep of life, and we can profit from that perspective. Although less familiar with technological advances than most of us, they often are in better touch with subtle, meaningful human values. Many elderly can be refreshingly fair-minded and open, in part because their concern is less with their personal future than with what life will be like for those who follow them. We are foolish to overlook such a resource. Many elderly individuals find significant activities and play important roles within their families and communities. These are the most satisfied of people, full of justified self-respect.

5. Growth. In the best of circumstances, old age is a time of growth. Fortunate elderly individuals discover that the insidious decline of later years can be offset by acquiring new knowledge and learning new skills. These people discard (and disprove) the prevalent stereotype of the deteriorating older person. They push their previous limits and learn that they still have room to grow. Their commitment to develop themselves adds immeasurably to their happiness. Their focus shifts to what they can accomplish next, making the troubles of old age seem trivial. Has your parent always wanted to write essays, study philosophy, become a stand-up comedian, play the accordion, build a garage, lay a brick sidewalk, learn to sail, weave, paint, or make pottery? Now is the time.

6. Money. Almost every scientific study of money and the elderly finds that those elderly persons with enough money to easily meet their needs are more satisfied with their lives than those who are just getting by. Money eases access to hobbies, classes, entertainment, sports, good health care, and social contacts. On the other hand, financial hardship is stressful and, if severe, makes enjoyment of anything difficult. Fiscal well-being is not essential for a successful old age, but it helps. Of course, the time for financial preparation is well before the money is needed. Are your parent's preparations sound? (See Chapter 24.)

56. *Healthy Sexuality*. Why spend a whole section discussing your elderly parents' sexuality? What could there possibly be to say? Isn't it something you would rather not talk about? Or think about? In spite of the importance of sexuality to each of us and in spite of our newly found liberation, most of us become exceptionally modest when talking about sex after sixty. This is especially true when we focus on our own parents. Often our parents become equally prudish and, in so doing, deny themselves an additional dimension in their relationship with a loved one.

The plain, unvarnished truth is that many elderly people are interested in, and most are capable of, a full sexual life. Many are sexually active. Such interests are natural. Older people who deny interest (and there are many) are usually reflecting the cultural bias which dictates that such desires are unnatural. The expectation of a sexless old age is an unnecessary burden to place on the elderly. Physical and sexual intimacy with a loved one can be comforting and renewing at any age and should be encouraged.

EMOTIONAL HEALTH AND COMMON EMOTIONAL PROBLEMS

Contrary to popular wisdom, sexual enjoyment should increase, not decrease, with age. The reasons lie in both psychological and physical changes. Psychologically, the elderly are more experienced, no longer distracted by concerns about pregnancy, and given to increased reflection and intimacy. Physically, they are thoroughly capable of pleasurable sexual activities. Although most older men are unable to have sex more than once nightly, and may wait several days before being able to bring intercourse to completion again, the length of time that they can stay sexually excited before orgasm increases markedly. The time between arousal and completion, which may have been measured in moments in youth, become half an hour to an hour or more in old age. Women, moreover, pass into their later years sexually unimpaired. That old bugaboo menopause does not usually physically inhibit sexual responsivity. Membranes may be drier, but local creams or estrogens can provide relief. Even a hysterectomy doesn't prevent a woman from pursuing a normal sex life. Thus there is normally no physical reason for elderly men or women to remain sexually inactive.

Nevertheless, why worry about our parent's sexual activity (or its absence)? The reason is that, enjoyment aside, the most crucial contribution of healthy sexuality to emotional health in old age is its capacity to enhance intimacy. The touching, caressing, and hugging which are such essential parts of the sexual experience continually renew the sense of closeness that is so important for health. Don't discourage your parent from maintaining an intimate relationship with someone because of your discomfort. A second reason to be concerned about a parent's prolonged abstinence is that, once abandoned in old age, sexual activity in males may be difficult to reestablish.

However, the major barrier to sexual intimacy among the elderly usually lies in their own reluctance to be active. They may require encouragement to see themselves as attractive. They may be put off by their own wrinkled skin and not even try to be desirable. They may be afraid that the rigors of lovemaking will threaten their health, or the health of their partner. In fact, sexual intercourse is usually no more rigorous than climbing one or two flights of stairs, and doesn't pose a danger to most elderly. Nonetheless, any uncertainties should be discussed with a physician. Some men may avoid sexual efforts because one or more recent attempts have been unsuccessful and they have concluded that they have become impotent. Old age is *not* a cause of impotence (see Section 144). A few elderly persons may never have enjoyed sexual relationships and may be glad to use old age as an excuse to withdraw. Finally, all too many older individuals avoid sexual activity because they believe it to be shameful at their age. It is not. Whatever the reason for abandoning or avoiding an intimate physical relationship, most lives are emotionally poorer as a result. Unfortunately, the most common reason for such poverty is lack of a suitable partner. Obviously, this is a particular problem for elderly women, many of whom outlive their husbands by decades.

COMMON EMOTIONAL PROBLEMS

Emotional problems are exceptionally common in old age. They can appear suddenly or slowly, and can develop whether or not your parent has had psychological problems in the past. One of the greatest services you can provide is to be alert to any emotional deterioration, and take appropriate steps if a difficulty occurs.

Is one of your parents experiencing an emotional problem? How can you tell? Why has it occurred? What can you do? What is the impact on you?

57. *Recognizing Emotional Problems.* Emotional difficulty may be obvious, or too subtle for easy recognition, or disguised as something else. What should you look for? Your parent may become more thoughtful, or slightly more forgetful, or more self-centered with age (Chapter 4), but none of these changes should be a cause for worry. On the other hand, if his or her emotions, thinking, or behavior become noticeably disturbed or disturbing—particularly if the change is sudden—suspect an emotional illness. Your parent may complain of feeling hopeless, anxious, unhappy, or overwhelmed, or he may deny or fail to recognize problems all too evident to you. Don't let your parents' obliviousness or resistance stop you from obtaining an explanation of, and help for, an obvious problem.

The elderly suffer from the same spectrum of emotional difficulties as everyone else, with the same spectrum of causes. But certain conditions and problems are much more likely late in life. Depression (Chapter 10), dementia or senility (Chapter 11), and severe reactions to losses (Chapter 9) are common. Paranoia (Section 109), hypochondriasis (Section 106), and alcohol and drug abuse (Sections 107 and 108) are not uncommon. All of these conditions can be serious, most should have a careful medical and psychiatric evaluation, and many benefit from treatment. If you are concerned or puzzled by either of your parents' behavior, become familiar enough with these common conditions to determine if any of them may be present.

However, there are a number of less debilitating emotional problems that should be recognized and treated. Stress may produce undesirable effects and anxiety can become chronic. Loneliness is an ever-present risk. Personality problems, usually evident for many years, may become overwhelming—to your parent, or to you. Although these problems tend not to become as severe as those psychiatric conditions described in other chapters, their presence can sour your parent's old age and impair your relationship with him or her.

58. *Stress and Stress Management.* Ours is the age of stress. It is pervasive and chronic, and we all bear its scars: increases in heart disease, high blood pressure, ulcers, colitis, cancer, unhappiness. Although there are tremendous individual differences, we are all sensitive to stress, the elderly particularly so. This may be due to the psychological and physiological frailty of age or to the accumulation of stresses over a lifetime. Whatever the reason, significant stress can cause serious emotional and physical problems: acute or chronic anxiety, depression, withdrawal, paranoia, despair. Moreover, old age is a time of frequent stress and loss, a time when your parent may need to weather blow after blow. Few older people escape. Some hold up well, others poorly.

Predicting who will be troubled by which kind of stress is currently impossible. Responses to the same stress vary enormously from person to person. However, certain stresses commonly produce problems among the elderly: loss of a loved one, poverty, sickness and physical impairment, isolation, a move to a nursing home. If your parent suffers one of these, particularly if it comes about suddenly, or there are several over a short time, he or she is likely to become emotionally distressed. For instance, if your father is crippled with arthritis, has recently lost his wife, and is watching his shrinking savings threaten him with loss of his home, expect some form of emotional disruption. The most common stresses afflicting the elderly are losses of one kind or another, and their impact and treatment are discussed in the chapter on loss (Chapter 9). The most common symptom among those elderly so stressed is depression (Chapter 10), although other common reactions include anxiety, suspiciousness, and hypochrondriasis.

If one of your parents is showing evidence of too much stress, help him or her understand and control the stressors. Do the worries center around finances? Help your parents evaluate the situation and take appropriate, realistic steps. Is it a health matter? See that your parent receives a thorough medical evaluation so that he isn't working from incomplete information. Don't accept your parent's perception about how dreadful the situation is—form your own opinion. Then help with the practical efforts to change things. In short, help your parent take control of his life.

Stress is only destructive if a person allows it to be. Your parent must learn to distance himself from his problems psychologically. Psychotherapy may help accomplish this. Just as important, your parent must learn to respond to the stress in a physically healthy way. In part, this means to learn to relax instead of being tense. Such an ability can be learned surprisingly easily. Numerous techniques, if practiced for ten to fifteen minutes several times each day, will allow your parent to escape many of the physically harmful effects of stress and enable him to view his situation from a new, more relaxed, healthier perspective. Encourage him to learn and practice biofeedback, deep muscle relaxation, Transcendental Meditation, or self-hypnosis. If used regularly and constructively, any one of these techniques permits your parent to take physiological control of his body and relax in the face of stress. Classes in these methods are plentiful in most locations. To such specific techniques, see that your parent adds exercise, good food, ample rest, and good friends. Unhealthy responses to stress can usually be controlled. But sometimes depression, anxiety, or some other common emotional reaction to stress and loss may require specific treatment.

59. *Anxiety.* After depression (Chapter 10), anxiety is probably the most frequent response to the buffeting of late life. Anxiety may be caused by concern about a new medical symptom, worry about a missing Social Security check, fright about the sudden illness of a grandchild, or concern that he can no longer measure up to a previous level of performance. It usually disappears when the situation which caused it changes, or when your parent has devised a new way of coping, or when he realizes that old standards of performance no longer apply. More significant and more disruptive, however, is the prolonged and profound anxiety which afflicts a few elderly individuals.

When anxiety reaches the severity of an illness, it is often free-floating, attaching itself to everything your parent experiences. He or she may have an insistent sense of apprehension or dread about the future and be unable to approach anything calmly. Your parents may be tense and irritable, constantly complaining that things are not going right or worrying about some disaster to come. He or she may have trouble falling asleep, sleep fitfully, and feel fatigued during the day. The feeling of anxiety may be accompanied by heart palpitations, shakiness and tremors, diarrhea, cold clammy hands, sweating, a dry mouth, a "lump" in the throat, "butterflies" in the stomach, and "pins and needles" in the hands and feet. Your parent may be unable to concentrate during a conversation, have difficulty making a decision, and experience memory lapses (causing the condition to be mistaken for senility). Full-blown anxiety can be unpleasant, exhausting, and frightening. Your parent is often chronically miserable. Not only is he worried about things going wrong, but about physical health and even sanity. Your elderly parent may be preoccupied with the state of his heart or become certain that he is developing cancer. A chronic headache may convince your parent that a brain tumor will soon be discovered. Brief episodes of panic may leave him exhausted and terrorized. Finally, a feeling of depression and of being overwhelmed so often accompanies symptoms of anxiety among the elderly that it frequently is difficult to tell whether your parent's primary problem is anxiety or depression.

If your parent's symptoms of nervousness or dread appear suddenly and without apparent cause, are severe, or last longer than you think they should, seek professional help. At the least, your parent should have a careful physical and psychiatric examination. Part of the reason such an evaluation is essential lies in the complicated nature of anxiety. At times it represents a prolonged reaction to too much stress and too many changes. But anxiety symptoms may also be caused by complex emotional conflicts or by alterations in brain biochemistry, each requiring a thorough evaluation to define and treat. An additional reason for obtaining an evaluation is that any associated depression must not be overlooked. Unrecognized depression, aggravated by painful feelings of anxiety, can become dangerously severe. Your parent may complain exclusively about anxiety, but the problem demanding immediate treatment may be depression. And the treatment for depression is often quite different from the treatment for anxiety. Finally, a medical examination must be included in the evaluation of your parent because certain medical diseases frequently cause nervousness, tremors, restlessness, and feelings of anxiety in the elderly before any physical symptoms appear. These medical causes can be as simple as drinking too much coffee, but may reflect illnesses like thyroid disease, low blood sugar, pneumonia, heart irregularities, early dementia, or the misuse of medications like steroids, appetite suppressants, or sleeping pills. If the anxiety is severe and sudden, it is probably caused by a new medical or psychiatric illness and should be treated.

It is first essential to be certain your parent is in good health. If a medical illness is responsible for anxiety, its successful treatment may be all that is needed. Once poor health has been eliminated as a potential cause of symptoms, treatment can focus on anxiety of primarily psychological origin. Psychotherapy is often helpful. A session or two with a skilled psychotherapist can often take the edge off even major episodes of acute anxiety. Sometimes it is necessary to search for the hidden roots of anxiety, but frequently a more matter-of-fact approach has a greater impact. This approach is supportive and helps your parent identify and remove important stresses. It encourages self-reliance and productive, rewarding activity. It focuses on decreasing your parent's sense of helplessness by seeking ways to provide social involvement, financial assistance, increased mobility, help around the home, and legal aid. It helps your parent identify the meaningful aspects of his or her life and can instill a better sense of self-worth. To this broad-based approach is often added specific psychotherapeutic techniques like biofeedback, meditation, and self-hypnosis.

Medication also has an important place in the treatment of severe anxiety among the elderly. Unfortunately, it is too often used inappropriately. Medication should not be used as a substitute for psychotherapy or for an improved understanding of the forces pressing on your parent. Mild tranquilizers (Valium, Librium, Serax) are useful for controlling symptoms during brief periods of increased anxiety but should *not* be used for more than several weeks. After that time they become ineffective at normal dosages, and side effects like grogginess and mild confusion often begin to worsen. They are much more beneficial if used only during periods of increased stress and anxiety. Antidepressant medications (Tofranil, Norpramin, Sinequan) may help relieve episodes of panic in those anxious people who are not otherwise depressed. Don't be surprised if the physician asks your nondepressed parent to try an antidepressant; just hope that it is effective, for the response can sometimes be dramatic.

A combination of these treatments will frequently improve your parent's emotional well-being. Failure to improve should be a signal for your parent (and you) to discuss long-range goals of treatment with the therapist. If the symptoms have appeared on and off throughout your parent's life (that is, if they seem to be a part of his or her personality) don't expect a major change at this late date.

60. *Loneliness.* Loneliness is the curse of survival. The longer a parent lives, the more his or her accustomed emotional supports drop away. Close friends, loved ones, favorite activities, familiar locations, all disappear into the past. They are replaced by a painful vacuum and a sense of emotional isolation which is not easily overcome. Your remaining parent may come to feel that there is no one left who can understand what he or she has experienced—no one who has "been there." It is the rare elderly person who does not feel the sting of loneliness at some time. A surviving parent feels a hunger for more than just companionship: he or she requires a special relationship of shared values and associations. Your parent needs someone to understand who he or she is and what he or she stands for. And that person must need such emotional contact as much as your parent. Loneliness is cured if your parent is valued, understood, and needed. Two hours of serious reminiscence with a daughter counts for more than innumerable hours spent in small talk. And a conversation with a stranger who happens to be from your parent's home town, and who shares old friends, can be strangely refreshing.

Loneliness can be destructive. It is a breeding ground for anger and resentment that can poison relationships. It can lead to depression or even suicide. It can sap your parent of the energy to reach out, make new contacts, and change things for the better. Perhaps worst of all, it can come to seem the normal state of old age.

You can help. Spend time with your parent, chuckle together and relive the good times. Share sorrows and help your parent come to terms with his or her failures. You can bring your parent up to date with your life. But your parent will be healthiest if he or she doesn't depend only upon you to interrupt his emotional isolation. A surviving parent needs to become active and develop new interests and friendships. Perhaps they won't be as close as past relationships, but they can be just as meaningful if they help him or her through the new challenges of old age. Elderly people encountering similar situations for the first time can benefit by comparing notes. Encourage your parent to get in touch with neighbors, church members, senior citizens groups. Natural gregariousness is one of the most useful qualities your parent can possess; new interests and causes can conquer loneliness. Pets can also help. You cannot conquer your parent's loneliness single-handedly (nor should you try), but you can get the ball rolling.

However, if things do not seem to be improving in spite of your best efforts, suspect that an emotional illness like depression may be involved, and seek a professional opinion.

61. *Personality and Personality Extremes*. Unless a mental disorder such as dementia or depression develops, don't expect your parents' personality to change much with age. If anything, expect prominent characteristics to become even more prominent. Your parents always may have been easygoing or high-strung, forgiving or hypercritical, trusting or suspicious, generous or miserly—expect more of the same. They have developed patterns of behavior which have fit their temperament and met their needs, and they are unlikely to change their styles now.

However, either parent may find that the personality from the past is mismatched to the changed circumstances of later life. Stresses such as poor health, decreased attractiveness, poverty, or failing memory can force surprising changes in your parents' personalities. Your mother's life-long reliance upon coquetry may be abandoned as her beauty fades. Your father's relaxed and cheerful personality may not survive years of debilitating arthritic pain and deformity. Poverty may turn generosity into stinginess, and the misperceptions arising from poor hearing and memory can result in chronic suspiciousness. Even a normal and healthy personality may undergo a major change if the stress is great or constant enough.

Some people, however, have personalities that have caused problems throughout life, both for them and for those around them. Such prominent personality styles, if maladaptive, are called personality disorders. One of your parents may always have been moderately paranoid, a loner, painfully perfectionistic, or overly passive. Any of these qualities, which we all have to some degree, will produce problems when taken to the extreme. What happens in old age to the person with a personality disorder? Will your parent's difficult personality change as he or she ages? Will the later years become more difficult or smoother?

Like most other elderly people, those with personality extremes continue to act as they always have. Many crotchety old people were crotchety young people, and the elderly man who warns neighbors away from his front door probably avoided them when younger as well. Only the person who has been extremely aggressive is likely to mellow with age. On the other hand, life frequently becomes more pleasant for people with certain personality extremes, and harsher for others. Why? This is due in part to the altered demands, expectations, and circumstances that accompany old age. Fewer demands are made, and behavior considered unacceptable during middle age becomes expected of many people when older. People who have always been criticized for being too dependent, submissive, and passive may find that these qualities are accepted easily in their later years. Has either of your parents always preferred being by him- or herself? This parent will encounter few problems with that behavior in old age. However, if one of your parents has been mildly depressed for a greater part of life, that personality style is likely to worsen under the impact of old age losses. If your parent has maintained a delicate emotional balance over the years by being compulsive and perfectionistic, poor eyesight or failing memory may make that impossible, and bring this parent to the edge of distraction. Perhaps worst off are the people who have long had a significant paranoid side to their personality: their stubbornness, suspicions, and accusations may drive away their few remaining friends and prevent them from seeking help from anyone.

Of course, those people who are outgoing, cheerful, and likable reap rich rewards at any age, and seldom need to change their style.

62. *Dealing with an Emotionally Ill Parent.* You suffer too. You are saddened by your parent's plight and want to help in any way you can. On the other hand, you may be driven to your wits' end by the problems created by your emotionally ill parent. For example, Mr. Spelling, 86 years old, had lived alone during the five years following his wife's death. He claimed he could take care of himself, but expected his daughter to supply meals several times each week and clean his house regularly. Always a critical indi-

vidual, he had become more so since the death of his wife, and he focused most of his complaints and dissatisfactions on his daughter. According to him, she was neglectful, a poor housekeeper, an inadequate cook, and had most of the many faults of her mother (whom she had loved dearly). And Mr. Spelling had recently begun accusing his daughter of intentionally trying to make his later years unpleasant. On several occasions he had called to berate her for stealing his checkbook (he later found it where he had hidden it), and when she called him to account for such unfair charges, he sincerely denied ever having said such things. In addition, he had become involved in a running battle with neighborhood boys: he would hurl accusations and threats as they passed his yard, and they would retaliate by upsetting his garbage can or simply by suspiciously "lurking" nearby until he became enraged. The boys' parents asked Mr. Spelling's daughter to stop him from swearing at their children, and warned that the police would be called if he continued to do so. When she discussed it with him, he minimized the problem, but then spoke vaguely about neighborhood people trying to ruin his health by keeping him up at night with their noise.

Doris Spelling Fanon, the daughter, felt at sea. She had spent a busy life raising four children, but now seemed about to repeat the process, since her divorced daughter had recently moved into her home with three children. Mrs. Fanon's husband was retiring two years early because of poor health, partially causing the long-awaited retirement years to lose their luster. She had expected to help her two brothers (now living in distant cities) take care of her father, but somehow the responsibility had fallen entirely upon her. Although she always had felt that she loved her father, she now wasn't so sure. Not only could she do nothing right in his eyes, his behavior had become so objectionable to others that to do nothing at all seemed equally wrong.

Mrs. Fanon was trapped between her sense of responsibility for her father and that for her own family and seemed unable to satisfy both. Moreover, the thought of neglecting either produced feelings of guilt. She felt things would have stabilized if only her father hadn't become so insensitive and strange as he aged, and she was convinced that her life would not change until her father died. It upset her to discover herself looking forward to that day.

Mrs. Fanon was making a mistake that complicated her life enormously. She assumed that her father's "peculiarities" were either normal for his age, or were something that couldn't be changed, and failed to consider that he may have been suffering from a treatable emotional illness.

In fact, his behavior suggested several possible mental illnesses. Perhaps he never recovered from the loss of his wife: the five years of increasing symptoms that followed could have been an abnormal grief response (Chapter 9). His increasing suspicion could have represented the development of a paranoid condition (Section 109), or the worsening of a suspicious, prickly personality (Section 61). Perhaps a dementia was responsible for his increasingly obvious memory loss (Chapter 11). Or, perhaps the memory loss, difficulty sleeping, and general sense that his life was getting worse reflected the gradual development of a serious depression (Chapter 10). Mr. Spelling's abnormal behavior was least likely due to normal old age.

Mr. Spelling became the focus of attention after Mrs. Fanon sought treatment from a psychiatrist for her own depression. A description of him by his daughter provoked an immediate medical and psychiatric evaluation. He was found to be depressed (accounting for his unhappiness, "crabbiness," insomnia, strange ideas, and failing memory) and to have mild heart failure (worsening his sleeplessness, and causing a loss of energy which made him feel "terribly old"). Treatment with medication, psychotherapy, and change in some of the previous family arrangements caused a marked improvement. He returned to his previous state of being, a state his daughter could tolerate. (Equally important, the rest of the family was called in to pick up their share of the responsibility.)

A few elderly people become very difficult for their children to deal with even though no emotional illness is present. Others have a condition for which little treatment is present. Whether you are anguished by your parent's behavior or infuriated by it, always ask if a correctable emotional illness is responsible. Only when such a condition has been excluded should you begin to evaluate how to live with your parent's problems.

The last year or two of an elderly person's life may be extraordinarily difficult for others in the family. Although many older individuals do not experience a prolonged decline, some do. Demands may be made on you and your family which tax, or exceed, your resources. At some point, you will need to take a hard-headed look at how much support you can provide. You will need to recognize that your physical and emotional reserves are not limitless. You will need to set priorities—and your parent may not be number one, or even number two. That may mean moving your parent out of his or her home, or out of your home. It may mean returning fewer telephone calls or making fewer visits. It may mean *insisting* that someone else help. It may mean applying the same rules to your relationship with your parent that would apply to any other relationship. Is your parent making outrageous demands or accusations on the phone? Don't talk with your parent until it stops. Does he or she insist on a visit every day, when such a strain may be fatal to your relationship with your husband (or wife)? Visit

EMOTIONAL HEALTH AND COMMON EMOTIONAL PROBLEMS

less frequently. Of course, the specifics vary with the situation and must be applied humanely. But the basic principle still applies: look after your own essential needs first. If you become exhausted, no one benefits. And, hard as it may be, try to subdue that nagging feeling of guilt and *excessive* responsibility with a healthy sense of reality.

9.

Losses

The loss of loved ones and loved things is the dark side of aging. Pauper or prince, neither of your parents will reach old age without experiencing significant personal losses. But will you recognize your parents' losses when they occur? Often they are obvious. When your father dies, you expect your mother to be shaken. The psychological impact of your mother's heart attack is plain to see. A parent's stroke is an obvious loss. But the cumulative effect of many smaller, less sudden, and more subtle losses is more insidious and often goes unnoticed. An elderly person's lack of enthusiasm and energy is not an inevitable consequence of growing older. Rather, it may be a response to the gradual falling away of abilities, friends, responsibilities, respect, familiar activities, and familiar places. It is a process that is encountered by all elderly—the piling of loss upon loss.

THE ACCUMULATION OF LOSSES

If unresolved losses are allowed to accumulate, gradual disheartenment and emotional poverty are inevitable. The normal and healthy response to a loss is to grieve. Whether loss is sudden, as in the death of a spouse following a heart attack, or slow, as in the loss of sight with aging, loss must be faced, thought about, and wrestled with—it must be grieved.

What are the expected losses of old age? What does it mean to grieve? How do you do it successfully and what are the results of failure? Probably nowhere can you aid your aging parents more than when helping them recognize and work through their losses. A decline can be reversed and years of enjoyment added to your parents' lives.

63. *Loss Is in the Eye of the Beholder*. A devastating loss to one person may be insignificant to another. Wrinkles may demoralize one person while they may be a source of amusement to someone else. If our parents have always fought bitterly, the death of one may be almost a relief to the other. We are often caught by surprise at how well or poorly our parents tolerate the blows of aging. Their responses depend on a mixture of their personalities, the suddenness and unexpectedness of the loss, the support they receive from family and friends, the expectations others have of them, how many other blows they have weathered recently, their physical health, their finances, and much more—all of which makes prediction extremely difficult. If they act in a totally unexpected fashion, however, it may be because they are unable to acknowledge and work through their grief.

64. *What Is There to Lose?* There are two types of losses that are traumatic for almost everyone: death of a loved one and loss of physical health.

Few people are able to remain unmoved, except at great emotional cost, by the loss of a loved one—a spouse, child, parent, or close friend. It is natural for psychologically healthy human beings to form close relationships with a few other people and to suffer when those ties are destroyed. Most commonly this is because of death, but similar problems can occur if the loved ones move away or are lost due to a disagreement. With such a loss, expect a parent to experience profound, and usually obvious, grief.

A second blow to your parents is their gradual loss of good health. The number of ways our bodies betray us in old age is almost limitless. After a lifetime of trust in their physical abilities, your parents may be shaken as one system after another fails. Painful joints, bad balance, failing eyesight and hearing, weakness, poor memory, frequent illnesses with slow recoveries, a heart attack or stroke, constipation, and a hundred other problems, both large and small, may conspire to reduce their abilities, pleasures, and spirits. These physical changes fundamentally alter the way they live their lives. Such impairments can be handled poorly or taken in stride, but for your parents to be truly comfortable with their new limits, this loss of what once was must be adjusted to, compensated for, and grieved.

The ultimate loss of good health is death. Nowhere is anticipatory mourning more appropriate. There are no second chances after death, no more visits from beloved children, no further opportunities to correct wrongs done, pursue interests, or fulfull ideals. Usually the death of a loved one or a severe illness sets your parent to thinking about life's transience and may begin him mourning his own decline. The very awareness that life is short or that they may not recover from their current illness may open doors long closed. Dying may be transformed into a growing process.

65. *Cumulative Losses Can Be Devastating.* The erosions of the hardwon gains, influence, and successes of a lifetime are often more devastating than one big loss. When every step becomes a step backward, optimism withers. With few exceptions, the world stops paying much attention to people when they pass into their 70s. Of course there is obligatory interest—medical care is provided, Social Security is mandated, food stamps are available, and politicians count their votes. Families continue to care. But who really listens to the elderly? With whom does their opinion really count? Your father is one day a boss and the next day a retiree. Your mother is a housewife only for your father, and when he dies . . . A friendly glance at the person seated next to them in a restaurant isn't even noticed—they have become nonpersons.

Besides being expected to accept a new, undesirable social ròle, the elderly suffer other diminishments. Independence, taken for granted for so many years, is lost on many fronts. They may become financially dependent and insecure. Their decisions may not be honored, even by those closest to them. Necessity may demand that they leave familiar quarters and the old neighborhood. Relocation, particularly when it is to a nursing home or other institution where a degree of regimentation and dependency is invariably forced on them, can strip them of their sense of individuality and can damage self-esteem. Even if they stay in their old neighborhood, it may so change over time as to be unrecognizable and undesirable to them. The loss of a driver's license signals the loss of the freedom to get around. Isolation becomes increasingly severe as they lose friends, activities, and mobility. Their world gradually shrinks to include just the town, then only the neighborhood, then the house, and, finally, perhaps, only their room. This is accompanied by a new sense of loneliness as they are separated from much they have treasured by failing vision and hearing, death of friends, dispersal of family, and loss of mental abilities. Their days may consist of waiting by the window for someone to come up the walk—whether friend, mailman, or salesman. Your parents may ultimately even refuse to make new friends or to try to develop new talents because they feel that these too will be lost.

The lesson for adult children concerned about their parents is clear—old age is a time of loss. But in spite of slowly accumulating limitations, old age can be a productive and pleasant time, if it is approached realistically and freed of expectations based on the past.

THE PROCESS OF GRIEVING

Mourning is natural, essential, thoroughly painful, surprisingly easy, and nothing of which to be ashamed. As a rule, we tend to carry a stiff upper lip too far. Our father weathers his stroke "like a trooper"—but he is not a trooper. He is an elderly man whose life has been turned around overnight and who has to get to know his new self and mourn the passing of the man he used to be. He must "talk it out," try to understand, ruminate, and cry. Grieving is a natural and healthy process with a fairly constant pattern of emotional responses—the grief reaction.

66. *The Shock of Loss—Denial and Numbness.* The initial reaction of many elderly to sudden and unanticipated loss often dismays their children more than all the trials to follow—their parents may deny the loss has occurred. If your father has suffered a massive heart attack, he may want to be up and about the next day in spite of the doctor's carefully reasoned explanations. Your mother may react to the unexpected death of your father by setting his place at the breakfast table the next morning. The more profound the shock, the greater their disbelief. No, your parents have not lost their minds. They are automatically and unconsciously employing one of the mind's most powerful defense mechanisms—denial. Unsettling as denial is to the observer, it is extremely useful in protecting your older parents until they can recover their emotional balance.

This type of reaction can develop with any type of loss and is most likely if someone close to your parents has died or if your parents have suffered a major physical impairment. A man who loses a leg may refuse to admit that it is gone. A woman may repeatedly insist that the physician who told her she is dying has her confused with someone else. Usually, this protective response is gone within hours or days. If it persists, a physician should be consulted, since the mourning process may have gone awry. Occasionally, however, it is wisest and most humane to let your parent keep the denial (if, for example, one of your parents has only days to live and refuses to admit it). This decision may best be reached with the aid of a physician.

The impact of a severe loss may also produce a sense of numbness. The mind protects itself, not by denying reality, but by slowing down and by creating a sense of unreality. They may become completely preoccupied with insignificant tasks like weeding the garden or cleaning cupboards.

They may be so distracted that conversation is impossible. Bear with them. Give them support. Assure them that you recognize their loss. Tell them it is all right to mourn. Don't immediately demand that they face facts—people set their own pace. Only when they pass the initial phase of denial and numbness and begin thinking about their loss does the real work, and triumph, of grieving take place.

67. *The Grief Reaction.* Successful grieving is an emotional roller coaster. Your parent may swing unpredictably from despair to anger to anxiety to numbness to hostility and back to despair. Grieving people may not understand their own emotions and are frequently caught by surprise as a powerful feeling washes across them in response to someone's offhand comment, a tune heard on the radio, or a fleeting memory. Some of these emotions are easily understood. Others are not. A close friend may be baffled when accused of not really caring or of not knowing what suffering is like.

In addition to turbulent emotions alternating with listlessness and depression, grieving parents may suffer a host of other symptoms. Feelings of guilt are common, frequently constructed around a grain of truth: *if only* he had not smoked in the house, his wife would not have developed lung cancer; *if only* she had been more careful with her weight, the arthritis wouldn't have developed; *if only* he had finished high school, he would have earned enough money to have avoided losing his house. Unfortunately, this kind of self-recrimination is unproductive and may delay the grieving process. Equally common are physical symptoms like headaches, shortness of breath, tightness in the throat, weakness, sleeplessness, loss of appetite, pounding in the chest, or abdominal distress. A person may go from doctor to doctor without satisfaction until someone recognizes that the medical symptoms are due to unfinished grieving. Other people become chronically anxious, begin to drink too much, or allow themselves to deteriorate physically. The variety of problems and symptoms which may develop in response to the losses of old age are almost limitless. This should be kept in the back of your mind as your parents begin to fail in one way or another.

The emotional upset and mental pain following a loss are not endless, but their disappearance does take time. Expect your parents to suffer the most during the first few weeks after a sudden loss, but realize that the symptoms may last for six months to one year following a major blow. If your parent continues to mourn after one to two years, suspect that a problem has developed. Grieving is rarely smooth and ups and downs are common, even after months or years. Expect symptoms to recur in situations that remind your parent of his or her loss and at special times like anniversaries and holidays.

68. *What You Can Do.* Rarely can we be of greater help to our parents than in the difficult task of grieving. Mourning is a lonely vigil, but it is also a social event that will succeed only with proper encouragement from family and friends.

1. Allow your parents time alone. They need to think about what they have lost, review the past, cry. They need to get angry—at themselves, at you, at life. They need to suffer—an offering to the sincerity of past feelings. And much of this is best done in private. You can facilitate this by allowing and encouraging them to spend time alone. They must have time to themselves amidst the whirl of funeral preparations or in the weeks following a serious illness. Don't become preoccupied with taking their minds off it or with making them feel better, since they will only really feel better after they have come to terms with their loss.

2. Be available. Although mourning is, by necessity, one of the loneliest of activities, it is often essential for the griever to have someone around who cares—someone to cry with, to complain to, to care about. Mourners need support and companionship. You shouldn't be with them constantly, but you should be available. Call frequently. Visit. Sit in the room with them, or in the next room. Get other key family members (or friends) involved.

Unfortunately, loss increases the likelihood of loneliness. Grieving individuals are sometimes among the least lovable of people. We all feel uncomfortable around someone who is shaken by a pain we cannot feel. If your parent complicates this by being alternately irritable, testy, caustic, hostile, despondent, apathetic, and withdrawn, you may find yourself shying away and finding reasons not to visit. Although this is understandable, and may be necessary if you are to maintain emotional balance, too much isolation can prolong your parent's unbecoming behavior and may cause their grief to harden and become chronic.

3. Encourage your parents to mourn. Unless you have been through this before, either with someone else or through your own grieving, you are likely to feel awkward when around your parent. Since your actions can be vitally important, what you need to do is usually quite simple—encourage your parents to mourn. Let them know that you understand what they are going through and tell them that their feelings are normal and understandable to you. Assure them that it is not only all right to grieve but is important and necessary. Encourage them to talk to you about their loss—about their sadness, fear, hopelessness, and anxiety. Urge them to reminisce.

Reassure them that things do get better and that they will begin to feel better. Be realistically hopeful but don't support false hopes (for example, that the cancer will disappear or that sight will return). Don't let them become too dependent on you for support—gradually encourage them to do more things for themselves and to become reinvolved in life. Finally, remember that you don't have to have all the answers. Instead, you need to be a listener—an active listener who is interested, tolerant, warm, and available. Throughout it all, let your parents set the pace. Some days they may wish to be left alone while the next day they may talk your ear off.

4. Help your parents rearrange their lives. The innumerable changes of aging gradually make difficult the old rules by which your parents have lived their lives. They must reorganize their priorities, goals, desires, and social supports—in short, they must build new lives. Careful planning and anticipation in earlier years will smooth the way. You can be enormously helpful by giving them support and encouragement, by suggesting new possibilities and new activities, and by helping them see themselves in an altered and favorable light. You can also help put them in contact with groups and organizations that will facilitate the grieving process (see Chapter 30). For example, widow-to-widow counseling is extremely helpful to many people who have lost a spouse. It is a chance to talk at length with someone who has suffered the same loss and has overcome it. There are several of these counseling services available, such as the Widowed Person's Service associated with the American Association of Retired Persons (AARP).

69. *If Your Parent Is Dying.* If your parent learns that he or she is fatally ill and will die shortly, the elderly parent usually experiences a typical grief reaction, with one exception—there are no second chances this time. Although younger people generally assume that this is the worst loss of all, the elderly are often more sanguine. Death may be viewed as a release from suffering, uncertainty, boredom, or loneliness.

The very finality of death makes its foreknowledge one of life's greatest opportunities for growth. When time is so limited, all the rules change. New priorities emerge. Old stresses and hindrances disappear. Your parent may be able to look at life and relationships, perhaps for the first time, without the distorting and obscuring lenses of anger, greed, envy, and prejudice. If weeks or months remain, he can be helped to lay to rest old problems, come to terms with current relationships, get his affairs in order, explore his most generous abilities for human contact, and consider how he will live the rest of his life. Grieving becomes an exploration. During this time, close contact with loved ones is vitally important. What is more, the hours spent with your father discussing how he has lived his life can be enormously enriching for you as well. Not everyone concludes life on such a satisfactory note—but it is worth a try.

Such an end to living is unlikely if your dying parent is isolated or crippled with pain or fear. Not everyone wants to talk about their coming death or to reflect with you about their past. Those wishes should be respected, but do make yourself accessible if the natural desire for life review begins to assert itself. Most people who are dying like the company of those close to them. It is not necessary to be with them continuously, but making frequent, short visits and being available for important conversations are vital. Severe pain should be controlled with medication, if necessary, but your parent shouldn't be so sedated that clear thinking is impossible. Communicate your concerns about a graceful and dignified death to the physician. Finally, do what you can to put your parent's mind at ease about common worries such as the fear of isolation, of being helpless, of leaving loved ones to flounder, and of losing control. These are such common fears that they are worth mentioning to your parent if he or she hasn't already raised them.

70. *Telling Your Parents Bad News.* Everyone dislikes being the bearer of bad news. Many doctors back off from that unwanted task as readily as do nonprofessionals. Often, sometimes with good reason, the job of "breaking the news" is left to a family member. How do you tell a parent that he is dying or that she has suffered some other serious loss? When? Where? Who should do the telling? What reaction can you expect? Would it be better not to tell your parent at all? How do you decide?

Although it is easy to rationalize and convince ourselves otherwise, it is usually better to tell our parents bad news. However difficult it is for us and however painful it is for them initially, such information provides them the opportunity to begin grieving—a process that is ultimately restorative. Besides, they usually discover the truth for themselves—accidentally or by noticing a new atmosphere in the house, wondering about our awkward answers to simple questions, or sensing the words that go unspoken. Occasionally, if our parent is too ill to be able to tolerate the shock, it may be better to delay the telling. Finally, a few individuals with shaky mental health from severe depression or anxiety or persons who have spent a lifetime avoiding shocks of any kind may be better handled by permitting continued denial. In general, however, a supportive presentation of the truth is healthier and less stressful for you and your parents in the long run.

Because you can serve as a major suport to your parents, it is often preferable for you to be involved in breaking the news. If the distressing information concerns their physical health, you can be there as someone to turn to when the doctor explains the finding. If you are to tell your parent, choose a quiet, private spot. Take your time. Break the news and talk about it briefly but allow your parent ample opportunity to respond. Use the response as an indicator of what to do next and of how much more to tell at this time. Don't monopolize the time with talk. Be truthful and realistically hopeful. ("The doctor says that the tumor is slow-growing." "We're all anxious to have you visit us at the seashore next month.") Most of all, be a warm, comforting presence. Your parent may want you there to look at and to touch for hours or days or he or she may initially withdraw. Don't be surprised if you have incorrectly anticipated your parent's reaction—it may be surprisingly mild or surprisingly severe. Strong negative emotions are to be expected as the first step in the chain of grieving and you must be prepared to accept them without embarrassment, without criticism, and without being overly sensitive should their anger be directed at the "bearer of bad tidings."

71. *When Grieving Does Not Occur.* Occasionally, the expected suffering following your parents' loss does not occur. Do not conclude automatically that they are callous and mean-spirited. There are several common reasons for overt mourning not taking place:

1. They refuse to face the loss. This is a major source of acute and chronic psychological problems and must be attended to.

2. They have already grieved. If your father has had one heart attack and may have another at any time, your mother already may have begun mourning. She daily may watch your father with the renewed fondness of those soon to part. This anticipatory grieving usually makes the time spent together more meaningful, but also prepares her for his death. Death comes as no surprise and, when it comes, her mourning is already partly completed. Premature grieving is common. Almost one third of elderly women have only a mild reaction to the death of their husbands. They have always expected the man to die first and are ready for it. This may occur whether or not the husband has been in poor health prior to his death.

Grief is typically more severe when its cause is sudden and unexpected. Loss due to heart attack or an automobile accident does not provide your parent as much time to prepare as does the relentless progress of a fatal cancer.

3. They can mourn only privately. Some people are exceptionally skillful at mourning by themselves. They cry and grieve only when alone. That's all right, but it is often the hard way to go—harder than if they share their sorrow.

4. They have become emotionally detached from the deceased. Sometimes the quality of a relationship is discovered by outsiders only after one of the individuals dies. The love between husband and wife or parent and child may have faded years before. At the time of death, they may not even like one another. Mourning, then, is typically brief. One caution is in order. Don't criticize your parent if you are disappointed that their marital relationship didn't measure up to your expectations. Regardless of how much you cared for both parents and wished them well, you are an observer. Only they could ultimately define how they felt about one another and only they knew the reasons why. Criticism of the surviving parent, either direct or implied, is often unfair.

72. *When Grieving Goes Wrong.* The majority of older people absorb numerous losses, compensate, and carry on. However, many elderly aren't so adaptable. They may respond to losses in ways that are self-defeating— from refusing to admit to losses and trying unsuccessfully to continue as before to giving up and sinking under their weight. It is difficult to predict how well your parents will adapt. One may tolerate the deaths of spouse and friends smoothly but be devastated by failing health while another may take illness in stride but be devastated by the death of a friend. However, there are a few general situations and personal characteristics which make a poor reaction to grief more likely.

1. Personal courage notwithstanding, it is difficult to endure the cumulative effects of many significant losses in a short period of time, particularly if some are unexpected.

2. Successful grieving is more difficult if done alone and without support. If family members are absent or if they are not sympathetic to a particular loss (such as death of a pet or death of a partner disliked by the family), a poor outcome is more likely. Sometimes your parent may try to ignore feelings of grief in deference to your wishes—with unfortunate results.

3. Some people try to maintain a "stiff upper lip." Others have always been inhibited or uncomfortable with any form of emotion. Still others have long been dominated by or dependent upon someone else who is no longer around. These people are at risk of having particular difficulties tolerating loss.

4. Your parents may have had mixed feelings, strongly positive and strongly negative, about someone close who has recently died. They may be swept with guilt now that the opportunity to do justice to the deceased is gone.

What behaviors and symptoms can you expect your parents to display if they are mishandling grieving?

1. Your parent may simply allow every blow to knock him down a peg. Rather than resolving each loss, making adjustments, and going on, he or she may gradually collect the losses, continually reflect on their sum, lose self-esteem, and become more and more depressed. Occasionally an older person may slip into a severe depression and show sleeplessness, significant weight loss, and suicidal ideas.

2. Some people suffer active grief for one to two years or more. They may seem to be perpetually in tears, withdrawn, angry, or depressed, or they may become chronically inhibited or anxious.

3. Other individuals may have exaggerated reactions to a loss. They may develop bizarre ideas or become euphoric.

4. Grief may be concentrated into physical symptoms—chronic abdominal pain, weakness, chest complaints, or headaches. Energy is focused on seeking medical help, thus avoiding facing the loss.

5. Some people indefinitely delay acknowledging a loss. Sometimes they may actually develop delusional ideas. For instance, they may believe that their heart completely repaired itself during the night after their heart attack or that they won't be evicted because a friendly neighbor paid their mortgage.

Whatever unsuccessful pattern of grieving your parent shows, a typical result is diminished life satisfaction and prolonged suffering. If you sense that your parent isn't grieving when he should be or is grieving when she shouldn't be or is displaying any of the other behaviors described above, discuss it. Your parents may have needed only a sympathetic listener. However, grief which has been twisted into some unnatural shape may need the help of a trained therapist. If your initial advances are repulsed, if your parent feels out of control or is overwhelmed by anger or guilt, consider seeking professional help from a psychiatrist, psychologist, or other psychotherapist. If your parent begins to develop signs of a major depression (see Chapter 10), he or she will require a thorough psychiatric evaluation and probably antidepressant medication. Progress is often rapid if your parent can be led into healthy grieving.

73. *Unresolved Losses Can Be Deadly.* Significant, unresolved losses may not only reduce your parents' enjoyment of life but can also shorten their lives. The likelihood that they will become ill increases markedly in the months following a major loss and they have an increased chance of dying during the subsequent years. This is most noticeable after the death of their marriage partner, after which life becomes more difficult, lonely, and stressful. If the loss is immediately accompanied by a move to a nursing home or some other institution, the probability of getting sick increases. The most reliable safeguard against these unwanted effects is to

see that your parents work through their losses and begin filling in the gaps with new interests, goals, and relationships.

74. *Your Losses.* The final element in all the losses your parents suffer over the years is the loss and grief you experience as you watch them change and decline. A part of your life is being stripped away as well. In order to help your parents, you must deal with your own feelings.

10.

Sorrow and Depression

Why aren't all old people depressed? They lose friends, physical health, their homes, their independence. What can they look forward to but more losses? Why don't they give up?

Some do! Some become chronically dissatisfied or seriously depressed. Some think of suicide, or attempt it. But most don't. Old age need not be that bleak. Most people are able to obtain real pleasure from their later years. Some find them the least complicated and most satisfying years of their life. We should not fall into the trap of assuming that sadness and depression are natural in old age—they aren't. And yet depression is more common after 65 than at any previous time. Suicide peaks in elderly men. Why? What can be done about it?

To answer those questions it is necessary to know something about sadness and about depression—to understand that they are not the same and to recognize that there are ways of dealing with each. In fact, of all the serious emotional illnesses of old age, depression is the most treatable. It should not be allowed to spoil our parents' final years.

75. *Sad or Depressed?* Sadness is a normal reaction to something undesirable, the way any of us would respond. Depression is an overreaction—sadness that has gone on too long, is too severe, has occurred for little or no apparent reason, or is life-threatening. It is important to recognize the difference. Although both conditions are unpleasant, sadness is often a necessary step towards feeling better, while depression is an illness that requires evaluation and treatment.

Every older person experiences sadness at some time and most are visited by it again and again. Even worse, as many as one out of three elderly people experiences a siginificant depression which, if neglected, steals precious months or years. In fact, depression is the most common severe emotional problem of old age, outstripping even dementia (severe senility) until a person is almost 80 years of age.

To make matters worse, depression often goes unrecognized. If your parent is a stoic, he may "put on a happy face" and thus prevent you from noticing his or her despondency. Unfortunately, this will prevent you from sharing the sorrow or discovering that your parent needs help with depression. Moreover, just as frequently depression appears in a disguised form; a preoccupation with aches and pains, a certainty that one is profoundly ill, grumbling and suspiciousness that push you away, or confusion or memory loss that suggest senility. You must learn what to look for if you are to avoid being misled.

SORROW

76. *Grief.* Most normal sorrow or sadness is caused by a loss. The longer your parents live, the more they stand to lose: physical health, financial security, independence, mental abilities, friends and relatives through death. These losses are real and the sadness is often profound, but normally the sorrow comes to a close and an elderly parent is able to continue to lead a happy and satisfying life. How rapidly this occurs depends on the severity of the loss, its suddenness, whether or not it is prolonged (as in a stroke), your parent's character, whether or not other losses also have occurred recently, and other factors. However, even in the most unlikely of circumstances, your parent can usually bounce back. As discussed in Chapter 9, you can help your parent to grieve effectively and to recover from a loss. But you also need to be able to recognize when grieving has gone awry. If your parent doesn't recover from a loss in a reasonable length of time, often a depression has supervened. In fact, a major loss seems to set in motion about half of all serious depressions in older people.

77. *Emptiness.* There is another kind of sadness that is not depression—that which springs from a sterile existence. Many older people become increasingly inactive as they age. They may not replace lost friends with new friends. They may not develop new interests when no longer able to pursue old ones. Financial limitations may cause them to go out less. Physical disabilities may further restrict them. These changes are often slow and subtle, but the result is an increasing spiritual poverty, a life less dense and less enjoyable. And, curiously, while some parents may complain bitterly

about this increased barrenness in their lives, others may be unaware of it or may accept it as the natural lot of the elderly. Their sadness may reflect a realistic appraisal of the quality of life they have come to lead.

Think about how your parents spend their day or week—visits from friends, trips out of the house, TV, books, meetings. Would it be interesting to you, or satisfying? If it isn't to you, it probably isn't to them. Of course, you have to take into consideration the differences in your interests and physical abilities. Yet your parents must fill their days with interesting and meaningful things just as much as you must yours. It is a mistake to think that as we age we are happy with less from life.

The solution to this spiritual poverty, of course, is to prevent this creeping sterility from developing or, once it is present, to reverse it. As countless elderly have shown, they can be active and involved, they can learn and create, they can teach and contribute, and they can grow until the last day of life. But they may need help in utilizing their potential and in recognizing that their life can be other than grim and empty. There are many opportunities to enrich the lives of the elderly (see Chapters 25, 26, and 27). Explore what is available in your area. However, if your parent is unhappy but sees no benefit from increasing activity, or is unable to generate the energy to improve his or her life, suspect that a depression has set in. If your parent lives an empty existence, don't assume that the life style has caused this demoralization. In fact, the depression may have come first and prevented your parent from taking any steps in his or her own behalf.

78. *Life Review.* It is natural for the elderly to reflect on life; to assess it and determine its significance. Normally, they conclude that their life has been well led and meaningful; this is a source of satisfaction and pride. However, if they conclude that their life has been wasted or of little value, their life review is unpleasant and produces a sense of low self-esteem and sadness.

You can help by participating in your parents' life reviews. Point out their accomplishments and past strengths. Note areas where they have had an impact and identify lasting achievements. If one of your parents is depressed, however, he may see things only in black and white, primarily black. If your parent has a sense of failure which seems unreasonable and which does not yield to your repeated corrections, strongly suspect that depression has unnaturally colored his point of view.

79. *Deprivation.* For a tragically large number of older people in the United States, life is hard. Although few people starve or are cold during the winter, many have few of the niceties that make life more varied, pleasant, and interesting. This can be a source of sadness for many, not only

because their world is thus made more sterile, but also because such deprivation can give them a sense of being cast off and forgotten. Some parents who are living a marginal existence attempt to hide that from their children, because of pride or shame; it requires careful detective work to discover that they don't go out because they can't afford to or that they keep the room cool because they need the money for food. Be aware of how your parent is living and do what you can to correct the deficiencies. There are a variety of public programs in most places that can help (see Chapter 29).

Loss, an unstimulating life, a sense of failure, or deprivation—these typically produce a sense of sadness among older people. However, if these are severe, occur together, or occur at the wrong time, they can precipitate a depression. Unhappy feelings become more profound, additional symptoms may appear, and correction usually requires professional help.

DEPRESSION

Depression significantly impairs the quality of life of more elderly people than any other emotional condition. It comes in many different forms (and disguises). It can be extremely severe, even fatal. And it probably goes unrecognized or is mistaken for something else more often than any other disorder. What is it? What does it look like? What can be done about it?

80. *Depression—What Is It?* There is no clear dividing line between sadness and depression. Often these conditions grade into one another, making it difficult to determine on which side of the line your parent falls. In depression, an elderly parent's unhappiness and other symptoms are worse or more prolonged than circumstances merit. Moreover, your parent is usually poorly able to function (work, read, have a conversation, etc.). He or she is unable to "snap out of it" for a short period of time. However, these criteria are obviously very vague and subjective. A parent saddened by the unexpected loss of a spouse may be profoundly distressed and temporarily inconsolable. On the other hand, a depressed parent may be able to be cheerful for a short while—for example, when entertaining guests. Even more deceptive may be your own perceptions of how justified your parent is in feeling unhappy. You may hear the situation described in the most disconsolate way. As your parent presents it, life sounds terrible and you may be totally convinced—yet this may be the depression talking. The depression may cause your parent to see only the dark side of things and to see no way out when, in fact, things are not that hopeless. Don't automatically accept your parent's view of the world and the future—make your own assessment. Only then will you be able to decide whether he or she is

unrealistically hopeless (and thus probably depressed) or whether life really is so excessively unrewarding or harsh as to explain this unhappiness.

Depression is an illness, or, more accurately, many illnesses. Several different types of depression can be identified in elderly people, each with typical characteristics, severity, and treatment. The points at which one form of depression stops and another begins are vague and confusing—and, not unexpectedly, experts disagree about those limits. One form of depression can change into another. And the causes of depression are uncertain and may differ from one type to another.

The primary cause of many depressions, and certainly the severe depressions, lies in our biology and our genes. Although a major loss or other stress may start a depression, ultimately brain chemistry is altered, hormones are thrown out of balance, and brainwaves during sleep (sleep EEG) are affected. Medication thought to correct the chemical imbalances in the brain often produces dramatic improvement. Certain medical conditions like diseases of the thyroid gland and pancreas can also cause depression. Physicians now appreciate the significant biological roots of many depressions and treat them accordingly. Thus your parents are likely to have their depression treated, at least in part, with medication and other physical means.

Some depressions are inherited. This is true of most severe as well as some minor depressions. Moreover, another condition of mood, mania, has also been shown to be related genetically to severe depression. A person with mania becomes overexcited and "high," usually for weeks on end. At other times that same individual may show a typical depression. Do your parents have any relatives who have become depressed or manic? If one of your parents is depressed, a careful record of the presence or absence of any depression or mania among close relatives can be of considerable help in determining the type of depression from which he or she suffers.

Some depressions have psychological roots. We have already seen that a major loss or stress can precipitate a severe depression (often in someone predisposed genetically to develop one). We also have noted that all of the conditions which produce sadness, if severe or prolonged, can generate a depression in some people. For example, depression often follows multiple losses, an acute medical illness (such as a heart attack), or a chronic physical disability (such as those caused by a stroke or rheumatoid arthritis). Certain types of people are particularly likely to become depressed: perfectionists who feel they are failing, dependent people who suddenly lose their support, people who have always prized their charm or beauty and who realize that these qualities are lessening with age, people who drink to excess, and people with chronically low self-esteem. Although none of these psychological dangers or personality characteristics can be used to predict with certainty who will develop a depression in late life, they are all found with increased frequency in elderly depressed people. Identifying these risks and characteristics can often aid in treatment.

81. *Types of Depression.* Depressions are difficult to categorize. They may be mild or severe. They may appear and disappear suddenly or develop slowly and last for years. They may be accompanied by bizarre ideas and suicidal impulses, or they may consist of little more than a profound sense of dejection. They may have afflicted their sufferer with depressed feelings throughout his life or only for a few weeks or months. Or they may have produced no sense of sadness at all, but rather anxiety, agitation, or preoccupation with physical symptoms.

And yet out of this tangle several kinds of depression can be identified. This splitting of depression into different types is vitally important. Because the different kinds of depression often behave differently, physicians frequently can make fairly accurate predictions about the course your parent's illness is likely to follow, choose the most effective treatment for that type of depression, and provide information about the likelihood of other members of the family developing similar difficulties in the future. Although there remain as many questions as answers about the classification of depression, examining your parent's symptoms in an effort to categorize the illness is the place to start in attempting to select the best way to help him.

Perhaps the most dramatic differences occur between mild and severe depressions.

82. *Minor (Mild) Depression.* Minor depressions come in all shapes and sizes, but even though they are mild they are worth worrying about. Some may be long-lived and depleting; others may cause your parent to become preoccupied with thoughts of suicide; still others may be mere way stations on the road to a severe depression. They may have predominantly psychological or biological roots and may respond best to psychotherapy, medication, or some combination of the two. Fortunately, most minor depressions do improve with treatment. Thus it is important to recognize them and to seek treatment, particularly since many older people are either unaware or are unwilling to admit that they are depressed. Although mild depressions may differ markedly from one another, some symptoms occur frequently enough to allow us to piece together a picture of a typical illness.

Most people who are depressed, feel depressed. They may describe themselves as sad, or depressed, or they may use words like unhappy, blue, dispirited, dejected, discouraged, demoralized, or despondent. They may complain of having no energy and of being constantly tired. They may lose enthusiasm for activities which had previously been of great interest, or they may have trouble experiencing pleasure in anything. Particularly in the elderly, depression may be dominated by moods other than sadness, such as agitation or irritability, anxiety, a feeling of emptiness, or wide emotional swings. Your depressed parent may be constantly complaining, restless and quick to anger; or he may worry that everything is going wrong, or he may deny feelings of depression altogether.

In addition to mood changes, the depressed person may be troubled by unpleasant or worrisome ideas. Your parent may become pessimistic, convinced that life is going desperately awry and that nothing can be done about it. For reasons unclear to you and that the person has difficulty explaining, he or she may feel worthless and as though life has been a failure. Or the person may be unable to stop thinking about death or the possibility of suicide.

A depressed person's thinking may seem changed. Your parent may have trouble concentrating on TV or a book. He may find maintaining a conversation difficult—his thoughts may wander or he may have brief mental lapses. Your parent may complain of poor memory and be convinced that he is becoming senile (repeated scientific studies have found little real memory loss in depressed elderly people who complain of failing memory). Your parent may become withdrawn and isolated and not seem to look forward to your visits; in fact, the depressed elderly person may no longer seem to care about anything.

Your parent may have difficulty completing a job, not only because he has little energy or enthusiasm, but because depression slows movements. The depressed individual may be tearful, often with little apparent provocation, and may be restless and pace constantly. Or he may wring his hands and mope.

Several other key symptoms should alert you to the possible presence of depression. (1) Insomnia. Does your parent awaken early in the morning and then not be able to fall asleep? Does he or she awaken frequently throughout the night? Less commonly, your parent may have difficulty falling asleep initially, or may sleep too much. If you have some concern that your parent is depressed, always ask how he is sleeping. (2) Weight loss. Has your parent lost appetite? Does he pick at his food? Has your parent lost weight or have you suddenly noticed that he looks thin? Is he constipated? Loss of appetite with an accompanying weight loss and constipation often accompanies a significant depression in an older person. (3) Daily variation. Regardless of the particular pattern of symptoms that your parent shows, are all symptoms less troublesome in the morning? People with mild depressions generally feel better in the morning, a time when people with more severe depressions generally feel worse.

Finally, depressed elderly people often feel that they are on their last legs. They complain bitterly about a variety of aches and pains. Any long-standing illness seems to worsen. Other medical symptoms appear for which the physician can find no explanation. They are genuinely distressed by these symptoms and, at times, these complaints may cause them to consider suicide.

No depressed person has all these symptoms. Usually they have a scattering of them, including some type of mood change, insomnia, and loss of appetite. Equally important in assessing your parent's depression is to note when it began. The majority of minor depressions in the elderly follow in the wake of a loss or some other undesirable change. Other older people have suffered from depression, off and on, for most of their life. Finally, some people have had a serious depression which improved but left chronic depressive symptoms that they have been unable to shake. Although individuals with these different patterns may look very similar when ill, the physician must know the particular course the disorder has followed in order to anticipate the future course or recommend treatment.

83. *Major (Severe) Depression.* Severe depression is a life-threatening illness. The risk of suicide is high, as is the risk that your parent may become medically ill by neglecting his or her health. If evidence of a major depression appears, seek medical help promptly (usually from a psychiatrist). You may need to insist that your parent see a physician, because he or she may be convinced that nothing can be done.

Your parent may display many of those symptoms found in a minor depression but in a severe form. Withdrawal may become complete isolation. Your parent may become mute and sit for hours without moving. He may see everything as hopeless and feel guilty, as though he brought all this to pass through some terrible or thoughtless action. If agitated, the depressed person may pace incessantly and be very difficult to talk to. He or she may cease eating entirely and undergo extreme weight loss. When enough of these symptoms become severe, your parent is considered to have a major depression.

New symptoms may appear—symptoms not found in a minor depression. (1) Your parent may become so withdrawn that he seems unaware of his surroundings. (2) A severely depressed person may develop bizarre ideas which have no possible basis in reality (delusions). For instance, the person may become convinced that his insides are rotting, that his body produces an odor that sickens people nearby, or that his past misbehaviors have led to the nuclear arms race. Depressed people will not be able to explain clearly why these things are so, but they feel certain that they are. And these convictions will be unshakable. (3) Your parent may become suspicious or noticeably paranoid, convinced that someone is bringing trouble down upon him. (4) Your parent may experience hallucinations. Most commonly, depressed persons may hear a voice disparaging or ridiculing them. They are not surprised by this, particularly since what is said fits perfectly with what they have come to believe about themselves.

Suicide is an ever-present threat among people this hopeless and confused. It must always be guarded against (Section 86). Equally worrisome, and an additional reason why professional help must be sought as soon as a severe depression is recognized, is that many of these people will allow themselves to slip into deplorable physical conditions. They may confine themselves to bed, stop eating, and stop cleaning themselves. As a result, they may develop a variety of medical conditions like bed sores, severe constipation, and clots in the blood vessels of the legs. If they weren't medically ill to begin with, they become so after a few weeks of this self-neglect.

The majority of severe depressions develop rapidly, over weeks or months, and if untreated may last for half a year or longer. Frequently, one or more similar episodes occurred earlier in life, but occasionally a first episode develops in old age. Some severe depressions may be preceded by a chronic mild depression that gradually worsens. Only about half the time is it possible to identify a specific event that triggered the depression.

As in mild depressions, knowledge of any past mood disorders is vital to predicting the course of the illness and to planning treatment. It is particularly important to know whether your parent has ever had a previous episode of severe depression or an attack of mania. (In mania, a person becomes excited, has boundless energy, sleeps little, is grandiose, impatient and irritable, and uses very poor judgment. A manic individual may spend all his money or conclude business dealings that are hopelessly unrealistic. Mania rarely develops for the first time in old age. Had your parent ever been manic, you probably would have known of it because mania is such a dramatic process.) There appear to be at least two different, inherited mental illnesses that produce severe depression in the elderly—one which causes a series of manic and depressed episodes during the adult years and another which causes only depressed periods. They are often treated differently, so it is important to determine from which (if either) your parent suffers. Since there are other routes to severe depression (for example, a severe loss or a major physical illness), it is equally important to be certain your parent has had no previous periods of depression.

84. *Medical Disease and Depression.* There is frequently a close tie between physical illness and depression. We have already noted that the symptoms of many different kinds of medical diseases worsen when a person is depressed. Degenerative joints ache more, constipation becomes

more severe, headaches become more frequent. We also have seen that the stresses from certain serious or chronic illnesses can worsen a depression. This is particularly true of heart disease (and heart attack), rheumatoid arthritis, and many types of cancer. Persons with any of these conditions should be watched closely for depression.

A few medical diseases actually can cause depression (through poorly understood biological mechanisms), in particular, Parkinson's disease, brain tumors, diseases of the thyroid gland, disease of the adrenal glands (both Cushing's disease and Addison's disease), diabetes, low blood sugar, multiple sclerosis (MS), some anemias, some cancers (particularly cancer of the pancreas), and serious kidney disease. If your parent has a history of any of these illnesses, be certain to mention it to the physician who evaluates the depression. Evaluation of your depressed parent should always include a thorough physical examination, since the recognition and treatment of an underlying medical illness is the primary means of treating this sort of depression.

In addition, some medications can cause depression. This is a particular danger in the elderly because they often take several (often unfamiliar) medications at one time, may receive medicine from several different doctors, may borrow medication from friends, may have trouble reading the small print on prescription labels, and may be mildly confused (medication itself often increases confusion). Moreover, many of the drugs useful for older people are the very medications that may cause depression as a side effect: heart medication (digitalis), high-blood-pressure medication (reserpine, Inderal, Aldomet, Ismelin, among others), steroids, cancer drugs, and antiparkinsonism medication (L-dopa). An even more common problem lies with the large number of sedatives and sleeping pills consumed by the elderly. All of these tranquilizers can have depression as a side effect, particularly when taken for a long time and in excessive doses. Moreover, the chronic drowsiness that results from too much sedative medication can be confused with depression and can lead to the use of inappropriate treatments. Do you know how much and what kind of medication your parents are taking? Do they know? Find out. Make a list. Keep track of *all* kinds, including vitamin pills, "water pills," and over-the-counter medication. If your parent is depressed, see that a physician reviews the entire regimen of medication. Not infrequently, a depression can be improved or relieved altogether by stopping the use of a drug or changing medications.

85. *Disguised Depressions.* Your parents may be depressed and you may not know it. If you visit only infrequently and for short periods of time, you may not notice the depression which he or she tries to hide. Or you may fail to identify signs of depression because they have developed so slowly as to

seem "natural." Or your parents may not seem depressed, but instead may appear to be ill in some other way.

Instead of feeling or acting depressed, some elderly people may be anxious, restless, irritable, or angry. Their personality may seem changed. They may become hostile and argumentative or clinging and dependent. Even if pressed, they may deny any feelings of depression. However, these people usually don't like the way they feel, and close conversation with them often reveals a sense of foreboding, pessimism about the future, or some other unhappy emotion. Unfortunately, they often may not want to seek treatment and they may try to raise their spirits by drinking too much or by using drugs, thus further complicating and obscuring the underlying problem. Because depression is so common among the elderly, always consider it as a possibility if your parents begin acting unlike themselves. Be particularly alert if the two most common disguises of depression appear: unexplained physical complaints and signs of senility.

Instead of complaining of sadness, your parent may become convinced that things are going wrong with his or her body. Feelings of weaknesses and tiredness and complaints of constipation are most common but headaches, stiff joints, backache, and abdominal pains occur frequently. Your parent may be unable to see himself as emotionally "deteriorated"— physical problems are a much more acceptable way of asking for help. If depression is behind your parent's bodily complaints, treating it usually removes these symptoms. Be aware that some older people with numerous physical complaints may have an undiscovered physical problem responsible, while others may have hypochondriasis (see Chapter 12), which requires a different form of treatment.

Either of your parents may complain bitterly and despondently about having recently lost their intellectual powers and memory. Do not conclude that your parent is becoming senile (see Chapter 11); it is just as likely that he or she is depressed. Perhaps the most common mistake made in diagnosing depression in the elderly is to confuse it with dementia (severe senility). Some older people who begin to experience the anxious and hopeless feelings of a depression decide that their mind is slipping. Worries about their mind and memory then dominate their complaints, confusing the family and the physician. If they then fail to receive treatment for their depression, months or years of unnecessary misery follow. This tragedy can be prevented only by making sure that the possibility of a depression has been eliminated when evaluating a person thought to be demented. Remind your parent's physician of that possibility if the doctor seems too quick to settle on the diagnosis of dementia. See Chapter 11 for some hints of how to tell the two conditions apart.

86. *Suicide.* If your parent is depressed, the possibility of suicide should be on your mind. The elderly kill themselves more frequently than any other group of people. (The highest rate of all is among white males in their 70s and 80s.) What's more, there is often little warning and few false tries—the elderly individual who attempts suicide is much more likely to be successful than is a younger person. You should not be unduly concerned or preoccupied about the possibility of suicide, because the likelihood that someone over 65 will kill himself is only 1 in 5,000 each year. However, since an older person who decides to commit suicide is likely to act in earnest, you should be alert to whatever warnings your parent may give that he or she is seriously considering it. All the while, recognize that you may not be able to anticipate the attempt.

What hints do you have? First of all, some people are at increased risk: those who have a serious physical illness or who are in constant pain, those who are severely depressed, heavy drinkers, people who are mildly demented or confused, hypochondriacs, people who have made a previous suicide attempt, men rather than women, and people who have suffered the loss of a loved one or a loss of self-esteem. These characteristics can serve only as warning signs, since most people who have experienced any one of them don't commit suicide. More important is how your parent acts. Does he appear despondent, irritable, tense, or agitated? Does he make comments like "You won't be bothered by me much longer," "I guess my time has about come," or "Being old is senseless and a drain on everyone"? Has there been a recent change in behavior that would suggest an altered perception about the future: making a will, giving away special possessions, buying a gun, having intense talks with friends? Has there been a sudden, unexpected change in the person's attitude: after a period of sadness, has your parent suddenly become withdrawn, or feverishly cheerful? Even if you are exceptionally alert, however, you can't always anticipate your parents' suicidal ideas or efforts. This is partly because many suicide attempts among the elderly are impulsive—they haven't been thinking about it or planning it, but suddenly the time just seems right.

If you have warning that one of your parents is thinking of suicide, or if he or she has made an unsuccessful attempt, what can you do to prevent another attempt? First, of course, your parent should be evaluated carefully—medically and psychiatrically—to determine if there is an underlying medical or psychiatric condition (depression, confusion, thyroid disease, etc.) which could have altered his mood or precipitated the action. If your parent has an uncomfortable medical condition which makes life difficult, can any improvements be made in its treatment? If possible, find out why he wanted to take his life but be aware that he might not know. Correct anything correctable. Try to reduce any isolation and improve your parent's social activities. Most of all, help him find something to live for. Help your parent realize that he is still important to you; that he still has a place; that he is still of value. However, recognize that you won't always be successful—that some people insist on the final say in when and how they die.

87. *Treatment of Depression—General Principles.* Most depressions in old age can be treated successfully. This has not always been the case. Severe depression often used to be a fatal illness. However, in the last ten years at psychiatric centers around the country and at the National Institute of Mental Health, there has been extensive research into the causes and cures of depression. This research has led to the development of new medications and improved psychotherapy techniques. Although your depressed parent may be successfully treated by the family physician, the increased complexity of the diagnosis and treatment of depression may require the expertise of a psychiatrist. Certainly, if your parent's depression is proving resistant to treatment, consult a psychiatrist.

Patients with a depression respond best to a combination of professional psychotherapy and a careful evaluation and correction of life stresses. In addition, most people also require medication. This is certainly true of the more tenacious depressions. The more severe the depression, the more likely it is to require medication, since major depressions often have biological roots. However, depressions of all degrees of severity may respond to the new antidepressant medications. Any distinct cause for the depression, however, such as an underlying medical disease, must be eliminated first.

Your parent can usually be treated as an outpatient. With severe depressions, however, treatment is usually safer if initially done in the hospital. Once medication has been stabilized, a thorough medical evaluation completed, and your parent no longer appears in danger of hurting himself, treatment can be continued outside the hospital. Most psychiatric services in private and university hospitals treat large numbers of seriously depressed persons every year and are thoroughly familiar with their care, so don't be reluctant if a physician suggests that one of your parents needs hospitalization in a psychiatric unit.

A few depressed individuals don't respond well to any form of treatment. Curiously, those patients least likely to improve are *not* those with the most severe depressions, but those whose depression has been of longest duration. If your parent has had a mild depression, but has had it off and on for many years, he is unlikely to respond dramatically to any form of therapy. It is as if the depression has become part of his personality.

88. *Treatment of Depression—Medication.* A breakthrough in treating depression has been the recent development of the antidepressant medications. Serious depressions are accompanied by biochemical changes in the brain, and antidepressant drugs appear to correct those changes. How they work is not understood completely, but it is clear that these medications have a specific effect on someone who is depressed but produce little effect on someone who is not. They do not work by "jazzing up" your parent (stimulant medications do this and may be useful in some depressed elderly), but by reversing the abnormal chemistry that causes the depression. Antidepressant drugs can raise your parent from depressed to normal but not from normal to excited.

The most common types of these drugs are called the tricyclic antidepressants. Some of the most frequently used are Elavil, Norpramin, Sinequan, Tofranil, Aventyl, and Vivactil. New medications related to the tricyclics, which are likely to be in common use soon, include Surmontil, Ludiomil, and Desyrel. If you parent is started on an antidepressant medication, it is likely to be one of these. You should know what to expect so that you can spot any developing problems before they have a chance to interrupt treatment.

These medications are usually begun at a low dose (given several times a day by mouth) and gradaully raised over one to three weeks to the normally effective dosage. An additional week or two may be required for a noticeable change in your parent's depression. If there is no improvement after four to five weeks, the physician usually either increases the dosage or changes to a different antidepressant and repeats the process. Once the depression improves and the dose of medication is stabilized, the drug is usually given as a single dose at bedtime. Occasionally the physician will take a blood sample to be certain that the level of the drug in the blood is adequate. The amount of medication that corrects the depression depends upon the type of drug chosen, the type of depression, and the person. A few elderly individuals respond to tiny amounts of medication, while most require doses similar to those needed in younger people. Two out of three people with a significant depression respond to the first antidepressant medication, while many of the other third improve with the second. If both trials fail, there are other treatments available, which are discussed later in this chapter.

If this is your parent's first major depression, he or she may need to continue the antidepressant for several months before gradually discontinuing it. Some physicians may want your parent to continue the medication in a reduced dosage for a year or more. If your parent has experienced several depressions in the past, it is likely that he or she will be asked to continue the medication, at a lower dose, for an extended period of time. Although long-term medication doesn't prevent the recurrence of all depressions, it does markedly decrease their likelihood of returning.

In general, the tricyclic antidepressants are safe and effective. However, there are some medical conditions in which their use would be risky, and there are some side effects that may make their use uncomfortable or impossible. If your parent suffers from heart disease, particularly if it is associated with an irregular heartbeat, the use of antidepressants should be carefully regulated by the physician. These drugs can still be used, but expect the physician to request frequent checkups that include a measurement of the electrical impulses in the heart (EKG). Other medical conditions in which antidepressants should be used with caution include severe high blood pressure, kidney disease, liver disease, an enlarged prostate gland, glaucoma, and alcoholism. The severity of side effects also determines how useful these antidepressants are likely to be. Most people experience some mild side effects, such as slight sedation, dry mouth, blurred vision, constipation, slight difficulty in urinating, a fine tremor of the fingers and hands, and a slight dizziness upon standing. These are generally tolerable and go away in time. However, if side effects are severe or if other effects appear, like an irregular heartbeat, confusion, or marked restlessness, one of the other antidepressants may work better. It is important that you become familiar with these possible side effects so that you can correctly identify them when your parents have physical complaints. Alert their physician to their presence. However, since most of these undesirable symptoms disappear with time, follow the doctor's advice as to how long to stick with the medication.

Since all of these medications are potentially lethal if taken in a sudden, large amount, be certain you understand the doctor's assessment of your parent's likelihood for suicide. It may be necessary for you to keep the bottle of your parent's medication until the worst of the depression has passed, since a bottle of these pills taken on impulse could be fatal. An overdose of antidepressants is a medical emergency and your parent should be taken to the hospital immediately.

Besides the tricycles, the other major class of antidepressant medications is the monoamine oxidase inhibitors (MAOIs, for short). These drugs include Marplan, Nardil, and Parnate. If tricyclic antidepressants fail, many physicians prescribe a MAOI. Like the tricyclics, MAOIs are begun at a low dosage and raised slowly. Elderly people often tolerate MAOI side effects (insomnia, lightheadedness on standing, giddiness) better than those of the tricyclics. However, there is one serious caution in the elderly. A person who is taking a MAOI and who then eats certain foods may suffer a sudden and severe rise in blood pressure. When this occurs, the individual usually experiences a sudden headache in the back or the sides of his head, often accompanied by sweating, fever, a stiff neck, or sensitivity to light. If your parent reports any of these symptoms, a physician should be contacted immediately, particularly if your parent has recently eaten any of the prohibited foods. Foods to avoid include: pickled or kippered herring; dried, salted fish; chicken livers or liver pâté; spoiled meat; ripened sausages; red wine, especially Chianti; beer; strong cheese; old yogurt; chocolate; and broad beans such as fava, Italian green, and lima. Your parents should discuss the potential side effects carefully with their doctor and should seek help if symptoms develop.

There are two other medications which may help relieve your parent's depression. Those who have suffered from both depression and mania are often best treated with lithium carbonate. Lithium is often used to control an attack of mania. While it does not relieve an attack of depression, it is effective in preventing its recurrence. Thus your depressed parent may be treated with one of the antidepressants until he or she has recovered and may then be switched to lithium to prevent future attacks. Lithium has very few side effects at normal doses (mild tremor, mild thirst, and slight loss of appetite), but must be carefully monitored with regular blood measurements since a slight excess in the blood can produce dangerous side effects. Symptoms which suggest increasing blood levels include diarrhea or other bowel distress and increased restlessness. Be alert if your parent complains of any of these, because as the level of lithium in the blood rises the symptoms can progress to seizures and coma. Particularly at risk are elderly people who suffer from kidney or heart disease, who are dehydrated, or who take diuretics (water pills). In spite of this intimidating list of worries, lithium may be the best and safest way to prevent a return of a life-threatening depression. The other medication useful for treating depression in some older people is the stimulant Ritalin. Used in low doses in persons who are withdrawn and apathetic, it sometimes increases their level of activity. However, it usually doesn't reverse feelings of depression, and it may cause excessive excitement and confusion if used in too high a dose. The use of either lithium or Ritalin should be carefully supervised by a physician.

There are a few other types of medication which, while not specifically antidepressants, may be useful in treating some of the problems associated with depression. Minor tranquilizers (for example, Valium) may help the anxious, agitated individual feel more comfortable, but because normal dosages cease working after several weeks and because they are all too frequently abused, tranquilizers should be used only for short periods of time. Major tranquilizers (for example, Haldol, Mellaril, Stelazine, Navane) are useful if your parent is profoundly depressed *and* has delusions or hallucinations: a combination of an antidepressant and a major tranquilizer will be required if he is to improve.

89. *Treatment of Depression—ECT.* ECT (electroconvulsive therapy) or "shock treatment" has an undeservedly bad reputation. Anyone who has seen the movie *One Flew Over the Cuckoo's Nest* has been left with a thoroughly inaccurate impression of ECT. Far from being a painful and debilitating treatment, ECT is perhaps the most effective and least risky of any of the therapies for severe depression. Although antidepressant medication is useful in treating serious depressions, ECT is more effective, dramatically improving nine of every ten patients. Moreover, it works in days instead of weeks and it produces fewer side effects.

ECT is used most often for those people who suffer from the most serious of depressions—people with severe agitation or withdrawal, delusions of bodily changes, hallucinations, or severe loss of appetite and weight loss. It can be life-saving for these people, since some of them may have become so weak and malnourished as to be close to death. Because its effect is rapid, it is occasionally the first treatment used, particularly in those who are desparately ill. More commonly, it is used after one or two trials of antidepressant medication have failed. It is also used for people with serious physical illnesses that preclude the safe use of medication. ECT has a valuable place in the treatment of severe depression and we should recognize its validity.

If your parent is to receive ECT, what can he or she expect? First, your parent will almost certainly be hospitalized. The patient will be prepared as if for surgery, receiving no food the night before ECT is to be given. Your parent will be treated by a psychiatrist, or a psychiatrist and an anesthesiologist. The treatment will be done either in your parent's room, in a special room on the psychiatric ward, or in a room associated with the hospital recovery room. Your parent will be put to sleep, and will wake up when it is over. While he is asleep, he will receive a brief pulse of electricity, usually to the right side of the head. This procedure is repeated, one to three times each week, for a total of four to eight treatments. You may begin to see improvement in your parent after the first or second ECT but major change may take a week or more.

ECT is a simple and safe procedure, but there are some mild side effects which occur in most people, and your parents should be forewarned. Most individuals experience confusion and mild memory loss for a short while after each treatment. The confusion clears within several hours, while the memory may require slightly longer to recover. Occasionally, the loss of some memories may last for a month or two, but longer-lasting amnesia is rare. A headache that disappears later in the day is also common. Any other side effects or complications from ECT are rare. The treatment, however, should not be given to a person who has an active disease of the brain, such as brain tumor or brain infection, or to a person who has not fully recovered from a heart attack.

90. *Treatment of Depression—Psychotherapy.* In spite of recent emphasis on the biological roots of depression and the remarkable effectiveness of antidepressant medication, psychotherapy and social assistance remain crucial elements in the treatment of any depressed elderly person. Most often, psychotherapy is combined with medication, one complementing the other.

No treatment for depression is complete, or likely to be effective very long, that doesn't take into account the stresses on your parents and the conditions under which they must live. The elderly often endure enormous stress due to poor health, important and frequent losses, financial insecurity, and a shrinking social world. You need to help your parents realistically assess their life's major deficiencies and help correct them. Don't neglect to point out their strengths in the process. Perhaps most important is to help them replace lost social relationships by encouraging new friendships and by assisting them in joining clubs, pursuing (or developing) interests, and exploring organized activities for older people in the community. Become familiar with what is available: most communities have a selection of interesting and meaningful activities for the elderly. If your parents still haven't recovered from loss, help them to grieve (see Chapter 9). Do your parents need help with finances? They may not need financial assistance as much as a careful review of how their money is managed.

Help your parents become active. Ongoing social activities are essential for emotional well-being. Most people who become depressed have allowed their social life to wither. Social contacts are essential supports as depression begins to lift. Physical activity is equally necessary. Not only does it make living more enjoyable, but recent scientific evidence suggests that it helps reverse depression through some poorly understood biological mechanism. Within their physical limits, your parents should be encouraged to walk, swim, bicycle, bowl, etc.

You will inevitably need to face the question of whether your depressed parent should become involved in formal psychotherapy. What kind? How often? For how long? Unfortunately, there are no pat answers to these questions. So much depends upon the particulars—upon your parent and the reasons for the depression, and upon what kind of therapies are available in your area. Those who were well adjusted and happy before the depression struck and who have recovered quickly and completely with medication probably have little need for psychotherapy. On the other hand, people whose depression seems to have grown from a sense of chronic dissatisfaction with their life may not be able to recover without some sort of active psychotherapeutic intervention.

There is no single effective type of therapy. Elderly depressed individuals have responded to individual, group, family, and couple therapy. However, all successful types of psychotherapy share certain characteristics. Invariably, they seek to promote your parent's sense of self-esteem and self-sufficiency. They explore the impact changing physical health and loss of independence have on your parent. They help your parent wrestle with losses and come to grips with and resolve unsettled feelings about being old. They help your parent establish appropriate, realistic goals. Whatever type of therapy is settled on, most of the gains are made in the first several months; only very unusual circumstances should require treatment past six months or a year.

In recent years, cognitive therapy has been developed specifically to correct depression and has had unusual success. It recognizes that depressed individuals frequently explain everything that happens to them in the most negative light: they twist their experiences around so that they see themselves as inadequate or to blame. Cognitive therapists help correct these self-perceptions, thought by thought. Psychiatrists and therapists of many types have begun using cognitive techniques. You might use a familiarity with cognitive therapy as one criterion for choosing a psychotherapist for your depressed parent.

Some depressed individuals present a special problem. They may not see themselves as depressed, or they may feel so hopelessly depressed that they resist any treatment. They may insist on being bedridden. Or they may be dependent and demanding, and refuse to participate in self-care in any way. A depressed person may insist that he can't get out of bed, walk, or feed himself. He may feel so completely helpless and hopeless that his only relief is to get you to participate in his misery. You must avoid playing along with this self-destructive behavior. You must insist that he try to do things for himself. See that your parent gets out of bed and fixes his own meals. Demand that he obtain treatment and follow through with the physician's recommendations. This kind of reaction to depression is difficult for you to deal with, both logistically and emotionally. Obtain the help of a professional.

Finally, don't try to turn your parent's life around all by yourself. Encourage your parent's independence. Utilize groups, organizations, concerned friends, and professionals. Churches, your state's Department of Aging, and public mental health organizations all may offer valuable services.

11.

Mental Confusion and Senility

91. *What Is There to Worry About?* Are your aging parents' minds slipping? Have they become forgetful? Have they suffered personality changes? Are they not as sharp or as quick as before? Do they become confused or befuddled easily? Have they gotten lost in town, in the neighborhood, or in the home? Is one of them having trouble finding the right words when he talks? Is he restless and does he have trouble keeping his mind on any topic for very long? In short, are you worried that they are becoming senile, or that something else is seriously wrong?

At some time during old age, your parents are likely to display one or more of these symptoms, or they may show some other sign of mental decline that will worry you. You will need to know what to make of it. At such a moment, it is natural to jump to the most disquieting of conclusions—that the irreversible mental decline, commonly called senility, has begun.

More often than not, your fears will be groundless—for several reasons. (1) Most mild mental changes in old age are just that: mild. They are products of normal aging, never become extreme, and portend nothing more serious than a need for you to modify slightly the way you deal with your parents (see Chapter 4). (2) Senility (also known as dementia) is a disease. It is not something which happens to everyone as they age. Only one person in twenty over 65 and one in five over 80 becomes truly demented. Even so, it is the major mental health problem among the elderly. (3) Dementia is not always incurable. One person in five who begins to develop all the classic symptoms of senility has a treatable medical illness. (4) There is a typical pattern of symptoms often found in a person who is becoming senile. Most types of mental symptoms in old age are *not* due to senility, but are due to causes ranging from emotional stress to medical illness. Perhaps the most common serious mental symptom among the elderly is confusion, and yet it usually does not indicate the presence of dementia.

CONFUSION

Confusion is experienced by many elderly people at some point. Often it is of minor importance—merely a sign that the older brain has lost reserve capacity and cannot tolerate stresses and shocks as easily as before. Occasionally, it is serious. Any pattern of confused behavior in our parents should always be evaluated medically when it first appears. Potentially serious diseases may thus be recognized and treated before damage becomes widespread and irreversible. We should resist the tendency to pass off as normal mild degrees of confusion in the old and instead should seek a cause for the confusion.

92. *Degree of Confusion.* First ask two questions: how profound is the confusion, and, how sudden was its appearance? Has your father begun making mistakes? Does he fail to recognize them? Does he sometimes seem unaware of what is going on around him? Is he forgetful? Does he have trouble paying attention or following a conversation? Is he confused at night, but fine during the day? Has your mother become restless, irritable, or even aggressive? Does she make "silly" mistakes—using loose tea to brew coffee or putting her blouse on inside out? Has she gotten lost while out walking? Or have your parent's symptoms been more dramatic—a sudden inability to recognize you or to know where he or she is; mumbled, incoherent speech upon arising in the morning; marked confusion about everyone and everything. Has your parent "seen things"—for instance, a man climbing in the window at night or insects on the wall? Most commonly, these symptoms appear in a day or days; but they may develop more slowly and initially go unrecognized. The more severe and the more sudden the confusion, the more it should be treated as a medical emergency. However, even a brief period of mild confusion should not be neglected, as it may be an important forewarning of a serious condition.

93. *Confusion Is a Symptom.* Confusion is not a disease—it is a symptom of many diseases. Anything that stresses the aging body or brain can cause it. It can be produced by strange surroundings and unfamiliar people as well as by dozens of different medical conditions, only some of them connected with the brain. Heart diseases which slow the flow of blood to the

brain, pneumonia, cancer, kidney problems which change the blood's chemical composition, a fall in body temperature from living in an under-heated apartment, or a missed meal which lowers the blood sugar can all produce confusion. So can diseases which affect the brain itself, such as stroke, menigitis, or the loss of brain cells seen in senility. Severe depression frequently brings confusion with it. A very common cause of confusion in older people is medication—be certain that any evaluation includes a thorough review of all drugs taken (particularly sleeping pills, tranquilizers, antidepressants, high blood pressure medication, and alcohol). If your parents are rested, healthy, and free from major emotional stress, they are unlikely to be confused. Assume that confusion is abnormal and take it seriously until it is proven to be of little importance.

Unfortunately, older people are frequently not aware that they are physically ill; the only sign that they are sick may be sudden confusion. The unwary family may ignore this one warning sign and so allow the illness to progress. The unwary physician may give a mildly confused and agitated older person a tranquilizer. Yet tranquilizing someone who is confused due to medical illness invariably worsens the confusion, while the underlying illness goes untreated. A vicious cycle is started—increased confusion is treated with more sedatives, which in turn produce more confusion. All too often, this cycle leads to institutionalization. A thorough medical evaluation usually halts this process. Never push for institutionalization or for medication until your parent's health has been thoroughly checked.

94. *Care of the Confused.* Confusion is usually temporary and disappears with removal of the underlying cause. In the meantime, it is essential for you to limit its effects on your parents. Look out for their safety. Elderly persons who are confused are often restless and fearful, particularly at night. They may be combative or in danger of hurting themselves as they attempt to escape imagined pursuers. Remove from the bedroom sharp objects your confused parent might fall against or heavy objects he or she could throw. Keep a small light burning throughout the night—if your parent wakes to familiar surroundings, he is less likely to be confused. Move the bedroom downstairs in case your parent wanders at night. Help reduce his confusion during the day by keeping familiar objects around, reminding him frequently what you are doing there, tactfully describing what is going on, providing calendars and clocks to help him keep track of time, and using a television or radio to keep him in touch with the world. Anxiety about their own confusion is common—be calm, supportive, and sympathetic.

Although confusion is most likely to be due to some treatable medical illness, it also may be caused by senility. In that case, it is likely to have been a long-standing problem.

SENILITY

We seem to go out of our way to call someone senile. What we usually mean is that the person's memory has begun to fail, he is no longer as quick or able to understand things, or he is beginning to behave oddly. We raise the warning at the first sign of forgetfulness or the mildest eccentricity and then we wait for deterioration. We assume these changes can only get worse, inevitably leading to incapacitation and feeblemindedness. Consider what such a branding accomplishes. We have decided that our parent shall never recover; shall never again be a competent adult; is less than fully human. We feel justified in ignoring opinions with which we don't agree or in taking control of elements of our parent's life in defiance of his or her wishes. We are concerned and saddened, but we are also patronizing. So subtly as often to be unaware of it ourselves, we begin to draw away from our parent, to grieve, to write him off. If our parent really is becoming progressively and profoundly senile, many of these responses are realistic. But senility is not a term to be used lightly. We should know what senility is and whether our parent is really afflicted before we make those subtle but momentous changes in our feelings. For, in truth, "senility" doesn't mean anything—or, rather, it means too many things. It is a label too quickly applied, which covers too many conditions of widely varying significance.

Long-lasting mental changes which begin in old age can be divided roughly into three groups: (1) common, mild changes that rarely become severe and which usually are of little significance (see Chapter 4); (2) conditions which develop slowly and end in profound loss of intelligence and memory; and (3) diseases which may produce senility that can be reversed or cured if the disease is caught early. These three are quite different conditions and should not be confused with one another. In this book, senility will refer to the second condition. Don't do your parent the disservice of concluding that he has developed senility when all he is showing are the normal changes of age. And if symptoms suggestive of senility do appear, be certain that a correctable medical condition is not present.

95. *Symptoms of Senility.* The symptoms of senility are most effectively illustrated in the following case study. Harold Ellis, 68 years old, had always been a good provider. He finished high school, married early, and began a window-washing business which, although not highly successful, prospered. Most of his time in recent years had been spent running the business and supervising his two dozen employees. His four children had

been out of the house for many years but continued to visit frequently. He and his wife, always close, had become closer since the children left. Mr. Ellis had been generally happy and had been satisfied with his family and his work, and in addition, had long been well liked by his friends.

About two years ago his wife and children noticed that he was acting differently and they used to joke among themselves that "the old man was becoming senile"—until it was no longer funny. First, there were mental lapses—business appointments neglected and telephone calls unreturned. The family remembers that he appeared slightly preoccupied during that time, and in fact they were concerned that he was becoming depressed because he seemed to have no enthusiasm for most of his past interests. Ever so slowly, his personality began to change. He became more irritable and more quick to anger; squabbles developed with the men at work over issues he would have laughed off the year before; he began to imagine slights; he began to hold grudges.

The combination of his irritability and decreased business acuity produced a slump in his business. One former business associate and family friend confided to Mrs. Ellis that he was employing another firm because the job wasn't getting done and Harry wouldn't listen to complaints. Moreover, the one son who worked for the firm as his father's primary assistant had no more luck getting him to examine why they were losing customers—Mr. Ellis just didn't seem to recognize that there was a problem.

Invitations to friends' homes came less frequently—for good reason. Not only did Mr. Ellis rise to anger more quickly, but his sense of humor, formerly one of his most endearing qualities, turned sour. Although he had never been a puritan, his jokes became noticeably crude and embarrassing. People present, including his wife, became uneasy, but Mr. Ellis didn't seem to notice. When Mrs. Ellis approached him about his inappropriateness, he lost his temper with her and began to shout—unheard-of behavior which caught her completely by surprise.

By the end of the first year, it was clear to everyone that there was a problem. Mr. Ellis was different, but not so different as to cause the family to seek medical help. So, the family found explanations for his behavior—many different explanations. First, the changes were ignored or laughed off. When that became impossible, they concluded that he needed a vacation (with surprisingly little encouragement, he went with his eldest son to Las Vegas where he proceeded to lose all the money allotted for the trip within the first twenty-four hours). They then decided that he was depressed. He denied it and efforts to cheer him up failed. He remained listless and uninvolved in activities he previously considered important, but he insisted that he felt fine. Reluctantly, his family concluded that Mr. Ellis was becoming senile.

The second year seemed to prove their case. He became extremely restless and distracted, unable to concentrate long enough to read the paper or sit through the TV news. He was difficult to talk with because his train of thought and conversation wandered. His memory failed noticeably—he had difficulty remembering people he had just met, and his son had to take over all scheduling and bookkeeping at work. He began to confuse the date and to lose track of time; he misplaced things and several times left the TV on all night. Whereas his family formerly had felt that he was "not as sharp" as before, they gradually came to see him as "dull." Through it all, he seemed oblivious to the changes that were so obvious to others, and although he was frequently aware that he was being discriminated against, he did not appreciate the reasons. A year ago it was obvious to family members that he was different; now his symptoms were obvious to complete strangers.

A medical evaluation was sought and, on the basis of an initial interview, the physician immediately concluded that Mr. Ellis was suffering from moderately severe dementia or senility.

Mr. Ellis was demented. His family's early jokes about "the old man's senility" have turned bitter—his wife and children have experienced the tragedy of real dementia.

Dementia is devastating. It destroys a life just as surely as the most fatal of illnesses. It robs a family of a loved one and replaces him with a stranger. Is it a surprise that we search elderly faces for any sign of feeble-mindedness and blanch at the first forgotten name? We want to be forewarned. And, we can be. Even early on, there are hints that alert us as to what is, and is not, in store.

96. *Early Changes in Senility*. The essential quality of early dementia is its relentlessness. With normal aging, our parent is likely to experience mild memory changes, or a slowing of the speed of thought, or a subtle intensification or stiffening of some part of his personality. With early senility, he is likely to experience all three, simultaneously. Though these initial changes may be slight and we may wonder if our concern reflects our imagination more than reality, in true dementia the deterioration advances inexorably.

Your parent may act like a different person—not all at once, but over months or a year. Your father may retreat into himself and become more of a loner. He may become apathetic and lose interest in previous activities. Emotions may become more shallow. His grip on his emotions may be less firm—your stoic parent may now cry, sulk, or rage. Previous personality characteristics often become amplified. If your father was stubborn, he becomes more stubborn. If your mother was frivolous, her silliness increases.

Be prepared to be surprised by the person who emerges—often the outline is familiar but the features are changed. And, usually, you wish you could have the old person back.

The mind dulls. Your older parent no longer appreciates complicated jokes. The news no longer interests him—perhaps because he doesn't understand it. He has trouble solving puzzles and he avoids games. Couple this blunting of intelligence with increasing apathy and lack of interest and your parent becomes a less interesting companion; you may find yourself avoiding conversations because they never seem to go anywhere.

Your parent's memory also begins to slip. He may hide it at first, successfully. You may not notice his extra efforts—notes written to himself or pill bottles carefully arranged on a kitchen shelf. But growing memory loss cannot stay disguised forever. Inevitably, keys are unaccountably lost or are left in the car's ignition. Doctor's appointments are forgotten. Bills go unpaid. Gradually, the toll mounts and the problem becomes obvious.

A psychiatrist or psychologist, by careful testing, can detect even mild memory loss. There are differences between the kind of loss due to normal aging and that due to dementia, and it is often possible to learn early which type is present. Unfortuantely, such testing is complicated and not available everywhere. In addition, by the time you are suspicious enough to want to have it done, enough other symptoms may have developed to make the testing unnecesssary.

Other early changes are common and impair your parent's ability in everyday activities. He or she may pace, be unable to stick to a task, and be unable to focus attention on one thing. Initially, this may look like increased interest and energy, but, when nothing gets accomplished, the true nature of this activity becomes evident. Your parent is frequently perplexed and thrown off track by minor complications. You can easily confuse him by making rapid demands on him or by asking him to perform under stress. And your parent may become easily fatigued. Growing senility seems to sap his strength and he appears more frail.

Finally, as these changes become increasingly evident and worrisome to you, your parent becomes less aware and concerned. Initially, he may be worried about his growing confusion and memory loss and be vaguely aware that he is changing in other ways. During this period, he may respond to his failures by becoming depressed, frustrated, anxious, or suspicious. In time, however, he gradually loses insight into his deficiencies and ends up as the least concerned member of the family.

Yet suspicious symptoms are only part of the story. Numerous psychiatric and physical conditions can perfectly mimic all the early changes of senility. A careful medical evaluation is necessary. You will have to make sure that your parent receives appropriate examination and treatment for symptoms of senility, since he is unlikely to seek help.

97. *Causes of Senility.* As noted earlier, one person in twenty over 65 years of age develops severe dementia. And the probability of becoming senile rises steadily thereafter: one person in five over 80 is afflicted. Each one of those individuals has a disease. Most have some obvious physical changes in the brain. The cause for each person's disease must be discovered; one of every ten people can be cured, another one in ten improved, and a final one in ten kept from getting worse.

Treatable causes abound. Any older person with a major illness may experience mental dulling due to the effects of that disease. Major culprits include heart disease, infections of the kidney and bladder, cancer, pneumonia, and chronic lung disease like emphysema. Usually these people are obviously sick, and improvement in their mental symptoms comes with improvement in their underlying illness. In a person who appears otherwise healthy, symptoms of senility may be due to chronic overuse of medication, abuse of alcohol, malnutrition (surprisingly common among the elderly), disorders of the thyroid gland, anemia, a brain tumor, a slowly leaking blood vessel in the covering around the brain (subdural hematoma; see Section 258), or many other disorders. None of these causes of dementia is particularly common, but added together they afflict a large group of people who may be inadequately treated if their condition goes unrecognized.

Unfortunately, there are often no symptoms that distinguish reversible dementia due to a treatable illness from irreversible dementia. But there are hints. Suspect that a recent medical illness is to blame if your parent's mental changes have appeared suddenly, over weeks or a couple of months. Also, the more confused your parent, the more likely it is that a medical condition is present. In any case, the final diagnosis must be based on a careful physical examination and laboratory and X-ray tests. Like the rest of us, a few physicians jump too easily to the conclusion that slipping mental powers in old age indicate irreversible senility. Let the doctor know that you would like your parent to have a thorough evaluation. Gather detailed information about your parent's behavior over recent weeks—by interviewing other family members, if necessary. Provide complete information about diseases your parent has suffered from or is prone to. Ask about the results of tests. Such encouragement often induces the physician to take another look at his conclusions.

Stress can also drive an elderly person into temporary dementia. The many problems the elderly face come at a time when the natural ability to bounce back is ebbing. Occasionally, the stress can be so unsettling as to produce symptoms indistinguishable from dementia. The solution, of course, is to help make the stresses more endurable—see that your parent's living conditions are improved, review his finances, see that correctable physical problems are treated. Help him establish new friendships and see that he stays active. All common sense? Of course! But such measures are frequently overlooked in the rush to label someone as senile.

Severe depression is perhaps the most common cause of false senility. Usually your parent feels and looks depressed, but occasionally the depression may not be evident. Instead, the only signs may be slowed thinking, withdrawal, a lack of zest, a failing memory, and a concern over his deficiencies. In other words, he looks as though he is becoming senile.

Fortunately, there are ways to distinguish depression from senility. A person with depression may complain bitterly and despondently about severe memory loss while a person who has become truly demented may barely notice it. The depressed individual feels incapacitated by his failings and can describe them in detail (in fact, often insists on telling you about them) while the demented person is much less certain about what has gone wrong. True dementia develops gradually and almost imperceptibly; pseudodementia due to depression appears suddenly (over weeks) and rapidly escalates. These kinds of differences frequently clarify the diagnosis, but when they don't, treating the presumed depression usually will provide the answer. The "senility" usually disappears within weeks when the hidden depression is treated with medication. If the medication produces no improvement, electroshock therapy (ECT) may be worth trying. ECT is an effective way of treating severe depression (Section 89), but you should thoroughly discuss its pros and cons with the physician. In any case, the outlook for the depressed patient with pseudodementia is good— the symptoms appear quickly and disappear just as fast with proper treatment.

Unfortunately, we have been discussing the tip of the iceberg, the 20 percent of senile persons who can be treated. It is the iceberg itself that should worry us—the 80 percent of demented individuals for whom we can do little. Over one half of all profoundly senile people suffer from a single condition—primary dementia (Alzheimer's disease). Another 20 percent have a different condition (multi-infarct dementia), which is related to heart disease and atherosclerosis. A few other people are afflicted by a variety of other rare, untreatable forms of brain deterioration. Finally, Parkinson's disease (Section 244) produces dementia in a few of its sufferers, but the cause is rarely in doubt since the indvidual usually has been struggling with the disease for many years. Primary dementia and multi-infarct dementia are the most common forms of severe senility. These two diseases have given us a terrifying image of dementia.

98. *Primary Dementia (Alzheimer's Disease)*. Alzheimer's disease produces the stereotyped symptoms of senility. Deteroration is slow but inevitable. Memory, personality, intelligence, and physical health all go. And it is always fatal.

Primary dementia is one of the major unsolved riddles of medical science, a devastating disease of unknown cause and untreatable effects. It presses relentlessly forward, causing death five to ten years after the first symptoms. It is more common in women: if your father lives into his 80s or 90s, he has one chance in ten of dying from it, whereas your mother's chance is one in four. In either case, it is a major cause of death among the elderly.

In primary dementia the brain is shrunken and dotted with derelict cells and the refuse of cells. Millions of brain cells die; an uncounted number of interconnections are destroyed. Sometimes these changes are mild, particularly early in the disease, but usually they are glaringly obvious. They can be seen clearly on special X-rays of the brain (CAT scan) and in a sample of brain tissue examined microscopically. As time goes by, the deterioration worsens. Most of the symptoms of primary dementia are caused by the gradual disappearance of innumerable brain cells. Until it becomes possible to halt that loss, the disease will remain incurable.

In spite of extensive research, the cause of Alzheimer's disease remains elusive. There are a few good leads: particular chemicals are abnormal in certain small areas of the brain and aluminum occurs in such places in suspiciously large amounts, the body's immune (disease-fighting) system may be abnormal, and certain viruses can produce a similar disease in animals. Unfortunately, none of these has been shown to be the primary cause of the disease, if indeed there is a single cause. Evidence also suggests that dementia develops more frequently in certain families. Possibly some people are genetically predisposed to contract primary dementia— but we don't understand why. Clearly, more research is needed to understand the roots of Alzheimer's disease.

What symptoms can you expect? First, your parent will have displayed some combination of the early symptoms of senility listed in Section 96. The onset was proabably so gradual that you have difficulty determining just when the changes began. However, by the end of two or three years, there should be little doubt that something is amiss. By the time symptoms are clearly evident, the pace of change usually seems to be accelerating. Deficits of all types become more marked. Memory loss now prevents your parent from handling the simplest household business or managing his or her own affairs. Such a person may become lost in the neighborhood where he has spent the last forty years and he loses his way from the kitchen to the bathroom in his own house. You wake at night to find him wandering in the living room, deep in conversation with a schoolboy friend who is now long dead. Or your mother can't seem to keep the day of the week straight and confuses morning and afternoon. Conversations with her become increasingly empty—she may nod, smile, and chatter appropriately, but the talk is devoid of meaningful content. If you appear to doubt what she is saying, she may rush to convince you with an uninterrupted string of information of questionable accuracy. Your parent increasingly fails to understand what is going on around him and may come to depend on you to make decisions for him. Your parent's behavior becomes stranger and less socially appropriate. For instance, your father may spray passers-by with the hose while watering the lawn. He may use the bathroom sink as a urinal. He may become sloppy and careless about his dress and manners. Your parent increasingly slips beyond the bounds of normal behavior and into the region where he or she will need help to remain healthy and comfortable.

After one to five years, this middle stage gradually gives way to the final stage of Alzheimer's disease. Your parent becomes completely dependent and confused. Your father will frequently lose track of where he is, who you are, and even who he is. Wandering may become a major problem: he may seem to be constantly finding his way out of the house and into the street. His speech may become rambling and incoherent, or he may become mute. He may develop peculiar preoccupations, hallucinations, or strange ideas. You may find him talking to himself. Unreasoning suspiciousness or paranoia may make it difficult to help him, since he misinterprets what you are trying to do. Or, your mother's physical health may deteriorate markedly and she may appear increasingly frail. She may become incontinent, compounding the difficulty you encounter caring for her at home. Eventually, she becomes bedridden and unable to communicate in even the most rudimentary fashion. In that debilitated state, she falls easy victim to a variety of different illnesses, any of which could be fatal. (Pneumonia is the most common cause of death in those individuals who are severely demented.)

The later stages of Alzheimer's disease are steeped in tragedy, for our parents and for ourselves. What can we do to soften the blow? Is treatment available? How can we make our parent more comfortable? How can we be more comfortable? How long should he remain at home? These and other questions will be discussed in later sections.

99. *Multi-Infarct Dementia.* Although considerably less common than Alzheimer's disease, multi-infarct dementia is still the second most common cause of senility. Usually, the elderly person with this condition has widespread atherosclerosis (narrowing of the arteries) and known heart disease. He may also suffer from high blood pressure or diabetes. Because the arteries are in poor condition, the tiny branches of arteries in the brain occasionally become blocked, causing damage or death to the cells they normally supply with blood. In contrast, if a large artery to the brain is suddenly blocked, the person suffers a stroke (see Chapter 20). When enough small areas throughout the brain are destroyed, mental dulling occurs and the individual becomes demented.

Normally, once these blockages begin, others follow over months or years. They cause your parent to worsen unpredictably, by steps. Because the tendency to form such obstruction can occasionally be controlled with proper medication, it is important to recognize and treat multi-infarct dementia. Distinguishing such dementia from Alzheimer's disease can be difficult—the physicians will need your help. The history of the illness, which your parent often cannot give accurately, is of the greatest help in telling the two kinds of dementia apart. Have you noticed, for instance, any of the stepwise progression of symptoms so characteristic of multi-infarct dementia? Has your parent been clear one day and confused the next? Have there been brief periods of time when your parent's speech hasn't made sense or when he or she has seemed unable to form words clearly? Has your parent had any trouble swallowing or complained of weakness of a hand or of the face? Has he complained of dizziness? A rapid development of symptoms, over weeks or months, is another distinguishing feature of multi-infarct dementia. If you are not certain about how your parent's disorder has advanced, question relatives or friends who might be able to supply specific examples.

Although most people with this form of senility do poorly, the outcome is not as uniformly grim as with Alzheimer's disease. A few people experience some damage, stabilize, and then live the rest of their lives without trouble. However, the typical course is downward, towards increasing dementia. This deterioration may take several months or several years, and there may be periods of significant clarity along the way. Unfortunately, since many of these people were in noticeably bad health from widespread atherosclerosis to begin with, early death is frequent and is typically due to heart disease, stroke, or pneumonia. Treatment, the outcome of which is unpredictable at best, will be discussed below.

100. *Evaluation of the Senile Person.* Once dementia is clearly shown to be present, the search should begin for a treatable cause. The physician should insist on a careful physical and laboratory examination. Expect the doctor to look at the heart, lungs, kidneys, liver, and hormone system. Such a broad examination is necessary because the different dementias are too similar to be able to tell them apart by superficial testing. Brainwave tests (EEG) and computerized X-ray examinations of the head (CAT scan) are particularly useful.

Unfortunately, there is no one test which can identify Alzheimer's disease. However, a history of gradual worsening over years, evidence of brain shrinkage by CAT scan, and absence of other probable causes all point to this diagnosis. Ultimately, the diagnosis of Alzheimer's disease is made by excluding other possible diseases. For that reason, be wary of any conclusion too quickly arrived at—inquire about further testing. Mr. Ellis, who was discussed in Section 95 as an example of the normal early development of senility, turned out to be anything but typical. Testing revealed markedly low levels of thryoid hormone (hypothyroidism), and when this hormone was carefully restored to normal by use of daily medication, he improved dramatically. His recovery probably would have been more complete if his condition had been recognized and treated earlier. There are no "typical dementias." Each demented individual is unique and must be thoroughly evaluated if treatable conditions are to be identified.

101. *Treatment of Senility.* Obviously, if a medical disease is causing the senility, it should be treated. But what can be done for the 80 percent of people whose dementia is not caused by medical disease? There is some evidence that mult-infarct dementia can be helped, or at least stopped from progressing, through control of any high blood pressure present and through use of medication, like aspirin, which impairs the clotting of blood. This treatment is similar to that used in stroke (Section 252). It is of uncertain value, however, and should be discussed with your parent's physician.

Nothing at present can change the course of most other serious dementias, particularly Alzheimer's disease. However, the medication DEM (Hydergine) recently has shown promise in reducing some of the symptoms of mild to moderate dementia when used in doses of 4–6 mg. daily. Although research with this drug continues, it is clear that it will not cure dementia; at best it will only slow its progression for a while.

Some help is available if your parent is crippled by certain symptoms. If your parent appears significantly depressed, antidepressant medication is often very useful in brightening his outlook and making him more alert. If your parent is agitated, hallucinating, or paranoid, small amounts of tranquilizers like Haldol, Stelazine, and Prolixin often can improve his functioning. One caution: the useful amounts of these tranquilizers are tiny—increasing the dosage often makes matters worse instead of better by increasing confusion or by producing stiffness and unwanted muscle movements. If your parent becomes agitated or profoundly restless and sleepless at night, a small quantity of a mild tranquilizer, like Serax or Restoril, often will make him more comfortable.

There are no ready medical solutions to the treatment of those who are senile. Much more important and useful is what you and others can do for them in their everyday lives.

102. *Caring for a Senile Parent.* Eventually, you will need to wrestle with the problem of how best to help care for your senile parent. Should your parent live alone, with you, or in a nursing home? Can you make his or her life more satisfying and comfortable? Should one family member take charge or should the responsibility be shared? These and other questions demand answers as any parent becomes old and feeble, but are particularly crucial if your parent has become demented.

Although the stereotyped picture is of the demented person shambling along the barren halls of a nursing home, staring vacantly from the recesses of an easy chair, or being fed with a spoon, most senile individuals live independently in their own home. During the early stage, which may last years, they are quite capable of managing their day-to-day affairs. Frequently, they function so well that the dementia goes unnoticed until specific problems arise. The majority of these individuals require only minor overseeing—help with shopping or the bankbook, occasional tidying up around their house, and an ever-present watchfulness for a more precipitous decline.

And that decline will occur. Nothing you can do will make a difference in the final outcome. All you can hope is that your parent will remain self-sufficient and satisfied as long as possible. Fortunately, there is much you can do to prolong his independence.

1. Keep your parent in familiar surroundings, if possible. Most elderly people are happier in settings they know well. They frequently adapt to new environments poorly—a period of temporary or long-lasting confusion and deterioration often follows a move from the family home to an unfamiliar apartment or nursing home.

2. Avoid most forms of change. Establish and keep regular routines. If you visit three days each week, try not to alter the days. Encourage your parent to stick to his or her own regular routines, like going to church on Sunday morning or grocery shopping on Monday afternoon. Keep familiar objects around your parent—pictures of family, a well-used vacuum clean-

er, or a familiar pipe rack can be both reassuring and orienting. Encourage old friends to continue visiting and keep other family members engaged.

3. Keep your parent involved in the world. Encourage him to watch TV, listen to the news, and read the newspaper. Orient him frequently and tactfully during your conversations: "This is the warmest Friday we've had this January" or "It's almost ten in the morning so I'd better help clean up the breakfast dishes." Keep calendars conspicuous and use a clock with large numbers.

4. Keep your parent involved, but not overinvolved. Just as a solitary, isolated life can promote deterioration, so can too much stimulation. Even during family activities, give your parent time to rest and collect his thoughts. Increasing confusion, agitation, or withdrawal may be evidence that you have exceeded his ability to tolerate activity. Recognize that his tolerance for stimulation will decrease as the disease worsens.

5. Provide for good physical care. See that your parent attends whatever doctor's appointments are necessary. Keep an eye on his nutrition— many senile individuals inadvertently neglect good nutrition by eating what is simplest to fix and most familiar. See that your parent has glasses which fit, a hearing aid that works (and is used), and that he lives in a house which is as free as possible from hazards like steep, poorly lit stairs or a bathtub without a handrail. Install nightlights. A demented elderly person who is taking a complicated regimen of medication is prone to mistakes—mistakes which can be life-threatening. Make sure that your parent is taking the required medications in the recommended dosages at the proper time. Help your parent create a checklist of essential activities, and include medication times.

6. Help maintain your parent's self-esteem. Speak clearly and precisely but don't talk down to him. Treat him like an adult, even though he may be showing childish behavior. To treat demented elderly parents as though they were incompetent and foolish usually results in either debilitating dependency or a struggle for control. Try not to be excessively critical or domineering—recognize that much of your parent's undesirable behavior is beyond his control and should be tolerated and accepted as inevitable as long as it doesn't seriously threaten his well-being. Recognize that, because his ability to concentrate is limited, your parent's most strident demands may turn out to be passing whims if they are treated lightly until they are gone. Try not to become locked in battle over something transitory. Be supportive, hopeful, and encouraging but don't lead a demented parent into situations beyond his capabilities.

7. The home atmosphere should be kept as calm as possible. The senile individual is exceptionally sensitive to any uproar, particularly to any friction between family members. This does not mean that you must walk

on tiptoe, but try to keep family arguments out of range of your parent. It is frightening to be as dependent as the demented are, and a heated, emotional atmosphere can send them into a tailspin of anxiety and confusion.

There are several available sources of information about caring for a demented parent. A good one is the book *The 36-Hour Day* by N. Mace and P. Rabins (The Johns Hopkins University Press, Baltimore, 1981).

103. *Caring for a Senile Parent—You Are Not Alone.* Caring for a demented parent is an enormous, and frequently overwhelming, job. Although it can be fulfilling and meaningful, you will need help. Never attempt it alone if you have an alternative. Too often, arrangements are left to chance and the primary responsibility falls to whoever is nearby and willing to accept it. If one person, willingly and unwillingly, shoulders an excessive amount of the work and pain involved, the inevitable result is resentment, anger, and hostility on his or her part, and guilt on the part of the other relatives.

Early on, when it becomes apparent that your parent is developing senility, marshal your resources. Bring the family together and make plans. Openly confront the difficult course ahead. Be sure to address several fundamental issues: (1) who will do the work, (2) how will expenses be covered, and (3) how will important decisions be made? Recognize that it is too big a job for one person; divide the workload. Attempt to get a commitment from each appropriate member of the family for time as well as for financial support (if needed). Be reluctant to allow one person to "volunteer" to do most of the work. It may seem like a fine idea at first but it ultimately creates problems as the enormity of the task becomes clear. It is also usually unwise for one person to make all the decisions. The best way of sharing responsibility differs among families. Usually, one person is "elected" to be responsible for day-to-day decisions. The somewhat thankless job is often taken by the son or daughter who has "always been the most responsible," but it may fall to the oldest son, the oldest daughter, or to some other relative. Almost any scheme that is agreed upon by all family members will work. However, if major decisions about the parent's welfare are made without considering the feelings of all concerned, trouble is bound to develop. It is possible for a family to weather the gradual deterioration of a parent gracefully, and a few families may actually grow closer together. But if the situation is poorly managed, it is just as likely that lifelong bitterness will result.

Your parent may require little help initially, but over time your visits may need to become more frequent. It is usually wise to set up a schedule which includes such things as the days you visit, who helps with the shopping, when the laundry needs to be done, the days your parent needs transportation and who is responsible, when the house should be cleaned next, the day the bills should be paid, and much more. This schedule will obviously intensify as your parent's condition worsens.

Frequently, there are not enough hands to do all that needs to be done. Some help, though limited, is available from community agencies. Meals-on-Wheels will deliver one hot and one cold meal to your parent's home five days a week. Many communities have homemaker services available which allow you to hire someone to visit your parent's house to clean and do other maintenance. Occasional use of a visiting nurse may be helpful, although that service is usually expensive. Most communities have publicly funded community mental health centers that provide a range of services. Your parent may benefit from being seen there by a psychiatrist or other therapist. Such centers occasionally have special groups and day-care programs geared to the demented patient. Such services can give family members a badly needed break from their responsibilities. Unfortunately, most nonspecialized community activities for the elderly are not organized to cope with the special problems of the senile person.

Finally, look for support to those people and organizations that your parent supported throughout his life: close friends, neighbors, an employer, his or her church or social club. Although they don't have to help, you may be surprised at their willingness to shoulder some of the responsibility. Planning for your parent's care is not complete until you have carefully identified everyone likely to play a role.

Specialized clinics and support groups are springing up all over the country to help Alzheimer's patients and their families. They are often associated with a university hospital or other major health care facility. Perhaps the best resource and source of information about Alzheimer's disease is the Alzheimer's Disease and Related Disorders Association. It can help you identify specialized help in your locale.

Alzheimer's Disease and Related Disorders Association
360 N. Michigan Ave., Suite 601
Chicago, IL 60601
(800) 621-0379

104. *The Biggest Change—Moving Your Parent from His Home.* Although the move from home may be forestalled by employing a live-in homemaker, eventually your parent will become so frail or so inadvertently dangerous to himself that some other living arrangement must be made. He may leave the stove on or forget to turn off the water. He may eat spoiled food that had been left forgotten in the refrigerator, or he may forget to eat at all. He may become irritable, threaten neighbors, or become physically

abusive to his spouse or to you. Or she may insist on driving when no longer able. The home may become so soiled that her health is threatened. She may become regularly incontinent. She may take walks and become lost or may carelessly wander across busy intersections.

In addition, the family may become exhausted. The spouse, if living, may be aged and worn out from constant effort and continual problems. You may be beginning to experience health problems of your own.

Finally, enough is enough. You then face one of the most emotion-laden actions for any family: moving your parent out of his or her home. There is no right time for such a move—each case is different.

First, decide where your parent will go. Most commonly, a demented parent will move in with one of his children or will move to a nursing home. Either choice has pros and cons. Do not automatically feel that he must live with you and try not to feel guilty if you choose some other solution—the most important thing you can do for your parent is to take care of yourself. If you and your family become too stressed by adding your parent to the home, no one benefits. The turbulence in such a home often hastens your demented parent's deterioration. If your emotional resources become depleted, you will have less to give your parent, whether he is in the home or in a nursing home. In addition, a good nursing home (see Chapter 23) employs personnel skilled at caring for demented individuals, professionals who often can coax a higher level of functioning from your parent than you ever could at home. Moreover, profoundly senile elderly persons can become acutely anxious and confused in a changing, stimulating environment and do better in the closed, quiet, and secure setting of many nursing homes—a lesson learned by many children who return a markedly worsened parent to the nursing home after the "treat" of a Sunday dinner out.

Finances play a crucial role in the decision of where your parent should live. The expense of nursing homes often causes some parents to stay in their own homes or with their children long past the time it makes sense for them to do so. Most nursing homes cost $10,000–$20,000 each year and may rapidly exhaust the family savings. Your parent will receive no help from Medicare, unless he or she is judged to need "skilled nursing care." However, in most states Medicaid will help pay nursing home costs, but not until your parents' combined savings have been reduced to a few thousand dollars. This creates an exceptional hardship for the nondemented spouse, who may be healthy and likely to live many more years, but who may be forced to do so without his or her life's savings. On the other hand, because taking care of seriously demented parents is often a full-time task, keeping them home frequently means that either you or your spouse will be unable to hold a job, thus depriving the family of valuable income.

There are no easy answers. Given the proper circumstances, your parent can live satisfactorily in either your home or a nursing home. Each family must come to its own decision after a careful assessment of its desires, needs, strengths, and shortcomings. Consider involving a physician or experienced social worker in that decision.

Our worst fear often is that our parent will be devastated to learn that we are considering putting him in a nursing home. In desperation, we may wait until the last moment to "spring it on him," or we may go out for a drive and "just end up" at a nursing home. Such underhanded maneuvers almost inevitably backfire—the sudden, unexpected change usually causes the demented parent to become acutely anxious and confused, producing just the effects we feared. It is usually better to involve our parent in the decision as much as possible. You may be surprised at how readily he accepts the possibility of a change. Even if they initially resist, most older people will gradually adjust to the idea of moving if it is discussed with them repeatedly and in a relaxed way. Unfortunately, it is occasionally necessary to place an older demented person in a nursing facility against his will. This usually requires a court procedure in which he is declared incompetent to make decisions for himself. In addition, the senile individual frequently becomes so careless with money and other personal matters that a relative must seek legal guardianship to protect that person from himself. Expect to rely on the judgments of both a physician (often a psychiatrist) and an attorney in these matters (see Sections 300 and 301).

105. *The Final Years—Your Emotional Roller Coaster.* It helps to know that you have done everything possible for your demented parent. However, senility remains one of the most painful disorders for everyone. You will be scarred emotionally; it is unavoidable. You will watch your parent slip from reach. Many of your parent's finest qualities will remain to the last as reminders of what you are losing. Finally, your parent will be lost to you, even though still alive—a stranger, uncomprehending. And yet, unlike a loss through death, you repeatedly are confronted with the shadow of what once was. It is probably this inability to mourn cleanly—because a final loss has not yet occurred—that makes a parent's slow death from dementia so hard for so many children.

But there are other emotional hurdles. Fortunately, some are avoidable—to be forewarned is to be forearmed. All emotions become heightened in these difficult circumstances. You catch yourself thinking things and feeling things you don't like. Everyone does. You feel angry toward your parent. You may neglect family and career, feel trapped and cheated, and in anger hold your parent responsible. You may consider your parent's behavior an embarrassment. You may wish he were dead—both for his sake and for yours. You may be ashamed if you catch yourself treating him with unnecessary roughness. If a demented parent is living with you, friends may avoid your home and you may suffer loneliness and feelings of isolation. Guilt may be a constant companion—for not doing enough, for being insufficiently sensitive, for wishing an end to it all. Expect these unpleasant emotions, and take solace in the knowledge that millions of people have been through similar experiences.

Also, recognize that your effort may not be appreciated. Your parent may complain constantly, belittle you and your efforts, or demand that you leave him alone. Or he may continually demand more care, more time, and more consideration. Relatives (usually, it seems, the ones who contribute the least) may criticize your every move. It helps little to recognize that often their own guilt is speaking.

Moreover, you have to adjust to a new, and often uncomfortable, role. Your parent has not become a child, but has become childlike. This may require an intense, and unpleasantly familiar, level of care. You may need to give a bath to the person who raised you and whom you admired and respected for so many years. You may need to check your father's teeth or give your mother an enema.

The course is stormy by its very nature, but there are a few guides. (1) Don't expect too much. In the most common types of dementia, your parent won't get better. He or she will only get worse. Your primary task is to allow that to occur as comfortably and satisfactorily as possible—for *everyone* involved. (2) Don't do too much. Your first duty is to yourself. To change that priority is to risk exhaustion. Moreover, that extra effort often produces only a modest return since the demented person's capacity to respond and improve is so limited. (3) Take a break. You must get away from any regular duties periodically. Responsibility for a demented parent is draining. Let someone else take charge. Go out to dinner. Take a long weekend out of town with the family. Take a vacation. Seek out a day-care program so that your parent is someone else's responsibility for at least part of the time. At the least, hire a live-in homemaker for a day or a weekend. (4) Share the load. Other family members should be involved. (5) Develop a closer relationship with your parent's physician and with other professionals familiar with the problems of the senile elderly.

Is the struggle to keep your parent at home and independent worth the effort? Is it worth the endless hours spent in his or her behalf—the innumerable afternoons or weekend days spent at your parent's home instead of with your family; the countless number of shopping trips or loads of wash; the wet sheets, the honey dribbled on the tablecloth, the endless complaints by both parent and family when things don't go smoothly, and the hundred other minor irritations that are the lot of someone caring for a senile parent? The answer is rarely an unqualified "yes." More commonly, it is a qualified "it can be." It can be if your parent can be made noticeably more satisfied and at ease in a setting you make possible. It can be if you and your family don't suffer beyond what is reasonable. It can be if *you* feel your efforts have helped repay your parent's lifetime of devotion to you.

12.

Other Emotional Problems

In addition to depression and dementia, several other serious emotional conditions present problems for a few elderly persons. Each is capable of making a mockery of a gracious old age.

106. *Hypochondriasis.* We want our parents to enjoy good health and are willing to help however we can. If your parent has a physical complaint or worry, you want it to be evaluated thoroughly. If a specialist is needed, you want your parent to see one. If sophisticated tests and a short hospital stay are required to track down the problem, fine—you'll see that they get done. But, what do you do if your parent's complaints are endless; if all the medical tests uncover nothing; if new complaints are continually added; if no treatment helps? How long can you remain supportive and sympathetic of a parent who constantly complains, and for whom things only seem to get worse? Few conditions among the elderly are as frustrating as hypochondriasis—an unyielding, irrational certainty that one is physically ill.

Among the serious emotional problems of the elderly, hypochondriasis is exceeded in frequency only by depression and senility. Although some younger people also suffer from it, it often develops for the first time in old age. Men are not immune but women are its chief victims.

If worried about it, most of us can expand a minor symptom into something more ominous, but we don't become preoccupied with it, and we are reassured when a physical examination and laboratory tests prove us normal. On the other hand, persons with hypochondriasis are convinced they are ill and may angrily reject evidence to the contrary. They may demand additional tests and treatments and they frequently "doctor shop." Persons with hypochondriasis may dwell on the most minor aches and pains and may conclude from those "symptoms" that they are terribly ill with a disease the doctors for some reason can't identify. They may recite an unending list of symptoms—gaining a new one whenever one is lost—or they may persist with several intractable symptoms which no examination can clarify and no treatment remove. Or, they may be preoccupied more with a sense of dread than with specific symptoms.

However afflicted, the individuals with hypochondriasis are obsessed with their "illness." Explanations or reassurance don't work—at least not for very long. They are frequently irritable and chronically dissatisfied with the efforts of family and physicians to help. These people usually bounce from one doctor to another, both because they are always looking for a second opinion and because the doctors, thoroughly frustrated, often are quite willing to have them go to someone else. Remember, however, that even though you find a hypochondriacal parent's behavior enormously annoying, he is sincere. Even though it may seem that your parent makes continual complaints just to irritate you, he is genuinely troubled by his physical concerns. This is an unpleasant disorder for everyone involved, including your parent.

The cause is not known—in fact, it is likely that there is no one cause, but many. Some people have always been preoccupied with their health; they just become more so as they get older. People who always have been perfectionists will often become overly concerned about the minor ways their body has begun to malfunction in old age. People developing dementia (severe senility) occasionally focus on their medical symptoms as a source of worry and also as something they can understand and talk about without embarrassment or contradiction. Usually, however, your parent has been pushed into hypochondriasis by some major change in life or by depression.

Hypochondriasis usually follows close on the heels of a major stress like moving, loss of a spouse, a financial setback, or the development of a physical disability. Has your parent lost some crucial support to his life? Is he isolated? If so, he may concentrate on his own physical symptoms as a point of familiarity in a sea of uncertainty. Moreover, he has (unconsciously) selected a type of response almost certain to guarantee, at least for a while, that family and friends will rally around him. His children will listen to his complaints and try to help. Friends will visit more frequently. His doctor, or doctors, will listen, discuss, examine. In other words, the elderly person will have created a new social life built around his medical symptoms that replaces the social life lost when he moved, retired, or became a widower. He also will be freed of some responsibilities for which he feels unprepared. And what sets this condition apart from mere "faking" is that he is unaware of the roots of these symptoms. To your parent the symptoms are real and need attention; we should see them as a distress signal.

The majority of persons with hypochondriasis are significantly unhappy. Sometimes the worries of hypochondriasis create the depression, but more often the depression comes first and the preoccupation with illness develops from it. How depression produces hypochondriasis in some elderly persons is not known, but there is little doubt that depression and loss are the leading causes of hypochondriasis.

Occasionally, hypochondriasis is very difficult to treat, particularly in those elderly persons long overly worried about their health. But more often it can be treated fairly successfully. If your parent is depressed, treatment of that depression frequently diminishes the medical symptoms. Treating loss by helping your parent grieve and by keeping him involved in life (see Chapter 9) often relieves the hypochondriasis. Anything you can do that keeps him from being totally absorbed in his medical symptoms is useful. In the meantime, minimize your attention to his symptoms. If your parent begins to talk about them, change the subject. If he insists, leave the room. Be supportive, but not of his physical concerns. Discourage your parent from doctor shopping. Try to develop a relationship with one doctor who will oversee your parent's total medical care, will see him regularly, and will help him work through the hypochondriasis. Be aware that some physicians will be reluctant to become involved to the extent necessary— find someone who will.

However, several cautions need to be borne in mind. (1) Hypochondriasis is a complex condition which frequently mixes loss and depression with your parent's unique personality type. Often, a psychiatrist should be involved, usually to work in concert with your parent's primary physician. (2) Suicide is a constant risk in a person with severe hypochondriasis. Not only is the individual frequently depressed, but he often becomes hopeless about obtaining any relief for his seemingly real symptoms. (This is another reason for involving a psychiatrist.) (3) Your parent may develop a serious illness which goes ignored. Each new symptom should be evaluated medically; even hypochondriacs can become ill.

107. *Alcohol Abuse.* Is your parent drinking too much. How do you tell? What risks does he or she run? What can you do?

Alcohol abuse, a major problem in the United States, is less common among older people than among younger ones. About one half of all older individuals abstain from drinking altogether. Heavy drinking and alcoholism decrease in old age, in part because many alcoholics don't live to reach their later years and in part because, for some reason, many heavy drinkers taper off when they reach their late 50s and their 60s. Still, many of the elderly who have drinking problems (mostly men) have been drinking moderately or heavily for many years and just gradually drift into alcohol abuse as they face the problems of old age. This is particularly common among those who, when younger, used alcohol to cope during times of stress. Only a few persons start drinking in their later years, and then usually in response to major losses and stress.

If your parent is drinking too much, it will quickly become obvious to you. You may smell alcohol on his breath and find empty containers in the garbage. His neighbor may stop you to complain of your parent's irritable or outrageous behavior or to express concern over his welfare. Because of frequent falls, your parent may have scrapes and bruises. In addition, he may be quarrelsome, particularly when you ask about his drinking. Although a few isolated elderly persons (particularly women) successfully disguise the amount of their drinking, most are aware of, and embarrassed by, their problem.

There is no set amount of alcohol that represents too much drinking. The ability to tolerate alcohol depends upon a person's age, health, and psychology. However, tolerance decreases with age while the likelihood of alcohol-related physical problems increases. Alcohol abuse, as opposed to heavy drinking, begins when your parent's ability to function from day to day starts to decline because of drinking. Perhaps he may miss an important appointment because of intoxication, or forget to eat and become progressively more malnourished. Or, you may notice that your parent's memory has begun to flag. Any evidence of alcohol abuse is a sign to get professional help.

Even if your parent's behavior has not deteriorated, heavy drinking takes a physical toll. In fact, physical problems are often the major reason for him to decrease his drinking as he ages. Conditions most likely to develop after several years of moderate to excessive drinking include stomach irritation, stomach ulcers, cirrhosis of the liver, anemia, problems with the pancreas, impotence, insomnia, and a host of problems associated with malnutrition. Alcohol use also may prematurely worsen other physical changes due to age, such as hardening of the arteries, high blood pressure, and heart disease. If your parent is drinking heavily, his physician should be alerted to be on the lookout for these associated conditions.

The risks of excessive drinking are not entirely physical. The likelihood of depression and the risk of suicide are markedly increased. Your parent may become irritable or even aggressive. He may become isolated as friends and family avoid his company. He may neglect to care for himself or he may experience periods of confusion. His finances may fall into disarray because he spends too much for alcohol (and medical bills). All in

OTHER EMOTIONAL PROBLEMS

all, the older parent who abuses alcohol is in for a stormy and unsatisfying old age.

If your parent actually becomes physically addicted to alcohol, he or she has to face all the problems of withdrawal, such as the "shakes" and the "DTs." He also runs a severe risk of memory loss and even dementia. Scientific studies have shown that the brains of some severe alcoholics may shrink. Fortunately, few elderly people end up with a physical addiction.

Of those elderly people who drink, most drink moderately and sensibly. In fact, a glass of wine with dinner or a "beer with the boys" can be a very effective social lubricant and can contribute to a satisfactory life style. The risk lies in the obligatory heavy social drinking that may accompany some dinner groups or afternoon card klatches. Whether heavy drinking occurs because of psychological need or social expectation, the effect on the body is the same and should be avoided.

Fortunately, most excessive drinking that develops in old age can be treated successfully. It is usually a response to unpleasant happenings, boredom, and loneliness, and the solution lies in helping your parent correct these situations. If the heavy drinking or alcohol abuse is longstanding and getting worse, the problem may be resistant to treatment; but usually it is more easily treated in an older than in a younger person. Joining organizations like Alcoholics Anonymous and Helping Hands, coupled with attending family and group therapy, appears to be the most effective way of obtaining lasting control over heavy drinking. If things are thoroughly out of control, your parent may need hospitalization in one of the alcoholism inpatient treatment units found in most moderate- to large-sized cities. To be effective, such hospital stays generally need to last at least several weeks, possibly several months, and they need to be followed by some form of continuing contact with an outpatient treatment group.

108. *Drug Abuse.* The kind of drug abuse which we associate with modern times, the use of narcotics and "street drugs," is very uncommon among the elderly. However, there is another form of drug misuse which is not at all uncommon—the abuse of prescription and over-the-counter medication. This is partly because the elderly use more medication than any other group in the population. People over 65 consume one quarter of all drugs prescribed in the United States. Almost any of these medications can be abused, but particularly common is abuse of sleeping pills, tranquilizers, pain medication, and laxatives.

One in seven elderly individuals uses some kind of tranquilizer, and almost one half of those people feel they would have trouble getting along without it—in other words, they are psychologically dependent. Tranquilizers can be used for several days at a time to help your parent tolerate brief periods of stress, but should not be used over weeks or months to control chronic anxiety. Sleeping pills can be used for occasional nights when sleep comes slowly, but should not be used every night (see Section 147). As many as 5 percent of the elderly misuse sleeping pills and tranquilizers. Some of this abuse is inadvertent—a person innocently takes more than the prescribed dose or takes several prescriptions simultaneously. To his dismay, he then may discover that he needs an ever-increasing amount of the medication to feel comfortable. Other individuals are aware that they are consuming too much medication but continue because they like the effect or because they don't like the unpleasant feelings that accompany trying to cut down.

Once your parent has begun abusing sleeping pills and tranquilizers, he often finds it difficult to stop. He may be convinced that he can't sleep or remain calm without them and may refuse to try. But if he continues to take any of these medications long enough (several weeks or longer) and in sufficient amount (usually slightly more than a normal prescription), he will become physically addicted.

What are the signs which suggest that your parent may be misusing these drugs? Expect him to appear mildly intoxicated during periods of the day or evening. He may be unusually talkative or irritable, or he may do or say things which would normally embarrass him. He may appear chronically sleepy, lethargic, apathetic, or confused. His speech may be slurred or he may be uncoordinated and stumble when he walks. You may be convinced at one moment that there is something seriously wrong with him, only to see him return to normal several hours later. If you notice your parent displaying any of these symptoms, be alert to the possibility of drug misuse, but recognize that other medical or psychiatric conditions can cause them as well. A few elderly people who have poorly functioning liver and kidneys (the organs that usually remove drugs from the body) and who take their medication in a correct fashion may accumulate drugs in their blood and may have symptoms associated with medication abuse.

If your parent has been taking excessive medication long enough for his body to become adjusted to its presence, a sudden decrease or absence of it will produce symptoms of drug withdrawal. Within hours, or by the next day, a person experiencing withdrawal will become anxious, restless, apprehensive, or irritable. He may lose his appetite and have severe insomnia. He may feel weak, nauseated, and shaky. If your parent experiences these symptoms anytime he forgets to take his medication, he is physically addicted. If that addiction is severe—that is, if the daily dose he requires is large—failure to take the drugs may result in confusion, fever, hallucinations, and even seizures. This form of drug abuse can be life-threatening.

OTHER EMOTIONAL PROBLEMS

If you suspect that your parent, knowingly or unknowingly, is using any of these medications to excess, his physician should be alerted. Whenever possible, this should be done with your parent's knowledge. If one of your parents becomes addicted, he or she probably should be admitted to a hospital for withdrawal—a procedure that usually takes several weeks, depending upon how much medication your parent has been taking each day. In the hospital the daily dose of a drug is slowly decreased until he is comfortable without any. If your parent was taking too much medication because of confusion or through a misunderstanding of how the drug should be used, often stopping the medication is all that is needed. However, if he was taking too much medication knowingly, it is just as important to deal with the underlying distress in his life as it is to withdraw the drug. Any hope of a long-term solution will depend upon your parent's feeling that it is possible to be comfortable and satisfied without the help of drugs. Consider involving a psychiatrist or other psychotherapist to try to identify the important issues that led to the problem.

Many other medications can be misused as well. Many are taken in excess by mistake—your parent misunderstands the prescription or neglects to mention to the physician that he is receiving medication from another doctor. Other medications are abused because your parent becomes psychologically dependent on them. Pain medications are frequently taken inappropriately by elderly people who believe that their aches and pains would be intolerable without them. When they continue to have pain in spite of the medication, they take this as a sign to increase (on their own) the amount of medication they consume, creating a vicious cycle which frequently leads to addiction or physical damage. Likewise, a parent who suffers constipation is often lured into depending upon laxatives. Eventually, his bowel will function only under the stimulus of a laxative, and then only poorly. And yet, he is psychologically unwilling to consider any alternatives. Such patterns occur, perhaps with less frequency, with numerous other medications (aspirin compounds, cold medications, etc.). Because many of them are physically harmful when taken in excess, it is important that your parent take medication only as prescribed and in the smallest possible quantities. You can help by familiarizing yourself with the drugs your parent takes, by making certain that they are what the physician prescribed, and by seeing that they are not duplicated by some other physician. Few elderly people actively hunt for drugs (for example, by getting the same prescription from many doctors), but, if your parent becomes caught in that unfortunate trap, contact both his or her physician and a psychiatrist for help.

109. *Paranoia*. Paranoia is unreasonable, unshakable suspiciousness. We are all suspsicious of someone or something from time to time but lose our worry when presented with reasonable evidence to the contrary. The paranoid individual, on the other hand, will not let go of his suspicions. Paranoid persons tend to be anxious and tense, and to never forget an insult. This often leads to an underlying current of hostility in all their dealings with others. Their numerous accusations drive others away and they are too suspicious to become close to anyone. They may develop elaborate and carefully reasoned explanations for their fears but can rarely see the errors in their logic. They tend to see everything that happens around them as somehow directed at them (the bagger at the grocery store dropped their shopping bag just to irritate them; the neighbor painted his house tan because he knew they disliked the color; etc.). This collection of traits and beliefs ensures that the paranoid elderly person lives a pathetically lonely and insecure life.

Mild suspiciousness is fairly common among older people; unyielding paranoid ideas occur much less frequently. A few elderly individuals become flagrantly paranoid—they may believe things which are obviously untrue, and even impossible. They may also have hallucinations, such as hearing insulting voices. If your parent is unfortunate enough to develop a late-life paranoia, treatment is available.

What causes paranoid ideas? No one knows for certain, but there are some ideas. (1) The most severe form of paranoia, paranoid psychosis, probably has an inherited, biological component, and may be a type of schizophrenia. If your parent or some other close relative has ever suffered from schizophrenia, the roots of your parent's current paranoia probably lie in that illness. (2) For reasons poorly understood, some people with serious depression or severe senility become paranoid. Perhaps it helps lighten a depression to feel that someone else is to blame for your plight. (3) Isolated paranoid ideas may have other roots. Some older persons need to explain seemingly peculiar happenings. If their vision is poor, perhaps they didn't notice the scratch on the refrigerator when they made it, but when they finally do see it they must find some explanation for it. Occasionally, that explanation is a paranoid one ("My sister-in-law did it during her last visit"). If their memory has been slipping, they may not remember telling the milkman to come only once each week, and thus feel purposely excluded. Their mild confusion may produce a variety of misperceptions that must be explained. If, in addition, these elderly people are lonely and isolated, they have ample time to construct explanations—without the constant touch of reality that regular exposure to people brings.

However paranoia develops, it is frequently treatable. Severe paranoia usually requires medication—antipsychotic drugs (also known as major tranquilizers) such as Prolixin and Haldol. Prolixin, which can be given by injection every two to three weeks, is usually the best choice. If this treatment is ineffective, it is often because your parent either develops side effects such as stiffness, tremor, sleepiness, dizziness, dry mouth, or inadvertent movements of his face or mouth, or because he refuses to take the medicine in the first place. You may need to encourage your parent to accept and follow through with treatment.

Lesser degrees of paranoia, from vague suspiciousness to one or two fixed paranoid ideas, may respond to medication but should first be treated with a heavy dose of reality. You should make certain that your parent understands that you do not see things his way. Don't belittle him or vigorously criticize his paranoid ideas—you are only likely to make him wary of you. Moreover, a point-by-point analysis of these ideas rarely changes his views. Sidestep confrontations such as "You mean you think I am lying." Instead, tell him you don't agree with his perceptions and point out the undesirable consequences of his way of thinking and behaving. A person who is paranoid usually has a running battle with someone (the neighbors, old friends, other family members, the power company, you) and is doing things that will provoke retaliation (turning over the neighbor's garbage can, refusing to pay the electric bill). Point out the consequences of this behavior. Concentrate first on getting your paranoid parent to stop what he is doing, rather than stop what he is thinking. Refuse to listen to his complaints or accusations. His ideas may change as his behavior changes; more likely, he may behave better but insist that he was right. If the pattern of your parent's life is changed in some major way, the paranoia often disappears. If your initial efforts fail, consider consulting a psychiatrist or other psychotherapist for additional ideas. Finally, medication may be useful. More often than not, your parent can be lured away from his preoccupation with paranoid ideas, but it may require concentrated effort on your part.

Medical Problems

13.

Fostering Good Health

110. *Health and Exceptional Health.* With age, the body begins to run down. Everything becomes less efficient; performance may flag. But poor health does not necessarily follow. Instead, your parent may enjoy exceptional health, the best of his life. How is this possible?

It is possible in part because good health consists of more than a physical machine that works. Complete health is a combination of physical health and emotional health. Such total health is a match between what our bodies can do and what we require to fulfill our needs, wishes, and goals. In a very real sense, good health is a state of mind. If your parent suffers from arthritis, diabetes, and heart disease, and yet is making new friends, having new experiences, expanding his horizons, and loving life, he is healthy. If he "is never sick," but dreads each new day, he is unhealthy. Old age should be a time of growth, enjoyment, and exploration. If the body allows that to happen, do we need anything more? Any physical health that carries us as far as we are capable of going, at any age, is exceptional health.

Of course, complete health depends upon a base of good physical health. And this is where the surprises lie. Older people are capable of greater physical health than has previously been thought possible. With proper habits, many elderly can perform like people thirty years younger. Although the essential groundwork for good health is laid in youth and middle age, determined health-seeking pays dividends at any age. Moreover, good physical health and good emotional health comprise more than the sum of their parts. A physically active and healthy person is more likely to flourish emotionally, and an emotionally vital person will see his physical health respond in kind.

How can your parent begin this climb towards total health? Since many older individuals have allowed themselves to deteriorate or have become ill, they need to treat diseases and change old habits if they are to begin their renewal. (1) Physical diseases must be recognized and tended to (see Chapters 14–22). Physical incapacitation is an abnormal, not an expected, condition of old age. (2) Mental diseases, common among the elderly, must not be allowed to persist untreated (see Chapters 8–12). (3) Good health must be actively promoted. The majority of serious illnesses among the elderly are life-style diseases that can be prevented, to a greater or lesser extent, by a change in habits. Good medical care, exercise, activity, proper nutrition, prevention of accidents, control of stress, and the elimination of destructive habits are essential.

111. *Regular Medical Care.* Ultimately, your parents are responsible for their own health, although if they are too old or too frail you may need to help. They should not depend upon their doctor, a clinic, or a hospital to look after them. They need to learn how to take care of their own physical health—this includes learning how to obtain good medical care, how to prevent disease, and how to promote health. This may sound like a tall order to people who have spent their lives believing that health care lies exclusively in the hands of physicians. But no one can monitor your parents' health half as well as they can. They should be encouraged to assume the primary active role in their own care.

Although a sensible life style is the cornerstone of good physical health, regular, high-quality medical care is equally essential. Your parents should plan for such care. They should have a physician they trust. They should understand and follow the principles of exercise, nutrition, stress management, and accident prevention. They should determine how various kinds of care will be paid for (see Chapter 24). They should know how often each of them needs a checkup, and what should be checked for. They should be ready for medical emergencies: put important numbers (physician, ambulance, taxi, emergency room, 911, fire and police departments, pharmacy, neighbors, you) in an obvious place, know the route to their doctor's office or the closest emergency room, be familiar with the hours they are open, research the quickest available transportation at different times, prepare in advance a summary of critical medical information. But, most of all, your older parents should understand and participate in whatever decisions affect their health: what medication either is asked to take, and why; how frequently, or infrequently, both of them are seen by the physician; what illnesses they suffer from and what additional treatments might be available for them; whether or not to consult a specialist or obtain a second opinion. A person who becomes involved in his own care is more likely to coax extra performance from an aging body.

Finding the right physician is crucial, but it is not always easy. Because the ideal doctor-patient mix depends partly upon the intangibles of personality and style, there is no one doctor who is right for everyone. What should your parents look for? (1) The best care usually is provided by a physician who has gotten to know your parent over the years, coordinates all necessary treatments, and participates in all medical decisions. With few exceptions, your parent's physician should specialize in general medical care, and usually should have completed three or more years of specialty training in either internal medicine or family practice. (2) The other primary requirement is that the physician be well qualified. But, how can you tell how qualified a doctor is? Specialty training is one measure. An even better measure is whether or not the doctor is board-certified in that specialty. (You can find out by looking in your local library's *Directory of Medical Specialists* or by inquiring at the local Medical Society office.) A recommendation from a friend is not enough: it merely indicates that the friend liked the doctor. Better is a recommendation from another physician you know and trust. Faculty members at medical schools and in university hospitals generally practice high-quality medicine, as do the physicians on a medical school's clinical faculty who serve as part-time teachers of doctors in training in other hospitals. Since being a clinical faculty member is considered an honor and a mark of professional quality, ask the physicians (or their secretaries) about the relationship. Another technique useful in finding a good doctor is to pick the name of a board-certified internist or family practitioner from the list of physicians allowed to practice at a nearby respected hospital. (Hospitals have their own screening procedures to help them eliminate poor physicians from their ranks.)

However, a physician needs to be more than knowledgeable and technically well qualified; he or she also needs to be compatible with your parent. Your parents must have confidence in and be at ease with their doctor. The physician should treat your parents with respect and be willing to answer any questions openly and at length. Neither parent should ever leave the doctor's office shaking his or her head in confusion about what the doctor had just said. No questions should be off limits, and answers should be frank and complete. The physician should encourage your parents to participate in their own care, and should be willing to help them design an exercise program, a better diet, or other preventive measures. Try to get a sense of how the physician feels about old age: is he optimistic about the possibilities for growth during the later years, or does he view old age as a period of hopeless decline? Is the physician ready to bring in specialists if he feels "over his head," and would he be comfortable if one of your parents were to seek a second opinion for a major decision? He must be available: the best doctor in the world is of little value if your parents must wait weeks to get an appointment to check a worrisome new development. Most physicians will honor within a day or two an urgent request to be seen. Is it almost impossible to reach the doctor by phone because he doesn't return calls or because his secretary is overly protective? Does the doctor work with a group which provides twenty-four-hour coverage in case of emergencies? Are his fees reasonable? Ask several physicians about their charges; comparison shop. The answers to some of these questions may come only after your parents have been seen by the physician several times. If the relationship is not working well, your parents should not stick with an unsatisfactory physician out of mistaken loyalty. They should be willing to shop around until they find someone who meets their needs.

Most older people should have an annual medical checkup. It should include a review of your parent's symptoms and any medication he or she is taking, a careful physical examination, and performance of crucial laboratory tests, and should also review your parent's life style, any stresses and concerns, emotional difficulties, and the results of any preventive measures he follows. A regular medical examination of an older individual has a number of essential parts.

1. Blood pressure should always be measured, since its elevation raises worrisome questions about possible development of heart disease and stroke.

2. Vision and hearing should be checked. Their deterioration can pose increasing problems for the elderly. Moreover, corrective measures sometimes can return the failing senses to near normal.

3. Men should receive a rectal and prostate examination, since the best safeguard against the common cancers in these structures is early detection.

4. Women should receive yearly breast, rectal, and pelvic examinations. They should also be schooled to give themselves careful breast examinations monthly. Those women at increased risk for developing breast cancer (for example, those who have had family members with breast cancer) may also need regular X-rays of the breast (mammography). A Pap smear should be part of the annual pelvic examination. Diligent use of such regular evaluations will do more than any other thing to prevent those serious killers of elderly women: cancers of the breast, intestine and rectum, cervix, uterus, and ovaries.

5. Important laboratory tests that should be performed yearly include: a measure of red blood cells (a hematocrit, which detects blood loss

from serious illnesses, among other things); a measure of blood sugar (to check for diabetes); an examination of a stool sample (to look for blood from a cancer of the intestine, among other things); and an examination of a urine sample (a urinalysis, which checks for kidney problems and diabetes, among other things).

If either of your parents suffers from a chronic disease, he or she may need other specific tests regularly. Careful treatment of known disease, regular screening for developing disease, health promotion, and disease prevention are the linchpins of a vigorous old age.

112. *Exercise.* Exercise creates miracles. Who would have thought that an 80-year-old man could run a marathon, or an 85-year-old woman climb a 13,000-foot peak in the Rocky Mountains? Seventy-five-year-olds who swim a mile or run several miles every day have become commonplace. Swimming, cross-country skiing, bicycling, jogging, and dancing are just a few of the vigorous activities which are usually within easy reach of the elderly. But exercise is not just for fun: it is a necessity. At one time, experts thought that the elderly should slow down and take it easy. No more! If anything, they should become more physically active. They should engage in energetic physical activity several times each week. Not only will such exercise make their life richer, but it is the single greatest safeguard to good health. If they do not use their physical abilities, they will lose them.

Exercise, like a nutritious diet and adequate rest, is for everyone. Its benefits are numerous. Regular and appropriate exercise can lower weight, strengthen muscles and bones, make joints more limber, and improve balance. It can control the increased blood sugar of diabetes, lower blood pressure, and prevent constipation. It can reduce the risk of heart attack and heart failure. It can relieve nervous tension and cause mild depression to lift. Self-esteem and emotional well-being invariably rise as physical competence develops, and life takes on richer possibilities. Life itself may be extended—not just life, but meaningful life.

If your parents don't exercise regularly, find out why. Encourage them to do so. Help them to understand the importance of exercise, and to develop an exercise plan and follow it. If one of them is living in a nursing home or similar facility, make sure that exercise is included as part of the daily routine. If they have been physically inactive, they should be evaluated medically and then develop a program with the help of a physician. The doctor, after identifying any limitations, may then refer your parent to a local exercise group to work out a specific plan. Such groups are available in most communities—through the YMCA, YWCA, churches, spas, company programs, or public agencies for the elderly. However, if your parent's doctor discourages him or her from participating in such a program, consider getting a second opinion—it is that important.

What kind of exercising should they do? The easy answer is any kind that they enjoy and will continue over the months and years. A full answer is more complicated. Well-designed exercises try to accomplish at least three things: (1) strengthen the heart and make it more efficient, (2) increase flexibility, and (3) increase muscle strength and tone. To strengthen the heart, an exercise must make the heart beat moderately faster than normal (usually 110–150 beats each minute, depending upon a person's age and physical condition), for fifteen minutes or more, several times each week. Such exercise will make your parent breathe hard at first, but, as the heart wall becomes stronger and more capable, it will take longer to become short of breath. To increase flexibility, the exercise must be smooth and gradual and must encourage an older person to bend and stretch in normal directions but with greater than normal enthusiasm. To increase muscle strength, the exercise must gradually increase the amount of force the muscle has to exert, until the arms and legs are comfortably tired.

Put all these requirements together and what do you have? You have a long list of enjoyable activities: swimming, dancing (square and otherwise), walking, hiking, jogging, running, bicycling, calisthenics, roller skating, ice skating, energetic tennis, cross-country skiing, and others. By no means should exercise be the grim regimen of toe touches and push-ups your parents grew up with in school or in the service. It should become increasingly enjoyable as your parent's fitness improves. By the end of two or three months, the weariness that may have plagued the initial weeks of a new exercise program will have disappeared and your parent should have a renewed sense of vigor and a desire to extend himself further.

Be aware, however, that only certain kinds of physical activity are useful or advisable for the elderly. In fact, some types of exercise can be harmful. Exercises or sports should not be rough or jarring. They should not stress joints or ligaments unduly. They should not cause pain or exhaustion. Sometimes older people are lured into overdoing it in the name of competition. Don't allow this—such exercises may cause physical damage. Some activities, on the other hand, although enjoyable and well worth doing for social reasons, provide little lasting physical benefit. Golf and bowling are good examples.

Most of all, your parents should begin exercising with caution. They should first obtain a medical clearance, and then allow time for the body to become comfortable with the new demands on it. They should begin each exercise period slowly. They can start with ten or fifteen minutes of stretching exercises as warm-up before launching into something more strenuous. At the end of the activity, they should take an equal amount of time (complete with stretching) to cool down.

There are plenty of people and classes around to help your parents get started. Even if one of your parents has serious physical limitations, a program can be tailor-made for him. The rewards are much too great for such an undertaking to be ignored.

113. *Activity.* If there is one theme in old age more important than all others, it is the elderly person's need for activity—for staying involved in life. I have made this point several times (see for example Section 55), but it needs to be made again. Continuing one's activity into the later years is absolutely essential for physical and emotional well-being. "Activity" means more than exercise; it also means maintaining intellectual interests and emotional ties. A vital and meaningful life is a major support to good physical health. Not only do involved people naturally gravitate towards healthy habits such as exercise and a good diet, but such involvement itself produces physical changes. The active older person puts many of the changes of aging on hold and lives a fuller, healthier life.

114. *Nutrition.* Most of us give little thought to nutrition. We assume that if we eat enough food (or, often, too much food) we will be adequately nourished. By and large that is true: few of us are malnourished. Few of us consume too few vitamins, minerals, or protein for good health (although we may consume too *much,* and endure all the problems associated with obesity). So, why worry about our parents? Aren't they eating the way they always have? Shouldn't they be as well nourished as we? No! In fact, undernourishment and dietary deficiencies occur frequently among older individuals, particularly among those living by themselves or in institutions. The causes are partly physical and partly psychological.

Physical changes may damage the appetite or impair the body's ability to handle food. Some of the worst problems occur in the mouth. Teeth may be missing, gums sore, or dentures ill fitting—all of which can make eating difficult and drive your parent toward soft, overprocessed, unnutritious food. With age, the mouth becomes dry, making swallowing difficult and soft food tempting. Taste buds become less sensitive; food may seem to lose its flavor. Sensitivity to sweet and salt tastes are often lost first, causing many older people to gradually replace worthwhile foods with sugared foods and drinks and to oversalt their meals. Many serious illnesses common among older people can cause long-standing nausea and loss of appetite (this is particularly true of advanced heart disease, and disease of the kidney, gallbladder, and intestine). Certain medications can promote malnutrition, either by depressing appetite (such as, for example, digoxin, if its level in the blood gets too high during the treatment of heart disease; or chemotherapeutic drugs, during the treatment of cancer), by impairing absorption of food from the stomach and intestines (antacids and laxatives, when used too vigorously), or by interfering with the body's use of vitamins and minerals (for example, some antibiotics, diuretics, steroids, and anticonvulsants). Finally, some elderly individuals, because of disease or aging, absorb fewer nutrients from their food and become malnourished in spite of a good diet. Be alert if your parents complain of their teeth or how foods taste, if they suffer from chronic illness, or if they are taking a number of medications. An elderly person's appetite may fall below a safe level without his being aware of it.

Social causes of a poor diet or malnutrition are often more important than physical changes. Loneliness, apathy, and depression are common roads to an inadequate diet. Lonely or isolated individuals (particularly widowers, who often lack cooking skills) wonder why they should bother fixing a "fancy" meal just for one person. The apathetic person is inactive and has little interest in anything, including meals. Depression allows little energy for the complicated task of preparing a varied, nutritious meal. The result of all these conditions is a shift to quick and easy food: a TV dinner, a jelly sandwich, a bowl of sugared cereal, or a dish of ice cream. Moreover, a vicious cycle often starts in which a poor diet leads to weakness and listlessness, which worsens apathy or depression, causing eating habits to deteriorate further. Since physical activity is a natural stimulus to the appetite, the inactive older person is at increased risk to slip into this destructive pattern. Restricted income may cause some people to skimp on the more expensive foods (meat, fruit, vegetables) in order to pay the rent or the utilities bill. Others may be unable to get to a source of good food: they may be crippled by arthritis or a stroke, have no ready transportation, or fear going outside in a dangerous neighborhood. Some older individuals are unaware of what constitutes a balanced diet and thus choose the wrong foods. Finally, mental illness of all kinds can impair a person's ability to concentrate on a healthful diet. Abuse of alcohol is perhaps the worst offender, since not only does the person fail to eat good food, but he drinks an excessive quantity of a harmful chemical as well.

There are ample reasons to be concerned about your parents' nutrition, especially since all too often your parents are unaware that there is a problem. They may recognize that they aren't eating as well as they should, but neither is likely to feel that he or she is malnourished. Familiarize yourself with your parents' diet. How many meals do they eat each day? How large are these meals? How well-balanced? How many are hot? Do they snack? Do they become confused and miss meals? Do they eat what they are served, or do they discard everything but the ice cream? Take a careful look at what your parents actually eat. Would it satisfy you? Do they choose the right foods? Do they overcook, overseason, or oversalt them? Only in this way are you likely to learn whether they eat well enough to stay healthy, since physical evidence of early malnutrition is limited.

Poor nutrition may go undetected for a long time. You can't even count on your parent to lose weight—a poorly balanced diet which has too little protein or too few vitamins but too many calories is common and produces a malnourished, obese person. Some people will become gradually weak or listless, but even that is not certain. Only when deficiencies of certain vitamins or minerals are advanced will effects appear, like cracking of the lips, painful fissuring of the tongue, loss of night vision, loss of hair, pins and needles in the limbs, or mild confusion and loss of memory. Probably the two most common deficiency diseases are anemia caused by a lack of iron in the diet (Section 260) and weakening of bone (osteoporosis; Section 240) caused in part by consumption of insufficient amounts of calcium during the adult years.

But this is not the whole story. If it were, your parent could just take a few vitamin pills and feel relatively safe (although some vitamins are absorbed poorly in old age). Just as important as the diet that leads to malnutrition is the poor diet that produces diseases of excess. Too many calories lead to obesity and that leads to diabetes in a few older people. Too much fat and sugar encourages hardening of the arteries (atherosclerosis; Section 158). Too much salt leads to high blood pressure (and often heart disease and stroke). Too much soft food causes constipation and bowel disease (Section 183). Thus, too little or too much of many different substances can produce diseases which develop almost imperceptibly but which can be devastating in their effects. See that your parent receives a healthful diet.

A healthful diet provides enough (but not too many) carbohydrates, proteins, and fats in sensible proportions and supplies adequate amounts of essential vitamins and minerals, fluid, and roughage. It is no more than that. Unlike exercise or education, more is not better. The key to a good diet is variety. The food consumed during a single day, and preferabaly during a single meal, should be a mixture of the four basic food categories: milk products; vegetables and fruits; grains, beans, and nuts; and meat, poultry, fish, and eggs. Select exclusively from only one or two classes and trouble lies ahead. If your parents eat an adequate number of calories each day from a wide selection of foods within these categories, they will not need to keep count of vitamins or minerals.

However, there are other important elements in a good diet.

1. An elderly person requires fewer calories than a younger one. This

is partly because most older people are less active and thus burn less energy, but also because there is a gradual decrease in the rate an older person's body uses energy to maintain vital functions and because the amount of muscle in the body decreases with age. Men of average size who are mostly sedentary require approximately 2,400 calories daily, while women require about 1,800 calories. Of course, that amount varies with a person's size and increases if the individual is unusually active or is suffering from an acute illness. Exceed the required number of calories every day, even by a little, and obesity—which is a form of malnutrition—will inevitably result. Moreover recent scientific evidence suggests that life may be extended and health improved if a person remains on the light side of normal. It pays to count calories. However, less food eaten every day means that a person has to pack adequate nutrients into smaller meals—an additional reason to concentrate on a balanced diet.

2. Consumption of fats, sugars, and salt should be kept down. Fats should make up only about 10–15 percent of the calories in the diet, and the majority should be unsaturated (vegetable oils, mayonnaise, and margarine). Keep foods containing cholesterol and saturated fats (liver, eggs, red meat, hard cheese, etc.) to a minimum. Refined sugars (as found in soft drinks, snack foods, and canned fruit) should also be minimized, since they add "empty calories." Salt raises blood pressure and causes water retention. It is an ingredient in many of the foods we buy, and we all eat too much of it. The amount of salt in the diet can be reduced to reasonable levels by removing the salt shaker from the table and by not salting food while cooking. Since many prepared foods contain salt in large amounts (ham, sausages, pickles, olives, catsup, smoked meats, etc.), packaged foods should be selected carefully. A physician can tell you if there is a need to control salt more vigorously. See *Low Salt Secrets for Your Diet* (Longevity Publications, Berkeley, CA, 1981) for food suggestions.

3. Fruits, raw or lightly cooked vegetables, and whole-grain products should be emphasized. All contain necessary vitamins, minerals, complex carbohydrates, and proteins; all have limited saturated fats and refined sugars; and all are low in salt. If these foods make up the majority of calories and are supplemented by low-fat dairy products and wisely selected meats, your parent's diet will be nearly perfect.

4. Adequate protein is essential. This does not (and should not) mean meat at every meal, but it does mean a healthy serving of high-quality protein several times each week. Poultry and fish can fill the bill as satisfactorily as red meat, and have the added advantages of being comparatively low in cholesterol and saturated fats and of being less expensive. With adequate knowledge and enthusiasm, it is also possible to provide all the nec-

essary proteins healthfully and cheaply by eating combinations of vegetables. To learn the principles of this creative form of cooking, see *Diet for a Small Planet* by Frances Moore Lappe.

5. Your parent must drink ample liquid every day. One and a half quarts usually will do, except when the weather is hot. Water is ideal, but skim milk and fruit juice are nutritious and have few drawbacks.

6. Adequate roughage is important. Fruits, vegetables, and whole grains may be supplemented by a tablespoon or two of bran added to a bowl of cereal in the morning.

Several good guides to planning a good diet exist, including:

Frances Moore Lappe, *Diet for a Small Planet* (New York: Ballantine Books, 1975, paperback).

Jean Mayer, *A Diet for Living* (New York: Pocket Books, 1976, paperback).

Center for Science in the Public Interest, "New American Eating Guide" (available for $2.00 from CSPI Reports, P.O. Box 7226, Washington, DC 20044).

Scientific studies have found that older people are most likely to be deficient in calcium, iron, and vitamin A. Other substances that may be deficient include: vitamins B_6, B_{12}, C, and D (in the winter); folic acid; thiamine, potassium; and protein. A varied diet which emphasizes vegetables, dairy products, fruits, and meats will supply ample amounts of all these essential substances. Only calcium and iron are difficult for a few elderly to eat in sufficient quantity. Those people may benefit from daily supplemental tablets (the standard dose is one gram of calcium and 10–18 mg. of iron daily).

You can help your parents improve their diet by encouragement and education. Help them learn how to shop for food and how to prepare it to meet their needs now that they are old. Your parents may have developed their own complex collection of vitamin pills that they take on some elaborate schedule. Usually such practices do no harm (or much good, either), although you should ask about them if they appear outlandish. However, be certain that your parents are not spending so much money on dietary supplements that they are unable to buy healthful food. The mood and atmosphere surrounding eating are also crucial—dining is a social activity. If only one of your parents is alive, does that parent eat by himself? Is the pantry bare because of lack of knowledge, interest, or money? There are food supplement programs available in most communities which help when money, transportation, or isolation are problems. The most common ones include Meals-on-Wheels, food stamps, and daily meals provided at Title III nutrition sites. Ask your state or local service for the aging for details.

If your parent is in a nursing home or other institution, be sure he, or you, has talked to the dietician (if there is one), or inspect the menu yourself. All too often, the diets in such facilities emphasize processed breads and pastries, eggs, sweet dishes, and foods prepared "from the grill." And older residents may go for long periods eating only part of each meal (often the least nutritious part), unnoticed by staff. Intercede. Point out deficiencies in the food or in meal supervision. If worse comes to worst, supply healthful snacks during visits and obtain a medical opinion about the need for vitamin supplements.

Of course, no program or diet plan will insure a healthful diet for your parent if he or she won't cooperate. Dietary restrictions are often hard to follow, particularly when they go against long-standing habits or when they make food unpalatable (as is the case with special diets for certain diseases). Your parent must be willing to develop new habits, and that willingness depends a lot upon how well he is coping with old age. He may be so demoralized as to care little about a good diet (or anything else). Nutrition is only one part of a whole pattern which must be fit together.

115. *Accident Prevention*. The term "accidents," when applied to older people, usually means falls. Although minor burns and cuts are common, although elderly individuals are at increased risk for many other kinds of accidents (to be hit by a car, to be injured by machinery), and although they may make more frequent mistakes with their medication, falling is easily their most common form of serious accident. A fall is serious for an older person: one quarter of all accidental deaths occur among the elderly, and most of those are the consequences of a fall. If your parent has had a serious fall, it is important to understand why (see Section 138), since there often is an underlying medical problem. Seek medical evaluation if the cause of the fall is not apparent.

Since most falls and other accidents occur in the home, there is much you can do to prevent them. Evaluate your parents' home to be sure it is safe. It should be on one level, if possible. See that stairways and corners are adequately lighted. Eliminate slippery linoleum or waxed wooden floors. Choose nonskid and rubber-backed rugs, and be sure their edges are not curled, or make carpets wall-to-wall. Put handrails on stairs and bathtubs, and install ramps on difficult low stairs. Are the kitchen utensils in good condition? Is the stove safe? Use a timer as a reminder to turn off

FOSTERING GOOD HEALTH

the oven and burners. Is the bathroom (and medicine cabinet) well lighted? Are yard and garden paths level and clear? "Accidents waiting to happen" are everywhere in the home of an older person. Correct as many as you can find before the accidents occur.

116. *Immunization.* There are several serious diseases in the elderly that can be prevented by regular immunizations. All tetanus, most influenza (Section 172), and most pneumonia of the pneumococcal type (Section 171) are preventable. See that your parent develops a schedule of regular immunizations.

The basic series of three injections of tetanus toxoid, plus a booster every ten years, provides complete protection against tetanus. If your parent hasn't had the basic series, or hasn't had a booster in many years, see that this is done.

Pneumococcal pneumonia is a frequently fatal pneumonia among the elderly. Now there is a vaccine available (Pneumovax) that protects about 80 percent of people from the illness. If your parent is over 65, particularly if he or she suffers from a chronic disease (most dangerous are diseases of the heart, lung, kidney, or liver), your parent should be immunized. Some physicians feel that only debilitated elderly individuals should receive the vaccine, while others recommend it (and a booster every three years) for all older people. Discuss the matter with your parent's doctor.

The third critical vaccine is against the influenza virus. Because this virus frequently changes its nature, immunizations with updated vaccine must be given every year. Such protection is especially crucial in older people with chronic heart or lung diseases, or in those who are especially frail.

117. *Stress and Its Management.* The effects of late-life stress are discussed elsewhere (Section 58). However, it bears repeating that too much stress or poorly tolerated chronic stress produces major physical problems. Heart disease, high blood pressure, ulcers, colitis, and cancer all are made much more likely and more difficult to treat by excessive stress. If your parent is to be healthy as well as happy, he must develop ways to control the stresses upon him.

118. *Eliminating Bad Habits.* The best health care will come to naught if your parent continually undoes it with self-destructive behavior, such as poor diet, sedentary ways, and self-imposed isolation. Other bad habits to watch for:

1. Your parent should stop smoking. The likelihood of cancer of all types, infections, respiratory diseases, and high blood pressure is higher in

people who continue to smoke than in those who stop even during their later years. People who quit (at any age) feel healthier. It is never too late to stop.

2. Your parent should not drink excessively or use drugs unwisely (Sections 107 and 108). However, some recent evidence suggests that people who drink one or two glasses of wine each day may actually be healthier than abstainers.

3. Your parent should not neglect his rest. He may need seven to eight hours of sleep at night, although certain older persons prefer sleeping less at night and supplementing with daytime naps. In either case, the test is that your parent should not feel sleepy when he wishes to be awake during the day.

Encourage your parent to part with bad habits in the interest of better health. Surprisingly, the later years may be the easiest time to make a change—the effects of poor habits are beginning to be felt and mortality is becoming obvious. Your parent may be "scared straight."

119. *Helping Your Parent Live with Chronic Disease.* Chronic diseases are common during the later years. Diabetes, arthritis, heart disease, stroke, thinning of bone (osteoporosis), digestive disturbances, emphysema, glaucoma, and cataracts may hound elderly people for years. Your parent may suffer from one or two of these diseases, or many. Does he take his illness in stride, or does it incapacitate him physically and emotionally?

Most elderly sufferers are tough. They realize that chronic disease can't be cured, but they continue to fight it with sensible habits, good medical care, and determination. They seek treatment and persevere with regimens that are both tedious and uncomfortable: daily exercise for painful and deformed joints, or speech practice following a stroke. They go on living with their disability and its new limitations as best they can. At times their resolve approaches the heroic.

However, some people give up, often with unfortunate consequences. As any physician or physical therapist can attest, the greatest barrier to treatment of any chronic disease is poor motivation on the part of the sufferer. Just as most diseases can be improved with determined care, so many of these conditions worsen if neglected. Elderly individuals who reject treatment, stay in bed, insist on being dependant upon others, or insist that their illness is incapacitating, are in trouble. Such behavior is self-destructive and condemns a person to a life of gradually decreasing function. If your parent has fallen into this pattern, intervene.

Individuals give up in the face of chronic illness for many different reasons. The illness may be physically exhausting, or it may have destroyed important physical or mental abilities. Your parent may have always been dependent, and chronic illness may offer the perfect opportunity to be cared for. Your parent may suffer from a major depression and need specific treatment for it (Chapter 10). Perhaps he or she has never worked through the loss of physical ability or self-esteem due to the disease (Chapter 9). If your parent is resigned to or content with a deplorable but remediable chronic illness, find out why, and try to change his attitude.

Unfortunately, motivation is difficult to create. Your parent may resist improvement. Your endurance, and that of your family, may be stretched painfully by a parent who is both demanding and passive. It is too easy to allow your concern and compassion, or your frustration, to blind you to the level of effort your parent could and should make. Don't resolve your parent's plight, and yours, by doing for him what he has trouble doing for himself. You, your parent, and the physician should develop a plan of expected activities for your parent. Stick to it. It is in his best interest to do as much for himself as possible. See that he understands this. If your parent complains bitterly about the impossibility or inhumanity of what people demand of him consider consulting a psychiatrist or a psychologist.

If your parent is becoming increasingly unwilling to take care of a chronic illness, take time to listen to his fears about his illness. Let him vent his anger and discouragement. Make certain he understands his disease—what the treatments are meant to accomplish, and what the future holds. Emphasize what your parent should be capable of doing, and what is *not* expected of him. Voice your concern about his condition, but also your expectation that he is capable of more. Get your parent involved in planning his own care—give him a sense of control over this part of his life, if possible. Emphasize that he must remain active in every possible way. Encourage and compliment him whenever he succeeds. Remind your parent of his remaining strengths and help him utilize them. Interest your parent in things beyond his own physical condition: the needs of others, the development of new skills. A focus on growth can keep a person from dwelling on his physical deterioration. In spite of your best efforts, however, your parent may gradually sink under the weight of multiple chronic illnesses, old age, and the resulting demoralization. Try to prevent this, but don't be crushed by a sense of your own failure if it occurs.

14.

Common Physical Symptoms

120. *Abdominal Pain* (see Chapter 16).

121. *Anxiety* (see Section 59).

122. *Back Pain* (see Section 233).

123. *Belching* (see Section 181).

124. *Bloating* (see Section 186).

125. *Blood in the Sputum* (see Section 177).

126. *Blood in the Stool* (see Section 187).

127. *Blood in the Urine* (see Section 210).

128. *Chest Pain* (see Section 175).

129. *Confusion* (see Chapter 11).

130. *Constipation* (see Section 183).

131. *Cough* (see Section 177).

132. *Depression* (see Chapter 10).

133. *Diarrhea* (see Section 184).

134. *Difficulty Hearing* (see Chapter 18).

135. *Difficulty Swallowing.* This complaint must not be ignored. If your parent remarks that food has begun sticking in his throat or "on the way down," or that all bites seem too large, have him see a doctor. Common causes of this problem include a dry mouth, weakened muscles of the esophagus, and scarring of the esophagus due to burns from stomach acid. Serious, and often fatal, causes include cancer of the esophagus and a lung cancer which is squeezing the esophagus shut from the outside. Are there other symptoms, like shortness of breath or a chronic cough? Early detection is essential. Evaluation usually includes a barium swallow: X-rays taken while a thick "barium milkshake" is drunk. The physician also may want to look down the throat with an endoscope if he has any questions after evaluating the X-rays.

136. *Dizziness.* Dizziness is an unpleasant sense of spinning or whirling, but sometimes it can be the feeling of losing balance and being pulled to the ground. To physicians, it suggests possibilities quite different from the symptoms of fainting or lightheadedness (see Section 137). Although it is common and usually not cause for concern, any sustained dizziness demands a thorough medical evaluation because a few of its causes are very serious.

The primary organ of balance is a matching set of fluid-filled tubes and chambers (the semicircular canals, utricle, and saccule), one buried deep alongside the inner ear on either side of the skull. Most severe dizziness is due to problems in these chambers, in the nerves which lead from them to the brain, or in the brain itself. The causes of dizziness include infection in the semicircular canals, a decrease in the blood flow to these areas, residual effects of a blow to the head, anxiety, a brain tumor, low thyroid hormone in the blood (hypothyroidism), and many others. Symptoms depend on the cause and may last only a few hours, be constant for weeks, or continue, off and on, for years. Whether your parent is dizzy continuously or only when he or she moves, the experience is invariably an unpleasant sensation. Many sufferers endure associated symptoms like nausea and sweating. Because the anatomic source of most dizziness lies so close to the inner ear, many people also experience varying amounts of deafness and ringing in the ears. A careful physical examination and laboratory, hearing, and X-ray tests may be required to determine the cause and its seriousness. Expect, at the least, an examination of your parent's hearing, eyes, and balance, as well as a measure of his blood thyroid level. Since the true nature of some dizziness cannot be determined until time has passed, your parent will probably need to be checked several times over the following weeks and months.

In most cases, treatment usually consists of lying in bed until the symptoms improve. Some people obtain relief from antimotion medication like Dramamine, Marezine, Antivert, or Bonine, or from sedatives like Valium. A serious underlying physical problem should be treated, if possible. Your parent can take solace in knowing that, uncomfortable as the condition may be, dizziness usually passes.

137. *Fainting (Lightheadedness, Blackouts).* A person who faints has a sudden, brief loss of consciousness. Someone about to faint may feel it "coming on" over a few seconds or a few minutes, but occasionally there is no warning. The loss of consciousness may be preceded by dimming vision, spots before the eyes, ringing in the ears, or a cold sweat. Fortunately, there may be time to lie down and thus prevent injury from a fall.

Most causes involve the transient interruption of blood flow to the brain. Disorders of the heart such as a "silent" heart attack or heartbeat irregularities are common offenders. Even more common is the drop in blood pressure that follows rising from a chair or bed (postural hypotension). Postural hypotension can be a side effect of certain medications, particularly antihypertensive drugs, tranquilizers, sleeping pills, antidepressants, and medication for Parkinson's disease. Atherosclerotic narrowing of the arteries to the brain may cause blood flow to be temporarily shut off when the head is tilted backwards to look up. Small strokes or transient ischemic attacks (TIAs; see Section 249) may lead to fainting. Moreover, any drop in the amount of blood (for example, blood loss caused by an ulcer) or in its quality (for example, anemia) can produce a fainting episode, particularly when your parent changes position.

A "slow faint," which may take place over several minutes, can be caused by low blood sugar (hypoglycemia) or by breathing that has become too rapid (hyperventilation). On the other hand, an instantaneous loss of consciousness is more likely caused by a seizure.

Obviously, there is a spectrum of causes for fainting. However, fainting should not be ignored. A careful physical examination, blood tests, electrocardiogram, and electroencephalogram usually can determine the cause. Occasionally a more extensive evaluation must be completed, including a CAT scan of the head to check for brain disease, or a twenty-four-hour heartwave recording (Holter monitor) to check for heartbeat irregularities. Usually, fainting episodes can be explained and their causes treated.

138. *Falling.* Has your parent fallen? Find out why! Although common, falling is abnormal among the elderly and demands an explanation. Moreover, it is dangerous—damage sustained during falls is one of the major causes of death among the elderly.

Causes are numerous. Vision, hearing, balance, reflex speed, sense of position, and muscle strength are all reduced in old age. The elderly sway more when standing and shuffle their feet when walking. As a result, they are at risk of falling, running into something, or being run into as they go about their daily activities. A variety of medical conditions may increase this risk. Falls may be caused by a number of different heart conditions, all of which suddenly lower blood pressure and cause fainting: a mild heart attack, a sudden irregularity of the heartbeat (arrhythmia), or a fall in blood pressure upon standing (postural hypotension). Other causes of fainting (see Section 137) may be responsible: anemia, blood loss, medication side effect, seizure, hypoglycemia, stroke. Dizziness (see Section 136) may be to blame. Uncover the cause, so that future falls, and the life-threatening injuries that often accompany them, can be avoided.

Unfortunately, your parent may not know why he has fallen. He "just went down," and is as surprised by it as you are. Nevertheless, close questioning can sometimes identify obvious hazards. Did a loose rug slip out from underneath her? Did she trip? Did she lose her footing in a poorly lighted stairway? Did it happen in a part of the house where she has always felt a little uneasy? Is your parent drinking? Ask her how she was feeling at the time of the fall and what she was doing. Had she just risen from bed or a chair? Did she feel dizzy? Did she black out? Did your parent urinate while unconscious (suggesting a seizure)? Did she experience any other symptoms (for example, chest pain, suggesting a heart attack, or heart palpitations, suggesting an arrhythmia)? Obtain information from anyone else who witnessed your parent's fall.

A brief hospitalization may be needed to pursue the issue further, even though your parent now feels well. A number of tests may be needed to solve the riddle, including blood tests, an electrocardiogram, an electro-encephalogram (EEG), and a CAT scan of the brain. Even at that, the original cause for the fall may have been transitory and nothing will be found.

Whatever the results of the medical evaluation, try to make your parent's environment safe. Make sure the home is well lighted and preferably on one level. Is the bathroom safe and are there adequate handrails throughout the home? Are the floors cushioned, or are they hard and slippery? Is everything in the kitchen within easy reach? Does your parent have a safe route to neighborhood stores? Any effort to make the surroundings safer can prevent falls, or avoid serious injury in case your parent does fall again.

139. *Fatigue (and Weakness)*. Neither fatigue nor weakness automatically accompanies old age, but they are common complaints. Why?

First, it is necessary to differentiate between the two. Fatigue is a feeling of tiredness and of lack of energy which may be recent or have been present for years. Weakness is a feeling of lack of strength. Although they often occur together, they don't have to, and they may be due to different causes.

Fatigue is commonly caused by boredom or depression. Your parent may have nothing to look forward to and no reason to be active. Life may also be limited by blindness, deafness, or a deteriorating physical condition. The solution, of course, is to get your parent reinvolved in activities, both social and physical. He or she should reestablish contacts with friends and social organizations, pick up old hobbies, start an exercise program, or take a class at the local college. However, if signs of depression are present (see Chapter 10), your parent should see a physician and perhaps begin a trial of medication.

Fatigue can also be caused by illness. The leading offender is heart disease. Chronic heart failure or "silent" heart attacks (see Chapter 15) can cause a sense of fatigue before either condition is recognized. Other chronic illnesses can be at fault, including lung disease, kidney disease, anemia, infections, and brain disease. Finally, fatigue can be a side effect of medication. This is particularly true of sedatives and sleeping pills, which may gradually be taken in increasing amounts, and antihypertensive drugs, which can lower the blood pressure too far or cause blood-chemical imbalances. If your parent complains of significant fatigue, whether acute or chronic, the condition should be evaluated medically.

If weakness occurs separately from a feeling of fatigue, there is likely to be a medical cause. Although the elderly do lose some strength with age, they shouldn't find this loss incapacitating. Have any complaint of weakness checked carefully. The answer may be as simple as a lack of exercise; however, the more severe the weakness, the more likely a disease is to blame.

140. *Headache*. Any headache of recent onset in an elderly person should be taken seriously. Headaches that occur among the young, such as tension and migraine headaches, decrease in old age. Headaches caused by serious medical conditions occur with increased frequency. Any headache without an obvious cause and which doesn't quickly improve should be evaluated. The common underlying causes differ depending on whether the headache is acute or long-standing.

Acute headaches are the most worrisome. The more severe, the more dangerous they are. If your parent develops a sudden, splitting headache, he should be evaluated medically as soon as possible. Although the cause may be insignificant (something he ate, sun exposure), life-threatening illnesses produce headache often enough to demand a careful examination. Of particular concern are infections of the brain such as meningitis and encephalitis, bleeding into the brain such as a subarachnoid hemorrhage, or sudden slowing of the flow of blood to the brain such as sometimes occurs before a stroke. Many of these conditions can be treated successfully if your parent sees a physician early enough. Be aware of any other symptoms your parent may be experiencing (fever, weakness, confusion) and report these to the doctor.

A slowly developing headache is also a cause for concern. Unfortunately, the type of pain may not help determine its cause; headache pain varies widely from person to person. A number of causes for chronic headache are minor: constipation; anxiety; allergy; infection of the sinuses, ears, or teeth; overeating; glaucoma, stiff neck or arthritis in the neck vertebrae. Severe depression and elevated blood pressure, while not immediately life-threatening, are serious conditions which can produce a headache that is relieved when the underlying conditions are treated. Finally, causes of chronic headache which are potentially fatal include brain tumor, impending stroke, and slow bleeding into the brain. No constant or recurrent headache in an elderly person should go unevaluated.

To this complex list of headaches must be added two unique types which develop for the first time in late middle age or after; cluster headache and giant cell arteritis. (1) The pain of cluster headache is throbbing, occurs on one side, lasts for about an hour, returns several times over several days, and then may disappear for weeks or months. Medication may help. (2) Giant cell arteritis produces a severe pain in the temple on one side of the head, accompanied by tenderness over the area and a mixture of fever, loss of appetite, weight loss, anemia, and fatigue. Occasionally, permanent blindness may occur in the eye on the affected side, so it is important to seek immediate treatment if these symptoms appear. Fortunately, treatment is usually effective. Look for symptoms which suggest that either of these specific headache syndromes is present, and alert the physician.

141. *Heartburn.* Heartburn is a mild to severe burning sensation in the middle of the chest which may last just a moment or may be almost constant. It is common among the elderly. It is usually caused by the squeezing of stomach acid up into the esophagus, and occasionally all the way to the back of the throat and mouth. Usually heartburn is simply unpleasant, but in severe cases the pain may be constant and extreme. Heartburn is usually most severe shortly after eating, particularly after a large meal, fat-

ty or spicy food, or alcohol. It also occurs or gets noticeably worse while lying down, bending, laughing, or with any kind of straining, such as while on a toilet or while lifting a heavy object. Complications may occur, such as bleeding from the raw walls of the esophagus or the gradual scarring and closing of the esophagus.

If the pain appears after a meal and disappears after swallowing an antacid (like Maalox, Mylanta, and many others), your parent is suffering from typical heartburn. If the pain doesn't disappear with antacid, however, it almost certainly isn't heartburn. It is probably not serious but should be discussed with a physician, because it sometimes can be caused by an abnormal position of the stomach called hiatus hernia (see Section 191), which may require surgical correction. Since heartburn is a pain in the center of the chest, older individuals may worry that they are having a heart attack. However, heartburn usually produces a burning sensation rather than the feeling of intense cramp or pressure common in a heart attack. For final confirmation of the diagnosis, your parent may need an X-ray of his esophagus and stomach, usually after swallowing a milk-like barium solution.

Treatment of esophagus irritation is usually effective and requires adopting habits like not lying down after a meal, not eating before bed, elevating the head of the bed at night, eating slowly, and avoiding large, spicy meals and excessive alcohol. It may also be necessary to take an antacid after meals and at bedtime, either temporarily or on a regular basis.

142. *Hip Pain* (see Section 232).

143. *Hypochondriasis* (see Section 106).

144. *Impotence.* The misty, myth-enshrouded topic of impotence in old age needs considerable clarification. Old age does not cause impotence—your parent should not expect it. A consistent failure to have an erection always requires an explanation. However, some changes in sexual performance do accompany aging and may be confused with impotence. Older men take longer to reach a full erection, their penises are softer, collapse more quickly after ejaculation, and they may not be able to repeat for hours or days. Moreover, most elderly men are no longer able to get an erection by just thinking about something arousing: they require direct physical stimulation. None of these changes are impotence, nor do any of them regularly lead to impotence. All may so worry an older man, however, that impotence results.

Most impotence has psychological roots: misinterpretation of normal changes as oncoming impotence, fear of an inadequate "performance," loss of sexual desire due to boredom or fatigue, anxiety over health ("Will I

COMMON PHYSICAL SYMPTOMS

have a heart attack?"), loss of self-esteem, marital conflict, or a psychiatric illness such as depression. Four out of five cases are explained by one or more of these causes. Many are successfully treated by instruction and psychotherapy. It is most important, however, that your parent appreciate that sexual activity is, at its core, an enjoyable interpersonal experience based on a trusting, intimate relationship—*not* just a sexual exercise.

Physical causes of impotence occur often enough that they should always be looked for. Any sudden illness can produce temporary impotence, which disappears when the illness is cured. Of greater concern is the chronic impotence caused by chronic illness. This impotence may or may not improve if the underlying medical condition is successfully treated. Diabetes is perhaps the most frequent cause of chronic impotence. Other common medical causes include heart disease, kidney disease, high blood pressure, obesity, and prostate enlargement. Medications are frequent offenders: tranquilizers, sleeping pills, antidepressants, high-blood-pressure medication, and others. Finally, excessive use of alcohol is a surefire way of becoming impotent, at least temporarily. Despite the fears of many elderly men, abdominal or prostate surgery produce impotence only rarely. Obviously, the treatment of impotence in any of these situations depends upon treating the underlying condition or removing the offending medication.

More than half of all elderly men with impotence can be successfully treated by a careful medical evaluation and sound psychological intervention. In spite of popular wisdom, hormone therapy is of little value.

145. *Incontinence of Bowel* (see Section 185).

146. *Incontinence of Urine* (see Chapter 17).

147. *Insomnia.* Lack of sleep is one of the most common complaints of the elderly. There is usually substance to the complaint, but the underlying problem is generally minor.

Normal sleep in the elderly differs from that of younger people in two major ways: there is more daytime napping and more frequent waking during the night. Many older individuals mistakenly conclude from this pattern that they aren't sleeping enough. A better measure of insomnia is whether your parent feels rested during the day.

One in five elderly people are troubled by insomnia at some time. Most often they can't fall asleep at night. Occasionally they wake too early and can't fall back to sleep. There are numerous causes. Perhaps the most common is boredom: they don't have enough to fill their days, go to bed too early, and consequently can't stay asleep all night. Lack of physical activity also plays a role—many elderly rarely exercise enough to feel truly fatigued. Minor (or major) pains and discomfort awaken them and break up sleep. The usual causes of these discomforts include: arthritis, shortness of breath from mild heart failure or chronic lung disease, and awakening to go to the bathroom. Anxiety (often about whether they are getting enough rest) sometimes interferes with sleep. Depression can be a major disrupter of sleep; most commonly it causes early awakening rather than difficulty falling asleep. Sleeping pills taken too long and in too great quantity can actually disturb sleep—sleep becomes unsettled at night, while the sleeping pill "hangover" causes excessive daytime napping.

Most insomnia can be improved. It helps to maintain a standard bedtime and to develop a "sleeping ritual," a specific set of things to be done before getting into bed. The room should be dark and quiet. Your parent should arise promptly in the morning. He should exercise each day, but avoid vigorous mental or physical activities just before bed. A bedtime snack may help. He should be reassured that, no matter how fractured his sleep, he is probably getting enough if he doesn't feel groggy most of the day. Your parent should become more socially active during the day and avoid excessive daytime naps. Biofeedback, self-hypnosis, or meditation may also be useful.

Sleeping medication probably won't help. The only legitimate reason for sleeping pills is to promote sleep on that occasional night when falling asleep can be expected to be difficult (the day has been exceptionally exciting, or the next day will be anxiety-provoking). They should not be used longer than two weeks at a time—after that length they lose their effectiveness. The most effective and least problem-fraught sleeping medications appear to be the benzodiazepines (Dalmane, Serax, Restoril). Your parent should discuss their use fully with his physician. If pain is keeping your parent from sound sleep, occasionally a mild pain medication (aspirin, codeine) may help. Care must be taken in using these medications as well.

148. *Itching.* Itching is very common among the elderly. Usually a limited area itches, like the legs, arms, back, or groin. Dry skin is the most common cause. Older skin produces less oil and holds water poorly. Thus it becomes dried by too much bathing, hot water, strong soaps, vigorous rubbing with a bath towel, dry air, cool air, and rubbing alcohol. Often it becomes cracked and scaly. A careful review of your parent's habits will usually clarify the cause of the itching.

Treatment for dry skin involves: taking short baths no more than once each day; using warm water; switching to a mild soap (Basis, Dove, Lowila); toweling gently; using bath lotions (Lubriderm, Nutraderm) or bath oils (Alpha Keri, etc.; but be *very* careful that your parent doesn't slip in the bathtub); avoiding extremes of temperature (both hot and cold); using a humidifier; and avoiding wool and tight clothing. A mild anti-itching medication (Atarax, Vistaril) may help, but should be considered as a treatment secondary in importance. If the skin has become noticeably cracked, a steroid cream may help return it to normal, but should be used only temporarily.

There are other less frequent causes for itching. Diseases of the liver and kidneys, anemia, thyroid disease, widespread cancer, and various medications can all cause itching that is resistant to treatment. Does your parent have one of these diseases? Discuss the possible side effects of any medication your parent is taking with his or her physician. Another cause of itching, which can become epidemic in some nursing homes, is lice.

149. *Joint Pain* (see Section 231).

150. *Leg Pain* (see Section 178).

151. *Loss of Appetite.* Many older people gradually lose interest in food. Most often the reasons are easily understandable; they may or may not be a cause for worry. Is your parent really eating very little or is she snacking on the sly? Does she say she is just not hungry or does she have another reason for not eating (for example: "It hurts to swallow" or "I'm already constipated enough")? Does she become nauseated when she eats? Is her poor appetite a recent change, a gradual change, or has she always eaten "like a bird"? Is she losing awareness of other daily routines besides eating? Has she developed any physical problems that make shopping for food or preparing it difficult? Does the food your parent eats look, smell, and taste edible? In spite of how little you think she is eating, has she lost weight? Is your parent weak? Does she have a chronic illness?

Most often a gradual loss of appetite results from a minor or correctable cause. If an elderly person's weight is stable and she feels good, perhaps she doesn't need more food—particularly if she is much less physically active than in previous years. Perhaps the food your parent is eating is bland and uninteresting—powers of taste and smell are less acute in old age, so food must generally be more highly seasoned to be stimulating. Improving the food's quality or getting your parent active again may yield a dramatic improvement in her appetite.

A frequent cause for an unhealthy loss of appetite is a waning interest in life or a serious depression. Occasionally a person concludes that she is too old, tired, or sick to go on and decides to stop eating and "just waste away." Often this individual has other signs of a serious depression, like difficulty sleeping, frequent crying, and a sense of hopelessness. However, a poor appetite may be the dominant problem. If your parent seems to be consciously neglecting herself, she needs to be evaluated by a physician, and possibly by a psychiatrist as well.

Illnesses of many different types—many acute diseases (particularly if fever is present), severe heart and lung problems, kidney trouble, various cancers, liver disease, and many types of intestinal problems—can also cause loss of appetite. Finally, poor appetite may be a side effect of medication (particularly heart medication like digitalis and some sedatives); ask your parent's doctor if this could be a cause.

152. *Ringing in the Ears* (see Section 227).

153. *Shortness of Breath* (see Section 176).

154. *Suspiciousness* (see Section 109).

155. *Vomiting* (see Section 182).

156. *Weight Loss.* A person's weight usually decreases with age. However, any unexpectedly large decrease in weight should be investigated. Perhaps the explanation is simple: your parent does not like the food available, or bad teeth make eating difficult. Unfortunately, more serious causes for unexplained weight loss are frequent. Any serious illness can cause it: chronic infection, heart disease, chronic lung disease, cancer. Serious depression, with its accompanying loss of appetite, is a frequent cause. If your parent is suddenly looking thinner, look into it.

157. *Yellowing of the Skin.* A gradual yellowing of the skin, the fingernails, and the whites of the eyes, over a period of days or weeks, is known as jaundice. Although it is not especially common in old age, if it occurs a doctor should be contacted. Jaundice is due to abnormally high levels of the chemical bilirubin in the blood, which can be caused by a variety of different, and often serious, medical conditions. Bilirubin is produced by the normal breakdown of red blood cells. After it is chemically changed by the liver, it is passed from the body in the stool. However, if red blood cells are breaking down unusually fast, if the liver is diseased and can't process the bilirubin, or if there is a block which keeps bilirubin from being excreted from the body, the level in the blood rises and jaundice occurs. A common cause of jaundice in younger people is the acute liver disease known as hepatitis. In the elderly the causes include blood diseases, scarring of the liver from alcohol, an unwanted side effect of medication, a complication of gallstones, and cancer. There are many specialized tests available that allow the physician to correctly identify the cause of jaundice; it is vitally important to bear with the doctor throughout the many procedures, since jaundice must never be neglected in the hope that it will "go away."

15.

Disorders of the Heart, Lungs, and Blood Vessels

The heart, lungs, and blood vessels all work together as an interlocking unit; a failure of one part usually has repercussions elsewhere in this system. Symptoms are shared as well: a heart disorder may produce symptoms easily confused with those of a lung disease. Disorders within this system are so common in old age that few elderly escape them. This chapter begins with a discussion of heart disease (angina, heart attacks, heart failure) and high blood pressure, since one of every two elderly people will be afflicted with such problems. Then follows a discussion of lung disease (asthma, bronchitis, emphysema, pneumonia, cancer). Next the chapter describes common symptoms related to both the heart and the lungs (chest pain, shortness of breath, wheezing, cough). The chapter ends with a discussion of the two most common problems affecting the blood vessels, damaged arteries and veins in the legs.

The Heart

Disease is as common as health in the aging heart—heart disease is the most common serious physical disease faced in old age. It is the major cause of death among those over 65, and it is a major cause of physical incapacitation and chronic disability. Much of the fatigue, weakness, and swollen legs and ankles so common among the elderly is due to heart disease.

The heart gradually changes with age. Its beat becomes quicker and less forceful. It may become stiffer as fibrous tissue replaces some of the muscle cells. However, unless disease intervenes, the aging heart will meet normal daily demands upon it. Only when sudden, excessive exertion is demanded does the heart show its age.

A vast array of heart disorders occur in the elderly. Some symptoms are related to abnormal valves, abnormal heart rhythms, or past rheumatic fever; these will be discussed later. The majority of problems, however, including most heart attacks, heart failure, and heart-related chest pains, are caused by atherosclerosis, often in combination with high blood pressure.

ATHEROSCLEROSIS AND HEART DISEASE

158. *Atherosclerosis.* Atherosclerosis is the gradual collection of irregular, fatty patches inside large arteries. These patches begin to form during the first several decades of life as smooth streaks on arterial inner surfaces. During the following decades, they slowly enlarge, begin to project into the arterial passage, and become hard and fibrous. They may even become calcified and bony. We all have them, to one degree or another. Their cause is unknown. Patches develop only in the larger arteries, most commonly in the arteries to the heart (coronary arteries), brain (cerebral arteries), and legs (femoral arteries). These patches, by slowly restricting the flow of blood to the tissues supplied by damaged arteries, may produce weakness and leg cramps due to poor circulation in the lower extremities. Because the blood flow often becomes sluggish and rough around the patches, a clot may form which suddenly shuts off the flow at that point, as in a stroke or heart attack. Atherosclerotic narrowing is the primary cause of many of the major ills which afflict the elderly: heart attack and heart failure, stroke, and poor circulation in the legs.

Although the cause of atherosclerotic patches is unknown, many factors which encourage them to grow have been identified. Atherosclerosis is more likely to occur if a person has high blood pressure, smokes, has high levels of blood fats (such as cholesterol and triglycerides), is markedly obese, or is diabetic. Controlling these factors helps prevent the development of the fatty patches.

In addition, the longer a person lives, the more likely he is to have developed atherosclerosis sufficient to cause symptoms. However, by the time a person reaches his 70s and 80s, many of the irreversible changes in his arteries will be present, and the risk factors that led to their development will be less important. Controlling high blood pressure and diabetes remains crucial in later years, but an overly rich diet and smoking, while important to control for other reasons, play less of a role in the further development of stroke or heart disease.

DISORDERS OF THE HEART, LUNGS, AND BLOOD VESSELS

Unfortunately, atherosclerotic patches are irreversible. They don't dissolve with medication or disappear with a change in diet. In special circumstances they can be removed surgically, but those situations are unusual. Prevention during youth is the only "cure." Once they are present, your parent will need to learn to live with the limitations and dangers they create.

159. *Angina.* Angina (the full name is angina pectoris) is chest pain which occurs when the heart becomes starved for oxygen. The most common cause for this condition is atherosclerotic narrowing of the coronary arteries, which supply the heart muscle with blood and oxygen. During an anginal attack the heart is stressed but little permanent damage is done. However, repeated attacks eventually do produce permanent scarring and a weakened heart.

Usually, during an anginal attack, a person feels an uncomfortable sense of tightness or pressure in the middle of the chest, a pain which may spread to the neck or down the left arm. However, angina in the elderly is often atypical; it may be sharp or dull and may be located anywhere from the head to the abdomen. Typically, the pain appears when the heart works hard and thus needs more oxygen—for example, during exercise or emotional stress, or after a heavy meal or exposure to cold. It lasts for a few moments, but then eases as the heart slows. Most often angina is suffered for years and is predictable enough for an elderly person to learn what activities produce it and how to avoid it.

An attack of angina is not a heart attack, but it is a warning of the increased possibility of a heart attack. Some people may experience angina for years without developing any more serious problem, but almost half the people with chronic angina eventually suffer a heart attack. Two types of angina are particularly worrisome. (1) Anginal pain that changes in frequency and severity over days or weeks is of greater concern than pain which is stable and predictable. It suggests that conditions in the heart may be changing. (2) Pain which lasts for more than a minute or two has a special name, acute coronary insufficiency. Typically, the pain of insufficiency may last for half an hour or more and be accompanied by nausea and sweating. As with angina, the temporary starvation of the heart muscle in acute coronary insufficiency produces no long-lasting damage, yet it is one step away from a heart attack and is a medical emergency. If your parent's anginal pain persists, he should see a physician or visit a hospital immediately.

A history of typical chest pain accompanying stress or exercise is the best indication of a diagnosis of angina and may be all that is needed for treatment to begin. Usually the physician will further confirm the diagnosis by asking your parent to exercise while recording his or her heartwaves (electrocardiogram, ECG or EKG). As the pain begins, the ECG pattern should change in a predictable way. If your parent then takes a medication like nitroglycerin which usually relieves anginal pain quickly, the disappearance of the pain makes the diagnosis almost certain. However, if your parent's pain is particularly severe or worrisome, more extensive diagnostic measures are often called for to be certain that a heart attack is not imminent. The most dependable test for a diagnosis of angina is to inject dye into the suspected coronary arteries and then obtain their outline by X-ray (coronary arteriography). This examination determines where the blocks are, how severe they are, and whether they are amenable to surgical correction.

Although the arterial narrowing that gives rise to angina can be reversed only by surgery, attacks can be partially prevented by sensible habits and can be stopped by medication. Your parents should learn their physical limits and should allow them to guide their activities. They should avoid situations likely to produce an anginal attack—not because each attack is terribly dangerous but because each does carry the risk that it might develop into something more serious. They should avoid single heavy meals in favor of several smaller ones. They should not exercise immediately after eating and should avoid exercising in the cold. Their symptoms will tell each of them best what they can and cannot tolerate; they should be encouraged to listen to those symptoms.

Several medications are available to treat angina. The mainstay is nitroglycerin. It works by dilating the blood vessels throughout the body (including the coronary arteries), which lowers the blood pressure temporarily, thus decreasing the work the heart has to do. Your parent should keep a supply of nitroglycerin tablets on hand, and, when an attack of angina begins, should put one under his tongue. The pain is usually rapidly relieved. If it isn't, he should use another tablet of this safe medication. Taken before stressful activity, nitroglycerin may prevent an attack of angina. Your parent will gradually learn the most appropriate times for the medication. Unfortunately, the effects of nitroglycerin last only a few minutes. For this reason, isosorbide dinitrate (Isordil), which is not as effective as nitroglycerin but which works for up to an hour, may be useful for some people who have frequent bouts of angina.

Several back-up medications useful in treating angina fall into at least two classes: beta blockers (Inderal, Lopressor) and calcium antagonists (Procardia, Isoptin). They operate, in part, by slowing the speed and strength of the heart beat, allowing the heart to relax. These medications, usually taken three or four times each day for long periods of time, help

DISORDERS OF THE HEART, LUNGS, AND BLOOD VESSELS

decrease the number of episodes of angina. Because these drugs work through different mechanisms, often a person may take nitroglycerin, plus a beta blocker, plus a calcium antagonist for maximum benefit.

If chest pain continues to be severely limiting in spite of control of a person's activities and medication, surgery may be necessary. Coronary artery bypass is the preferred operation, during which the clogged artery (or arteries) is removed and replaced with a vein that has simultaneously been removed from some other part of the body (usually from a leg). This operation has been perfected to the point where the risk is low for surgery of this magnitude. Most people find that the surgery relieves their symptoms. Unfortunately, the beneficial effects usually last only for a few years; most people develop atherosclerotic patches in their new arteries and begin once again to experience angina.

160. *Acute Myocardial Infarction (MI, or Heart Attack).* A heart attack or myocardial infarction (MI) occurs when the blood flow feeding the heart muscle is interrupted sufficiently to cause cell death and permanent damage to the heart wall. Usually a heart attack occurs in coronary arteries that are already narrowed by atherosclerosis; then the blood flow through one of them is decreased further or stopped suddenly by a clot or a spasm. However, anything that rapidly reduces the amount of well-oxygenated blood passing through the coronary arteries, such as a sudden fall in blood pressure or damage to a lung, can produce an MI.

Heart attacks are common, and are usually unexpected. Although some elderly people have been forewarned of an attack by months or years of angina, most people either have no alerting symptoms or have symptoms they don't associate with their heart. And, particularly among the elderly, heart attacks may go unrecognized for a short period of time after they have occurred. Why?

Younger people who suffer an MI usually have a characteristic set of symptoms. (Only one in four elderly persons have those same "classic" symptoms.) A typical heart attack in a younger person consists of the sudden onset of a prolonged "heavy" or "crushing" pain in the center or left side of the chest, accompanied by sweating, nausea, and occasionally unconsciousness. The victim is usually rushed into treatment because of these profound symptoms. An elderly person is more likely to have no symptoms or to experience sudden shortness of breath, faintness, dizziness, weakness, extreme fatigue, confusion, or abdominal pain. The older the person, the more likely he is to have one of these atypical symptoms instead of chest pain. In fact, it is common for a heart attack in an 80-year-old individual to be mistaken for the rapid onset of pneumonia; thus valuable time is lost before his sudden breathlessness, nausea, and sweating are correctly diagnosed. Sudden, acute discomfort in the head, chest, or abdomen should always be considered possible signs of a heart attack.

Not only do some heart attacks mimic other illnesses; some occur completely without symptoms or with only a vague symptom such as sudden fatigue. Many an elderly person has shown evidence of an old, unrecognized MI during a routine physical examination and electrocardiogram. Such a discovery is always of concern. Although a silent MI is preferable to an acute, life-threatening illness, it is important to be aware of a past heart attack because the heart has been damaged and made susceptible to failure.

Not all heart-related catastrophies are due to heart attacks. A major cause of sudden death is the rapid development of irregular rhythms in a chronically diseased and overstressed heart. The heart begins to beat inefficiently and blood flow slows markedly, causing fainting and often death. Many people who suffer this type of sudden, life-threatening episode have heart disease which has required treatment for years. It is important to distinguish this type of episode from a heart attack, however, since the problems and the potential for recovery are different.

Heart attacks in the elderly are frequently difficult to diagnose. Numerous other diseases can produce similar symptoms, including disorders of the lung, esophagus, stomach, and gallbladder. If a physical examination is completed shortly after the start of symptoms and electrocardiograms are taken during the following hours and days, often an accurate diagnosis can be made. The diagnosis may also be confirmed by the use of two specialized tests. (1) Damaged heart-muscle cells release the enzymes creatine phosphokinase (CPK) and lactic dehydrogenase (LDH) into the blood. If, during the days following the start of symptoms, these enzymes are measured and their amounts in the blood rise and then fall in parallel with the active destruction of the heart cells, the diagnosis of a myocardial infarction can be made with relative certainty. (2) Certain mildly radioactive chemicals are concentrated in damaged heart cells, while other similar chemicals are excluded from those cells. Measuring the concentrations of one of those chemicals in the various parts of the heart following its injection into the blood determines areas of damage.

A combination of these various diagnostic techniques usually allows the physician to determine whether or not your parent has suffered a heart attack. Unfortunately, the weak link in this chain of evidence that leads toward diagnosis is at the beginning—the possibility that your parent has suffered a heart attack must be thought of as early as possible.

An MI is a medical emergency that requires immediate hospitalization in an intensive care (ICU) or cardiac care (CCU) unit. Above all, the

DISORDERS OF THE HEART, LUNGS, AND BLOOD VESSELS

heart must rest. Thus your parent will be given a powerful painkiller (usually morphine) to make him more comfortable, oxygen to ease the heart's work, a sedative to reduce his anxiety, an antiarrhythmic drug (such as lidocaine) to help prevent dangerous heart irregularities, stool softeners to prevent constipation and straining, and possibly anticoagulants to prevent further formation of clots. He will be kept in bed for three to four days and during this time his only exercise will be to sit on the edge of the bed (with help) or to use a bedside commode. And he will be fed a few small meals.

Perhaps most important, your parent will be watched constantly by trained nurses, and his heart will be under continuous electrical surveillance by an electrocardiogram. This surveillance is necessary because the electrical conduction system in the heart may have been damaged by the MI. In fact, most deaths from heart attack during the first two days are caused by the heart's abnormal rhythms, which may result in erratic beats or in the complete cessation of beating. Constant monitoring of the heartbeat allows correction the moment the heart's normal rhythm changes.

Most elderly people recover from a heart attack. Of those who do not survive, a few die within minutes or hours of the attack, but most succumb after days or weeks to a complication like shock, heart failure, collection of fluid in the lungs (pulmonary edema), a blood infection, or pneumonia. The older a person is at the time of a serious heart attack, the more likely it is that his MI will be fatal; thus the majority of 65-year-olds recover, while most 90-year-olds do not.

For those who survive a heart attack, a return to a normal life should be possible. A complete recovery requires a comprehensive program of rehabilitation, which begins in the hospital. A cornerstone in any recovery program is regular, carefully selected exercise. Your parent must work with his physician to develop a schedule of gradually increasing exercise: walking, jogging, bicycle riding, swimming. This should be done regularly but gently during the first two to three months (occasionally with cardiac monitoring to look for unsuspected dangerous heart rhythms, as is possible on a treadmill in the physician's office), and more vigorously thereafter. Many people who rigorously follow such a program find themselves in better physical condition after their heart attack than at any time since their youth. Other rehabilitative efforts after a heart attack center around decreasing smoking, losing weight, and reducing fats and calories in the diet. The stress of a heart attack often provides the push necessary for your parent to adopt a more sensible, and often more fulfilling, life style.

For some people, however, the narrowing of their coronary arteries continues to severely limit their activities and ability to function. Once their heart has recovered from the acute MI, they may choose to have a coronary bypass operation (as is done for severe angina; see the preceding section). This operation is often quite successful at restoring normal function.

Unfortunately, a person who survives a heart attack has survived with a weakened heart. The affected portion of his previously healthy heart wall has been replaced with scar tissue, tissue which is stiff and does not contract. As a result of the presence of this abnormal tissue, the heart is at risk not only to develop dangerous irregularities of its beat, but to falter in its job of pumping blood throughout the body. Repeat heart attacks are common. Moreover, as the heart becomes less able to perform its task, a serious condition may appear: congestive heart failure.

161. *Congestive Heart Failure.* The "frail heart of the elderly" is real. Although the normal deterioration of the heart with age usually causes no problems, almost one half of older people eventually develop symptoms due to cardiac weakness. Why? Because those people have other things wrong with their heart in addition to the changes of old age. Leading the list is damage to the heart muscle caused by chronic oxygen starvation from narrowed coronary arteries, repeated bouts of angina, or past heart attacks. Other common stresses on the heart include the excessive pumping needed to force blood through a narrow, damaged valve, to supply the body adequately if the blood is anemic, or to create the elevated pressure in the person with hypertension (high blood pressure). Severe illnesses of any type may stress the heart past its coping point. Infections, especially of the lung, are particular culprits. When these stresses are severe or prolonged the heart frequently ceases to perform.

What happens when an aging heart is gradually stressed too much? Usually, it begins to swell and the walls thicken. This process takes place over months or years. Even though the heart looks larger and stronger, it is actually less efficient. The heart may try to pump more blood with each beat, but generally it pumps less. Blood backs up, not just in the heart but throughout the body. Fluid begins to collect in the lungs, producing a cough and shortness of breath. Older people with a failing heart are at first breathless with mild exercise, gradually becoming short of breath even when they are not active. They may not be able to lie down comfortably without having their head raised on pillows, since their lungs become moist if they lie flat. They may awaken at night breathless. Fluid also collects in the extremities, most commonly swelling the feet, legs, and ankles. As blood circulates less vigorously throughout the body, people with a failing heart feel fatigued and weak. As the brain receives less nourishment, they may become mildly confused or may suffer symptoms of anxiety, sleeplessness, headache, or failing memory.

This condition of gradually increasing breathlessness, fatigue, and

DISORDERS OF THE HEART, LUNGS, AND BLOOD VESSELS

fluid collection is known as chronic congestive heart failure. The heart is failing to meet the demands of the body for blood. Usually, heart failure develops over years, as repeated insults take their toll on an aging heart. The symptoms gradually become more noticeable and limiting. Your parent's feet become more swollen, his breathing more wheezy and distressing, his sleep more broken. Occasionally, though, heart failure may appear to develop rapidly. An acute illness may make too great a demand on the heart, blood may begin to back up, and breathing may become markedly more difficult over a period of hours or days. This medical emergency actually has its cause in a heart that has been slowly weakening over the years. It is a condition that requires immediate treatment in a hospital; treatment likely to be very similar to that received by someone who has had symptoms for years.

Before any treatment begins, however, the diagnosis of congestive heart failure must be confirmed, since certain other conditions resembling heart failure (such as some kidney diseases) require quite different therapies. A careful physical examination is the most helpful test, since there is a particular combination of findings, like certain heart and lung sounds, which is characteristic of congestive heart failure. When the physical exam is supplemented by blood tests (which help exclude conditions like anemia and kidney disease), an electrocardiogram, and a chest X-ray, the diagnosis usually becomes clear. Thus congestive heart failure is usually recognized shortly after your parent enters the hospital. More time may be needed, however, to determine what medical condition underlies it (for example, infection, mild heart attack, thyroid disease). Occasionally, considerably more sophisticated tests, such as heart catheterization or surgical sampling of the heart muscle, are required to pinpoint the precipitating medical cause.

If the onset of heart failure is sudden and severe, your parent must be hospitalized. He or she is likely to appear acutely ill: breathing with great difficulty, coughing and bringing up large amounts of sputum, feeling cold and clammy. Treatment, which is two-pronged, must be started immediately. (1) The underlying cause for the acute episode must be identified and treated. (2) The acute symptoms must be controlled. Treatment includes strict bedrest in a semiseated position, pain medication (usually morphine), oxygen, a diuretic medication (such as Lasix or Edecrin) to remove excess fluid from the body, and a type of digitalis medication (such as Lanoxin or SK-Digoxin) to make the heartbeat more efficient and stronger. If the underlying medical condition can be controlled, the congestive heart failure usually improves after several days of vigorous treatment in the hospital. Then long-term care must begin.

Nearly one out of three elderly individuals suffers from chronic heart failure. For most, the condition is mild, displaying itself in slightly swollen ankles and a limited tolerance for exercise. For others, it makes breathing difficult and severely limits activity. Those with a weak heart must carefully follow a specific, individualized treatment plan developed by a physician. Such plans make several typical recommendations. (1) The diet should be as salt-free as possible (see Section 114). (2) Exercise should be limited to what can be tolerated comfortably. It is important to continue some physical activity in order to maintain muscle tone and preserve blood circulation in the legs. However, too vigorous exercise can push a weakened but stabilized heart into acute congestive failure. (3) Most people with a chronically weakened heart need to take a digitalis preparation (for example, Lanoxin) and a diuretic (such as Esidrix, HydroDIURIL, Diuril, Aldactone, or Dyazide) for an extended period. Taken together, they reduce excess fluid in the body tissues and increase the heart's efficiency. However, side effects can be a problem, particularly if your parent inadvertently takes too much medication. If the digitalis level in the blood becomes too high, your parent may experience nausea, vomiting, diarrhea, weakness, blurred vision, and abdominal pain. Side effects associated with diuretics include nighttime urinary incontinence, fatigue, muscle weakness, and depression. If your parent develops any of these problems for no other obvious reason, call them to his physician's attention. (4) As with angina, a few elderly people with chronic heart failure benefit from regular treatment with nitroglycerin or a similar medication—often a nitroglycerin ointment (Nitro-Bid, Nitrol) or isosorbide dinitrate (Isordil, Sorbitrate).

Although the regulations concerning your parents' activity and diet and the complicated schedule of medication may appear oppressive, such treatment can keep them functioning and add years to their lives. It is worth the effort.

NONATHEROSCLEROTIC HEART DISEASE

Not all heart disease among the elderly is due to atherosclerosis. A few older people even suffer from heart disease present since youth. Although the spectrum of heart diseases includes heart infection, heart-muscle deterioration, and the effects of thyroid disease on the heart, most of these conditions occur infrequently. However, two types of nonatherosclerotic heart disease are common: deterioration of the heart valves and development of undesired, irregular heartbeats (arrhythmias).

162. *Abnormal Heart Valves.* The heart is divided into four chambers, each with a different task. The hardest-working chamber is the one responsible for pumping blood throughout the body, the left ventricle. It is also the one most prone to problems. The left ventricle receives blood

DISORDERS OF THE HEART, LUNGS, AND BLOOD VESSELS

through the mitral valve and pumps it to the body through the aortic valve. Deterioration of either of these one-way valves is common in old age, and each produces its particular set of symptoms. Deteriorated valves may produce a characteristic murmur, and frequently develop bone-like calcium deposits visible on X-ray.

The mitral valve may become stiff and narrowed, allowing less blood to pass into the left ventricle (mitral stenosis). Or it may become floppy, allowing blood to pass either way (mitral regurgitation). This may be a delayed effect of rheumatic fever in childhood, but there are many other causes as well. Most mitral valve disease produces shortness of breath and fatigue. If the valve suddenly breaks open, however, breathlessness can be sudden and extreme. Although the symptoms of mitral valve disease resemble those of other heart diseases enough to be confusing, usually a murmur helps establish the diagnosis. Sophisticated techniques like the use of sound waves (echocardiography), though, are occasionally required to pinpoint the abnormality. Many people with mitral valve disease never have significant problems. Others slowly develop incapacitating shortness of breath and congestive heart failure. If the symptoms become severe, surgery is indicated, either to open the valve or replace it with an artificial one.

The most common disorder of the aortic valve is aortic stenosis: the valve leading out of the heart becomes narrowed, making the left ventricle work exceptionally hard pumping blood throughout the system. People who develop aortic stenosis were usually born with a misshapen valve, which with age has gradually become calcified and tight. Years of pushing blood through a small opening finally causes the heart to become overextended and to fail, producing shortness of breath, chest pain, and fainting (particularly with exertion). A heart murmur and a calcified valve (detected by chest X-ray) are other characteristic symptoms. If the symptoms become severe, surgical replacement of the damaged valve with an artificial one is the only useful treatment.

163. *Irregularities of Heartbeat.* To pump effectively, the heart must beat with a steady rhythm and the various parts of the heart must beat in coordination. The heart achieves such efficiency by means of a specialized web of conductive tissue embedded in the heart muscle. The key to this conduction system is a small knot of sensitive muscle cells at the top of the heart, the S-A node, which regularly produces the electrical signal that leads to contraction. This electrical impulse then is conducted through specialized cells across the top two chambers of the heart, causing them to contract simultaneously. That impulse continues uniformly across the lower two chambers, causing them to contract in unison and forcing blood

throughout the vascular tree. Irregularities of the heartbeat stem from disturbances of this conduction system: (1) the S-A node may become irregular or some other part of the heart may begin contracting on its own, or (2) the cords of conducting fibers may be interrupted, causing an irregular spread of the electrical impulse across the heart.

Minor, unimportant irregularities of heartbeat occur at any age, but are more common in elderly persons. However, many of these abnormalities are the warning signs of serious heart disease such as early heart failure or an unsuspected heart attack. Acute heart attacks and obvious heart failure are frequently accompanied by extremely serious heart arrhythmias—those irregularities represent one of the most common causes of death in these conditions. In addition, some serious, and even life-threatening, irregularities result from changes and deterioration in the heart's conduction system.

What's more, there may be few signs of their presence. Although your parent may experience symptoms caused by these irregularities, often there are no symptoms and the irregularities are first discovered during a routine physical examination or an annual electrocardiogram. The symptoms that do occur are often nonspecific and range from palpitations and dizziness to chest pain and shortness of breath. No matter how they come to the physician's attention, these symptoms demand an explanation and may precipitate a more extensive evaluation of your parent's heart.

Irregular beats and disturbances in conduction come in a confusing variety of types, each with different symptoms, causes, and degrees of seriousness. Correct analysis requires the skills of a specialist—an internist or cardiologist. Because proper treatment depends upon a correct understanding of the problem, your parent should insist on being evaluated thoroughly. An electrocardiogram (ECG) is a standard part of any evaluation, but it may be augmented by ambulatory heart monitoring (Holter monitor), a procedure in which your parent wears a small heart recorder for a day. Such a long period of recording allows identification of abnormal rhythms that otherwise would have been missed. The rest of the evaluation depends upon the specific rhythm abnormalities found as well as your parent's symptoms. The entire spectrum of heart evaluation techniques and equipment may be called into play.

Treatment for heartbeat irregularities depends on their cause. If there is underlying heart disease, it must be treated. In addition, medication is available which is useful in "quieting" irregular beats. The particular medication chosen, if any, also depends upon the cause and may include quinidine, procainamide, lidocaine, phenytoin, disopyramide, or propranolol. Unfortunately, each of these medications is useful for only a limited range of conditions, and each has significant side effects. Thus your parent

DISORDERS OF THE HEART, LUNGS, AND BLOOD VESSELS

should use them only under close supervision. Used appropriately, however, they can be extremely helpful.

For some conditions, the only solution is to install a pacemaker, which provides the heart with an artificial heartbeat. Usually it is set to stimulate the heart at a certain rate and only sends signals if the heart's natural rhythm falls below that level. Pacemakers are safe and easily installed: the electrode wires are usually threaded through a vein into the heart, a procedure which does not require a major operation. Most pacemakers are problem-free, needing only to be checked periodically for the strength of the battery. However, your parent must avoid strong magnetic currents (which can change the pacemaker's rate temporarily) such as those associated with microwave ovens and magnetic sensors in airport terminals. Overall, a pacemaker can free your parent from unpleasant and dangerous symptoms and produce a marked improvement in his sense of well-being.

HIGH BLOOD PRESSURE (HYPERTENSION)

164. *Hypertension—What Is It?* Most people can remember their most recent blood-pressure measurement, but few people really know what those numbers mean. Yet those numbers are crucial, since they may be the only evidence of high blood pressure. Other symptoms are often completely absent. Moreover, blood-pressure readings alone may cause a person to be prescribed medication and to alter his diet and life style for years, even though he feels fine.

For all practical purposes, our system of blood vessels forms a closed, watertight circle. With each squeeze of the heart, a high-pressure wave of blood pushes through the arteries into the tissues. The blood later returns to the heart at a lower pressure by way of the veins. Two measurements of this process are vital: the highest pressure in the arteries at the peak of the wave (systolic pressure), and the lowest pressure reached in the arteries in the trough of the wave (diastolic pressure). Both of these blood-pressure measurements are made on the arteries; pressure in the veins is much lower and is usually of little concern.

When a blood-pressure cuff is placed around your arm, it is tightened just enough to completely stop the flow of blood through the arteries, even at the peak pressure. The physician then listens to your arm with a stethoscope as he slowly loosens the cuff. The measurement of the blood-pressure cuff at the moment the physician hears the first whooshing sound of blood just able to force its way through the compressed artery indicates the highest pressure in the artery (systolic pressure). With further loosening, a point is reached at which the blood flows smoothly and quietly past the cuff, because even the lowest pressure in the artery is greater than that of the cuff (diastolic pressure). Thus any blood-pressure measurement consists of both a systolic and diastolic pressure (usually spoken of as one number over the other; for example, 120/80, or 120 "over" 80).

Ideally, your parent should maintain a blood pressure under 140/90, although pressures up to 160/95 are so common among the elderly as to be considered normal. If either your parent's systolic or diastolic pressure is constantly above 160/95, he has hypertension and should be seriously considered for treatment. The higher the pressure, the more certain he is to need treatment. Since blood pressure tends to rise with physical activity and emotional excitement, a single measurement in the doctor's office may not represent a constant state. Repeated recordings, often weeks or months apart, must be made to be certain that the pressure is regularly elevated.

The cause of high blood pressure is usually unknown. Although in a few people hypertension may be produced by specific medical conditions, such as certain kinds of kidney abnormalities or disease in particular endocrine glands, in the vast majority of people it develops without explanation. With age, artery walls become stiffer, which partially explains the gradual upwards creep of systolic pressure after age 40. However, most high blood pressure seems to be related to abnormal changes in the tendency of arteries throughout the body to chronically contract and thus represents a pathological condition.

165. *Hypertension—Its Consequences.* Hypertension among the elderly is both common and serious. Untreated, it is one of the leading causes of heart disease and stroke. Even minor chronic elevations of blood pressure can increase the likelihood that your parent will develop hardening of the arteries (atherosclerosis), suffer a heart attack or heart failure, or experience a stroke. Constant pumping against increased pressure often causes an aging heart to work beyond its natural limits and gradually to fail. The problem becomes more severe with each rise in pressure. All of these slow changes often take place unnoticed. The only hint is elevated blood pressure—a warning which should not be ignored. Moreover, the risk of atherosclerosis and related heart attack and stroke increases markedly if your parent not only suffers from high blood pressure, but smokes, drinks to excess, is obese, or has diabetes.

In a few people, usually those with moderate or severe hypertension, blood pressure can rise suddenly to very high levels. This is a medical emergency. These people often become irritable and confused over a period of a few hours or a few days; they may experience a severe headache, a severe pain in the back, or some other acute symptom. They should be evaluated medically, and often hospitalized. Be alert to any such symptoms in your hypertensive parent, and take them seriously.

166. *Hypertension—To Treat or Not to Treat.* There is little doubt that an older person who suffers moderate to severe hypertension (for example, a diastolic pressure above 105–110) should be treated for it. Younger persons with mild hypertension (above 140/90) must be treated if they are to avoid an increased risk of heart attack or stroke in the future. But doctors disagree on the benefits of treating mild hypertension in the elderly. The elevated pressure does seem to increase the risk of later complications, yet many of these complications may have already developed, and may be irreversible. Moreover, lowering the blood pressure in some elderly individuals can produce symptoms such as mild confusion. A good rule of thumb is that hypertension of any degree should be treated, but the lower the pressure, the more gentle and gradual the treatment. If side effects due to the treatment develop, the need for treatment should be reassessed.

Treatment should not be undertaken until your parent's overall physical condition has been evaluated and any specific causes for the high blood pressure identified. A careful physical examination, electrocardiogram (ECG), and blood tests for sugar, cholesterol, and kidney function are usually all that are required. Occasionally, findings are suggestive enough to require more extensive tests of your parent's cardiovascular system, kidneys, or endocrine glands.

167. *Hypertension—Nondrug Treatment.* Only the mildest high blood pressure can be managed without medication. However, several other therapies are valuable, even essential, for use in combination with drugs.

Habits which can worsen hypertension or make the risk of complications greater should be changed. Smoking, for instance, should be severely limited or stopped. Your parent should not drink heavily. He or she should avoid or control stressful situations and should seek out relaxing activities. Sedentary ways should be replaced with regular exercise such as walking, swimming or bicycle riding. A few medications can produce or worsen high blood pressure and, if your parent is taking any of these, it should be mentioned to a physician: hormones such as those used in treating skin conditions, certain drugs (such as Indocin) which are used for arthritic conditions, thyroid medications, and stimulant medications such as those found in diet pills.

Diet is crucial to controlling some hypertension for two reasons. (1) Merely reducing obesity can often reduce blood pressure significantly. Thus a diet which restricts calories should be part of your parent's treatment if he is overweight. (2) Excessive salt intake can worsen high blood pressure; and moderately restricting salt consumption can lower the pressure. Many of the prepared foods we eat, such as potato chips, catsup, canned soups and vegetables, frankfurters, smoked meats, ham, olives, cheese, and TV dinners, have an exceptionally high salt content. Merely eliminating them and not salting other food can reduce blood pressure over a period of months. A thorough listing of the salt content of most foods may be found in *Low Salt Secrets for Your Diet* (Longevity Publications, Berkeley, CA, 1981).

168. *Hypertension—Drug Treatment.* Medication is necessary for controlling blood pressure in most older persons with hypertension. Most elderly people will improve sufficiently by using only one type of drug, but occasionally two or three will need to be taken simultaneously. The choice of which medication(s) to use is often complicated. Certain rules guide the physician's selection.

The doctor usually prescribes one of the common, milder drugs (antihypertensives) for a few weeks. If satisfactory improvement fails to occur, the doctor may switch to another, or add a second medication of a different kind. If improvement again is insufficient, a third drug may be added. Most hypertension requires no more than three drugs for control. All drugs are begun in small dosages. Any changes in medications are also made carefully. It may take many months before your parent's blood pressure is in an acceptable range. Expect this, and consider it a sign of cautious and considered care.

The most common first medication used by physicians to treat hypertension is a diuretic. These medications reduce the amount of water in the body and blood stream. Although there are a number of different diuretics, those most commonly used include hydrochlorothiazide (under various names like HydroDIURIL, Esidrix, and Oretic), chlorthalidone (Hygroton), triamterene (Dyazide), metolazone (Diulo), and furosemide (Lasix). Although one of these medications may be all that is needed to control mild to moderate hypertension, and may be taken safely for years, there are cautions. To prevent loss of potassium from the blood, your parent may have to take potassium supplements. Diabetes may worsen. Serious problems may result if a person with severe kidney disease takes diuretics. Nausea, vomiting, diarrhea, or mild confusion may occur in a few people. In spite of these problems the diuretics, taken with care, are safe and vital medications for many people.

People with a more severe degree of hypertension often need to take one or two medications in addition to a diuretic. This becomes a very complex business, since these supplementary drugs work in a variety of ways, and different combinations work for different people. Common second-

and third-step drugs include Inderal, Lopressor, Apresoline, Minipress, Serpasil, Aldomet, and Catapres. Your parents and the physician will have to determine the safest and most effective combination. Unfortunately, these drugs have a variety of side effects, so be alert to any new complaints or symptoms. Each of the drugs has its own spectrum of common problems; taken together, some of the most frequent side effects include dizziness on standing, nausea, mental confusion, depression, sedation, giddiness, and chest pain. Work with the physician closely until the medication becomes regulated.

The Lungs

CHRONIC OBSTRUCTIVE LUNG DISEASE (COLD)

Although the term chronic obstructive lung disease (COLD) sounds like a single disorder, it really represents a group of related diseases which includes asthma, bronchitis, and emphysema. All these lung diseases have a common feature: in each, the sufferer has great difficulty moving air in and (especially) out of the lungs. The basic features of each disease are often so mixed together in certain persons that some physicians prefer to say that the patient has COLD rather than trying to be more specific. This group of diseases is both common and severe, and it produces more disability among the elderly than any other lung condition.

169. *Asthma.* We tend to think of asthma as a lung disorder of childhood, but many asthmatics don't develop the disease until their 40s or 50s. The disease that these older people develop, however, is different in several respects from that experienced by children. It is usually more severe; it is less likely to improve spontaneously or disappear for periods of time; and it often responds less well to medication.

What causes asthma? For reasons that are still not clear, the muscles which surround the small tubes (bronchi) that conduct air into the air sacs of the lung are exceedingly sensitive and hyperreactive. Exposure to any of a long list of irritating factors—a list which varies from person to person—can stimulate these muscles to go into spasm. This contraction causes the bronchi throughout the lung to narrow. At the same time, the inner lining of the bronchi often becomes swollen with fluid and mucus, further narrowing the size of these small tubes. Air forced through these narrowed tubes encounters increased resistance and produces the whistling, wheezing sounds that are so characteristic of an asthmatic attack.

Although it is not understood why asthma develops, the numerous irritants which set off an attack are well known. With childhood asthma these irritants are usually substances to which the child is allergic and which produce an allergic reaction throughout the body that becomes focused in the lungs. However, in adults the irritants appear to stimulate the bronchi directly, causing those tubes to narrow. Common stimuli that the elderly person may have to guard against are dusts, cigarette smoke, fumes, atmospheric pollution, and cold air. Even breathing hard, as in exercise or laughing, may precipitate an attack. An attack can also follow the flu (influenza), an upper-respiratory infection, or sinusitis. In fact, few people who have contracted asthma as adults can weather the flu without suffering an associated bout of asthma. Finally, emotional stress can begin or worsen an attack of asthma.

The patient with asthma usually experiences periods of few symptoms interspersed with acute attacks, although this pattern is less true of older asthmatics. Elderly persons are more likely to have fairly constant symptoms which worsen, sometimes dramatically and dangerously, following heavy exposure to an irritant. Their narrowed bronchi cause them to wheeze when breathing. Increased mucus in the lung causes them to cough frequently. They may be chronically short of breath and, during acute attacks, the difficulty of getting air into and out of the lungs may be terrifying and exhausting. A serious attack is a medical emergency. Your asthmatic parent should plan for such an attack and know how to relieve the initial symptoms. Finally, other medical diseases can develop on top of asthma and can complicate its course. The most common is infection of the lung with bacteria (pneumonia). If the sputum produced by your parent at any time becomes foul-smelling or foul-looking, particularly if your parent also becomes feverish or ill in some other way, suspect that an infection has developed and consult a physician.

The treatment of asthma is complicated. The first step, of course, is to be certain that asthma is the correct diagnosis. That is usually straightforward (and is the physician's responsibility), but be aware that some forms of chronic heart disease as well as other lung conditions like bronchitis and emphysema may occasionally be confused with asthma in the elderly. It may be useful to document your parent's degree of impairment by having him blow into a machine that measures his ability to force air out of his lungs (spirometry).

Once the diagnosis is certain, the first effort in treatment is to identify and avoid whatever is irritating the lungs. Few asthmatics smoke, but they may have to avoid smoke-filled rooms. The air in their homes may need improvement through installation of an air conditioner, a more effective filter on the furnace, or a room humidifier. If all else fails, they may have to move to another climate. If exercise induces asthmatic attacks it should be moderated. In the few cases where the irritant is causing symptoms by

DISORDERS OF THE HEART, LUNGS, AND BLOOD VESSELS

producing an allergic reaction, desensitization injections may help. A blood test and skin-sensitivity tests may be needed to verify the allergy. However, it is often hard to demonstrate a close connection between a few irritants and a person's symptoms. Generally, elderly asthmatics continue to have symptoms (but perhaps less frequently) in spite of their best efforts at avoiding irritants, and their continued well-being will depend on their diligence at following a carefully planned medication schedule.

The treatment of asthma with medication requires the active participation of the patient. He should learn as much about the drugs taken as possible. Several different medications are useful in treating asthma. Since they act in different ways, it is often possible to use more than one at a time. Moreover, if one type doesn't work, a second type may. (1) Two classes of drugs used to treat asthma relax the muscles of the bronchi and thus allow them to dilate: the sympathomimetics (epinephrine, isoproterenol, metaproterenol, terbutaline, salbutamol, fenoterol) and the methylxanthines (theophylline, aminophylline). None of these drugs is perfect. They all stimulate the heart (undesirable in the elderly) to a greater or lesser degree and all produce muscle tremors. Also, some last only minutes in the body, and are useful only by injection. (2) Another type of drug, cromolyn, prevents certain cells which line the bronchi from releasing chemicals that can precipitate an asthmatic attack. This is effective in preventing an acute episode in a few people but is of no value in treating asthma once it has started. (3) Steroids are exceptionally effective for controlling severe asthma, but because of severe side effects they must be used for only short periods and in the lowest possible doses.

Treatment of asthma with medication consists of beginning with the mildest drugs and gradually moving towards larger doses or more potent medication until your parent's symptoms are controlled. If his symptoms are only sporadic, your parent may be able to use an inhaler with a drug like metaproterenol (Alupent, Metaprel). Be certain that the physician has carefully explained the use of the inhaler and that your parent understands: frequently this treatment fails because the elderly patient is not using the inhaler correctly. If the wheeze or cough continues, your parent may need to use an inhaler more frequently, and may need to take a medication like theophylline (two to four times daily) or terbutaline (three to four times daily) in addition. If symptoms continue, the next steps include use of an inhaler plus both theophylline and terbutaline; a trial of a cromolyn inhaler; and finally a trial of steroids. This last has several steps: brief use of a steroid like prednisone taken by mouth and then discontinued, a trial of a steroid inhaler (Beclovent, Vanceril), and then the regular (usually every other day) use of oral steroids. Obviously, this complicated procedure for determining the ideal treatment schedule for your parent must be supervised carefully by his physician, but that does not exempt either you or him from trying to understand what is going on. Be sure you know the possible side effects of each of the drugs.

Treatment for a severe asthmatic attack requires hospitalization. Many of the same medications used during routine treatment are indicated, but they may have to be given in higher-than-normal doses and by injection.

With thoughtful and aggressive treatment, many elderly persons will obtain significant relief from their symptoms. Unfortunately, many others will continue to experience often severe symptoms daily. With close medical supervision, deaths from acute asthmatic attacks are few.

Often, asthma does not occur alone but in the company of one of the other chronic obstructive lung diseases like bronchitis or emphysema.

170. *Chronic Bronchitis and Emphysema.* Taken together, these two diseases are a major cause of physical disability among the elderly. They are both chronic conditions, and the physical changes in the lungs that accompany them are usually permanent. They often appear in the same person. Their primary cause is the same: cigarette smoking. Both diseases impair movement of air in and out of the lungs. And frequently it is difficult to tell where the one condition leaves off and the other begins. What are these diseases like?

Regular cigarette smoking irritates the bronchi leading to the air sacs of the lungs. Other conditions, like severe air pollution or chronic exposure to toxic fumes, can do the same, but less predictably. After several years of such abuse, the walls of the bronchi become thick with mucus. The persistent seeping of mucus from the walls produces a chronic cough as the body tries (unsuccessfully) to rid itself of the irritating mixture of mucus and cigarette ash. When the cough ("smoker's cough") is present daily for at least three months of the year, the person is considered to suffer from chronic bronchitis. He coughs, brings up sputum, wheezes at times, and experiences a declining ability to exercise. He may find himself severely limited during bad weather. He is prone to frequent and severe chest colds, and even pneumonia. And the longer he smokes the worse it becomes.

Chronic bronchitis is the penalty most smokers pay for their habit. However, a few unfortunate people pay a much higher price—the development of chronic obstructive bronchitis, emphysema, or both. Bronchi may not only become thickened and ooze mucus; they may become narrowed, plugged, and chronically infected (chronic obstructive bronchitis). Air moves through them with difficulty. Those affected cough, wheeze, produce foul-smelling sputum, feel short of breath during exercise, suffer repeated chest infections, and may gradually take on a slightly grayish or

DISORDERS OF THE HEART, LUNGS, AND BLOOD VESSELS

dusky hue. On the other hand, in some people the damage to the bronchi is minimal while the damage to the air sacs is profound (emphysema). The oxygen-absorbing walls between the tiny air sacs may break down, producing large, inefficient, flaccid pouches. The lung, which is elastic and normally expels air by collapsing like a rubber balloon, loses its resiliency and its ability to evacuate air. The resulting sluggish movement of air produces air hunger (breathlessness, sometimes profound) and a dry cough. However, destruction to the bronchi and air sacs often occurs simultaneously and symptoms usually reflect both obstructive bronchitis and emphysema. Both conditions develop more frequently in men and in people who are genetically predisposed to a more rapid deterioration of their bronchi and lungs with smoking, that is, persons who have had a family member suffer from COLD.

The diagnosis is often not obvious. Other lung conditions like asthma and lung cancer may produce gradually increasing cough and sputum, wheezing, and shortness of breath. The diseases must be looked for, particularly if your parent's long-standing, mild symptoms have recently worsened. To complicate the picture, many people with chronic bronchitis also have hyperreactive bronchical walls, making it difficult to determine where asthma leaves off and bronchitis begins. Moreover, persons who have smoked for many years may contract both COLD and lung cancer, so clear evidence of either chronic obstructive bronchitis or emphysema does not mean that cancer cannot also be present.

The physician's evaluation of your parent's lung condition will include a thorough physical and X-ray examination, microscopic examination and culture of the sputum, and measurement of how well your parent exhales air (spirometry). If there is a suspicion of cancer, the evaluation is likely to be more detailed (see Section 173). Simple chronic bronchitis requires little more than the correct group of symptoms to make the diagnosis. On the other hand, the diagnosis of either obstructive bronchitis or emphysema requires proof that your parent has chronic difficulty breathing out, a difficulty that doesn't disappear after treatment of conditions like asthma or lung infections.

Treatment of simple chronic bronchitis, obstructive bronchitis, and emphysema consists of several parts. However, the overall approach must be realistic, and must acknowledge that the changes of COLD are both permanent and physically limiting. Moreover, your parent should understand his disease and know why it is necessary to persist in lengthy, complicated, and sometimes unpleasant treatments.

1. Your parent must stop smoking.

2. Any underlying illness must be treated. Chronic infection, as indicated by foul-smelling sputum, should be treated with antibiotics. Heart

disease and high blood pressure are common in elderly smokers and can dramatically worsen their breathing difficulties. Influenza (Section 172), which can be devastating to a person with COLD, should be prevented by a yearly vaccination.

3. Any asthma-like spasm of the bronchi should be treated with the appropriate drugs (see the preceding section). Often the best way to determine if a degree of asthma is present is to treat with medication as though it were, and see if improvement occurs. Moreover, steroids, as they are used in asthma, can help some persons with COLD but must be used with caution.

4. Emotional distress and symptoms like depression, hopelessness, and anxiety are common and often need aggressive therapy. People are frequently frightened by their disease and feel helpless and out of control. All too often they conclude that they are never going to improve, and become severely depressed. The effort and exhaustion associated with breathing can produce a sense of desperation. Some of these feelings of hopelessness can be relieved by recognizing that their own determined efforts to follow careful treatment plans can often significantly improve their symptoms. Formal psychotherapy is also often helpful. However, if a depression is severe or persistent, antidepressant medication (Tofranil, Aventyl, Sinequan, Vivactil) may make a dramatic difference.

5. The bronchi should be kept clean. The mucus and sludge that collects in them needs to be removed through regular (often once or twice each day) treatments. Diligence in following the treatment regimen closely separates those whose symptoms improve from those whose symptoms remain unchanged. These treatments should first be done with the close supervision of a physician and physical therapist; ideally your parent will then learn to do them alone. There are several different techniques, but most have a common pattern: (1) your parent breathes a mist containing bronchi-dilating medication; (2) after several minutes the bronchi have opened and your parent then switches to breathing water vapor; (3) after several more minutes, he attempts to cough (by then it is easy); and (4) he taps on his chest to further loosen the mucus and lies in certain positions designed to help his lungs to drain.

6. Other equipment and habits are also useful. Air conditioners, air humidifiers, and room precipitators may help. Training in slow, deep "abdominal" breathing is vital. Your parent should be evaluated for an exercise program which will improve his overall fitness. Portable oxygen equipment is readily available and may allow your parent to become considerably more active. Discuss other possibilities with the physician.

Although simple chronic bronchitis can usually be readily treated by a change in habits, obstructive bronchitis and emphysema are chronic and irreversible conditions that can make your parent's later years considerably less pleasurable. However, with persistence and careful medical attention, your parent can often continue to get about and function in spite of severe lung disease.

OTHER LUNG DISEASES

171. *Pneumonia.* Pneumonia is an infection of the lung, usually caused either by one of several types of bacteria or by a virus. The tiny air sacs in the involved portion of the lung become filled with fluid, white cells, and bacteria (or viruses). As the infection worsens, it spreads to other parts of the lung and the most seriously affected parts may become solid with infected material. Both lungs may be infected ("double pneumonia").

Pneumonia is common and serious in elderly people: two out of three of them have bacterial pneumonia. Unfortunately, there is no easy way to prevent infection. Although a few types of pneumonia are usually contracted only in the hospital, most develop at home without any known exposure to the bacteria. And they occur much more frequently and in a more serious form in those people who are ill or debilitated from other causes. In fact, many people who are seriously ill and hospitalized with some other disease also develop a pneumonia because their resistance is so low. However, a major advance has been the recent development of a vaccine against one of the most common and serious types of the illness, pneumococcal pneumonia. This vaccine, given once by injection, provides protection to four out of five people. Although the vaccine is available to everyone, many physicians who are wary of giving unnecessary medications to the elderly recommend that only debilitated older persons and those with emphysema receive it automatically.

Bacterial pneumonia commonly begins with slight, cold-like symptoms which escalate rapidly (over hours or a day or two) to fever, chills, cough, shortness of breath, the production of large quantities of foul-looking and foul-smelling sputum, and sometimes a stabbing pain in the chest. Microscopic examination and culture of the sputum, a physical examination, and a chest X-ray usually allow the diagnosis to be made. Occasionally, however, pneumonia has a deceptively mild early course in the elderly. The person may have no symptoms or may experience a mild cough, fatigue, loss of appetite, headache, a sudden change in personality, or mental confusion. By the time these mild symptoms worsen, the disease may be well advanced. Any symptoms of chest infection in an older person deserve attention.

Viral pneumonias are often less severe. The person may feel as though he has the flu (influenza): mild fever, cough, aching in the chest, lethargy, headache, and muscle aches. The cough plus some shortness of breath may cause the physician to order a chest X-ray, which then shows the presence of a pneumonia. Unlike most people with bacterial pneumonia, who require hospitalization, those with a viral infection may be able to be up and around ("walking pneumonia"), and may be treated at home.

Bacterial pneumonias are treated with antibiotics. The choice of drug depends upon the type of bacteria causing the disease, which is determined by careful examination of sputum samples taken early in the illness. Before the type of pneumonia has been determined, seriously ill individuals are often treated with an antibiotic that is moderately effective against a variety of bacteria (a broad-spectrum antibiotic) in an effort to kill as many different kinds of bacteria as possible. Those people with advanced disease may also require oxygen and special respiratory drainage procedures in the hospital. Treatment for a viral pneumonia consists mainly of watching to be sure that the symptoms don't become too severe and that a bacterial pneumonia doesn't develop in addition. To guard against a secondary bacterial infection and because some mild pneumonias are caused by organisms other than viruses, many physicians use an antibiotic (like erythromycin) for even minor lung infections.

Most pneumonia disappears in four to six weeks with treatment. However, as many as one in ten elderly people with severe bacterial pneumonia die. The likelihood rises even further in the very old.

172. *Influenza.* All of us suffer from colds and the "flu" on innumerable occasions throughout our lives. With few exceptions, each illness is caused by a virus to which we are not immune. Of the variety of different viruses that cause these episodes of runny nose, cough, sore throat, fever, and fatigue, the influenza virus is of particular concern to the elderly. Influenza virus causes severe illness in older people, one which all too often results in the death of the very old. Influenza occurs in local outbreaks, or in national or worldwide epidemics. When such an epidemic is worldwide, it often attracts the attention of the news media and receives a name such as the Asian flu, the Hong Kong flu, or the Swine flu, although these illnesses differ little from influenza that occurs locally during the years between the big epidemics.

An attack of influenza usually begins suddenly with the onset of fever, shaking chills, severe headache, weakness, and muscle aches. These usually last for two or three days and as they start to relent, a dry cough, runny nose, and sore throat begin. The sense of weakness and fatigue, as well as the cold-like symptoms, usually last for one or two more weeks but may last for a month or more. We have all experienced such an illness, but for the elderly there is more: life-threatening complications. The liver, kidneys, and nervous system may all be compromised dangerously, but far and away the most common complication is pneumonia. If, after a day or two of illness (when symptoms should be beginning to taper off), your parent develops a cough, worsening fever, shortness of breath, or blood-streaked sputum, suspect pneumonia. The pneumonia may be caused by the virus, or by a secondary bacterial infection. In either case, it is a dangerous development in an elderly person, usually requiring hospitalization.

Unfortunately, there is no cure for influenza (or for other viral illnesses), but there are ways to help prevent it as well as to treat it after it has developed. Influenza vaccine is available and probably should be taken each fall (since most influenza occurs during the winter) by the elderly, the frail, and by those with heart, lung, or other chronic diseases. The vaccine should certainly be used by the elderly during an influenza epidemic. A medication called Symmetrel has recently become available to treat influenza. Used either immediately after exposure to someone with the disease or within the first day or two of symptoms, Symmetrel will reduce the symptoms and the length of the illness in many people. It also reduces thereby the risk of life-threatening complications. The medication produces some side effects (nervousness, difficulty in concentrating) and treats only one of several kinds of influenza. If Symmetrel were used regularly, many people would be treated with it who did not have influenza, but rather had an illness due to some other virus; for this reason, many physicians prefer to use it only during an epidemic, when they can be fairly certain that influenza is the cause of your parent's symptoms.

173. *Lung Cancer.* Lung cancer is a serious worry for many elderly people, and for good reason—it kills more older men than any other cancer, and it is second only to breast cancer as a cause of cancer death in older women. We know what causes it: smoking. Although a few cases are due to working in uranium mines, asbestos factories, or polluted environments, most of them are due to smoking cigarettes. The risk increases with the number of cigarettes smoked daily, the number of years a person has smoked, how deeply he inhales, and the kind of cigarettes used (regular or low tar). Add smoking to a risk like exposure to asbestos, and you have a truly deadly combination. And still people continue to smoke. The best thing your parent can do to prevent lung cancer is to stop smoking. You probably have told him that many times. The risk goes down the day he stops and continues to decline thereafter. However, smoking is an addiction—one of the most tenacious known. If your parent has been smoking for many years and shows no signs of stopping, perhaps it is better not to push this issue too far, since too aggressive an effort on your part to get him to stop may jeopardize your relationship. On the other hand, if your parent

ever decides to quit, help is usually available locally through the American Cancer Society, the American Heart Association, and the American Lung Association.

Lung cancer often develops silently in its early stages. An elderly person should be alert to those early symptoms found in most people who develop cancer of the lung. A cough is the most common symptom of early lung cancer. This is less helpful than it might seem, since most people who develop cancer are chronic smokers and most chronic smokers have chronic coughs. It is more important to watch for a change in a chronic cough; a cough that is different—is more persistent, or suddenly starts producing sputum. Traces of blood in the sputum is another sign. Usually this is merely slight red streaking of the mucus, but occasionally it may be a significant amount of blood produced during coughing—a symptom which demands immediate evaluation. Newly developed shortness of breath also requires an explanation since, in addition to appearing in many other conditions of the heart and lungs, it often develops in lung cancer. As the cancer enlarges and spreads, many other symptoms may occur, including chest pain, fever and chills, loss of weight and of appetite, hoarseness, difficulty swallowing, and bone pain. These usually begin after cough, reddened sputum, or shortness of breath, but not always. Suspicious symptoms should be evaluated at once, since cancer of the lung which is caught early is much more likely to be treated successfully.

Unfortunately, lung cancer is usually not identified until the elderly person has developed enough new symptoms to alarm himself, his family, or his physician. By then, the cancer is well advanced. Since cancer at times may be seen sooner on a chest X-ray, some physicians recommend yearly X-rays for the elderly. Other doctors feel that such regular X-rays are necessary only for heavy smokers. Your parent should consult his physician.

How is the diagnosis of lung cancer made? Most commonly, the physician becomes suspicious of your parent's symptoms or of an abnormal X-ray. A physical examination may add additional information but doesn't tie down the diagnosis. What is required to make a definite diagnosis of lung cancer is a sample of tissue which, when examined microscopically, shows cancer cells. The physician may obtain the needed cell sample in several ways: collection of sputum, sampling through a tube threaded down the throat (bronchoscopy), using a needle to take a piece of tissue from any suspicious spot located near the surface of the skin (biopsy), or, in some cases, by an operation on the chest to explore the suspected area (thoracotomy).

If the tissue is cancerous the doctor will discover one of four types of cancer cells. Each of these types of cancer (oat-cell, adenocarcinoma,

DISORDERS OF THE HEART, LUNGS, AND BLOOD VESSELS

squamous cell, and large cell) has a different severity, with oat-cell carcinoma being the most serious and adenocarcinoma the least. The physician will then obtain other information, including: how widely the cancer is spread throughout the lungs; what structures (if any) in addition to lung tissue are involved; whether cancer is found in the lymph nodes that drain the lung; and whether the cancer has spread to other parts of the body (the most common sites are the liver, bone, the neck, and the brain). Assessing this information, the physician will decide on appropriate therapy and estimate your parent's likelihood of recovery.

The most common treatment for lung cancer in the elderly is radiation. Although surgical removal of the tumor carries the only significant possibility of cure, it is not indicated if your parent's health is poor or if the cancer is too widespread. When surgery is used, it is commonly combined with radiation or anticancer drugs (chemotherapy). Chemotherapy is of significant value only with the oat-cell type of lung cancer.

In spite of recent advances in treatment, the chance of a person's survival after the discovery of lung cancer is not very high. The majority of people die within two years and only one person in ten is alive after five years. However, the survival rate is better if the cancer is caught early, before it spreads throughout the lungs or to other parts of the body.

174. *Tuberculosis.* Tuberculosis (TB) was once the major health problem in the United States. Today it is much less of a worry, and therein lies a danger: it is easily forgotten and overlooked. TB is an infection of the lungs, and occasionally other parts of the body, with tuberculosis bacteria. At the turn of the century it was most common in children and young adults, but today it occurs most frequently in the elderly. And in them it often appears in a disguised form.

A person who contracts a typical case of TB develops a fever, profound tiredness, weight loss, night sweats, and a productive cough that is often streaked with blood. Faced with these classic symptoms, a physician will usually confirm the diagnosis with a chest X-ray, a skin test for TB (PPD), and a microscopic examination and culture of the sputum. In a typical case, all of these would point directly to tuberculosis. Unfortunately, all too often an elderly person shows no symptoms until the disease is far along, may have only a mild cough or a slight fever, or may suffer only chronic fatigue. The X-ray may look normal or may mimic some other condition of the lungs, and the skin test may be negative. Occasionally the only evidence that something is wrong is a mildly abnormal X-ray noticed during a routine checkup. Often, only diligence yields the correct diagnosis; that is, a refusal to assume that a chronic, unexplained cough or a slightly unusual X-ray is probably normal.

Most cases of tuberculosis in old age are not due to a recent exposure but to a reactivation of an old focus of TB, contracted many years ago, which has lain dormant ever since. When your parent was young, TB was considerably more common. Often, he never knew that he had been exposed to or had contracted the disease. But with age and failing health, when the body's defenses are down, the TB organisms begin to stir and become active. Was your parent exposed to someone with tuberculosis as a child?

Fortunately, once TB is recognized treatment is routine. Unless it has already progressed far enough to produce major damage to the lungs, medications like isoniazid, rifampin, ethambutol, and streptomycin will kill the organisms and halt the disease.

COMMON SYMPTOMS OF HEART AND LUNG DISEASE

175. *Chest Pain.* Every elderly person worries about chest pain, fearing that it may signal a heart attack. But most chest pain has other origins. It is important to understand what conditions can produce pain in the chest and when to worry.

Any pain in the chest should be taken seriously. There is no easy way to distinguish pain due to serious conditions from that caused by minor problems. This is particularly true in the elderly, because their pains are often mild and have unusual characteristics. They may suffer a heart attack without being aware of it, experiencing only shortness of breath, a mild tightness in the chest, or a pain in the jaw. Although only a few causes of chest pain are medical emergencies requiring immediate treatment, all unexpected, rapidly developing, or severe pains in the chest should be evaluated by a physician. Most mild but persistent pains should be checked as well.

There are only three common causes of sudden chest pain which are medical emergencies: heart attack, aortic dissection, and pulmonary embolism. (1) A heart attack (Section 160) occurs when the blood flow to the heart wall is interrupted sufficiently to cause heart-muscle death. Although the resulting pain is usually "crushing" in quality and is felt in the center of the chest, almost any symptom can occur in its place. Some of the most common of these symptoms in the elderly are sudden shortness of breath, profound fatigue, faintness, and confusion. Your parent will probably (but not always) feel acutely ill with nausea, vomiting, sweating, and dizziness. More important in identifying pain caused by heart attack is the fact that the pain worsens with any sort of exercise or emotional stress. If

DISORDERS OF THE HEART, LUNGS, AND BLOOD VESSELS

the pain does not become more severe when the heart beats faster or works harder, it is probably caused by some other condition. (2) Aortic dissection is the sudden splitting or tearing of the large artery (the aorta) which conducts blood from the heart to the smaller arteries that pass throughout the body. Located in the back of the chest, it is often made inflexible by atherosclerosis and deposits of calcium. Occasionally it will tear, particularly if high blood pressure is present. The pain is extremely severe and sudden, and has a ripping or tearing quality. This condition often requires immediate surgical treatment. (3) Pulmonary embolism is the lodging of a clot in the arteries that supply the lungs. If the clot is large, the victim may be short of breath (as in a heart attack), and may have associated, pressure-like pain. Although a person may also feel faint, be sweating and confused, occasionally these other symptoms may be absent. Unfortunately, even with these three serious causes of chest pain, the diagnosis is not always obvious. What is obvious is that any sudden severe chest pain is reason for an immediate medical evaluation, preferably in a hospital.

However, most chest pain has other causes. Not all of the causes are located in the chest, and most are considerably less severe than the three mentioned above. The heart can produce pain which is unrelated to a heart attack. Chest pain can be caused by lung conditions like pneumonia, TB, and pleurisy (inflammation of the covering of the lungs). Ulcer pain, gall-bladder disease, and inflammation of the esophagus all can produce pain that is centered in the chest. The muscles of the chest and the ribs can be sites of pain. Finally, anxiety and depression can cause a sense of tightness or aching in the chest that resembles a heart attack but is probably produced by an unconscious, prolonged tightening of chest muscles. Many of these conditions cause pain which is sharp, brief, and stabbing, rather than prolonged and crushing as in a heart attack or prolonged and tearing as in aortic dissection. However, a sharp, intermittent pain in the chest can still be related to a life-threatening condition and should be evaluated.

176. *Shortness of Breath.* Shortness of breath is a deceptive symptom among the elderly. Most people expect to become a little "short-winded" as they age and make no complaint when they find taking a walk or climbing the stairs more tiring than before. Although mild shortness of breath with exercise is common among those in their 60s and 70s, breathlessness which develops rapidly or becomes limiting is almost certain to be caused by disease. Moreover, many people unconsciously decrease their activity to avoid unpleasant episodes of breathlessness without being aware that they are doing so. Eventually they may become breathless with the mildest of activity, and the symptom can then no longer be ignored.

The diseases which produce this symptom vary depending upon

whether it develops suddenly (over days or weeks) or slowly (over months or years). In either case, the problem is most likely to lie with the heart or the lungs. The sudden appearance of breathlessness is most commonly caused by pneumonia, asthma, acute bronchitis, pulmonary embolism, or a heart condition like acute heart failure or a heart attack. Acute anxiety can also produce a sense of not getting enough air. Any sudden breathlessness demands an explanation, and possibly a medical evaluation, unless the condition is well understood (for example, an asthmatic attack). Often it is caused by a serious medical condition and requires hospitalization.

Slowly developing shortness of breath is most likely to be caused by a chronic lung condition like chronic bronchitis or emphysema, by gradual heart failure, or by both. However, it may also be due to lung cancer, anemia, obesity, or many other less common conditions. Most often a diagnosis of the cause can be made after a physical examination, chest X-ray, blood tests, a measure of breathing ability (spirometry), and an electrocardiogram. This can usually be done in the doctor's office. Occasionally, much more sophisticated tests must be employed, including a complete lung-function study, a measurement of blood gases, exercise testing, and more. These may require a brief hospitalization to complete. In any case, a cause for the increasing breathlessness must be determined if proper treatment is to begin.

177. *Cough.* Coughing increases with age. This is partly because lung tissues gradually deteriorate and secretions collect. Coughing clears waste material from the lungs and airways. In addition, with age the mucus linings of the throat and airways become thin and dry and are more easily irritated. However, frequent coughing may indicate the presence of disease and require a medical evaluation. Be wary of any cough that is severe, begins suddenly and without obvious cause, or won't go away. The majority of sudden coughs are caused by an identifiable acute illness, like the flu or pneumonia. Although coughing may be the first symptom to appear, others usually follow. Thus, a person with the flu also develops a runny nose and fever while one with pneumonia produces a foul-smelling sputum with coughing. However, a few acute coughs are caused by a serious, unsuspected medical illness. If a steady cough lasts longer than several days, see a physician.

A chronic cough, even if mild, also bears watching. The reason to be alert to such a common symptom is that the older lung (and chest) is prone to develop serious medical conditions which may first signal their presence by producing a cough. Most chronic coughing among the elderly is caused by cigarette smoking. Bronchitis and emphysema also cause a chronic cough, as does living in a severely polluted environment. Unfortunately, there is a risk that a person with a known condition like chronic bronchitis or smoker's cough will look for no other explanation for a worsening cough, and thus will overlook the development of a more deadly illness like lung cancer. The rule of thumb is that a chronic cough that suddenly changes its character should be evaluated.

Of even greater concern is a cough that is accompanied by bloody sputum. Although pink- or red-streaked sputum is not uncommon after forceful coughing, if a significant amount of blood is produced during coughing, have it evaluated immediately. Blood from a nosebleed or from the gastrointestinal tract (for example, from a stomach ulcer) is sometimes mistaken for blood coming from the lungs. However, if the blood is mixed with air and appears foamy, it is almost certainly from the lungs. Most causes of bloody sputum are serious (for example, bronchitis, tuberculosis, lung cancer). Hospitalization is often required to evaluate your parent thoroughly; besides blood tests, chest X-ray, and examination of the sputum, serious bleeding often requires bronchoscopy. During bronchoscopy, the patient is sedated and a hollow tube is slid through his mouth into his trachea (airway). Sites likely to cause bleeding are examined and usually a diagnosis is confirmed. The more rapid your parent's bleeding, the more it should be considered a medical emergency.

DISORDERS OF THE BLOOD VESSELS

Both arteries and veins are prone to serious problems as the years go by. Most abnormalities of the arteries are caused by atherosclerosis, while those of the veins stem from the increasing physical inactivity of the elderly. Both sets of problems were preventible during your parent's earlier years.

178. *Damaged Arteries.* With age, most large arteries in the body develop areas of narrowing caused by atherosclerotic patches. This happens earlier and is much more severe in people who have smoked, eaten fatty foods, suffered from high blood pressure or diabetes, or have a family history of atherosclerosis. Arterial narrowing is the primary cause of three of the most debilitating conditions that afflict the elderly: heart attacks (Section 160), strokes (Chapter 20), and poor circulation in the legs (see below).

Blood is distributed throughout the body from the aorta, the main artery from the heart. The aorta lies against the backbone inside the chest and abdomen and branches out to the arms, the brain, and the various organs. The aorta ends at the base of the spine, where it splits into two branches, one extending down each leg. The bottom of the aorta and the main artery in the leg are very prone to narrow with atherosclerosis in the elderly. When that occurs, acute and chronic symptoms can be severe.

These points of narrowing can be the sites of a sudden blood clot or other rapid blockage of blood flow. When that occurs, your parent will usually experience sudden coldness and numbness in the leg below the point of the block. Over a period of hours, the leg may become darker, mottled, painful, and then insensitive to pain. After twelve to eighteen hours without blood, the leg is certain to develop gangrene. If your parent develops such symptoms, get him to medical care immediately. Occasionally the block can be relieved by a few hours of treatment with anticoagulants, but if that is not successful, surgery to clear the artery may be necessary.

More common than a sudden block of an artery are symptoms caused by the slowly progressive narrowing of the arteries in the leg. Your parent may first notice that his calf or thigh begins to ache if he walks more than a few blocks. Eventually he may have to stop walking after a block or two because the pain has become too severe, although the pain usually disappears after a few minutes rest. As the arterial narrowing worsens, additional symptoms may appear, such as numbness, pins and needles, pain after walking only a few yards, and pain in his foot when it is elevated (as when lying in bed). Finally, the symptoms may progress to ulcers and gangrene in his foot and in his leg below the narrowing. The location of the symptoms is a good indication of the location of the block.

Chronic arterial narrowing is a potentially incapacitating condition. Your parent may have increasing difficulty getting around. Treatment is available, although it is markedly beneficial to only a few individuals. First, the location and severity of the narrowing must be determined. That can usually be done with a careful physical examination and by sophisticated techniques like the use of ultrasound measurements to determine the blood flow in the leg. If surgery on the leg is contemplated, dye must be injected into the artery above the block (arteriography) to determine the exact location of the narrowing.

The most common treatment is watchful waiting. Your parent must stop smoking and control any diabetes. He must take scrupulous care of his legs and feet, keeping them clean and avoiding any injury or infection. Little can be done to reverse an atherosclerotic block, but a regular exercise program may keep the muscles strong and allow other arteries to enlarge to help supply blood to the leg. Ultimately, the wisest course may be to encourage him to live with a moderate limitation.

However, if the limitations are too severe, or if the condition appears to be worsening and gangrene threatens, surgery may be necessary. Essentially, two operations are available: making a lengthwise cut in the artery and removing the atherosclerotic growth (endarterectomy), or cutting out the narrowed section and replacing it with either artificial tubing or a piece of vein removed from some other location in the body. Both operations carry risk and neither is completely successful, but either one can improve your parent's symptoms dramatically. Discuss the possibility of surgery with your parent's physician. Unfortunately surgery may not be possible, and the only alternative is amputation. Every effort should be made to leave as much of the leg as possible, although the cut must often be made well above the damaged section to ensure success of the operation. Be sure your parent understands how much of his leg will remain after surgery.

Perhaps the most important aspect of the presence of arterial narrowing in the leg is not the symptoms produced but the realization that atherosclerosis is widespread. Few people develop leg symptoms without also having significant narrowing in the arteries to the heart and brain. Thus your parent should be evaluated carefully for any evidence of impending heart attack or stroke.

179. *Damaged Veins.* By far the most common problems with the veins occur in the legs. Blood returns from the limbs through two systems of veins: superficial veins that lie immediately under the skin and deep veins, which are covered by layers of muscle. The problems in each set of veins differ markedly in severity.

Disorders of the superficial veins are usually mild. The most common condition is varicose veins: dilated, twisted, unsightly veins usually found along the inside of the thigh or the side of the calf. Every few inches along the length of these leg veins, there is a fragile valve which prevents the blood from flowing backward toward the foot. If these become damaged, blood backs up and produces swollen, sluggish varicose veins. Heredity plays a role in the development of these abnormal veins, as do chronic lack of exercise and prolonged standing, tight-fitting clothes, obesity, and the damage to blood flow suffered during pregnancy. In short, anything that impairs the flow of blood back to the heart helps to create varicose veins. Fortunately, they are not serious and rarely require treatment. Exercising (such as walking), avoiding prolonged standing, elevating the legs occasionally during the day, and using support stockings are usually all that is required to keep the veins from worsening. Except for the severe varicosities that develop when the deep veins become blocked (see below), the only common reason for treating them aggressively is cosmetic. They can be closed by injecting them with a scar-producing solution (often done in the doctor's office), or they can be removed surgically.

The deep veins can produce more serious problems. Most of the blood returning from the legs to the heart travels through these veins. Any time an elderly person is inactive (simple lack of activity, recovering from an operation, immobility during depression, long car trips) or develops mild heart failure (Section 161), the blood flows more slowly in the legs and the person risks developing a blood clot in the deep veins. If it occurs, the leg rapidly swells and may feel "full," painful and tender to touch, and warm. These symptoms should not be overlooked. The clot that has formed, if it is not treated, can destroy the valves in the deep vein, making repeat episodes of swelling and pain much more likely. More important, the clot can break free of the vein and drift "upstream" through the heart to lodge in the lungs (pulmonary embolism). Pulmonary embolisms are potentially life-threatening. Contact your parent's physician if there is any evidence of such a clot in the deep vein. Treatment must be started immediately, usually in the hospital. Your parent will be given anticoagulant medication by vein for a week or more to prevent further extension of the clot. He or she then will need to take anticoagulants by mouth for several months until the risk of redeveloping the clot has decreased. If your parent then gives evidence of having permanent damage to the deep veins (lower legs are chronically swollen, skin becomes dry and scaly, ulcers develop about the ankles), he or she will need to wear support stockings, elevate the leg frequently, take care to avoid injuring the leg, and begin a program of regular exercise. Deep vein clots are dangerous and every effort should be made to treat them promptly.

16.

Gastrointestinal
Disorders

Few problems of old age are more common than those of the mouth, stomach, and bowels—disorders of the gastrointestinal (GI) tract. The GI tract is our great consumer and our greatest grumbler. It begins with the mouth and teeth and ends with the rectum and anus—all problem-fraught. And the stops in between read like a who's who of medical malevo-lence: the esophagus and stomach are the location of heartburn, nausea, ulcers, bleeding, and stomach cancer; the small intestine is a source of pain, obstruction, and occasional bleeding; the large intestine is the loca-tion of constipation, cramps, diarrhea, bleeding, appendicitis, cancer, and much more; and the liver, gallbladder, and pancreas give us cirrhosis, jaundice, and gallstones. However, the GI tract is also one of our most dog-gedly faithful companions, considering the abuse to which we subject it. Some of its failures are preventable and represent responses to our mis-treatment of it, while many of its other problems are readily correctable.

Many elderly bring to their old age a panoply of GI complaints collect-ed over the years. The first rule of thumb is that the *new* complaint, not the old problem, should demand our primary attention. Whether that symp-tom be constipation, heartburn, or bleeding, it is much more likely to signi-fy that something worrisome is developing if it is new. A second rule is that problems like constipation or soiling are not shameful. All too often they are felt to be unmentionable and thus are ignored for far too long.

180. *Diagnosing GI Disorders.* In the last two decades medical science has vastly improved our ability to recognize and treat disorders of the GI tract. In times past, the stomach and bowels were a black box—we usually knew when things were wrong but we couldn't look inside to determine the problem. All that has changed. There is now very little of the GI tract that cannot be looked at directly or measured indirectly both safely and in relative comfort. In addition to the still useful upper-GI X-ray, which outlines the esophagus, stomach, and small intestine; the barium enema, which outlines the large intestine on X-ray; and the sigmoidoscope, which allows the physician to look directly into the last two feet of the large intestine, recent technology has added the following:

1. Endoscopy. By carefully threading a long, thin, sophisticated fiber-optic cable (endoscope) through the mouth, a physician can see clearly almost any structure from the mouth to the first section of small intestine (duodenum). A similar instrument may be threaded through the anus, allowing the physician to see all of the large intestine (colonoscopy). Some instruments with additional features allow the doctor to sample tissue, inject dye, seal some bleeding points, and remove abnormal growths—all without an operation.

2. Radiology. New techniques using sound waves (ultrasonography), computers (CAT scan), and radioactive material allow much more precise diagnosis than ever before.

3. Angiography. Physicians can now safely inject dye into the arteries which supply the GI tract and thus can often accurately determine bleeding points or the location of tumors.

4. Laparoscopy. By slipping a fiberoptic tube through a small hole made in the abdominal wall, the physician can see the outside of most organs.

5. Blood tests. Specialized analysis now permits the detection of some kinds of GI cancer from blood samples.

Common GI Complaints

181. *Belching.* Burping is usually a sign that a person is unconsciously swallowing air either because of nervousness or because of some mild stomach distress such as heartburn. It is a habit rather than an illness and can sometimes be eliminated by making the person aware of the habit or by treating any GI problems underlying it.

182. *Vomiting.* Vomiting is so common that we almost expect it when we are ill. Although it is frequently associated with intestinal flu or some dietary foolishness, it can usher in a variety of serious medical illnesses as well. Does your parent have any other symptoms, such as abdominal pain, blood in the vomitus, high fever, or confusion? If so, call a physician for advice. Is your parent taking any medications which may be causing illness? Has he vomited more than a couple of times? Beware of vomiting that lasts several days.

Prolonged vomiting may indicate a serious underlying medical illness, and can cause severe dehydration and chemical imbalances. Older people who vomit may lose body water quickly and become weak and confused. Your parent needs frequent checking when ill and vomiting.

183. *Constipation and Fecal Impaction.* Constipation, which afflicts one in three older people, is usually something we bring on ourselves. It is *not* an automatic result of aging, and by taking the proper measures most people can avoid it altogether. Your parent may complain about not "going" often enough, or having hard, painful stools, or both, or related symptoms like a bloated feeling, crampy abdominal pain, or mild nausea. Although you may tire of your parent's seemingly endless ruminations about his bowels, constipation can be a real problem. At the least it is uncomfortable, and at the worst it can be a signal that some more serious medical illness is developing.

The first task is to determine if your parent really is constipated. Many people hold strange ideas about elimination and may believe incorrectly that they have a problem. It is not necessary to go to the bathroom daily. In fact, no harm is done by a delay of one to two days, whereas problems may develop if a person tries too hard to produce something each day. Defecating three times a day or three times a week are both normal. Good bowel function is marked not by frequency but by stools that are soft, that move easily, and that are produced without strain. Even hard stools may indicate only that your parent drinks too little water and eats mostly soft food. Be more concerned if he has to strain excessively to produce a stool, if it is particularly painful, if four or five days or more pass between eliminations, or if your parent experiences a definite sensation of incomplete emptying.

Constipation occurs when food moves too slowly through the large intestine. Although the elderly are at risk of becoming constipated because their age-weakened abdominal and intestinal muscles push the food less forcefully, that is not the major cause of ordinary constipation. Much more important to its development—and the secrets to its prevention—are the following:

1. Soft food. The rule of thumb is that eating soft food produces hard

stools and hard food makes soft stools. It's the indigestible roughage and fiber in our food which holds water and keeps the feces from becoming dried and compressed. The elderly, who typically eat too much soft food like meat, starch, dairy products, and sugar, could help prevent constipation by eating bulkier foods, like rough vegetables (peas, beans, carrots), minimally processed cereals, whole-wheat bread, and bran. Two full tablespoons of bran on a bowl of whole-grain cereal in the morning can make an enormous difference in bowel habits.

A vicious cycle can develop when the nausea due to constipation causes elderly people to decrease the amount and bulk of the food they eat. Unfortunately, this understandable reaction only worsens their constipation.

2. Poor fluid intake. The elderly don't drink enough liquids. They either forget or decide not to because they feel a little bloated from constipation. Poor fluid intake, together with older kidneys which conserve water poorly, is a second major reason for dry, constipated stool. Those elderly who live in a hot, dry climate, such as Arizona, are doubly at risk to become dehydrated and constipated. The remedy is to make a point of drinking several glasses of fluid daily—even if it means leaving notes at the kitchen sink to help remember.

3. Inadequate exercise. The person most certain to suffer from constipation is the older individual who is physically inactive, either because of habit or because of immobilization through illness or injury. General physical activity (walking, working, bowling) improves muscle tone throughout the body and helps food pass more rapidly along the intestine.

4. Poor bathroom habits. Elimination is usually an automatic and natural function, but it can be frustrated. If we resist when the pressure in our rectum signals that we need to defecate, or attempt too often to go when there is nothing present, it becomes increasingly difficult to establish a routine that works. The trick is to establish a flexible habit that takes advantage of natural rhythms, such as heading for the bathroom after breakfast when the natural reflex from food entering the stomach has started the bowels stirring. If that routine doesn't work, don't worry. It's more important for an individual to simply remain alert to his own internal signals than to try to force the issue or to go to the bathroom by the clock.

5. Laxative misuse. Although laxatives may be useful at times, often they are not necessary and frequently they are part of the problem. Approximately 25 percent of older persons take a laxative at least once weekly, and some depend on them. Unfortunately, they are not without problems. The stimulant type of laxatives (for example, Dulcolax, Senokot, castor oil) may be valuable if used infrequently. If used daily, however, they often cause weakening of and degenerative changes in the bowel muscles and thus

make it even more difficult to defecate normally. Regular use of mineral oil can produce unpleasant leaking of oil from the rectum and poor absorption of some necessary vitamins. Stool softeners (for example, Colace, Surfak) and bulk laxatives (Metamucil) are useful for short periods of time when a person is having a problem, but they are expensive and unnecessary for routine use. In short, frequent laxative use makes it more difficult to establish a healthy normal pattern and should be avoided.

Take seriously your parent's report of recent (not life-long) constipation. Such a change requires a careful medical evaluation. The cause may be no more serious than a change in eating habits or a decrease in exercise, but if a serious medical illness is responsible, it must be caught early. Medical illnesses causing constipation can range from a failing thyroid gland (hypothyroidism), to a serious depression, to a drug's side effects (for example, iron, some kinds of antidepressants, tranquilizers, and pain medication), to cancer of the intestine. Constipation may be the only tip-off that one of these serious conditions is developing. The other advantage of identifying and treating constipation is that it is then possible to avoid some medical conditions which are aggravated by chronic constipation, such as hemorrhoids, varicose veins, outpouching of the large intestine (diverticulosis), and hiatal hernia.

What if your parent is already constipated? If not treated properly, the constipation may worsen. As stool increasingly backs up in the end of the intestine (the sigmoid colon and rectum), it can gradually form a hard, dry mass known as a fecal impaction. This mass, which occasionally may fill the greater part of the large colon, is both uncomfortable and potentially dangerous. It may cause severe abdominal pain, low fever, vomiting, and even chest pain and confusion. Your parent may become quite ill, even if no serious underlying medical condition is discovered on evaluation.

Your parent can usually relieve a mild impaction over two or three days by taking several glasses of fluid, a stool softener, and mineral oil by mouth; by exercising; and by applying one or more gentle enemas. Usually enemas can be administered at home by your parent alone or with your help; however, if you desire professional help, often a home visit by a nurse can be arranged. A few elderly find it necessary to take an enema every week or two until they develop a successful bowel routine. A physician should help make the decision whether to use enemas for an extended period.

More serious impaction may become a medical emergency and need hospital treatment. Your parent may become totally obstructed, and his condition may closely resemble other medical emergencies, like acute appendicitis or intestinal blockage from some other cause. The doctor will need to know how long and how severely your parent has been constipated, whether he has had any bleeding with his stool or vomitus, what his pain has been like, and what he has done to try to relieve the problem. Attempt to have that information available if your parent is not up to talking. Usually, severe impaction can be successfully relieved by repeated enemas, fluids, and stool softeners, but it frequently takes four or five days or more to become completely "cleaned out." Then the most important effort starts—beginning new and better habits which will prevent a recurrence of the constipation and impaction.

184. *Diarrhea*. Although many older people will experience a brief bout of diarrhea when they have gastrointestinal flu or have eaten too much rich or spicy food, major problems with diarrhea are uncommon. However, diarrhea that is severe or that lasts for several days or more should be investigated.

Significant diarrhea poses special problems for the elderly. It can cause rapid dehydration in someone who is not drinking additional fluid, resulting in weakness, elevated temperature, confusion, and a host of other symptoms. And it may be caused by a more serious illness than just the flu. One study of elderly people admitted to the hospital with diarrhea found that about one half cleared up quickly with rest and fluids, one fifth were significantly dehydrated on admission, and some had diarrhea caused by conditions such as bacterial infections of the bowel, side effects of medication, misuse of laxatives, and fecal impaction. Diarrhea which either does not improve quickly or is particularly severe needs to be evaluated by a physician.

Three of the major causes of diarrhea can be avoided if recognized: laxative abuse, medication side effects, and severe constipation. Just as excessive use of laxatives paradoxically can cause constipation, so it can cause diarrhea. Curiously, some individuals will continue taking laxatives, even though they now experience diarrhea instead of constipation. If the laxatives are stopped the diarrhea usually quickly disappears. Other medications can produce diarrhea as an unwanted side effect. A physician should review your parent's medications. Major offenders include some antibiotics (particularly after prolonged use), iron, some heart medications (digitalis preparations like Lanoxin and Crystodigin), and some arthritis medications (for example, Indocin). Finally, constipation can cause diarrhea. This diarrhea is not the kind associated with that common, chronic intestinal condition, the irritable bowel syndrome (in which constipation may alternate with diarrhea; see Section 196), but rather is a watery diarrhea that forces itself around a solid fecal impaction of the large intestine. Your parent may be convinced that the problem is diarrhea when, in reality, liquid stool is all that can pass through a blocked bowel. Recognizing the onset of constipation and taking steps to prevent it are the keys to avoiding this kind of diarrhea.

185. *Incontinence of the Bowel.* Few possibilities are more dreaded by the elderly than losing control of their bowels. Few occurrences are more embarrassing. However, only a few older people ever become incontinent of stool. If it occurs, they must find out why!

Fortunately, the most likely causes are preventable. One-time accidents may occur if individuals become acutely ill, are feverish, or become confused. Accidents may also occur during episodes of acute diarrhea. The most common cause of occasional or regular incontinence, however, is constipation and fecal impaction—a person's large bowel becomes chronically stretched and blocked; he loses awareness of regular signals to defecate, loose stool pushes vigorously to get out, and an accident happens. Also, getting quickly to a toilet may be hard for some elderly individuals suffering from stiff joints or other difficulties in moving around. Is it any wonder that they are occasionally embarrassed? The remedy, once again, is to prevent constipation by establishing regular bowel habits, eating a sensible, high-fiber diet, drinking ample fluids, and getting regular exercise. However, remember that a few people who have recently developed incontinence may have a more serious illness, like cancer of the rectum. A physician needs to be consulted whenever unexplained fecal incontinence crops up.

Other individuals have a more chronic form of incontinence. Due to disease, they have lost the ability to sense when the rectum is full. Others, because of serious damage to the brain, such as a stroke or developing senility, have developed fecal and often urinary incontinence. Some of these people, only partly aware of the problem, may not suffer as much embarrassment, but treatment is still important to prevent infections and other complications. Because their intestine is often out of their control, treatment is frequently difficult and lengthy. Since they often can't participate in their own care, the usual practice is to give them medication over several days that makes them mildly constipated and follow with a laxative or enema every three to five days. By taking advantage of the body's natural reflex to defecate when food enters the stomach, some elderly may be trained to eliminate at a certain time and place and upon a certain cue, such as immediately after the evening meal.

186 *Bloating and Expelled Gas.* Although the sense of being bloated and the uncomfortable need to release gas from the anus may occasionally be caused by chronic constipation, fecal impaction, or some other process that blocks the intestine, most intestinal gas is caused by swallowed air or

by particular kinds of food. Excess gas is often produced by beans, cabbage, celery, lettuce, broccoli, other rough vegetables, raw fruits and fruit skins, and rough wheat products. Although we certainly don't want to eliminate roughage from the diet, when treating an elderly person for excess gas it is often useful to try excluding several of the major offenders temporarily. If the bloating improves, experiment with fiber-containing foods until a combination is found that does not produce gas.

187. *Blood in the Stool.* Because blood in the stool may signal a serious disease, it is essential that this condition be recognized. It is also important not to mistake this condition for other causes of reddish stools, like that due to eating red beets. Frequently, blood is passed in such small quantities that it can't be seen (occult blood). If blood is visible, however, it can take two different forms. The stools may be streaked by or mixed with bright red blood, indicating that the blood is very fresh and probably came from near the end of the intestine. On the other hand, blood which has been changed by the chemicals in the intestine may not resemble red blood at all, but may instead be very dark or black and be either liquid or sticky and "tarry." Often this strange-looking stool comes from a bleeding point in the stomach or high in the intestine, and there may not be any other symptoms.

Although most bleeding is due to correctable conditions, the sudden appearance of any blood in the stool requires a prompt call to a physician and a careful evaluation, since the elderly are at risk for several serious diseases, such as cancer of the intestine, which may produce bleeding long before any other symptoms appear. It is vital to recognize these serious diseases as early as possible.

188. *Other GI symptoms* are discussed elsewhere:
Difficulty Swallowing (Section 135);
Heartburn (Section 141);
Loss of Appetite (Section 151).

From the Mouth to the Stomach

189. *The Older Person's Mouth.* Mouth disease is prevalent among the elderly. Several scientific studies have shown that at least two of every three older people are in need of dental and mouth care. More than 10 percent of elderly individuals restrict their social activities because of embarrassment over bad teeth or poorly fitting dentures.

Over 50 percent of all older people are totally without teeth, and by age 75 three quarters are edentulous. In most cases, that loss is preventable, and even in old age teeth may be saved. In youth, teeth are damaged and lost primarily due to dental caries (cavities). In later years, decay still takes its toll but gum (periodontal) disease and wear are more important. Your parents can slow all these processes if they wish. At any age, decay can be retarded by brushing after meals with a soft toothbrush and a fluoride toothpaste, frequent rinsing with water, daily use of a fluoride mouth wash, a low-sugar diet, and regular visits to the dentist for cleaning and fluoride applications. The more important problem of periodontal disease often goes unnoticed by elderly people until the gums become red, swollen, and painful and the teeth become loose. By then, much permanent damage has been done. Fortunately, some periodontal disease can be prevented by good tooth care and, particularly, by regular (at least yearly) visits to a dentist for cleaning and polishing. Finally, although teeth ultimately wear out, they can last one hundred years with gentle treatment. Exceptionally rough and gritty foods, hard-bristled toothbrushes, nervous grinding of teeth, and prolonged exposure to citrus foods and soft drinks should be avoided over the years.

Once many or all their teeth are gone, the elderly often spend the rest of their lives in a constant battle with ill-fitting dentures. Partial dentures which can be anchored to healthy teeth are usually more problem free than a full set—an important reason to preserve any remaining teeth. Once a good fit is attained it is unlikely to last, since the bones of the mouth gradually change shape with age, particularly if teeth are missing. Poorly fitting dentures are uncomfortable and a constant worry to many elderly who expect them to come out at the most inopportune time. To smile, talk, or eat with friends is to risk potential embarrassment. Denture wearers are also plagued by an overgrowth of gum tissue around the denture edges and by painful bruising and infection of the gum or mouth tissue where the dentures rub. The correction for these problems is to try to improve the fit of the dentures and to keep them scrupulously clean. The older individual who forgets to take them out at night and neglects to clean them invariably has problems. But the picture is not all bleak—particularly when you consider the alternative. Dentures improve the appearance and make eating and talking easier. Without them, the bones of the mouth shrink markedly, making a person look much older and eliminating many foods from the diet completely. Obviously, it is important to save as many teeth as possible— vigorous dental care in old age is as vital as any other medical attention.

Sores occasionally appear in the mouth. Most are harmless; a few are not. At some time, almost half the population will experience small, painful, whitish ulcers (aphthous ulcers or canker sores) on the inside of the cheek or the tongue. They usually disappear after a week or two and are not dangerous. If they are extremely uncomfortable, mild pain medication and mouth rinses can make them tolerable. However, what looks like a canker sore may actually be a white patch called leukoplakia, which is usually painless or only mildly painful, may remain for years, and may become cancerous. Canker sores also resemble cancer of the mouth and tongue. *Any* sore in the mouth which has lasted more than two or three weeks is cause to consult a physician. Mouth cancer may vary from a painless reddened patch to an extremely painful ulcer. It is more common in men and in people who smoke pipes and cigars or who drink a significant amount of alcohol. Any suspicious plaque or sore in the mouth should be biopsied and examined for cancer as early as possible, because the likelihood of survival goes down dramatically if mouth cancer has a chance to become established.

190. *The Esophagus.* The muscular tube which connects the mouth to the stomach bears watching in old age. It is the source of at least two problems—one very common and one very serious.

Everyone, at one time or another, experiences that burning sensation in the center of the chest that results from stomach acid briefly squeezing upward into the lower esophagus (reflux). If the muscular sphincter at the bottom of the esophagus functions poorly, acid reflux may occur regularly when a person lies down, during meals, or even between meals. The result, reflux esophagitis, may produce frequent or constant heartburn, and the walls of the esophagus may become inflamed or even ulcerated and scarred. Because reflux esophagitis can get worse and because it is uncomfortable, the parent with regular heartburn should be evaluated for its presence. Treatment is usually effective and involves eating an increased number of smaller meals, avoiding lying down after a meal, not eating before bed, elevating the head of the bed at night by three to four inches, lying on the right side so that gravity helps the stomach to empty, and taking antacids after meals and at bedtime. Since it is more common in people who smoke, drink significant amounts of alcohol, eat large spicy or fatty meals, or who are overweight, changing those habits is important in its control.

Cancer of the esophagus, more common in the later years, is the reason any recent complaint of painful or difficult swallowing must be evaluated *promptly*. The only real chance of surviving this particularly devastating form of cancer lies in early detection and treatment. Over several months, the cancerous esophagus gradually closes, making solid foods, and later even liquids, difficult to swallow. Treatment usually involves surgically removing the diseased portion of the esophagus and is often combined with radiation therapy.

GASTROINTESTINAL DISORDERS

191. *Hiatus Hernia.* This common condition in older people occurs when the upper part of the stomach slides from below the diaphragm—where it belongs—up into the chest. Almost half of all people with a hiatus hernia have no symptoms. Those with symptoms suffer primarily from heartburn caused by stomach acid reflux into the esophagus. However, they may have more severe problems from acid scarring, such as ulcers in the esophagus and blood loss severe enough to cause weakness and anemia (blood containing too few red blood cells). The diagnosis is made by X-rays taken as your parent swallows a barium drink. If there is evidence of an ulcer, scarring, or bleeding, the physician may also want to look at the esophagus-stomach area directly with an endoscope. Treatment is the same as that described for heartburn due to reflux esophagitis (Section 190): improved eating habits, antacids, and making gravity work for you rather than against you. Infrequently, surgery may be required if these measures fail.

192. *Ulcers.* Throughout adult life, ulcers of the stomach (gastric ulcer) or of the intestine just below the stomach (duodenal ulcer) are common and serious medical problems. Gastric ulcers are more common in old age than at any other time, while duodenal ulcers, although less common than in earlier years, remain a significant problem. Because ulcers of either type can usually be treated successfully with medication, and because procrastination in seeking treatment can lead to life-threatening complications, it is essential to recognize the early symptoms of ulcers and to seek help if they appear.

An ulcer is a hole eroded through the superficial lining, or even through the underlying muscular lining, of the stomach or duodenum. Most ulcers are a little less than an inch across and form when damage to the protective coating overlying the cell lining allows stomach acid and other digestive chemicals to attack the walls, much as those juices would digest food. Scar tissue and areas of degeneration make up the bottom and sides of the ulcer. If the ulcer happens to involve a blood vessel, it may produce serious or life-threatening bleeding. If an ulcer works its way completely through the stomach or duodenal wall (perforation), severe pain and widespread infection result. Only one person in ten suffers these serious complications. Fortunately, the body is usually successful in walling off an ulcer so that it doesn't continue to grow.

What are the symptoms that should make you suspect an ulcer? The primary one is pain in the middle of the abdomen, just below the edge of the ribs. There may or may not be a feeling of nausea, or some vomiting, or a sense of bloating or indigestion, but there is usually a burning, gnawing, boring, or aching pain which comes and goes throughout the day. It is usually absent early in the morning, appears an hour or two after meals and at bedtime, may wake your parent in the night, and generally disappears with eating. It is a chronic pain which may be severe for several weeks, disappear for weeks or months, and return later with equal force. However, the condition is not quite this simple because almost half of all older people who develop an ulcer do not have this "typical" pain. Or if they do, it is late in the ulcer's development. Some of these people go through their older years never knowing they have an ulcer, while others are found to have an ulcer only when a complication like bleeding develops.

If your parent's physician suspects an ulcer, he will want to investigate further and will almost certainly order an "upper-GI X-ray series." After your parent drinks a glass of thick, milky, barium liquid, several X-rays are taken. If an ulcer is present, its center and walls will usually be outlined by the barium. This examination is done to be certain both that your parent has an ulcer and that another disease isn't producing similar symptoms. Cancer of the stomach, however, often produces similar symptoms and frequently shows a stomach ulcer by X-ray, so many physicians also look directly at the stomach and duodenum with an endoscope and take samples of ulcerous tissue for examination under a microscope. The combination of X-ray and endoscopy allows the doctor to differentiate between a benign and a cancerous ulcer in over 90 percent of people. In the other 10 percent the type of ulcer can be determined by treating the condition for three to four weeks as if it were an ulcer—a benign ulcer will be much improved at the end of that time, while a cancer should be the same or worse.

Since an ulcer can cause serious problems if untreated, it is comforting to know that medical treatment is generally successful. With medication and proper diet alone, 85 percent of patients with ulcers recover. The other 15 percent of patients are operated on, and most do well if they are not severely ill beforehand. Unfortunately, over 30 percent of people treated for stomach ulcers suffer a recurrence within two years and must repeat the same process of diagnosis and treatment.

Medical treatment for either a gastric or a duodenal ulcer has two parts: medication and diet. Until recently, the only useful medications were antacids. Still a mainstay, they work by neutralizing acid in the stomach and duodenum for the four to six weeks it takes for an ulcer to heal. Unfortunately, they must be taken in large quantities: two tablespoons of liquid antacid (such as Maalox or Mylanta; the pills are less effective) one and three hours after all three meals and at bedtime. Because these dosages can occasionally produce side effects like diarrhea, constipation, and imbalances of blood chemicals, a new medication called cimetidine (Tagamet) has been a very useful addition to the treatment of ulcers. It appears to be as effective as antacids in eliminating stomach acid and in healing ulcers, and the patient only needs to take one pill four times each day for a month. Moreover, another drug which has been used for years as an anti-depressant medication, Sinequan, has recently been shown to be possibly even more effective than Tagamet in healing ulcers. The future looks bright for ulcer sufferers.

People recovering from an ulcer need to control their diet. However, recent medical evidence shows that it is not necessary to eat bland food or to drink large amounts of milk, and that it is even inadvisable to eat frequent, small meals. Instead, your parents should eat three moderate-sized, tasty, well-balanced meals, not eat in the late evening or at bedtime, and avoid snacks. Also, they should not drink strong liquor, coffee, tea, or cola in large amounts. It would be wise for them to eliminate any food that regularly produces pain. Your parents should consult with their physician if they are taking medication known to irritate ulcers—particularly aspirin, some arthritis medications, and some steroids. Finally, they should try not to smoke, since nicotine seems to slow ulcer healing.

If medication and diet don't work, if a serious complication develops, or if the same ulcer keeps developing over months and years, surgery is usually the next step. Operations that may be effective with different patients include removing the ulcer and part of the stomach, cutting the nerves that supply the acid-producing segment of stomach, or some combination of both. As with medication, the primary goal of surgery is to reduce the acid in the stomach and duodenum, since if only the ulcer is removed another ulcer frequently develops. Because an ulcer of the stomach (but not of the duodenum) may be stomach cancer in disguise, and because early detection is the best hope for cure, be alert to any new symptoms and see that your parents keep their follow-up appointments.

193. *Stomach Cancer.* Cancer of the stomach is considerably more frequent in old age than at any other time of life. Fortunately, it has become much less common over the last few years, although the reasons for this decline are unknown. However, because it is such a dangerous form of cancer and because it can be mistaken for a less serious GI complaint until it is too late for treatment, it is essential to think of stomach cancer when your parent complains of intestinal distress.

Unfortunately, there are no clear-cut symptoms indicating the presence of stomach cancer. Your parent may lose appetite, feel bloated after a meal, or suffer from a gnawing or burning pain after eating. He may become weak or listless and lose weight. While these problems can be caused by stomach cancer, they are much more likely to be due to several other, less serious illnesses. No specific symptoms set stomach cancer apart, which is why any persistent, unexplained symptoms in the upper abdomen of an older person deserve a medical evaluation.

A careful medical check-up, including upper-GI barium X-rays and endoscopy along with the removal of tissue samples, will identify at least 95 percent of all stomach cancers. Unless the cancer is too far advanced or the person too weak, treatment is always surgical—removal of the tumor and any other involved tissue. In addition to surgery, cancer-killing drugs may be used (chemotherapy), but they are not very effective if used alone. It is distressing that cancer of the stomach is frequently caught late, since those patients who are treated before the cancer has spread have a long-term survival rate of 40–50 percent, as compared to 10 percent for those in whom it has spread.

The Intestine and Digestive Organs

Food enters the gastrointestinal tract in the mouth, is moved along to the stomach, where it is mixed with acid and other substances and where digestion begins in earnest. Digestion continues as food passes from the stomach into the beginning of the small intestine, where it is mixed with digestive chemicals from the liver, gallbladder, and pancreas. Bile, which is manufactured in the liver, is stored in the gallbladder and released several times each day to aid in digestion of fats. The pancreas produces enzymes which facilitate the digestion of proteins, fats, and carbohydrates. Bile and pancreatic juice each leave their respective organs through separate small ducts and flow into the duodenum through a common entry. Once the food and acid meet the bile and pancreatic juice in the duodenum, the resulting mixture slowly passes down the length of the small intestine. During this trip, digestion is completed and the nutrients are absorbed into the blood. What remains then passes into the large intestine, where water is removed and it is readied for passage out of the body as stool.

Most of the lower abdominal pain, diarrhea, and constipation that so trouble the elderly result from a poorly functioning or diseased large intestine. Although there are a number of things that can go wrong with the small intestine, they are uncommon, and it remains on good behavior through most of old age. The small intestine usually presents problems only in people who are severely ill from other causes. However, the digestive organs that drain into the small intestine do present a few problems of their own.

194. *The Liver and the Pancreas*. The liver is not prone to new diseases in old age. It does, however, show the effects of a lifetime of rough treatment. If your parent has long used alcohol excessively or has had his liver injured by hepatitis, he is at risk to have developed the weakened, scarred condition of the liver called cirrhosis, a serious illness that is one of the major causes of death in old age. Although there is no cure, often its progress can be slowed or halted by a well-balanced, nutritious diet and absolute abstention from alcohol.

The most common disease in the pancreas is a sudden or long-standing inflammation which results when an irritation, like severe alcohol use or a blocked pancreatic duct, causes the enzymes to leak and begin digesting the pancreas itself. Upper abdominal pain (which can be terribly severe in acute cases), nausea, and vomiting are typical symptoms. Since these symptoms resemble those of several other GI diseases, diagnosis depends on medical and laboratory evaluation. Similar symptoms, plus weakness and weight loss, accompany that other major pancreatic disorder of old age, cancer of the pancreas. It is usually a fatal form of cancer, in part because of the difficulty of diagnosing it early enough to treat successfully.

Of course, the most common pancreatic disorder is diabetes. Because that is such an important condition, it is treated at length in Section 263.

195. *The Gallbladder and Gallstones*. Almost one third of all older people have gallstones in their gallbladder. One half of these people never know they have stones unless the stones are accidentally discovered during a medical examination. Many of the other elderly persons with gallstones suffer indigestion and pain, off and on, for years as stones periodically block the duct from the gallbladder and cause it to become inflamed (chronic cholecystitis). Occasionally, they will have such a severe bout that they will become acutely ill and experience fever, chills, vomiting, and marked abdominal pain and tenderness (acute cholecystitis). In either case, these people should seek a medical assessment since it may be much to their advantage to be without their gallbladder.

The symptoms of gallbladder disease are fairly typical but, like most other illnesses of the gastrointestinal tract, can be confused with other conditions. The trick is to differentiate gallbladder disease from an ulcer, which it can closely mimic, as well as from hiatus hernia, inflammation of the pancreas, or even a heart attack. Fortunately, that can usually be done by a careful review of your parent's symptoms and by performing several simple and safe laboratory tests.

The most common gallbladder symptom is a severe, steady ache or cramp that lasts for an hour or two and is felt in the front, underneath the ribs on the right side. This pain is unpredictable—eating or changing position usually neither brings it on nor relieves it. It will probably make your parent feel sick to his stomach and may actually cause vomiting. He may have a fever as well. The pain gradually wanes, but it may recur hours, days, or months later.

Special tests are needed to prove that these symptoms are due to gallbladder disease; blood tests are only suggestive. With the most common test, an oral cholecystogram, your parent swallows a tablet of dye the night before an X-ray is taken. The dye normally should be concentrated by the gallbladder, making it show up nicely on the X-ray. If disease is present, the gallbladder may not work well enough to collect the dye and nothing will appear on the X-ray, or the shapes of gallstones may appear. Other useful tests include the application of high-frequency sound waves across the abdomen (ultrasonography), computerized X-ray scans of the abdomen (CAT scan), and the injection into the blood of a short-lived radioactive substance which is rapidly concentrated in the gallbladder (radionuclide imaging). Finally, if the diagnosis remains in doubt after all of this, the physician may thread a tiny catheter through the mouth, esophagus, and stomach, into the small intestine, and then into the bile duct itself—a procedure having a name only a doctor could love: endoscopic retrograde cholangiopancreatography (ERCP). Using ERCP, very specific X-rays may be made.

Most people who have gallstones but no symptoms require no treatment. However, if they have mild but persistent symptoms or if they have a severe, acute attack, their gallbladder should probably be removed surgically. Unless they are weak and in poor health or there are complications, this operation (cholecystectomy) is simple and safe. It can be done either at the time they are acutely ill or, in cases of chronic disease, at your parent's convenience. While surgery is the usual treatment, a new medication, chenodeoxycholic acid, has been shown to be capable of dissolving some kinds of gallstones. The physician will need to determine if your parent has the type of disease for which the medication is likely to be effective. Gallstones so treated tend to take one to two years to disappear. Unfortunately, they also slowly return in about one half of the people, so surgery may ultimately be needed. One other step which may help prevent a recurrence is for the obese person to lose weight.

196. *The Large Intestine.* The large intestine, or colon, confronts the elderly with more problems than any other part of the body. It is between five and six feet long and begins at the short, blind end that contains the appendix. It extends from the lower right of the abdomen up to the ribs on the right side, across to the ribs on the left side, and down the left side of the abdomen to exit as the rectum and anus. Its primary task is to dry the resi-

due of digested food and store it until it can be eliminated. The large intestine brings us constipation, diarrhea, hemorrhoids, cancer, infection, and much, much more.

One out of every ten elderly persons has one or more polyps in the colon. A polyp is a growth of the intestinal wall that projects like a small finger into the hollow of the intestine. Most produce no symptoms. Occasionally they may bleed into the stool or cause constipation or diarrhea. However, their real importance lies in the possibility that they may become cancerous. Polyps are most frequently discovered when they produce symptoms or when they are seen during inspection of the inside of the lower colon with a sigmoidoscope during a routine physical examination—another reason why regular, thorough physical examinations of the elderly are important. Unfortunately, it is usually impossible to determine by sight which polyps are cancerous—although the larger they are, the more likely they are to be early cancer. Since it is usually simple to remove them painlessly with the colonoscope, many physicians will do this and then examine them microscopically for cancer. If the polyp is of the type which is likely to become cancerous, it is essential for your parent to have regular checkups every two to four years. If the polyp actually contains cancerous cells, the doctor will need to determine whether additional tissue should be removed.

Although we tend to think of infection of the appendix (acute appendicitis) as a disease of young people, it occurs regularly in old age. It is a dangerous disease in older people because the warning signs are ignored until very late in its development. We expect appendicitis to produce severe abdominal pain and high fever, but if we wait for those symptoms to develop in our parents we will have waited too long. A persistent ache and tenderness in the lower abdomen on the right is the most common preliminary symptom, often accompanied by nausea, loss of appetite, and mild fever. Have your parent seek medical attention if this symptom pattern appears, since delay in getting to a doctor is risky.

The irritable bowel syndrome, or spastic colon, resembles many other gastrointestinal diseases. It is one of the most likely causes for your parent's abdominal complaints. It usually produces vague abdominal pain and a mixture of constipation and diarrhea, but may also cause heartburn, nausea, bloating, and other symptoms. It's a chronic condition, so your parent may have had many of these complaints in the past. An evaluation for these symptoms should be made as much to exclude the presence of other diseases as to make the diagnosis of irritable bowel syndrome. For unknown reasons, the muscles of the large intestine appear to be very irritable. It is not a life-threatening illness but it is an uncomfortable one. Unfortunately, there is no specific treatment that is sure to work. Best results occur with a high-fiber diet, good bowel habits, activity, and an effort to reduce stress as much as possible.

197. *Diverticulitis*. Diverticu*losis* is a condition in which small, blind pouches of intestinal lining (diverticula) extend from the inside of the intestine, through its muscular wall, and into the inside of the abdomen. Diverticula are found predominantly in the last part of the large intestine. They may be the size of a fingernail or of a thumb and are extremely common among the elderly—almost half of all people over the age of 65 have one or more. They are thought to be caused by soft food, hard stool, and a lifetime of straining. They are almost unheard-of among people who eat rough, fibrous food, as in some African tribes. Frequently people don't know they are present, or at most experience slight tenderness or cramping in the lower abdomen on the left. However, they are a common source of blood in the stool. Often these symptoms in an older person will cause a physician to perform a barium enema, in which the large bowel is filled with a barium mixture from below. Diverticula will show up as little pockets filled with barium sticking through the wall of the intestine. Except for recommending a high-fiber diet, nothing more is usually done unless your parent begins to have other symptoms.

The real importance of diverticula is that they can become inflamed (diverticu*litis*) and may develop a hole which sometimes allows the contents of the bowel to leak out. This condition, called perforated diverticulitis, can make your parent acutely ill. Diverticulitis is a common, serious medical illness in old age. The most typical symptoms are nausea, constipation or diarrhea, chills, fever, and sudden aching pain and tenderness to touch in the left lower abdomen. Some elderly, however, may have only mild symptoms. Often the symptoms will gradually disappear, but occasionally they get worse and produce widespread pain, infection, or bleeding.

If the doctor suspects diverticulitis, he will usually put your parent in the hospital, feed him only through the vein, and give him a course of antibiotics. As the condition improves, your parent will receive liquids to drink, then soft food with a lot of bulk and fiber. If your parent's symptoms are mild, he may be permitted to stay at home, drink only liquids, and take antibiotics. Once he is no longer acutely ill, additional tests like a barium enema may be done to confirm the diagnosis of diverticulitis. If your parent is getting rapidly worse or if he has had a series of acute episodes, surgery is usually the safest and best method of treatment. Approximately one quarter of all people with acute diverticulitis require an operation for it at some time. This usually means removing that short section of the large intestine which has been giving the trouble.

198. *Cancer of the Large Intestine and Rectum.* Cancer of the colon and rectum, cancer of the lung, and cancer of the breast are the three major cancers in the United States. Cancer of the large intestine is particularly common in the elderly, reaching a peak in the 70s. Thus it is important that you and your parents recognize its symptoms and that they receive regular medical checkups: it is much more likely to be cured if caught early.

Unfortunately, cancer of the colon often presents no symptoms until it is well developed. For that reason, annual medical checkups for the elderly are essential. Because about one half of these cancers are located at the very end of the intestine and can be reached by an examining finger, and because they will often leak small amounts of blood for months or years before any other symptoms appear, it is important that the annual evaluation include a rectal examination and a chemical test of the stool for blood. Some experts recommend that older people have a physician carefully inspect their colon with a fiberoptic sigmoidoscope every several years, since much more of the large intestine can be screened that way.

The first symptoms to appear are usually blood in the stool or constipation. Blood loss is often slow, but significant enough to make your parent weak. Listlessness or weakness may be the first symptom to appear. Anemia from the blood loss can be detected by standard blood tests. Constipation or increasingly smaller stools is frequently the first symptom of cancer located at the very end of the intestine. As the cancer grows, it slowly blocks the intestinal tube, making it harder for your parent to pass stool, and producing chronic constipation. He may have a sense that he can't defecate completely. He may have pain anywhere in the abdomen, or no pain at all. In the later stages, weight loss may be considerable. Because all these symptoms are so vague and resemble so many other less serious illnesses, it is essential for those in the older, at-risk age group to have regular checkups.

If the doctor finds something suspicious, the next steps are fairly standard. Evaluation for cancer of the colon and rectum involves several blood tests including those for liver dysfunction and anemia, a test of the stool for blood, a rectal examination, and an examination of the lower bowel with a sigmoidoscope. Next a barium enema allows the outline of the entire colon to be viewed. If questions remain, the physician may look directly at the entire large intestine with a fiberoptic colonoscope, taking samples of any suspicious spots if need be. Since this battery of tests is quite reliable, the doctor can provide an almost certain yes or no answer for your parent.

If cancer is present, surgery is the only promising course unless your parent is too weak or ill to tolerate it. How extensive the surgery should be depends upon how large the tumor has become. Usually the section of bowel with tumor can be removed and the two ends sewn together. Sometimes, particularly if the tumor is in the very end of the rectum, the free end of intestine must be attached to the abdominal wall so that it leads directly to the outside—a colostomy. Most people dread the thought of a colostomy, yet unless your parent has significant physical or mental impairment, it is quite possible to have this operation and still lead a normal life. Occasionally, surgery may be combined with anticancer medication (chemotherapy).

In comparison with other cancers of the gastrointestinal tract, cancers of the large intestine and rectum yield a good likelihood of survival. If the tumor is caught early, when limited to a small section on the inside of the intestine, there is up to a 90 percent chance of survival. Even when the tumor has gotten quite large, over half of sufferers will live longer than five years, unless cancer has spread extensively throughout the body. Regular medical examinations and early detection remain the key to the best prognosis.

199. *Hemorrhoids.* Almost all older people suffer from hemorrhoids. Hemorrhoids are dilatations of the normal blood vessels which lie under the skin around the anus. With time, straining at stool, chronic constipation, pregnancies, and the use of irritating suppositories, they gradually enlarge and begin to protrude from the anal opening. They are often uncomfortable, frequently itch, may bleed, and, at their most severe, become exceedingly painful. Fortunately, treatment is almost always successful. The specific kind of treatment depends upon how severe they have become. Very small hemorrhoids require no treatment other than a high-fiber diet, drinking lots of fluid, establishing regular bowel habits, avoiding straining at stool, and possibly using a stool softener. If hemorrhoids are large enough to be troublesome, they may be removed by either injecting them with a caustic solution or tying a band around their base. Both treatments need to be done by a physician and are usually fairly painless. Exceptionally large hemorrhoids may be removed surgically by a reliable operation known as a hemorrhoidectomy. No matter which technique is used, a change to a high-fiber diet to reduce constipation and straining is essential if hemorrhoids are not to recur.

17.

Bladder and Kidney Disorders

200. *The Anatomy of Urine Production.* The urinary system is troublesome for the elderly. We are born with two kidneys (one on either side of the spinal column just above the small of the back) that remove chemical waste and excess water from the blood to form urine. The urine trickles from the kidneys, through ducts known as the ureters, to be stored in the bladder and finally eliminated through the urethra. The kidneys age well but can produce serious illness when impaired. The bladder is the weak link in this system. Elderly people often have difficulty controlling the bladder. Males have an additional potential weak link, the prostate gland (part of the reproductive system), which sits at the base of the bladder, surrounds the urethra, and by enlarging can gradually interrupt the flow of urine.

INCONTINENCE

201. *Incontinence—The Myth vs. the Reality.* The stereotype of the aged person sitting in a puddle of urine or wetting the bed nightly is seldom accurate. Only a minority of the elderly are incontinent, many of them only occasionally, and much can be done to help those unlucky few.

We may be tempted to become angry at an incontinent elderly parent and feel as though we have been personally insulted. This "habit" may be considered dirty, disgusting, or childish. Spots on furniture, increased laundry bills, and the pervasive odor of urine may make this reaction understandable, but it is still unfair. The leaking of urine is terribly humiliating and frustrating to the parent who feels powerless to control it. He may go to great lengths to hide the symptom and its effects—to discard clothes rather than wash them, to hide caches of soiled laundry, to deny the problem to family and physician. This problem can completely upset his life, causing him to avoid friends and activities for fear of social embarrassment and to become angry and hostile or depressed and withdrawn. Family members, particularly those who do the cleaning, may believe that the wetting is willfully done—it rarely is, but the parent may have given up all hope of control and is just "letting it go." An unfortunate and often unnecessary result is that an otherwise beloved parent may be encouraged (and be willing) to enter a nursing home long before such a placement is appropriate.

202. *Bladder Function Is Complex.* The bladder is just a bag that holds urine, but it is a very intelligent bag. The bladder wall senses stretching (filling) and sends a signal to the brain, which usually ignores the signal until the bladder contains slightly less than one pint. Then the brain begins sending increasingly strident alarms to void. Urination occurs when a person relaxes the muscular valve on the urethra and the bladder automatically contracts. An interference with any one of several steps in this chain may result in incontinence.

203. *Incontinence Is Not a Normal Response to Aging.* When incontinence first develops, seek a medical evaluation. Not only is the problem more easily reversed in early stages, but the psychological costs of leaving it untreated are high. A thorough evaluation includes a careful physical examination, laboratory evaluation of the blood and urine, and cystometry (a measurement of bladder pressure as the bladder is artificially filled with water, which is then voided). In addition, an accurate description of symptoms is essential in distinguishing one kind of incontinence from another.

204. *Temporary Incontinence.* Illness may produce temporary incontinence in anyone, particularly in the elderly. Anyone who develops an acute bladder infection (signaled by burning upon urination) or an illness with a high fever, especially if accompanied by mental confusion, is at risk to be incontinent. This incontinence usually passes when the illness clears. Encourage your parent to treat it as the minor symptom it is. Just being confined to bed may also cause incontinence, which usually disappears after the person is up and active.

205. *Chronic Incontinence.* More troublesome are the numerous conditions that can lead to chronic incontinence.

If the parts of the brain that regulate urination are damaged, either slowly as in senility or suddenly as in a stroke, the most common form of incontinence in old age, an unstable bladder, may result. Only a small amount of urine in an unstable bladder is sufficient to start contractions, which are difficult for the person to stop. The contractions start shortly after or simultaneously with the awareness of the need to void; if a slow-moving older person hasn't planned to be near a bathroom, he or she will be incontinent. Because a person in this condition may need to void every hour or two, life can become an endless and anxious tour of community restroom facilities. The more mentally confused a person is, the more likely he is to be incontinent and the more resistant to treatment. The most difficult people to treat are the demented, who may actually be unaware of or indifferent to the symptom. (These individuals are likely to lose control of their stool as well.)

Any obstruction or blockage which keeps urine from leaving the bladder produces problems. If the block occurs suddenly or even over days the bladder painfully enlarges, and a physician may need to insert a catheter into the urethra to drain the bladder. This *urinary retention* is a medical emergency, but fortunately it is usually relieved easily. More common is the obstruction which develops slowly, often over months or even years, from causes like an enlarged prostate, cancer, or severe constipation and impacted feces, which squeeze the urethra shut. When that happens, the bladder slowly and painlessly enlarges to several times normal size. It may contain more than a quart of urine, even after voiding. A person with such an obstruction has trouble starting a stream of urine, dribbles urine throughout the day, and isn't always aware that his bladder is full. Incontinence disappears in these people as soon as the cause of the blockage is removed, particularly if they are treated early.

Dribbling incontinence from an enlarged bladder can also be the result of a medical condition such as long-standing diabetes mellitus (sugar diabetes). Severe diabetes can damage the nerves that supply the bladder. The bladder's signals to the brain never arrive, there is no sense of fullness, and so there is no normal voiding; the bladder empties by perpetually leaking. The patient usually needs to wear a bag with a catheter.

Finally, a form of incontinence common among women who have had many children and who have suffered stretching and distortion of the tissues near the exit of the birth canal is called *stress incontinence.* The muscles which control the flow of urine have been weakened, and these women typically leak urine when they cough, stand up suddenly, or laugh. Specific exercises and surgery are often helpful.

206. *Treatment for the Incontinent.* Whether your parent has frequent small accidents from an unstable bladder or dribbling incontinence, there are several things you can do to help. Success in eliminating incontinence usually depends more on the combined efforts of you and your parent than on anything the physician might attempt. Except where there is a clear-cut and easily reversed problem such as an enlarged prostate or fecal impaction, day-to-day management holds the key to staying dry. Discuss the problem in a matter-of-fact way with your parent. Don't make him feel anxious or guilty—these feelings can worsen the symptom. Consider what has been tried and why it has failed. Be certain that his general health and dietary habits are good. Although restriction of water and other fluids may seem logical, an elderly person's blood chemicals slip out of balance so easily that this is a dangerous practice and one which often actually worsens incontinence. At least two quarts of liquid should be drunk evenly throughout the day, but liquids should be avoided the hour or two before bedtime. A person who is up and active during the day is much more likely to be dry than someone who stays in bed, if only because it is difficult to get out of bed and to the bathroom in a hurry. Be sure that the physician has reviewed any drugs that may be aggravating the incontinence—the leading offenders are sleeping pills, sedatives, and diuretics (water pills).

The next step in dealing with incontinence is to evaluate and plan around your parent's established toileting habits and wetting patterns. Cooperation of everyone in the home is required. Does the wetting occur only at night? During the day? When during the day? Keep a chart for a week or two to be sure the facts are straight. When is the bathroom successfully used (both during the day and at night)? Where are the bathrooms in the house? How much lead time does your parent usually have to get to the bathroom? Are the chairs in the home easy to get out of? Are the bathrooms well lighted at night (and during the day)? Are the toilets easy to operate for someone with poor eyesight and trembling fingers? Would a grab-bar be useful? Are your parent's clothes easy to remove in a hurry? Add lights, make minor structural changes in the bathroom, or buy more appropriate clothing, if necessary. If your parent is in a wheelchair, is the house adapted for it? Encourage activity—the more mobile the person, the easier it is to reach the bathroom in time. Encourage regular trips to the bathroom just before your parent would be likely to be wet (refer to your chart). If your parent is forgetful, an alarm clock set regularly through the day and night can help. Encourage nighttime trips to the bathroom along a well-lighted path. If getting out of bed at night proves difficult, consider a bedpan (simple for men, less easy for women) or a bedside commode. Do not expect success with the first try, but work with your parent to fine-tune the routine.

Incontinence should not keep a person from having a normal social life, but it often does. Find out where the community restrooms are (public buildings often have them; many private stores do not) and plan trips accordingly. Tactfully visit the bathroom yourself and take your parent along. In a theater, sit near the aisle. Interrupt long car trips with rest stops. It may require planning and determination to stay dry in the community but it can be done. When incontinent elderly people discover that they can be socially active again, often their enthusiasm and motivation, and thus success at staying dry, increase dramatically.

207. *Exercises.* A series of exercises to strengthen the pelvic muscles which help shut off the flow of urine is useful for women with stress incontinence. The routine involves trying to stop the flow of urine in midstream and practicing similar movements several times each day when not voiding.

208. *Other Treatments Are Available.* If careful planning and exercises do not satisfactorily control the incontinence, there are numerous medical interventions of some value to a few individuals. The bladder may be artificially distended by cystometry. Medications may be useful for some people—for example, some elderly women may markedly improve with estrogens. Mechanical devices such as condoms for males, incontinence pants, incontinence pads for the bed, and temporary or permanent catheters with bag are available. None of this equipment, however, is problem-free. Surgery may be indicated for a few specific conditions. Raise these possibilities with the physician.

OTHER URINARY TRACT PROBLEMS

209. *Bacteria in the Urine.* An infection of the urinary tract is extremely common in people over 65, and in most people is not usually serious. A fresh urine sample examined for bacteria usually allows a diagnosis. If there are acute symptoms such as burning, itching, nighttime wetting, or urgency, treatment with antibiotics is valuable.

Chronic, mild bladder infections are common and are generally symptomless. They frequently occur in people who are in poor physical health, bedridden, incontinent, or who can't empty their bladders completely. When first discovered, the infection is generally treated with antibiotics. After the infection has recurred one or more times, however, medication is usually discontinued. Attention is then shifted to correcting those underlying conditions, like immobility and incontinence, which allow the infection to develop. In a few elderly people, bacteria causing the infection are being washed downstream from a chronic kidney infection. Encourage your parent to seek evaluation if symptoms of acute infection or poor urine flow develop.

210. *Blood in the Urine.* The appearance of blood in the urine (hematuria) is a dramatic symptom which must be medically evaluated. Some of the causes, such as bladder tumor and prostate cancer, are serious, but bleeding may also be caused by conditions like bladder infection or a kidney stone. Try to determine whether the red color is intense at the beginning or the end of voiding, or whether it is even throughout. Also notice whether any clots have been passed and whether their color is more red or brown. This kind of specific information will help a physician quickly identify the condition.

211. *The Prostate Gland.* Most males suffer gradual enlargement of the prostate gland after age 60. This may cause them to have trouble starting or stopping the stream of urine, to be unable to completely empty their bladder, or to develop dribbling incontinence and nighttime wetting. Called benign prostatic hypertrophy (BPH), the gland's excess tissue is fairly easily and safely removed by a surgical operation called transurethral resection. Impotence does not usually follow this surgery. With any symptoms of urinary dysfunction, your parent should visit a physician. Prompt treatment prevents later complications, and also permits early diagnosis of possible cancer of the prostate, a condition treated successfully only if caught soon enough.

Cancer of the prostate develops fairly frequently in men over 60. It often mimics the more common BPH, and it can be fatal. Thus it is essential that men who develop urinary tract problems receive a careful evaluation. If prostatic cancer is detected and treated early, surgical removal of the prostate will make a cure more likely. If early symptoms are ignored, the cancer spreads—frequently to the bones—producing additional symptoms such as back pain, weight loss, and shooting leg pain. Once the cancer has spread, the chance for survival is much less.

212. *Kidney Diseases.* Kidney disorders of all types are only slightly more common in the elderly. Because older people tend to be in poorer general health than the young, however, severe illness and death are more likely to occur from a kidney disorder. It is not uncommon for an older person who is seriously ill with some other disease to suffer from kidney failure, which may be fatal. Treatment for kidney disease in the elderly is usually similar to that received by younger people. Aggressive use of such sophisticated methods as hemodialysis and kidney transplantation is almost as likely to be successful in the old as in the young.

18.

Disorders of the Eyes and Ears

Eyes

Everyone's vision worsens with age, but four out of five older people continue to have serviceable sight throughout their later years. That is fortunate since the world of the poorly sighted is filled with hazards. Physical dangers abound—medication labels are misread, switches are turned to the wrong setting, moving cars go unnoticed, steps are not seen. Worse yet are the psychological dangers—the loneliness of self-imposed isolation; the confusion about a world indistinctly seen; the gradual wasting away of enthusiasm and health due to the forced immobility of the blind or near-blind. Your parent, who is otherwise intact, may become profoundly dispirited as his vision fails.

Many elderly can have their vision improved by modern techniques. A yearly visit to an eye doctor should be part of every older person's schedule—not just to ensure optimum vision at present, but to detect diseases of the older eye which can be treated successfully only if caught early.

The normal changes in sight with age have been described earlier (Section 21). Many of them can be improved with glasses, contact lenses, or other vision aids. In addition, there are three common diseases of the eye (glaucoma, cataracts, and macular degeneration), several uncommon but devastating ocular emergencies, and several common disorders of the eyelids which affect the elderly. These are all treatable, particularly if recognized early. It is important for you and your parents to be familiar with them so that you do not mistake the signs of a disease for normal changes due to age.

213. *Glaucoma.* This is the most serious common eye disease of the elderly and is the major reason your parents should have a thorough yearly eye examination. It develops slowly, and by the time symptoms become evident, permanent loss of vision may already have occurred. The *only* hope of recognizing it early is through regular eye examinations, because the noticeable early changes are in the interior of the eye. It must be caught early if irreversible damage is to be prevented.

Glaucoma is caused by increased pressure inside the eye. In the normal eye, the fluid which fills the front part of the eye is produced behind the lens, seeps forward through the gap between the lens and the colored part of the eye (iris), and is absorbed into the blood vessels at the outer edge of the iris. In the most common type of glaucoma, open-angle glaucoma, the absorbing vessels slowly become plugged, impairing the outflow of fluid, and pressure builds up which gradually destroys the nerves in the retina at the back of the eye. If this goes untreated, your parent may notice eye aches, headaches, nausea, loss of vision from the corners of the eyes, or halos around lights. Because these symptoms are sporadic, develop late, and are usually mild, they are often ignored. Loss of peripheral vision gradually worsens until that loss is severe—unfortunately, a person rarely notices mild loss of side sight. An examination at this point often reveals that vision is only directly in front of the eye, known as tunnel vision. This can progress to total blindness unless treated promptly.

One out of every twenty elderly people develops glaucoma. The open-angle type of glaucoma tends to run in families, so be aware if any relative has suffered loss of sight. The cause of this most common form of glaucoma is unknown, but it is usually easy to recognize if the proper tests are performed. Each year, your parent should have the following done:

1. A physician should carefully examine the interior of your parent's eyes with an ophthalmoscope. The first changes of glaucoma occur there, often long before any loss of vision.

2. The pressure inside the eye should be measured with a tonometer. With his eye anesthetized by drops, your parent either has the tonometer placed against his eye while lying on a table or, while sitting, he rests his chin on a more elaborate "applanation tonometer." Although valuable, the results are sometimes confusing for a couple of reasons. First, some people can develop glaucoma even though they have a normal pressure. Also, the pressure may vary throughout the day so that it may be normal when measured but elevated during the rest of the day.

3. The completeness of your parent's field of vision should be tested.

DISORDERS OF THE EYES AND EARS

The physician examines the visual fields by mapping where your parent begins to see things (for example, a pin or a finger) coming from the side while he is looking straight ahead. To be useful, this test must be done carefully and the results must be compared from year to year. Very accurate measurements of the visual fields can be made on specialized equipment found in the offices of a few general physicians and all ophthalmologists.

The certain diagnosis of glaucoma requires information from all three of the above tests. Once glaucoma is suspected, your parent should see an ophthalmologist for confirmation. The doctor will use specialized equipment, such as a gonioscope, to prove the diagnosis and to determine which of the several kinds of glaucoma is involved.

A much less common form of glaucoma, closed-angle glaucoma, appears as an acute attack that can result in permanent loss of vision within hours. Usually, only one eye is involved at a time, but the other eye is at risk to develop an attack in the future. Over a period ranging from minutes to hours, the eye becomes red and painful. Your parent may become nauseated, complain of headache and blurry vision in the painful eye, and see colored rings around lights. When this occurs, your parent must see a doctor, preferably an ophthalmologist, immediately. There are other, less serious causes of a red and painful eye, but don't take a chance by delaying a visit to the physician. Eye drops that control the acute attack are available. After the acute episode passes, however, your parent should have eye surgery to prevent further attacks. A small hole made in the edge of the iris (peripheral iridectomy) usually solves the problem.

There is no cure for open-angle glaucoma. However, several medications are available which if used faithfully usually decrease the pressure in the eye and prevent loss of sight. They are used alone or in combination with one another, and most (for example, pilocarpine, carbachol, epinephrine, and timolol) are taken as eye drops two to four times each day. One medication is available as a thin wafer which is slipped under the eyelid and lasts for a week (Ocusert)—unfortunately, it is expensive (seven to eight dollars per week). Another, Diamox, can be taken by mouth. These medications work in different ways, and thus it is reasonable to combine them if one does not do the job. Unfortunately, their use is often limited by the side effects they produce, which range from weakness, fatigue, nausea, loss of appetite, depression, and allergic reactions to the production of cataracts and kidney stones. For the few people in whom the medication is ineffective or produces unacceptable side effects, surgery may be necessary. Such surgery is delicate, and its success is not guaranteed; it should be postponed until medication has been thoroughly tried.

One caution: steroid eye drops or eye creams should be rigorously avoided. They are sometimes used to reduce eye inflammations or allergic reactions, but in someone with glaucoma they frequently raise the interior eye pressure markedly. Your parent should remind any unfamiliar physician (for example, one in an emergency room) both of the glaucoma and of this reaction.

214. *Cataracts.* Cataracts are the most common serious eye disease of the elderly—they afflict over 80 percent of people in their 70s and 80s. The lens of the eye normally yellows and darkens with age; cataracts seem to be an acceleration and extension of that process. Often they develop in both eyes, but they may enlarge at different rates. They can be caused by damage to the eye, as with a blow or infection, but most frequently they are due to gradual deterioration with age. The discoloration is in the lens itself, not in the fluid overlying it or in the cornea. Thus the variety of treatments available all involve removing the affected lens.

If and when your parent should be treated for a cataract depends primarily on how many problems the impaired vision is creating. Glare, dimness, and vagueness of sight are the major problems encountered. Your parent may not be bothered excessively now but may need to consider treatment in the future. If his interests and pleasures depend upon clear vision, such as is required for reading and sewing, it may be better to seek treatment earlier. If, however, your parent's preferred activities are cooking, watching a large-screen TV, or walking in familiar surroundings, treatment can be done anytime your parent is convinced of the need, as long as he or she is in fairly good health.

All of the available treatments for cataracts involve surgery, but all are safe and require at most only two or three days in the hospital. Although no treatment is perfect, some are better than others for certain patients. There are two steps to all of these treatments: removal of the lens and replacement of the lens.

There are two standard methods of removing the lens. The older, time-tested way is to make an incision on the cornea, cut the retaining structures inside the eye, and slip the lens out. A more recent method is to make a very small cut through the cornea, insert a needle into the lens, and vibrate the needle extremely rapidly. The lens is shattered into tiny fragments which are then drawn out through the needle. There are advantages and disadvantages to both techniques—the ophthalmologist will tell you which is the best technique for your parent. In either case, your parent should be able to leave the hospital in a day or two, or occasionally, on the same day.

Once the natural lens, which used to focus the light coming into the

DISORDERS OF THE EYES AND EARS

eye, is gone, it must be replaced by an artificial structure which does the same thing. Three types of lenses are available.

1. Glasses. Until recently, thick "post-cataract" glasses were the sole way to correct sight after surgery. They continue to be useful for some people, but they are frequently difficult to adjust to: they magnify everything and narrow the field of vision so that a person must continually be turning his head. Moreover, if the other eye has good vision, the contrast between the good eye and the corrected eye is so great that a person is likely to suffer constant double vision and may at times become disoriented.

2. Contact lenses. Hard contact lenses are a marked improvement over glasses for most people—they still magnify, but to a much smaller degree. Unfortunately, many elderly people find them difficult to manage. Trembling, arthritic hands manipulate them poorly, and they are small and hard to see with the uncorrected eyes of the cataract patient. The newer soft contact lenses which can remain in place for up to a month at a time are much more useful; an elderly person is more likely to stick with such a lens.

3. The most recent and most promising advance is a small, plastic lens which is placed directly in the eye, replacing the natural lens. Improvement in vision is dramatic and immediate. This was felt to be the perfect solution when it was first developed, but it has been found to produce a few complications like damage to the cornea and infection. However, as the quality of the lenses available has improved, the likelihood of complications has decreased substantially. In all probability, direct implantation of an artificial lens into the eye will eventually become the standard method of improving vision after cataract surgery. The surgical treatment of cataracts is not problem-free, but for most people it is considerably better than living with impaired vision.

215. *Senile Macular Degeneration*. This term refers to a gradual, irreversible deterioration of the retina that occurs in a few older people. The retina is the sheet of light-sensitive cells wrapped around the back of the eye, and the macula is that section of the retina on which light falls when we are looking directly at something. The macula allows us to make fine discriminations and to identify details—to read, recognize faces, tell time, or thread a needle. When it degenerates, we lose all these abilities, although our peripheral vision is intact and thus we can still get around.

Senile macular degeneration starts as early as the 50s and 60s, progresses gradually, and is common in people in their 80s. Fortunately, many sufferers do not lose all their central vision, and none go on to total blindness. However, it is extremely frustrating for many people and may force them to make radical changes in their life styles. The cause of the degeneration is unknown, although a similar condition occurs in people who suffer from severe diabetes (in fact, all of the common eye conditions of old age—glaucoma, cataracts, and macular degeneration—are found more frequently in diabetics). There is no known effective treatment. For people whose vision is not too profoundly impaired, magnifying glasses, telescopes, and other magnifying devices can be of great help. It is important to assure your parents that they will not completely lose their vision.

216. *Eye Emergencies.* Your parent may experience several eye symptoms which should be evaluated by a physician *immediately*. Not everyone who has one of these symptoms is in immediate danger, but each one of the symptoms may be caused by a condition that could blind your parent. Until the seriousness of the symptom is determined, it should be treated like an emergency.

1. Sudden eye pain. Acute eye pain is usually caused by some problem in the outer eye: a speck of dust, an infection of the eyelid or cornea, an eyelash scraping on the surface of the cornea. These require attention but are not usually medical emergencies. However, an attack of acute glaucoma is a medical emergency which if unattended could result in permanent loss of sight. Hours count. In all of these conditions, the eye suddenly begins to hurt and becomes red. Frequently, though, disorders that affect the eyelids or cornea are particularly painful with blinking, whereas blinking doesn't worsen the pain of acute glaucoma. In any case, take no chances—get your parent to a physician promptly.

2. Sudden loss of vision. This is a most worrisome symptom, since few of its causes are minor. Serious causes vary from blockage of a blood vessel to the eye, to hemorrhage of blood into the inner eye, to a peeling away of the retina from the back of the eye (retinal detachment). Many of these emergencies are due to the fragile and narrowed blood-vessel system found in the elderly and to the fact that diabetes, high blood pressure, and atherosclerosis (hardening of the arteries) are all more common in old age. If your parent suddenly loses sight in one eye, minutes may determine whether or not that loss is permanent.

3. Sudden double vision. The sudden appearance of two objects where one should be is often a frightening symptom. If it develops over minutes or hours (or even days or weeks), your parent should be evaluated by a physician. The symptom may be present continuously or only when your parent looks in a particular direction. In either case, the problem may be serious and should be investigated.

DISORDERS OF THE EYES AND EARS

217. *Problems of the Outer Eye.* Most problems of the eyelids, the cornea, and the whites of the eyes occur at any age, but there are a few conditions that your parents should particularly watch out for.

With age, eyelids begin to droop. This may affect your parent's appearance and thus his self-esteem, and occasionally significant medical problems follow. If the lower eyelid sags outward (ectropion), the delicate inner membrane may become dried, and this may encourage infections and excessive tearing. If the condition is severe, surgery to tighten the lid may be the only solution. If the eyelids turn inward (entropion), the lashes begin to scrape against the eye, causing the cornea to become raw and painful, producing a sense of always having something in the eye, and causing frequent infections. Antibiotics are useful in the short run, but surgery to correct the position of the eyelids is often the only permanent solution.

Many elderly persons gradually develop crusted, reddened eyelids. This common condition, known as chronic blepharitis, is usually due to inadequate washing of the face around the eyes, often occurring in a person who has become less aware of personal hygiene. Because the crusts of dried tears and secretions readily harbor bacteria, infections of the surface of the eye are frequent. This problem is easily solved by administering antibiotic drops for a few days to clear up any infection present and by scrupulously washing around the eyes with soap and water.

Complaints about wet eyes and dry eyes are common in old age. Some elderly people have chronically misty or teary eyes, usually caused by blockage of the tear duct which usually drains the tears that collect in the eye. Cure depends upon finding and treating a cause, such as a chronic tear-duct infection. Problems with dry eyes are equally frequent. The eyes feel dry, burning, scratchy, and as though there were something in them. They are prone to infection. Most people get relief from the use of artificial tears—two or three drops in each eye several times daily.

218. *Improving Your Parent's Vision.* With few exceptions, poor sight can be improved by use of one or more of the many vision aids available. The particular aid, or combination of aids, ideal for your parent depends not only on the specific eye disease and vision loss but also on his interests, activities, and personality. After a careful evaluation to determine which optical aids would be most helpful, he should have a complete explanation of the equipment as well as ample opportunity to try it out. If an elderly person is not comfortable with or does not understand his new tools for sight, he is unlikely to use them, and they will be of little value. In spite of your most vigorous efforts, your parent may be so demoralized and depressed by vision loss that he may lack the motivation to give potentially useful equipment a fair trial. This is more likely if your parent has lost vi-

sion suddenly rather than over years. Keep trying, but consider seeking help for the emotional difficulties.

The variety of aids is so broad and the rules for their use so complicated that only the briefest sketch can be given here. Seek out a qualified specialist for evaluation and prescription. There are books available for the professional which describe the range of equipment. You may want to read a book such as *Management of Low Vision* by Gerald E. Fonda (Thieme-Stratton, Inc., New York, 1981).

The various aids available all focus on improving central vision—little can be done to change damaged peripheral sight such as occurs with advanced glaucoma.

1. There are many different types of glasses, for a variety of purposes. Glasses that magnify for close work can allow your parent to continue reading long after he would otherwise be able to. However, your parent must bear in mind that the stronger the magnification, the closer he will have to be to the paper. Glasses come as bifocals and trifocals. Bioptic telescopic glasses allow your parent to view things at a distance through the upper lens and see more normally through the lower. The major difficulty with telescopic spectacles is that they so narrow the field of vision that your parent can see only what is directly in front—getting around requires continual scanning (turning the head from left to right). Walking becomes unsafe.

2. Numerous magnifiers are available for close work. Most are useful. Handheld magnifying glasses are popular—some even come with a flashlight attached for illumination. They also are sold on stands and as paperweights (the Visolett type sits directly on the page). Paperweight magnifiers have the advantage that they naturally increase the lighting on the page being magnified. An expensive but extremely effective magnifier is closed-circuit TV.

3. Contact lenses are often the most important of all the optical aids. To give maximum benefit, they require careful selection, expert fitting, and scrupulous maintenance. No evaluation of your parent's eyesight is complete without consideration of the possible value of contact lenses.

4. A basic rule of low vision is: the poorer the sight, the brighter the light. Although persons with cataracts are sometimes bothered by glare in bright light, most people who have trouble seeing do much better in strong light. Daylight is ideal, incandescent lights are a close second, and fluorescent lighting is useful but the least desirable.

There are numerous helpful tricks for providing useful lighting. Use nightlights. Keep a flashlight at the bedside. Paint the walls and ceiling a light color. Surround doorknobs and light switches with fluorescent tape.

5. Just as making objects look larger helps, so does using larger ob-

DISORDERS OF THE EYES AND EARS

jects. Your parent may profit from a large-screen TV, large numbers taped to the telephone, and large-print books. Most public libraries have a special section of large-print books, or they can be ordered directly from the publisher. *Reader's Digest* and the *New York Times* come in large-print form. Also, consider books which have been read onto tape cassettes—several companies sell them.

219. *Agencies Providing Information for the Visually Handicapped.* Several agencies provide information about specific eye conditions, lists of low-vision centers, lists of large-print books, or other information about blindness or near-blindness.

American Council of the Blind
1211 Connecticut Ave., N.W., Suite 506
Washington, DC 20036
(202) 833-1251

American Foundation for the Blind
15 West 16th St.
New York, NY 10011
(212) 620-2000

Associated Blind, Inc.
135 W. 23rd St.
New York, NY 10011
(212) 255-1122

Blind Service Association
28 E. Jackson Blvd., Rm. 714
Chicago, IL 60604

Braille Institute
741 N. Vermont Ave.
Los Angeles, CA 90029
(213) 663-1111

National Association for Visually Handicapped
305 East 24th St.
New York, NY 10010
(212) 889-3141

National Society to Prevent Blindness
79 Madison Ave.
New York, NY 10016
(212) 684-3505

Tapes for the Blind
7852 Cole St.
Downey, CA 90242
(213) 923-3388

Volunteer Services for the Blind
919 Walnut St.
Philadelphia, PA 19107
(215) 627-0600

Ears

220. *Hearing Difficulties in Old Age.* Hearing problems are common and can be incapacitating for elderly people. Almost one quarter of people over 65 lose a significant amount of hearing, as do half of those over 85. Deafness is frequently more devastating to our parents than loss of vision. Whereas blindness severely limits what we can do, deafness limits our ability to be who we are. It isolates. Elderly persons with a hearing problem cannot easily share thoughts, feelings, worries, or hopes. Often they do not understand others and are frequently misunderstood. As communication with friends fails, they lose contact with what is happening in their community. As television and radio become garbled and unintelligible, they lose touch with the world. The world becomes a more dangerous place—they don't hear whistles, sirens, or car horns. Life becomes more sterile—the pleasures of music are lost, as are innumerable random sounds like wind-rustled leaves and the cries of birds and children.

Most important, the world becomes less friendly. Friends and family draw away as our parent becomes harder to talk with. Our visits become increasingly easy to postpone when we feel that little can be accomplished or communicated. Although we don't mean to be unkind, talking with an individual who is hard of hearing is difficult, exasperating, and hard work. We both become irritable as our parent becomes dismayed by his own incapacity and sense of losing valued relationships and pleasures. Friends visit less often. Invitations to bridge games come less frequently. Telephone calls are fewer.

As the sounds of life begin to fade, older people often withdraw. They remain at home rather than risk the embarrassment of being publicly misunderstood. Loneliness and depression are the lot of too many deaf elderly. Moreover, a steady diet of garbled sentences and misperceptions can cause suspicion, which often leads to further isolation.

Many hard-of-hearing elderly can have their hearing noticeably improved by a careful medical evaluation followed by appropriate treatment. A complete hearing examination includes testing with an electric audiometer. Because of significant improvement during the last decade in medical therapies, from new surgeries to better hearing aids, your parents no longer need to feel resigned to deafness. Understanding the physical reasons for hearing limitations can relieve anxiety and encourage them to take an active role in planning around those deficits.

221. *How Do We Hear?* To understand the variety of problems that ears develop, it is necessary to understand the anatomy of hearing. The structure of the outer and inner portions of our ears determines what sounds we hear as well as what problems are likely to occur.

Sound waves from the environment are concentrated by the funnel of our outer ear, rush down the ear canal, and pound against the eardrum. The rapidly vibrating eardrum moves the first of three tiny bones (the hammer, anvil, and stirrup) which extend across the bone-encased cavity known as the middle ear. The last bone in this vibrating chain pushes one end of a fluid-filled tube (the cochlea), driving a fluid pressure wave up the tube to stimulate the sensitive hairs which line the way. The hairs lining this tube (the inner ear) are connected to the nerve which carries the signals for hearing to the brain. The exact sound heard depends upon the number of hairs stimulated, and that depends upon the strength of the pressure wave. Anything that interferes with the creation of that wave or with the nervous signal passing to the brain interferes with hearing.

Hearing loss is usually one of two types: conductive loss, in which the outer or middle portion of the ear is affected, and sensorineural loss, in which the cochlea or auditory nerve is at fault. These types of damage present two different sets of problems. Speech composed primarily of low-frequency vowels (*a, e, i, o, u*) would sound like a series of grunts, while a sentence made primarily of high-frequency consonants would be weak but understandable. Generally, conductive loss impairs the hearing of vowels while sensorineural loss affects the hearing of consonants. Thus, if your parent has outer- or middle-ear damage, speech will be fainter but comprehensible to him. In fact, he may be able to understand someone in a noisy room better than you can because he is not bothered as much by the background noise (since most such noise is low-frequency). However, in a quiet room you must speak up if he is to hear you. Inner-ear or sensorineural loss is more incapacitating. Because consonants are not heard well, speech is more likely to be unintelligible. Moreover, the low-frequency sounds tend to be amplified, so your parent hears a cacophony of background noise interspersed with guttural speech. Speaking loudly to your parent adds to the noise but not to the clarity of what he hears.

222. *What Can Go Wrong with Older Ears?* Any older person whose hearing begins to fail should be evaluated carefully—there are many correctable causes of hearing loss. The medical evaluation will attempt to determine whether the problem is due to age-related deterioration of the inner ear (presbycusis), the most common cause of deafness in the elderly (Section 225). To accomplish this, the physician will first make a thorough search for all other possible causes. If the doctor fails to find any other reason for the hearing loss and if the symptoms your parent exhibits are characteristic, he will probably conclude that your parent suffers from presbycusis.

Two initial questions need to be asked: "Is the hearing loss recent?" and, "Does it run in the family?" Deafness beginning in middle age and the deafness caused by inherited conditions tend not to be presbycusis. A third helpful question is: "Does significant loss occur in one ear only?" Such a one-sided problem is usually due to an identifiable, and frequently correctable, cause.

223. *Hearing Loss in the Outer and Middle Ear.* Any blockage of the outer-ear canal can make sounds become more faint. The most common cause is build-up of wax deep in the canal where it is out of sight. The ear canal bends forward and it is impossible to view its end without the help of a special instrument, the otoscope. The physician can instantly restore hearing by looking at the wax through the otoscope and removing it, either by means of a small, long-handled loop, by flushing with water, or by a wax-dissolving solution such as a Cerumenex.

The other major disorder of the outer ear experienced by older people is infection—otitis externa. It is typically caused by either bacteria or fungus. With this condition, your parent usually suffers pain in and drainage from his ears. Since ear canals normally produce a protective layer of oil and wax, infection often begins after too vigorous washing or picking of the canal or after long use of an inadequately cleaned or poorly fitting hearing-aid earmold. Treatment should be prescribed by a physician. Antibiotic eardrops and gentle care are usually successful. The moral is: ears should be clean but not too clean.

The middle ear, with its delicate bones and rigid walls, is an additional source of ear problems and hearing loss. Once again, infection is a culprit. When infected (otitis media), the middle ear fills with debris. Your parent may suffer ear pain, hearing loss, a sense of fullness, and even fluid draining from the ear if the pressure inside pushes a hole in the eardrum. Most occurrences of otitis media can be successfully treated by antibiotics, and at times it heals by itself. Even a ruptured eardrum usually repairs itself with little loss of hearing. What will impair hearing is repeated, severe, poorly treated infections or a chronic infection which damages the fragile internal structures. Although most afflicted elderly individuals are painfully aware of otitis media and seek treatment, the confused or senile elderly person may make no complaint, receive no care, and become deaf.

Otosclerosis is the other major middle-ear disease which afflicts the elderly. It is an inherited condition that usually begins to develop in a person's 20s, although your parent may not notice any hearing loss until decades later. Excess bone gradually forms around the last of the three bones in the middle ear, the stirrup (or stapes), where it joins with the cochlea. When that overgrowth of bone becomes too large, the stapes becomes immobilized and no sound wave is created in the cochlea. Look for evidence that your parent has been losing his hearing gradually throughout middle age. Also check for hearing loss in other family members (including yourself)—in half of all cases someone else in the family is similarly affected. Stapedectomy, a delicate surgical operation in which the stapes is removed and replaced with a tiny wire model, markedly improves hearing in most people.

Outer- and middle-ear diseases primarily impair conductive hearing—the cochlea and auditory nerve are still healthy and functioning. Even if the eardrum or the middle ear is hopelessly damaged, soundwaves are still transmitted to the inner ear through the slight vibrations of the bones of the skull. Thus your parent retains some hearing. Sounds with a prominent vibration, such as those transmitted through a telephone receiver pressed against the head, are easily heard. Such hearing usually can be improved by using an amplifier such as a hearing aid.

224. *Hearing Loss in the Inner Ear.* Much of inner-ear, or sensorineural, deafness occurs early in life—due either to an inherited condition or to damage suffered around the time of birth. If that is the case, your parent will have had hearing loss since childhood. However, there are several causes of sensorineural hearing loss which develop in old age. Some can produce deafness over days or weeks.

1. A few medications can damage the cochlea. The leading offenders include certain diuretics (water pills) such as Lasix and Edecrin; aspirin; some antibiotics (particularly neomycin, kanamycin, streptomycin, and gentamicin); and several metals, such as lead and mercury, that your parent may have been exposed to at work. Often it takes months or years of using these substances to produce damage (except for neomycin). Hearing frequently returns during the weeks or months after the medication

has been stopped. Your parent should be checked for hearing loss if he or she is taking any of these medications.

2. A blow to the head can damage the inner ear. Be suspicious of any hearing loss that follows an accident.

3. Infection can damage the inner ear (labyrinthitis). When that occurs, the center that controls balance, which lies nearby, also becomes affected and your parent may experience dizziness and nausea as well as loss of hearing. If your parent suffers from sudden dizziness and deafness, he should consult a physician.

5. Some chronic medical disorders occasionally produce deafness. The most common offenders are diabetes, rheumatoid arthritis, high blood pressure, and Paget's disease (Section 241).

An increasingly common cause of hearing loss in both the young and old is noise. Although it is possible to be permanently deafened by a single loud noise, such as a gunshot or an explosion, much more common is the loss of hearing suffered by people who have lived or worked in a noisy setting for many years. Your parent is very likely to show some high-frequency deafness after spending a lifetime working around industrial machinery, automobiles, airplanes, guns, or any other source of excessive noise—particularly if he took only minor precautions to guard against damage. Unfortunately, little can be done about this form of hearing loss once it has developed. If your parent avoids further loud noise, however, the loss should not worsen. The history of chronic exposure to noise is important because this type of deafness is almost identical to, and often confused with, that progressive and extremely common form of hearing loss in the elderly, presbycusis.

225. *Presbycusis*. Presbycusis is the most common reason for loss of hearing in old age, and affects about one out of every four people in their 70s. Its cause is unknown—the hearing mechanism may simply wear out or it may be damaged by a lifetime of too much noise, too many medications, or too many illnesses. In presbycusis most of the deterioration is in the sensitive hair-cells of the inner ear, and hearing loss is of the high-frequency, sensorineural type. One caution: as your parent's hearing fails, it is all too easy for everyone, the physician included, to assume that the problem is presbycusis and to search for no further cause. That is a mistake. Other, correctable types of deafness develop in old age and should always be tested for first.

Presbycusis develops slowly, over years, and most often becomes apparent in a person's 50s or 60s, though it may be detected earlier by careful testing with an audiometer. By the 70s a person is usually clearly impaired, although complete deafness is unusual.

With presbycusis, your parent may first notice an irritating inability to hear the high notes on the radio, an ambulance until it passes him, or the sound of a teakettle boiling. These losses, annoying at first, produce real frustration as they spread more widely throughout the higher-frequency sounds. Major impairment begins when your parent can no longer understand speech. Loss of high-frequency hearing creates an inability to hear the higher consonants (*c*, *ch*, *f*, *s*, *sh*, and *z*). Your parent hears speech, but not clearly; sentences become an unintelligible series of vowel sounds (for an example, see Section 42).

You can help your parent understand you by being careful to follow some basic rules. Speak slowly, clearly, carefully, and in low tones. Face your parent so that he can watch your mouth move and see your facial expressions. Move your lips naturally and don't cover your mouth with your hands. Speak slightly louder than usual but don't shout. Say the same thing several different ways so that he can understand you from the context of the sentences. Above all, do not become angry, or your parent may give up.

226. *Hearing Aids and Other Aids to Hearing.* Improvement in hearing often can be achieved through a balanced rehabilitation program. There are many useful techniques and much valuable equipment available that should be considered before concluding that a hearing aid is necessary. Whatever methods are chosen it is always useful to introduce them before your parent's hearing becomes severely impaired. It is much easier to learn lipreading, sign language, or use of a hearing aid while some hearing remains.

Lipreading or speechreading is a convenient and unobtrusive way for your parent to improve the ability to understand conversations, although some elderly people have difficulty mastering it. It is preferable for them to work with a professional trainer and highly desirable for them to begin training before all hearing is gone. Skillful lipreaders make sense of speech which otherwise would be incomprehensible. Sign language, though it is often markedly helpful to deaf children, is usually less useful to older adults. Much specialized equipment is available which can make essential sounds audible to the deaf. Telephones and doorbells can be fitted with loud buzzers, and phones can be equipped with amplifiers. Headphones allow better listening to television and radio. Some clocks can have loud alarms, and both clocks and telephones can be equipped with flashing lights rather than bells. Intercom systems can relay important sounds from one room to another (for example, from the bedroom to the kitchen).

Hearing aids have an undeservedly poor reputation. Too often they are bought at great expense only to be abandoned. Disillusionment sets in when a person finds that a hearing aid does not restore normal hearing—it only makes sounds louder. If speech sounded garbled without a hearing aid, it will probably sound garbled with one. Your parent should always obtain a professional hearing evaluation before deciding to buy a hearing aid. He should consider and try out different kinds. Part of the selection process is scientific and part is personal preference.

Other factors should be taken into account when considering a hearing aid. Inner-ear problems are often not helped by a hearing aid. People with presbycusis find that sounds become louder but not clearer. First-time hearing-aid users are often startled by how noisy it makes the world seem, and they may forsake the instrument in despair. The solution is to select the hearing aid wisely, understand its limits beforehand, and learn to use it correctly through a careful break-in and training period. The earmold must be skillfully fitted and service must be maintained: new batteries must be properly inserted, the earmold cleaned frequently, and the whole system regularly readjusted to your parent's changing needs. With care, practice, and realistic expectations, most hearing-aid users find them a benefit. Unfortunately, the more profound the loss, the less improvement to expect.

227. *Ringing in the Ears (Tinnitus)*. Almost everyone has experienced ringing in the ears. Most people can hear it anytime if they listen closely enough in a quiet room. However, for millions of individuals, it is a serious complaint that interferes with their ability to concentrate and leads them to question their sanity. The sounds heard vary from ringing to popping, buzzing, hissing, clicking, chirping, and roaring. The intensity of the sounds ranges from slight to louder than normal speech.

Significant tinnitus is usually accompanied by some deafness, which, surprisingly, is frequently overlooked by the sufferer. Because your parent focuses so closely on the noise in his ear, he often fails to notice that as the tinnitus has increased, his hearing has worsened. In the majority of cases tinnitus is caused by ear disease. Although just how the disease produces the ringing is unknown, almost any disorder of the eardrum, middle or inner ear, or auditory nerve may be responsible. Many causes are minor; some are significant. If complaints of ringing in the ears persist, your parent should obtain a thorough medical and hearing examination. If ear disease is not uncovered, examination should be done every year or two until the tinnitus is explained.

To cure tinnitus one must first treat the underlying disease. Antibiotics for a chronic ear infection, removal of ear wax, or surgery for otosclerosis often help. Second, a person's hearing should be improved, as that tends to decrease the ringing. Thus your parent should try a hearing aid

DISORDERS OF THE EYES AND EARS

even if he doesn't think that he is hard of hearing. Third, mask noises in the ears to make them more tolerable. For instance, listening to the radio at bedtime may help your parent fall asleep. Tinnitus "maskers" produce a constant tone designed to minimize the noise of tinnitus, and are worn like a hearing aid. Fourth, try a sedative. Although medication is generally ineffective, your parent may benefit from a sedative for a short period of time. Relaxation training, self-hypnosis, and biofeedback are all worth trying if your parent is overly concerned by the problem. Finally, he should be assured that ringing in the ears is not a sign of becoming deaf or going crazy. On the contrary, unless the ear disease is getting worse, most people with tinnitus find that their symptoms gradually improve with time.

228. *Additional Sources of Information for the Hearing-Impaired.* Direct general questions to:

The American Speech-Language-Hearing Association (ASHA)
10801 Rockville Pike
Rockville, MD 20852
(301) 897-5700

Better Hearing Institute
1430 K St., NW, Suite 600
Washington, DC 20005
(202) 638-7577

National Association of the Deaf (NAD)
814 Thayer Ave.
Silver Spring, MD 20910
(301) 587-1788

Obtain information about speechreading from:

The Alexander Graham Bell Association for the Deaf
3417 Volta Pl., N.W.
Washington, DC 20007
(202) 337-5220

Get the names of hearing-aid dealers from:

The National Hearing Aid Society
20361 Middlebelt Rd.
Livonia, MI 48152
(313) 478-2610

For the results of yearly evaluations of hearing aids, write to:

The Veterans Administration
Washington, DC 20420

Sufferers from tinnitus can obtain information from:

American Tinnitus Association
P.O. Box 5
Portland, OR 97207
(503) 248-9985

19.

Joints, Bones, and Muscles

229. *The Skeletal System—A Weak Link*. Most elderly suffer undesirable changes in their joints (rheumatic conditions) and their bones. Slight stiffness, aching in the joints, and decreased flexibility are expected and cause few problems. Other common changes are less tolerable—degeneration of the joints, gout, slipped discs, weakened bones, and fractures. Some diseases, like rheumatoid arthritis, may have afflicted your parents for years; others occur only in the later ages. All these skeletal conditions must be taken seriously, since they can impair your parents' ability to stay active and independent, and thus may remove much of the pleasure from old age.

Proper treatment for joint and bone disorders requires accurate diagnosis. However, the many possible causes for common symptoms, like joint pain and stiffness, sometimes make diagnosis difficult. Also, a disease which appears in an unmistakable form in one person may be unrecognizable in someone else. Thus a firm diagnosis can't always be made until additional symptoms appear. Since treatments may vary markedly from one condition to another, your parent should try to weather the series of tests often required in search of a specific diagnosis. Fortunately, evaluation of rheumatic and bone diseases has become more sophisticated, allowing diagnoses to be made earlier and more accurately.

In addition to the essential history and physical examination, a multitude of blood tests are now available, particularly for rheumatic conditions. Besides X-rays, which are always useful and often essential, there are also a variety of techniques for examining swollen and abnormal joints directly. These include collecting fluid with a needle (arthrocentesis), inspecting the inner surface of the joint by inserting a thin fiberoptic tube (arthrosco-py), and injecting dye into the joint and then taking X-rays (arthrography). In disorders of the back, it is often advisable to inject dye into the space surrounding the spinal cord and then, by X-ray (myelogram), determine if the cord is involved. Finally, complicated tests such as a computerized X-ray (CAT scan) can often give an excellent picture of certain structures like vertebrae.

Although most bone and joint problems among the elderly are chronic or only slowly progressive, a few develop rapidly and are very serious. For example, a swollen, hot, and painful knee may be caused by overuse of an arthritic joint or by gout, but the swelling could also be caused by infection in the knee—if so, the joint may be destroyed without immediate treat-ment. Likewise, a suddenly painful hip may simply be "arthritis," but it could also be the result of an unsuspected fracture. The sudden onset of symptoms suggests a more urgent need for attention; your parents should not delay in seeking treatment for worrisome new symptoms.

Treatments for joint and bone disorders include exercise, heat, medi-cations, surgery, or some combination of these. The specific treatments chosen vary with the type of disease and its severity. However, most chron-ic rheumatoid diseases are treated in part with aspirin or a similar medica-tion. Just because their use is so common, don't underestimate their value. But aspirin-like compounds may be a mixed blessing—used in high doses and over a long time, they may produce irritation or even bleeding of the stomach lining, and may occasionally cause stomach ulcers, skin rashes, and other problems. Since they are often the best treatment available, these compounds should be used when appropriate—but they should be used in the lowest effective doses, and your parents should be alert to side effects. Twelve to fourteen aspirin daily is not an unusual amount for pa-tients suffering from conditions like rheumatoid arthritis.

COMMON SYMPTOMS

230. *Typical Symptoms of Bone and Joint Disease.* Symptoms of bone and joint disorders range from mild aches to severe pain, swollen joints, high fever, and marked tenderness. Although most of these diseases devel-op in typical ways, they may break their own rules as often as they keep them. The same disease may have different symptoms from one person to the next. Moreover, it is sometimes very difficult to determine not only the specific location of the symptom, but even whether the problem is in the bone, the joint, or the surrounding tissues. In collecting information to clarify the problem, it is important to notice whether there are general symptoms such as fever, chills, or whole-body aching. Is anything swol-

len? Does the problem feel like it is in the joint? Is more than one joint involved? Does it hurt to move? Is your parent too stiff to move? Does the stiffness worsen or improve as the day wears on? From the answers to these and other questions, the doctor is able to narrow the number of possible conditions that could be causing your parent's symptoms.

231. *Joint Pain.* Four basic questions need answers here. Has the pain developed over the past several days or has it been developing gradually for weeks, months, or years? Are one or two joints involved or are many of them painful? Which joints are affected? Have other problems developed along with the painful joints, such as hot, swollen joints, fever, muscle aches, or a skin rash? Finding an explanation for your parent's joint pain is often difficult, but there are some rules of thumb. If one joint has suddenly become swollen and painful, the cause is more likely to be gout, injury, or acute infection. If one or two joints have become more painful over months or years, suspect degenerative joint disease. If many joints have become simultaneously swollen and painful, usually over days or weeks, rheumatoid arthritis is likely, particularly if your parent is also feeling feverish and sick. With answers to these questions the physicians may have some initial impressions, but the diagnosis will still depend on a careful physical examination and various laboratory and X-ray evaluations, as described for the specific diseases later in this chapter.

232. *Hip Pain.* Pain in the hip has a multitude of causes, most of which can usually be identified by a careful physical examination, X-rays, and laboratory blood tests. Pain and stiffness which develop over years are probably due to degenerative joint disease. If the problem appears suddenly or within several days, the cause is more likely to be gout, infection, or a fracture. If both hips are involved, rheumatoid arthritis should be suspected. Finally, sometimes cancer of another part of the body can locate in bone, and hip pain may be the first indication that the cancer is present. Pain which steadily worsens over weeks should be evaluated.

233. *Back Pain.* Most older people have back pain. Usually it is not severe, but occasionally it is incapacitating. Back pain typically comes in two varieties: a dull aching of the lower back which may extend around the sides or into one or both buttocks or partway down a leg, and a sharp, lightning-like pain which may shoot down a leg. The sharp pain usually means that one of the nerves which leaves the spinal cord through the backbone has been squeezed by an overgrowth of bone or by a vertebral disc. Either type of pain, or a combination of the two, can be caused by a number of different back disorders.

The backbone, a complicated stack of vertebrae, has many weak links where trouble can begin. Because the lower back carries most of the upper body's weight over a lifetime of twisting and turning, it is most frequently affected. Each of the many vertebrae is separated from the others by a disc of soft cartilage and by two joints. Problems are usually due to the gradual deterioration of this system. The vertebral edges and connections may become worn, deformed, painful and stiff, and may develop bony spurs—all characteristic of that most common cause of back pain in the aging, degenerative joint disease, or osteoarthritis. On the other hand, the discs may deteriorate over time and slowly produce pain by bulging from between the vertebrae, or they may create acute pain by suddenly pushing out from between the bones—a ruptured or slipped disc. The bones provide a third weak link, since they frequently become more porous with age, either through loss of calcium (leading to the condition known as osteoporosis) or through a bone disorder like Paget's disease (Section 241). These weak, porous bones often collapse, producing pain and actually causing your parent to become shorter.

Any rapid worsening of chronic back pain should be evaluated by a physician. It usually means that one of these slow degenerative conditions has taken a sudden step in the wrong direction, and treatment may be necessary. It may also indicate that one of the other less common, but very serious, causes for back pain is present, such as cancer in the bone or an infection in one of the joints or disc spaces.

Treatment for back pain begins with a careful evaluation, since the specific treatment depends upon what condition is responsible. Some acute conditions require surgery. A few may require immediate antibiotics. More commonly, back pain is chronic and a regular program of treatment should be worked out with the help of your parent's physician. These programs frequently require regular exercise, weight loss for those who are obese, heat treatment, massage, relaxation exercises, and possibly self-hypnosis or biofeedback. Potentially harmful activities like contact sports, skiing, and horseback riding may have to be avoided, while swimming and walking are usually encouraged. Aspirin and other mild analgesics may be of value for short periods of time, as may the periodic use of braces and traction. Finally, some surgical procedures may help relieve specific causes of chronic backache, but these should not be attempted until more conservative treatments have been thoroughly tried.

DISEASES OF THE JOINTS

Joint diseases in the elderly include the serious conditions of rheumatoid arthritis, osteoarthritis (degenerative joint disease), and polymyalgia rheumatica, as well as the less serious but thoroughly troublesome conditions of gout, bursitis, and spondylosis.

234. *Rheumatoid Arthritis.* Although most people who develop the chronic joint disease rheumatoid arthritis do so in their middle adult years, some individuals don't encounter the first symptoms until old age. Though not nearly as frequent after the age of 65 as degenerative arthritis (osteoarthritis), it is both common and serious. Modern treatment may help prevent the frequently associated crippling and deformities, but a cure is not yet in sight.

Rheumatoid arthritis usually begins slowly, over weeks or months. Your parent may feel weak and tired and may be slightly feverish. Joints and muscles begin to ache and stiffen—particularly the joints of the fingers, wrist, and feet but also those of the knees and hips. Affected joints gradually become swollen and warm, lose flexibility, and may assume unnatural positions. Marked stiffness and difficulty getting around in the morning, which gradually works itself out but which returns after vigorous exercise, is characteristic. This acute form of rheumatoid arthritis may continue for a long time or may improve, only to return in weeks or months. One in four persons who develop the disease in old age, though, have a much more stormy course in which all of the symptoms occur more rapidly and are more severe.

Whether rheumatoid arthritis begins slowly or quickly, it is chronic and prone to complications. Although one quarter of affected people may have minor symptoms, most can expect some degree of joint swelling, pain, and stiffness off and on for years. It is a lifelong illness. With time, complications may develop. Particularly dreaded are permanently deformed and painful joints and frozen, unusable fingers and limbs. These are more common if the disease is exceptionally severe, but can occasionally be avoided by meticulous, long-term treatment.

Because there are a number of complex and confusing diseases which resemble rheumatoid arthritis but which differ considerably in prognosis and treatment, it is essential to try to make an accurate diagnosis in order to improve the specificity of treatment. When all the classic symptoms are present, it is usually easy to make the diagnosis, but at other times several specific laboratory tests prove invaluable. Although an X-ray examination is useful, the most telling changes occur in the blood. Expect the physician to check the blood for an abnormal erythrocyte sedimentation rate (ESR), for the presence of "rheumatoid factor" (by a latex-fixation test), and for anemia—all three routinely occur in rheumatoid arthritis. Although no single test proves that rheumatoid arthritis is or is not present, combinations of abnormal results are very suggestive. If there is any question, the doctor frequently will sample the fluid in a swollen joint (arthrocentesis) and even take a small piece of tissue (biopsy) from the surface of the joint. Chemical and microscopic evaluation of these samples help exclude other conditions. Occasionally, the diagnosis remains uncertain and the physician must wait for symptoms to change before the disease tips its hand. If your parent's condition continues to appear vague and complicated, consider consulting a specialist in this area, a rheumatologist. Once the diagnosis is clear, proper treatment can begin.

There is no cure for rheumatoid arthritis. Your parent must expect to wrestle with it for many years. Treatment over those years focuses on controlling the acute episodes, promoting good functioning between episodes, and preventing complications. Fortunately, with proper care, symptoms can usually be controlled and your parent can expect to continue leading an active life. Success is dependent on a close working partnership between your parent and his physician and on your parent's willingness to participate actively in his own care—without daily and hourly attention to treatment by your parent, the doctor's efforts are seriously handicapped. The goals of treatment which can realistically be attained by many people include decreased joint pain and swelling, increased joint flexibility and muscle strength, limited permanent damage, and improved ability to perform daily tasks. Treatment is two-pronged—physical care and medication. Both are essential. Physical care, such as exercise and heat, is difficult to apply without the control of pain and swelling by medication. Likewise, even with medication, the joints gradually stiffen and become immobile without proper physical care.

Physical treatments proven to be useful in controlling or restoring function in the arthritic patient include a careful balance of exercise and rest plus the use of massage, heat and cold, and splinting. Each person requires an individually tailored schedule of physical treatments. Because the wrong kind or amount of physical therapy or the right treatment done at the wrong time can be exceptionally harmful, your parent's treatment plan must be developed with the help of his physician. The doctor may wish to consult an expert in this area, a physiatrist (a physician who is an expert in physical medicine and rehabilitation) or a physical therapist. However the specific schedule is created, several general rules should be followed by anyone suffering from rheumatoid arthritis.

1. Do not exercise an acutely painful, inflamed joint. It has no beneficial effect and is clearly destructive to joint tissue. Rest the joint instead,

baby it, but avoid prolonged bed rest. Preserve function in the acutely swollen joint by gently moving it through its full range of motion two or three times each day.

2. Exercise less acute joints regularly and gently unless it increases inflammation or prolongs pain. Always strike a *comfortable* balance between rest and exercise. Which joints and muscles to concentrate on should be decided with a physician's help. Isometric exercises (tensing, without movement) often are best.

3. Splints designed to keep the fingers, wrists, and knees in a natural position (worn at night or during the day) help prevent contractions. Canes and walkers may be invaluable in getting around, but walking should not be encouraged during flare-ups of the disease.

4. Apply heat to troublesome joints—it often decreases pain and increases flexibility. Try warm baths or showers, an electric blanket in the morning, or a heat lamp (be careful of burns). Cold water, curiously, may help some people.

5. Arrange for a deep, gentle massage. A family member may be trained to do this.

6. Lose weight if necessary.

All of these treatments can usually be done at home. Is a family member willing and available? If not, is there a local visiting nurse program? Question the physician or the local Arthritis Foundation about possible help. An additional valuable source of specific hints for living a more active life is *The Arthritis Helpbook* by K. Lorig and J. Fries (Addison-Wesley Pub. Co., 1980).

All those with active rheumatoid arthritis should receive medication. Of the many effective drugs available, the most common ones decrease the inflammation of swollen joints and, in so doing, decrease the pain and allow freer movement. Unfortunately, not all of the medications work for everyone, most do not control the underlying destructive changes of the disease, and all are limited by their side effects. Expect the physician to choose one medication for a trial and, if it fails, to try another and then another. Trial and error remains the best way to identify the drug which is right for your parent. Don't become discouraged if a trial seems to drag on forever—a month or more often may be needed to see an effect. The most commonly used drug is aspirin; it is usually the first medication tried in anyone who has developed arthritis, and it may be the only medication needed. If aspirin proves ineffective, the doctor usually proceeds along a chain of drugs with increasing side effects, beginning with those known as nonsteroidal anti-inflammatory agents (for example, Motrin, Nalfon, Naprosyn, Clinoril, Tolectin, or Indocin), then gold compounds (Solganal, Myochrysine), and then antimalaria drugs (chloroquine, penicillamine). A few new medications (like benoxaprofen and piroxicam) may be as effective as aspirin but have fewer side effects. Or they may be most effective in combination with aspirin. The last step is usually steroid therapy—effective but problem-fraught. Once a person's illness has been controlled with steroids, it is often difficult for that person to do without them, and the serious side effects of chronic steroid use, like stomach ulcers and weakened bones, become major problems. However, if most of the arthritic problems come from one or two joints, steroids may be effective and safe if injected directly into those joint spaces, as long as they are used no more than several times each year. Throughout treatment with any of these medications, the goal is to produce the best improvement with the smallest dose of the safest drug.

One final treatment, surgery, may be useful after all else fails. Successful replacement of an unusable hip with an artificial one has become common, and it is likely that replacement of other severely crippled joints will become routine in the future.

Rheumatoid arthritis may dramatically change your parent's style of living. He or she may need extra help around the house. The physical layout of the home may need many special changes like larger handles on cupboards, ramps in place of stairs, additional railings beside the bathtub, and easy-to-open medication bottles. Your parent's emotional health requires particular attention, since depression and withdrawal are common responses. And yet, arthritis also represents an opportunity to succeed—to best a debilitating disease through one's own efforts.

235. *Gout.* Gout, the butt of many jokes but actually a serious joint disease, usually develops during middle age but continues to be a problem in old age. Crystals of the chemical urate form in the joint fluid and cause both acute attacks of pain and gradual deterioration of the joint. Acute attacks begin with sudden redness, swelling, heat, and extreme pain in the larger joint of the big toe or in the wrist, knee, or ankle. Usually there is no obvious cause, but occasionally the attack may be set off by a blow to the joint, too much food and drink, a medication like penicillin, a diuretic (water pill), or a sudden illness. Attacks often become more frequent over the years and, if not treated aggressively, will ultimately produce irreversible damage to the affected joints. Accurate diagnosis is essential, since there is a very effective and specific treatment for gout which is of little value for those conditions which occasionally mimic gout, like rheumatoid arthritis, degenerative joint disease, and joint infections. In addition to the presence of characteristic symptoms and an increase of urate in the blood, diagnosis usually requires identification of urate crystals in a sample of joint fluid. Indocin, Butazolidin, Motrin, and several other drugs are very effective in

treating acute attacks. Different medication, like probenecid (Benemid) or alopurinol (Zyloprim), is usually required if your parent has recurring attacks. These drugs do not control acute attacks, but they do prevent new attacks. As with rheumatoid arthritis, your parent needs to become actively involved in caring for his own joints, since that provides the best assurance that function will be preserved.

Pseudogout, a closely related condition also marked by crystals in the joints, develops primarily in old age. It has similar but less severe symptoms, requires a needle sample of joint fluid to diagnose, and frequently does not respond as well as gout to medication. Pseudogout is often caused by a serious illness like diabetes or hyperparathyroidism.

236. *Polymyalgia Rheumatica.* This condition occurs primarily in the elderly, appears suddenly, is easily treated, and can have extremely serious consequences if untreated.

What should you look for? Think of this disease if your parent complains of stiffness, sore muscles, or aching joints of the shoulders or hips. It may appear so suddenly that your parent goes to bed feeling fine, only to awaken the next morning barely able to move, or it may develop over weeks. The primary symptom is shoulders that are extremely stiff, painful, and tender first thing in the morning but which gradually improve as the morning wears on. The hips may be similarly affected, with pain being felt primarily in the buttocks, groin, and thighs. These symptoms are always worse in the morning or after a period of lying or sitting during the day. Those affected feel sick, have a slight fever, lose interest in food, and may begin to lose weight. Although it feels like the muscles are to blame, the disease probably lies in the joints or in the small arteries that supply the muscles. Diagnosis is not made by one specific test but is suggested by a typical cluster of symptoms, an abnormal result on the blood test called the erythrocyte sedimentation rate (ESR), and a mild anemia. Treatment is the final proof—polymyalgia rheumatica almost always improves dramatically within one week of starting steroids (like prednisone). If there is no change, the doctor will probably look for another explanation for the symptoms.

The consequences of failing to recognize and treat this condition are real and severe. Twenty percent of people with untreated polymyalgia rheumatica ultimately develop an inflammation of one of the arteries to the head. Symptoms that suggest that this complication is developing include headaches, extreme tenderness of the scalp above the ear, and pain in the jaw muscles. Worst of all, permanent blindness can result if treatment is delayed. Fortunately, with steroid treatment blindness can be avoided altogether.

237. *Bursitis.* Although a person of any age can develop bursitis, the elderly certainly have their fair share of problems with it. A bursa is a small sack with slippery walls located between muscles or between muscles and bone which allows these structures to slip freely across one another as a person moves. There are dozens of bursae located throughout the body in places of movement like the shoulders, elbows, knees, and ankles. Bursitis is the painful inflammation of a bursa and usually develops suddenly after trauma to the area or after the muscles around the bursa have been strained and overused. However, often it begins "out of the blue." Although the typical symptom is pain when trying to bend the knee or raise the arm at the shoulder, the region around the affected bursa may be hot, swollen, and tender as well. Usually the symptoms disappear in several days with rest, hot packs, massage, and strict avoidance of the activities that produced the bursitis. If symptoms are particularly severe or if they last longer than a couple of days, a physician should be consulted, since other conditions such as gout, muscle or tendon tears, or rheumatoid arthritis can sometimes mimic or accompany bursitis. Aspirin or a similar medication may help relieve your parent's symptoms during the first day or two, but should not be necessary very long.

238. *Degenerative Joint Disease (Osteoarthritis).* With passing years, joints deteriorate. A careful X-ray examination would probably already show signs of wear and tear in some of your joints and almost certainly would provide evidence of degeneration in those of your parents. This degeneration is so common as to be considered almost normal among the elderly. Fortunately, most joint deterioration is without symptoms; pain and other problems occur in only about one quarter of the elderly. Even at that, degenerative joint disease, or osteoarthritis, is the most common disorder of the joints in old age. Although occasionally confused with other joint diseases like gout or rheumatoid arthritis, osteoarthritis is a chronic condition which can usually be recognized long before it causes serious problems. And since it develops slowly, over years, there is often ample time to make changes in habits and activities which may prevent its progression.

Some people appear to inherit a tendency to develop osteoarthritis, but, for most people, the reasons their joints deteriorate are not clear. It used to be thought that joints just wore out with normal use, but that view has had to be modified since many people who exercise vigorously throughout their lives do not develop joint problems. There probably needs to be some element of trauma to the joint, as in an exercise that repeatedly strikes the joint from an abnormal direction or in the exercising of a joint which fits together poorly. Joints that experience excessive use or trauma throughout life are at risk to wear out quickly and become painful—the knees of a football player, the ankles of a ballet dancer, the hips of someone very fat, or the wrists and elbows of the jackhammer operator. Often your parent can identify the particular activity which appears to have caused his specific problems. Sometimes a single trauma is all that is necessary to start the process—the joint of a stubbed finger becomes more painful and stiff with the years. Any joint disease, like an infection or rheumatoid arthritis, can lead to similar long-term problems. Once a joint becomes irregular or roughened, the rate of wear increases and symptoms become more likely.

When symptoms appear, your parent may first notice mild aching and stiffness in one or two joints. These are likely to be finger joints, a hip, the knees, a wrist, or an ankle. Occasionally, the aching may be in the neck or the small of the back. Later, the aching may worsen into outright pain deep in the joint. The joint is most likely to stiffen, but may swell and become tender as well. By this point, the cartilage which lines the inside surface of the joints has worn thin, and stiff fibrous tissue or bony spurs may have developed at the edges of the joint. The fingers may look gnarled—some of the joints may become decorated with hard, bony lumps. It may be difficult to pick up a heavy object due to pain in the wrist or to shake hands due to finger pain. Your parent may limp from pain in the hip or have difficulty rising from a chair or walking because of knee pain. The joints may feel, and be, unstable and may make crackling sounds with motion. The back of your parent's neck may hurt, the neck may become stiff, or shooting pains may develop in the arms as a vertebral spur compresses a nerve. There may be stiffness after rest or periods of inactivity which rapidly disappears as he gets up and moving. Unlike in rheumatoid arthritis, in osteoarthritis the pain worsens with exercise, improves markedly with rest, and morning stiffness lasts for a few minutes rather than for an hour or more. And all of these problems are limited to a few problem joints. Without proper care, the joints gradually become enlarged, deformed, and immobile. Although your parent may not be seriously impaired if only the fingers are involved, he can be crippled if the knees or a hip is compromised.

Osteoarthritis is generally easy to recognize but may be confused with rheumatoid arthritis if several of the larger finger joints are simultaneously affected, or with gout if a joint flares up suddenly. The only blood tests that will help the physician are those which test for the presence or absence of other diseases. The diagnosis is usually confirmed by the combination of typical symptoms and X-rays of the painful joints which show characteristic narrowing of the joint spaces and fibrous, bony spurs around the joint.

Occasionally it becomes necessary to sample the joint fluid—in degenerative joint disease it is usually normal but may contain fragments of cartilage.

With medication and a sensible life style, most people do well. Much can be done to improve the symptoms of osteoarthritis, although the damage already done to the joint cannot be reversed. Medication should be avoided in mild cases. If osteoarthritis causes significant pain or loss of function, the medications found most useful are mild anti-inflammatory drugs with pain-relieving qualities, like aspirin. Two aspirin, three to five times each day, usually decrease both the swelling and pain, but other medications such as Indocin, Butazolidin, Mortrin, Naprosyn, or Clinoril may be beneficial if aspirin fails. A new medication, diflunisal, shows promise of being safer and more effective than aspirin. The muscle spasms that occasionally accompany an acutely painful joint can often be helped by a muscle relaxant like Valium or Robaxin, taken for a *short* period of time. Although the steroid therapy used in rheumatoid arthritis is both ineffective and too risky in osteoarthritis, steroid injections into troublesome joints may be of some help. The physician should decide which joints are likely to respond—generally the small joints (fingers, wrist, ankle) improve with injections while the knee and hip do not.

Sensible care of the joints is usually more important than medication. They should be protected. A parent with osteoarthritis should avoid injuring a painful joint and should heed the warnings of increasing pain and fatigue. If fingers or wrists are affected, your parent should avoid heavy lifting, scrubbing, or other activities of the arms or hands which cause pain. If ankles, knees, or hips are painful, he should minimize walking or climbing stairs. Resting in bed or on a couch for an hour each day is often helpful if the problems are in the hips or knees. Free use should be made of such supportive equipment as canes, walkers, and wheelchairs. While protecting joints from additional injury, it is essential to continue to exercise limbs in order to keep muscles strong. This can usually be done safely by isometric exercises or by moving the extremities without any weight or resistance. The physician can help your parent develop a beneficial and safe exercise program. Frequently, exercises are made easier by hot packs, a warm shower, a whirlpool, or by the use of ultrasound. If your parent is heavy, he or she should lose weight. The goal in any physical therapy program is two-fold: to avoid further injury to the joints, and to maintain joint flexibility and muscle strength. If the muscles become weak, the joint becomes more unstable, which leads to the vicious cycle of greater joint injury and worsened disease. With sensible treatment your parent can expect additional years of use from osteoarthritic joints.

Occasionally there may be one or two large fragments of bone or carti-

lage loose in a joint. These may be removed surgically (debridement), in-
stantaneously returning function to that joint. However, there may come a
time when, despite his best efforts, your parent is incapacitated by a frozen, painful joint. But even then all is not lost. A dramatic improvement
can often be achieved by surgically replacing a deformed, deteriorated
joint with an artificial one. Most of the success has been with hip replacement and, recently, replacement of the knee. Insertion of artificial finger
and wrist joints is not yet common. If a deteriorating hip or knee has
caused your parent to become confined to his house, wheelchair, or bed,
discuss the possibility of an artificial joint with a surgeon—it often can provide a new lease on an active life for him.

239. *Cervical Spondylosis and Lumbar Spondylosis.* Spondylosis is present in two thirds of older people. As the vertebral discs deteriorate, bony
spurs develop around the edges of the vertebrae. This condition, spondylosis, usually causes no symptoms. Occasionally, however, if the spurs are
too large or in the wrong location, serious problems may result. Spurs in
the lower back may produce low back pain, shooting pains in the legs, or
muscle weakness in the lower back and legs. Bladder control may be lost as
the spurs press on the nerves which lead to the bladder. The most common
symptoms of spurs on the neck vertebrae include a painful, stiff neck and
pain and weakness in the arms. X-rays of the neck or lower back along with
a myelogram or CAT scan to look at the spinal cord usually allow an accurate diagnosis. These bony growths usually slowly enlarge and the symptoms may gradually worsen. Occasional traction at home may help the
symptoms, and wearing a cervical collar frequently improves neck and
arm pain. If the symptoms become too constant and too limiting, surgery is
usually recommended.

DISEASES OF THE BONES

240. *Osteoporosis.* Osteoporosis, the presence of normal-looking but porous and weakened bones, is the most common skeletal problem of older
people. The bones have a normal size, shape, and appearance—only the
quantity of calcium has changed. Several million older people are affected,
and older women are particularly at risk—one of every three suffers from it.
In all of us, calcium is constantly washed from bone to blood and then re-
plenished by the calcium we eat. However, over the years, the loss exceeds
the gain. A loss severe enough to make the bones fragile and prone to
breaking is called osteoporosis. Falls with subsequent fractures are the
leading cause of accidental death in older women. Presumably, if we lived
long enough, we all would have osteoporosis. Unfortunately, this condition

seems to be irreversible. Once bones become weakened by loss of calcium, they are unlikely to recover, and the most we can hope for is to prevent them from losing any more material or strength.

It is not known why this normal thinning of bone proceeds more rapidly in some people. Osteoporosis is most common in small women, which suggests that, because they had less total calcium to start with, they have less to lose to reach worrisomely low levels. Female hormones clearly are involved, because calcium loss typically accelerates after menopause. Also, since calcium is poorly absorbed by older people, they need more calcium in the diet than younger people. Thus osteoporosis is very likely to occur in people who avoid calcium-containing foods like dairy products. In addition to sex, physical size, and diet, a fourth contributing factor is probably the reduced physical activity of many older people. It is well known that any type of immobilization, such as that imposed by a plaster cast or a brace or forced bedrest, will quickly cause calcium to disappear from the rested bones. Finally, although some mixture of these causes accounts for most osteoporosis, other factors can help produce it and must be checked for: thyroid disease, diabetes, chronic alcohol use, steroid medication, and possibly heavy cigarette smoking. Some other serious illnesses, such as bone cancer, may initially mimic osteoporosis; evaluation should not be delayed.

Unfortunately, osteoporosis usually goes unrecognized for many years until a fracture appears. Since the bones first and most severely affected are usually the vertebrae in the middle and small of the back, the most common initial symptom is a severe backache that occurs when one of these vertebrae partially collapses into itself. This is typically not a sharp pain, but rather a constant dull ache or a tired feeling in the back which gets better with rest but which worsens with any kind of stress or activity like walking, standing, bending, or lifting. Twisting and turning may become difficult as the muscles beside the fracture tighten. Because the bones are already weakened, the most minor trauma, like lifting a twenty-five-pound sack of sugar, may cause the bone to break. The pain usually goes away after several months, but may last as long as a year, and may return if further fracturing occurs in the same, or a nearby, bone. After repeated fractures of the vertebrae, a hump gradually develops between the shoulder blades where the bones can no longer hold the back straight. Also, your parent may lose several inches in height because the bones of the back have become flattened. Another bone that may be severely affected, the thigh bone, presents a much more serious problem. If the narrow neck of this bone where it enters the hip becomes thin and fragile, even a minor fall or blow may produce a fractured hip. This particularly dangerous fracture in older people has been treated in the past with prolonged

JOINTS, BONES, AND MUSCLES

immobilization in the hospital, which too frequently has led to muscle weakness, pneumonia, blood clots, and weakness of other bones throughout the body. It is more common now for the physician to get the elderly person up and moving at the first opportunity in order to prevent these complications.

It would be extremely useful to be able to spot developing osteoporosis before the first fracture, but this is not currently possible. There are usually no early symptoms. The diagnosis of osteoporosis is usually made by noticing thinned bones on X-ray in someone who has already had a bone break. However, by the time bones begin to look weak on X-rays, they usually have lost up to 50 percent of their calcium. Moreover, there are no specific blood tests with which to diagnose osteoporosis. It is possible to get information by sampling the bones directly with a small needle (a bone biopsy), but that is usually done only after symptoms appear. In short, there is no reliable way to make the diagnosis early, and we are relegated to suspicion: looking for the condition in women who are small-boned, who passed through menopause several years before, who are sedentary, and who don't eat well. However, a new radiological technique called quantitative computed tomography (CAT) of the limbs and spine shows real promise in early detection of people at risk. It is not available everywhere—ask the physician.

How can you treat a condition which you can't know is present until significant damage has been done? Since most people have sustained a fracture by the time they visit a doctor, the first order of business is usually to treat that fracture. Except for serious breaks, like that of the thigh, little treatment is required. The vertebrae generally sink into themselves, hurt for a while, and then cause no more trouble, except that the back has now changed shape. Only a few elderly individuals experience so much pain and muscle tightness that they need treatment. Mild pain medication, heat, massage, and specific exercises are generally effective and usually are necessary for only a month or two. The more important question is how to prevent further calcium loss in people who are at risk for osteoporosis as well as in those who already have damage.

The gradual weakening of bone with age may be substantially slowed in most people by several simple practices.

1. The diet should contain ample calcium. Ideally, we should begin to focus on calcium when we are still middle-aged rather than waiting for symptoms of calcium loss to appear. The standard recommended adult daily allowance is probably not enough for the elderly—they should eat 1,500 mg of calcium (roughly the equivalent of eight ounces of hard cheese or six 8-ounce glasses of milk). Since a normal American diet contains approximately 600–800 mg of calcium, your parents must carefully plan their diet

to be assured of eating enough calcium. All dairy products contain it, as do beans, broccoli, cauliflower, kale, rhubarb, beets, turnip greens, sardines, shell fish, and almonds. Calcium tablets are also available in many stores, and your parents may prefer to take one or two each day, particularly if they feel they are consuming the entire vegetable garden just to eat enough calcium. A standard daily amount is one gram of calcium carbonate (for example, two Tums has one gram) divided among three meals, but, since calcium carbonate may produce constipation, calcium gluconate may be substituted.

One additional dietary caution is in order. It has recently been shown that excessive protein in the diet causes calcium loss from the body. Although your parents need adequate protein, too much may do them more harm than good.

2. Estrogen therapy should be considered. Replacement of female hormones (estrogens) slows down calcium loss. However, taking estrogens can be risky and must always be discussed with a physician. They increase the risk of cancer of the uterus, stroke, and heart attack and they may produce high blood pressure. They should always be taken in the smallest useful dose, and the benefits and risks of long-term use should be thoughtfully weighed. Usually they are taken in cycles of three consecutive weeks with a week's break in between or with the use of progesterone (another female sex hormone) during the break. Vaginal bleeding can be expected at the end of each cycle.

3. Regular physical exercise should be part of everyone's program to prevent osteoporosis. Walking and swimming are particularly valuable. Anything that contributes to lack of exercise should be avoided, if possible—like bed rest, casts, braces, or just "taking it easy until I recover."

4. Other substances can be added to the diet which may be effective in preventing calcium loss. Vitamin D (50,000 IU weekly) and fluoride (50 mg daily) appear to be most useful. Because Vitamin D is synthesized when sunlight strikes the skin, older people who are house-bound are most likely to benefit from vitamin supplements. The usefulness of sodium fluoride has not yet been proven, and it should be used only after a discussion with the physician.

5. Other habits which appear to contribute to bone weakening, like excessive alcohol use or smoking, should be curtailed.

241. *Paget's Disease.* Paget's disease is a bone disorder of unknown cause which is rare in younger people but which afflicts one of every ten people in their 80s. The bones of the hip, skull, back, and sometimes throughout the skeleton show patches where the bone material is being

destroyed and other areas where new bone is being deposited. The result is often moth-eaten-appearing bone which is very weak in places.

In many people the process progresses quietly and is discovered only when they have an X-ray for some other reason. In others, there is intense bone pain, fractures of the weakened bone, and obvious deformities. As in osteoporosis, the first symptom may be a fracture of a vertebra, but often the person with Paget's disease experiences considerably more pain. Also, as bones break and become deformed, they often press on nearby structures and produce symptoms like deafness, dizziness, headaches, pains in the legs, weakness, and pains in the joints. Finally, a most worrisome complication which affects 5 to 10 percent of people with severe Paget's disease is the development of osteogenic sarcoma, a particularly dangerous type of bone cancer. If a person is going to be troubled with symptoms from Paget's disease, problems will usually appear before age 70.

The doctor can generally make the diagnosis without difficulty, since the X-rays have a typical appearance of "holes" in some parts of bone and dense areas in other places where new bone is being laid down. A chemical in the blood, alkaline phosphatase, and one in the urine, hydroxyproline, are often abnormally high as well. If there is any question that one of the bones has developed cancer, a needle biopsy of the bone is the immediate next step.

Treatment, which used to be of little value, has recently become successful for most people because of the development of three medications: calcitonin (Calcimar), EHDP (Didronel), and mithramycin (Mithracin). All three produce remissions in the majority of people, and if one of the three is ineffective another may be tried. Usually, the pain rapidly disappears and some of the complications like dizziness and weakness improve as well. Throughout the course of the disease it is necessary to be alert for any change which might signal the onset of cancer. In some patients in whom the pain in a particular bone is not controlled by medication, and in all patients who develop cancer, surgical removal is necessary.

242. *Fractures.* As noted above, the loss of calcium over a lifetime produces osteoporosis—porous bones which may break with even minor blows or falls. The bones of the spine and those that make up the wrist, hip, and knee fracture easily. This is particularly true of women, whose bones are weaker. Such fractured bones, especially the hip, have a deservedly bad reputation—fifty years ago, four out of every five elderly people with a broken hip died. That is no longer true. Today most fractures can be treated successfully because of advances in surgical technique, like artificial joints and bone glue, and because of improvements in medical care, like

effective antibiotics and the practice of getting a person active soon after surgery. A serious fracture in an elderly individual is no longer the beginning of the end—in many cases that person can expect to return to near-normal levels of function.

Two fractures require special attention—the hip and the knee. Two thirds of all hip fractures occur in the elderly, usually after falls. Because an older person is more likely to be unstable on his feet than someone younger, falls are more frequent. The fracture usually occurs in the knob and shaft at the upper end of the thigh bone, the femur, where it fits into the hip joint. Because this segment of bone has a very poor blood supply, healing is slow. In days past, when convalescence was long, deaths were common—usually due to the many complications that occur when an elderly person is bedridden, such as blood clots, blood infections, and pneumonia. The much more successful modern treatment is to repair the hip surgically within the first twenty-four hours if possible, using either an internal metal support through the fracture or an artificial ball and shaft. In either case, the patient can be active and exercising within several days. There are also a variety of successful operations available for treating a fractured knee, and several different artificial parts which can be used. As in the repair of a hip, success depends on getting a person up and active as soon as possible following surgery.

DISEASES OF MUSCLE

243. *Diseases of Muscle.* Not all old-age aches and pains are caused by skeletal conditions; some originate in the muscles. Many older individuals have allowed themselves to slip into such poor physical condition through lack of exercise that their muscles protest at the slightest effort. In addition, older muscles and tendons are more susceptible to strains than are younger ones—the elderly must warm up longer before exercising if they are to avoid pulling a muscle. The remedy for these common causes of muscle aches is simple—a sensible daily exercise program.

Because some muscular weakness is due to treatable medical causes, an evaluation should be sought if weakness or shrinking of muscles develops over a short period of time. The rule is: if there is a significant, unexplained recent change, check it out. However, the most common causes for recent weakness are conditions which keep your parent from being active, such as a broken bone or sore joints.

20.

Diseases of the Brain

Our nervous system remains reliable throughout life in spite of the tremendous demands for performance and flexibility we make on it. Memory, reasoning, and reflexes function more slowly with age, but continue to function well. With three or four exceptions, diseases afflict the brain and nerves infrequently, and are the same disorders that can strike at any age. However, the few exceptions are of enormous significance: Parkinson's disease, stroke, and senility. (Because senility is complex, common, and profoundly disabling, it is discussed separately in Chapter 11.)

PARKINSON'S DISEASE

With the exception of stroke, Parkinson's disease is the most common serious neurologic disease of old age—there are nearly one-half million sufferers in this country.

244. *What Is Parkinson's Disease?* A person with well-developed parkinsonism is almost unmistakable—you have probably seen such an individual but may not have known what was wrong. Afflicted persons shuffle slowly when walking, are bent at the waist, and look as though they are perpetually falling forward. Their movements are slow, whether they are raising a fork to their mouth or reaching out to shake your hand. When relaxed, their fingers appear to be constantly stroking their thumbs, but they become steady when they move their arms or hands. Victims of parkinsonism develop a rigid posture, and their muscles feel stiff and tense to

the touch. Their faces are often expressionless, or they may appear angry, depressed, or unfriendly. This appearance usually is due to a neurological inability to summon the complex variety of smiles, frowns, and other facial movements that punctuate and give meaning to our conversations and relationships. The voice becomes soft and they speak in a monotone. Handwriting becomes small and tremulous. Persons with parkinsonism may have great difficulty initiating movement. They may be unable to rise from a chair, not necessarily because they are too weak and unsteady (although they may be), but because they can't seem to get a movement started. So characteristic are the motions of individuals with moderately advanced Parkinson's disease that they can often be recognized across a room or while they walk along the sidewalk.

These symptoms worsen with time. Patients with advanced disease are often bedridden, their muscles stiff and immobile. One out of three individuals develops senility, and one out of four becomes significantly depressed. Many patients display a variety of other mental symptoms such as agitation, aggressiveness, and unpredictable irritability. This instability can make treatment difficult. The whole course of the disease, from first symptoms to final immobility, may take five years or thirty years. Usually, it develops over a decade or more, beginning in a person's 50s or 60s. Its development is slow enough that many people die of other causes before its symptoms become profound.

It is surprisingly difficult to tell whether your parent is developing parkinsonism, because the early symptoms are subtle and easily overlooked. Your parent may complain of feeling stiff, weak, and tired. He may lose some dexterity, move more slowly, or display a slight tremor of his hands. It may take several years, and a steady progression of these symptoms, before we (and the physician) recognize that the problem is parkinsonism, not simply changes due to aging.

The trouble is in the brain. Certain cells located in a small center deep within the brain, the substantia nigra, slowly begin to fail. The signals these cells used to send to surrounding centers, by a means of a chemical named dopamine as a messenger, aren't sent. Interruption of the smooth and regular flow of messages through this area of the brain in turn interrupts the smooth and free movement of the body. Why those cells fail remains unanswered. In a few people it is due to an infection or a small stroke. Certain medications (primarily some powerful tranquilizers used to treat severe mental illness) can cause the same group of parkinsonian symptoms, but these symptoms usually rapidly disappear when the medication is stopped. In most cases there is no explanation for the onset of parkinsonism—it is a degenerative disease without known cause.

And there is no cure. The goal of current treatment is to minimize the symptoms. All the while, the deterioration of the substantia nigra slowly progresses.

245. *Treatment of Parkinsonism.* Even though the underlying process remains untreatable, there has been spectacular recent improvement in the treatment of symptoms. It is now possible for a person to replace the missing chemical messenger, dopamine, by taking a very similar substance, L-dopa. In the brain L-dopa is chemically changed to dopamine, supplementing the low amount present in the deteriorating cells of the substantia nigra. When L-dopa was first developed it was felt to be a "miracle drug," much like insulin was for the treatment of diabetes. This initial unbounded enthusiasm has gradually waned, although L-dopa remains the best medication available for treating Parkinson's disease. L-Dopa is taken several times a day by mouth. One out of three people experiences a dramatic improvement, particularly in correcting slow movements and rigidity (mental changes are less affected). Another one in three taking L-dopa shows less spectacular benefits, while the final third of all people struggles with significant side effects. Most bothersome to many people are unwanted, involuntary movements—facial tics, grimacing, writhing motions of the arms and shoulders, movements of the tongue and lips, and general restlessness. Many people lose their appetite and develop nausea and constipation. Insomnia may develop, as may agitation and, at higher doses, confusion and bizarre behavior. Since many of these symptoms only develop at higher doses, a combination medication, Sinemet, is available, which combines L-dopa with another substance that retards the breakdown of L-dopa in the body, allowing lower doses to be taken each day. A few people who are unable to tolerate L-dopa alone do well taking Sinemet. Unfortunately, regardless of how good the initial response to L-dopa, it gradually loses its effectiveness in most people, and many individuals become exquisitely sensitive to changes in dosage, developing side effects with little provocation.

Other treatments are available. Standard medications long used to treat parkinsonism, but which have recently been supplanted by L-dopa, remain effective, particularly if used in combination with L-dopa or Sinemet. Some of the most common include Artane, Akineton, Cogentin, Kemadrin, Pagitane, and Tremin. Unfortunately, these medications also frequently cause side effects, including sleepiness, blurred vision, constipation, dry mouth, and confusion. Symmetrel is another medication of a different chemical class which is occasionally effective when the more standard medications either do not work or produce severe side effects. Usually, all of these drugs are most effective if used in combination with L-dopa, thus lowering the total daily dose of L-dopa.

Years ago, surgery on the damaged brain center was a mainstay of treatment for people with severe parkinsonism. Since the development of L-dopa, this treatment is rarely used and is appropriate only if all else fails—if even then.

Regardless of the medications available to alleviate the symptoms of parkinsonism, we need to remember that a person with Parkinson's disease is chronically ill and debilitated. As the disease progresses, your parent will have increasing need for physical therapy and a regular, active exercise program to forestall stiffening of the muscles and immobility. Are there structural changes that can be made around the home that will allow your parent to do more—high-seated chairs, railings in the bathroom, oversized eating utensils? Equally important is attention to your parent's emotional health. Parkinsonism is exceptionally frustrating and, moreover, carries with it an inherent risk of depression, senility, and agitation (probably due to biological changes in the brain). The emotional problems associated with the disease are often as crippling as the physical ones; you may want to consult a psychiatrist. Antidepressant medication and other psychiatric therapies often produce a marked lifting of depression.

STROKE

Just as senility is the great fear of those who dread becoming foolish and inconsequential, so stroke confronts us with the equally frightening specter of permanent helplessness. But this need not always be the case.

246. *What Is a Stroke?* Stop the flow of blood to a part of the brain, even for a few moments, and that section dies. The brain must have a constant supply of nutrients. A stroke occurs when the brain is deprived of blood long enough to cause damage.

There are two common ways the flow of blood to the brain can be stopped. All blood gets to the brain through two sets of arteries—the carotid arteries in the front (the ones you feel pulsing when you press underneath your jaw on either side of the windpipe) and the vertebral arteries behind (buried deep against the spinal column on either side of the back of the neck). These arteries can be blocked or they can burst. Either way, the result is likely to be a stroke.

Three out of four strokes are caused by blockage. A clot (thrombus) may form inside the artery—this is the most common type of stroke (thrombotic stroke), and is particularly likely in people whose arteries have become narrow and rough due to atherosclerosis (hardening of the arteries; the same process that causes heart attacks when the arteries to the heart are affected). Blockage can also occur when a solid object (an embolus), carried through the blood stream, plugs the first artery too small for it to squeeze through (causing an embolic stroke). Anything solid in the blood is abnormal—in the case of a stroke, that object is usually a clot that has formed on a valve of the heart and has broken free to float "downstream" until it lodges in an artery of the brain. People with heart disease are more likely to form clots within the heart, and people with irregular heartbeats (arrhythmias) are more likely to have these clots break loose— one of the reasons why such people are at increased risk to suffer a stroke. Another common type of embolus consists of small fragments broken from an atherosclerotic patch on the inner wall of an artery. Embolic strokes are second only to thrombotic strokes in frequency among the elderly, making up almost one third of all strokes.

Rupture of an artery in the brain causes approximately one out of every five strokes in the elderly (hemorrhagic stroke). The blood rushes into the substance of the brain, damaging that tissue and interrupting the flow along the rest of the vessel. This type of stroke is most common in people suffering from long-standing, poorly controlled high blood pressure.

Similar to a stroke, but generally more devastating, is the damage done when the blood is shut off to the entire brain. This can be caused by anything that stops blood circulation throughout the body, such as a severe heart attack. If the interruption is prolonged enough, the result is what doctors refer to as "brain death." Even if the circulation can be started again (for example, if the heart can be restarted), the brain has been irreparably damaged and cannot sustain life.

Along with cancer and heart disease, stroke is the great killer of the elderly. But, more significantly, it is a great disabler. Each year, more than one-quarter million people suffer a stroke in the United States; 75 percent of them are over 65, and half die. But one half of them do survive. Of the almost 1.5 million people in the U.S. who have survived a stroke, half of them are seriously disabled. People often fear surviving a stroke more than dying of one, and frequently for good reason, yet many people recover almost completely from strokes. The difference in degree of recovery is often a matter of luck and commitment to a rehabilitation program. It is even occasionally possible to anticipate a stroke and to successfully prevent it (see Section 249 below).

247. *What a Stroke Is Like.* No two strokes are the same. The characteristics of any stroke depend upon how rapidly changes are taking place in the blood stream, which branch or branches of which artery or arteries are involved, what kind of stroke it is, the pattern of your parent's unique map of blood vessels, whether he or she has two arteries that go to the same region, how old your parent is, whether he is left- or right-handed, and

many other factors. But though different types of strokes have slightly different patterns, the general outline that strokes follow as they develop is often surprisingly similar.

Strokes are sudden. Your parent may become paralyzed in an arm, become speechless, or collapse into unconsciousness within seconds, but this is infrequent. Much more common is the stroke which develops over minutes or hours. Your parent may become mildly confused and show one or more symptoms such as paralysis of a limb or of a side of the face, confused speech, numbness, dizziness, or partial blindness. A few strokes are accompanied by headache, but many are painless. Particularly common are strokes which occur at night, while your parent sleeps, or which develop when he rises to go to the bathroom at night. Typically, symptoms remain unchanged for a few minutes or an hour or more, then they quickly become more severe and new symptoms are added. Several such worsenings may occur during the first twelve hours. As the stroke progresses over the early minutes and hours, there is no way to determine how extensive it will finally become. The acute stroke is usually completed by the end of twenty-four hours and almost always by the end of several days.

However, the uncertainty does not end when the stroke is completed. After the symptoms have developed, they usually begin to recede. The weeks and months after a stroke are a time of concerned, and hopeful, waiting for both you and your parents. Speech that had been lost returns. Paralysis becomes weakness and weakness becomes strength. There is no way to predict how much function will be recovered. The more extensive the stroke, the more likely it is that your parent will be left with a significant, permanent deficit. On the other hand, a person who suffers a comparatively minor loss, such as weakness in one leg, stands a good chance of recovering completely during the weeks after the stroke. Although improvement is the usual course following a stroke, be aware that your parent is at marked risk to suffer an extension of the stroke or a second stroke during the following few weeks. The conditions which led to the first episode, such as a narrowed artery or clots on a heart valve, may still be there. Don't be caught off guard and have your hopes dashed by a second stroke—rather reassess the condition in light of these new changes and watch for signs of recovery.

What happens in the brain during the early minutes and weeks following a stroke which leads to these peculiar patterns of symptoms? The most rapid symptoms are usually caused by an embolus, which suddenly blocks an artery. An artery that ruptures produces some sudden symptoms also, but continued bleeding then steadily adds more problems as the minutes pass. Clotting of blood in an artery (thrombosis), the most common form of stroke, produces symptoms more slowly. The first symptoms appear as the thrombus begins to form, but it often takes many hours for it to reach its final size. As it grows up and down the artery, symptoms are added. At times, clots will form around emboli and at the site of a hemorrhage, causing these types of strokes to slowly progress also. In any stroke, there is a core of brain tissue that is irreparably damaged, surrounded by tissue that is injured but will recover. Initially, the injured tissue doesn't function well and adds to your parent's symptoms, but, as it regains health over the ensuing weeks, the symptoms it caused disappear. Clots and emboli may break up and disperse with time, and brain tissue which is still alive may be restored to health. However, all of these changes occur in the first weeks or months—any major problems remaining after three to six months are probably permanent.

248. *Who Is Likely to Have a Stroke?* There are populations of people among whom strokes are almost unheard of—mostly third-world people used to vigorous physical labor and who eat enough to get by from day to day. Clearly, our diet and life style encourage strokes.

The majority of strokes are related to atherosclerosis. Anything that promotes it, promotes stroke. As described in Section 158, in atherosclerosis fatty scar tissue begins to grow in patches on the inside walls of arteries. The arteries become narrowed, allowing less blood to pass. Clots frequently form at these narrowed spots. The plaques of fatty tissue occasionally break off, creating emboli. Atherosclerosis is the major cause of heart attacks and chronic heart failure, and such heart diseases encourage strokes. And what promotes atherosclerosis? High blood pressure. Diabetes. Eating fatty foods and eating too many calories. Becoming fat. Smoking. To control any one of these factors when young is to move a step further from a stroke in old age. To control them all is to stand a good chance of avoiding a stroke altogether. The most important condition to control is high blood pressure—not only is it a powerful stimulus to the development of atherosclerosis, but the increased pressure it creates in the arteries makes them more likely to rupture (hemorrhagic stroke). High blood pressure can be treated in old age with some expectation that your parent's risk of having a stroke will be decreased.

249. *TIA—A Stroke's Only Warning Sign.* Most strokes are unexpected. Widespread atherosclerosis in the arteries to the brain, narrowed vessels, a clot on a heart valve, or an artery ready to rupture—none of these produces noticeable symptoms. However, there is one forewarning of a stroke which is all too often overlooked, frequently with disastrous results—the TIA.

A TIA, or transient ischemic attack, is a "mini-stroke"—a *brief* complete or partial interruption in the flow of blood to a part of the brain. Your parent may experience any of the symptoms that accompany a stroke though usually in milder form: weakness on one side, difficult speech, temporary confusion, one-sided blindness, dizziness, stumbling gait, or some combination of any of these. These symptoms may last for only a few seconds, although usually they last for a few minutes. Recovery is complete. Unfortunately, in their mildness and brevity lie the seeds of tragedy. The symptoms, so strange and unexpected, are gone as quickly as they appeared. Like a mirage, they are forgotten or ignored. It is only too natural to want to forget a frightening experience—to pretend that the suddenly slack arm or momentary incoherence never happened and make no appointment for a medical examination. There may be only one TIA or there may be dozens—over days, weeks, or years. Do not ignore them. Many people have TIAs and nothing more, but TIAs are the only warning that your parent will get of an impending stroke. One of every three people who begins having TIAs ultimately suffers a stroke at some time in the future.

A TIA may be due to a clot that begins to form but then disappears, or to an embolus that blocks a small artery for a moment and then disperses. A medical examination is essential, but by the time it is performed the immediate cause of the blockage is usually gone. The value of the examination is to pinpoint the underlying cause of the TIA your parent has experienced, either to locate the narrowing of an artery or to identify previously unrecognized heart disease. Some of the conditions that ultimately lead to stroke can be successfully treated. On the other hand, even if no explanation for the TIA can be found, treatment may still help prevent a stroke (see Section 252).

250. *After a Stroke.* It is not the day of the stroke that so frightens us—it is the years that follow. We fear being bedridden, paralyzed, crippled, confused, blind, or mute. And for good reason. Almost half of all people who survive a major stroke remain significantly disabled. However, a few people recover completely from even a major stroke. The majority of victims, while remaining damaged, are able to care for themselves and to take up life pretty much where they had left off.

By three months after a stroke, the natural recovery of damaged brain tissue will have occurred. The remaining deficits are permanent. However, that doesn't mean that your parent will never get any better. Vigorous participation in a rehabilitation program can transform your parent from bedridden and essentially helpless to independent. The person who gives up after a stroke invariably deteriorates and becomes dependent; the fighter frequently improves. Thus, anything that compromises vigor and motivation promotes failure. This explains why the person with widespread paralysis often does better than the person with damaged thinking. Expect greater resistance to improvement if your parent has developed marked senility, confusion, difficulty understanding, or distorted sensation such as blindness, deafness, or extensive numbness. The severe demoralization and depression that often accompany a stroke and which can profoundly sap your parent's ability to fight back is another major block to improvement—fortunately, one which often is successfully treated. On the other hand, weakness and paralysis can be overcome and worked around (see Section 253). So powerful are factors like motivation, vigor, and clarity of mind that they can be used as guides in predicting the degree of recovery.

251. *Medical Tests*. The most important examination of all is the one that attempts to anticipate a stroke—the one that evaluates TIAs. If your parent experiences one or more TIAs, he should have a medical checkup that includes both a thorough physical examination and a careful history of any symptoms which might suggest trouble. Because so many of the conditions that cause TIAs or produce TIA-like symptoms are located in places other than the head (particularly in the heart), a general examination is essential. Depending on the physician's assessment of the likely cause, the examination may include chest X-ray, blood tests, electrocardiogram (a recording of heart waves), electroencephalogram (a recording of brain waves), CAT scan (a computerized X-ray of the brain), cerebral arteriography (X-rays of the head after dye is injected into the arteries to the brain), and a few sophisticated tests for special situations. Most often a cause for the "spells" is discovered and treatment to correct the condition is started. Since little treatment is effective once a stroke has begun, if your parent has had the luxury of a warning, don't allow him to neglect it.

After a person has suffered a stroke, a careful medical evaluation can often determine the type of stroke, the cause, the site of the block or rupture, the location and size of the brain damage, and the likelihood of a second stroke. The physician will first attempt to determine what part of the brain has been damaged and, next, what has caused it. In addition, the doctor will be alert to any evidence that suggests your parent has not suffered a stroke. A few other conditions, like a brain tumor that has bled into itself, can mimic a stroke and can result in confusion and inappropriate treatment.

Because different parts of the brain control different parts of the body and different sensations, a meticulous listing of symptoms usually permits an accurate estimate of which areas of the brain have been affected. The physician can usually determine the extent of damage and can make a good estimate of the likely causes and the likely sites of blockage or rupture.

Sophisticated X-ray tests now available allow almost complete certainty about the nature and causes of a stroke. The CAT scan, unknown ten years ago, has become the most important tool in evaluating a stroke. Although it is expensive to perform, its uncanny accuracy makes it a bargain. It can determine the cause and location of the vast majority of strokes—identifying with almost 100 percent certainty those who have suffered a ruptured artery and correctly identifying three quarters of those who have suffered an artery blockage. A CAT scan is usually performed as soon as possible after your parent has developed his first symptoms, because the information it provides may affect the choice of immediate treatment. The other mainstay of evaluation is arteriography—the injection of a dye into one of the major arteries to the brain, followed by a rapid series of X-rays of the head. This test shows the outline and condition of the suspected artery. Although extremely useful in determining the location of any narrowing of the artery, cerebral arteriography is usually delayed until absolutely essential because it occasionally causes a stroke to worsen during or shortly after the test. Another useful test is radioisotopic scanning—injection of a short-lived, radioactive chemical into a vein followed by measurements of the amount of radioactivity that collects in the brain over the ensuing days. This technique, used in combination with a CAT scan, can determine the cause of most strokes.

These tests, and others, usually can be done at a leisurely pace during the days after a stroke if the physician has sufficient understanding of what is going on to prescribe any immediately necessary treatment and if he is positive that your parent is undergoing a stroke and not something else.

252. *Treatment of a Stroke.* The first day or two following a stroke are filled with uncertainty. You don't know if your parent will live or die. You don't know how damaged he or she is. You want to help, but don't know what to do. For the first day or first week, a major stroke is a medical emergency. In most cases, your parent is in the hospital. The medical team is concentrating its primary effort on keeping your parent alive and preventing spread of the stroke. The hospital room will contain an IV apparatus for giving him fluids by vein. Possibly he will have a catheter draining the contents of his bladder into a bag by the bedside. Other life-support treatments may be in progress. Do not be overawed by them—your own contribution will begin after your parent is more medically stable. And that won't be long; most questions of life or death are answered in the first two days. A first estimate of the prospects for recovery can be made almost as quickly.

No treatment corrects a stroke. Once it has occurred, we can only cross our fingers and hope for natural improvement. What we must concentrate on is preventing a stroke, but even there our weapons are meager.

Fortunately, both TIAs and a stroke that has just started can be treated. Unfortunately, the treatment is both controversial and only moderately effective. If tiny emboli or a clot begin to cause symptoms, they often can be stopped and prevented from recurring by the use of medication that impairs the clotting of blood. Most useful is aspirin, but anticoagulants like heparin and Coumadin are also of value. If your parent is placed on one or more of these drugs as soon as the first signs of a thrombotic or embolic stroke appear, occasionally the stroke may be stopped. Likewise, regular use of aspirin following a first TIA may prevent both further TIAs and a stroke. But there are several problems with this treatment. First, the medication doesn't always work. Even more important, if the stroke is due to hemorrhage rather than blockage of an artery, halting the clotting may be precisely the wrong thing to do—it may worsen the bleeding. The physician must be absolutely certain of the type of stroke before beginning anticoagulant medication. The development of the CAT scan has made that easier. The use of medication must be decided on an individual basis, but anticoagulants are of value for many people.

The only other available treatment is surgery, but there are only a few situations where it is indicated. If your parent has suffered a hemorrhage into the brain, occasionally the hemorrhage can be drained surgically. If your parent has a significant narrowing of one of the carotid arteries that seems to have been responsible for TIAs or a small stroke, it can sometimes be removed (carotid endarterectomy)—a mildly risky operation which should be discussed fully with the physician beforehand.

Since treatment of stroke remains inadequate, we must focus on prevention. The most effective prevention of stroke is lifelong control of diet, obesity, smoking, high blood pressure, and diabetes. Such sensible habits could make the rest of this chapter incidental for the majority of older people; but few of us are so disciplined.

253. *Rehabilitation—The Long Haul.* You may be still reeling from the shock of your parent's stroke when the doctor asks you to help with his treatment. How can he be so callous?

In fact, the doctor is not being insensitive or rushing things at all. Long-term rehabilitation begins the day after a stroke, even if your parent is unconscious—and you are likely to be one of the people most involved in that care over the months to come.

Experts in rehabilitation, the physiatrist (a physician) and the physical therapist, begin working with your parent within the first day or two in the hospital—even though your parent may be barely aware of their presence. Your parent may be paralyzed, but if his limbs aren't moved and his muscles aren't stretched, they rapidly become frozen and useless. Also, your parent must be turned frequently so that bedsores (decubitus ulcers) don't develop on his skin. Special pillows and sheepskin mats may be needed. His arms and legs should be placed in positions that prevent contractures and distortions from developing. All of this is essential if your parent is to have a good start in recovering function after the medical emergency is over. If you don't notice such activity after your parent has spent two or three days in the hospital, ask about it.

Your parent's medical condition is most likely to have stabilized within the first two days. At that point, the rehabilitation effort should shift into high gear. Vigorous treatment appears to be considerably more effective than a more relaxed pace. Do not be upset if the doctor insists that your parent, whose arm and leg are newly paralyzed, sit or walk by the second day. Early efforts seem to promote the most complete recovery. Such activity keeps joints mobile and flexible, helps prevent muscle weakening, and gives your parent the sense that recovery is expected.

The crucial time for any rehabilitation program is the first three months. It is during that time that deterioration must be prevented and new patterns of activity established. Your parent's physical limits should be determined and ways around them created. As much of the lost ability as possible should be recovered: through exercise to develop strength, biofeedback to relax stiffened muscles, or therapy to clarify speech, if necessary. Substitutes should be found for skills that have been lost. If it appears that function is unlikely to return in one arm, your parent can be taught to do whatever he needs with the other one. Special equipment can make up for specific deficiencies: Velcro straps instead of shoe laces, a three- or four-footed walking cane, grab-bars for the toilet and a transfer bench for entry into the bathtub, a one-handed electric can opener, a lower leg brace if he has no strength at the ankle, and much more. By the end of the first month or two, he should have a well-defined set of daily exercises designed to preserve the strengths and abilities that remain. He should also have a new set of equipment and skills that will replace lost abilities. With such an aggressive approach to rehabilitation, most people who have suffered a major stroke can take care of themselves and become independent, whether they live by themselves or with family.

But there are special hurdles for some people—a few which are almost insurmountable. Marked deterioration in your parent's intellectual ability makes his participation in a rehabilitation program unlikely. The loss of the ability to speak or to understand speech presents unique problems to recovery, which may occasionally be overcome through use of a few sensible, basic principles (see Section 44). If contractures or frozen joints have already become well established, they may be very difficult to relieve, and efforts will have to be made to work around them. If the nerves that control the bladder or bowel have been damaged, retraining should be attempted—it is often tedious and difficult, but is frequently successful (see Sections 206 and 185).

A variety of emotional problems plague the stroke victim. His life has been turned upside down in an instant. His body and mind have changed and can't be depended on. His memory, and with it his present and much of his past, may be lost. The stroke victim must also reassess his future. He may consider himself a social outcast. He may be treated like one. The result of these multiple losses and changes is usually a profound grief reaction (see Chapter 9)—he may be depressed, angry, bitter, anxious, hopeless, or a combination of these. After a stroke your parent may become excessively dependent on you or someone else and be reluctant to attempt anything on his own. Often these reactions last for months or longer, or they can color the rest of his life. Don't let this happen. Consult a psychiatrist or other psychotherapist. Not quite as common, but more difficult to treat, are the emotional problems due to strokes that reflect destruction of brain tissue. Almost any symptom may appear, but most common are signs of emotional instability like temper outbursts, marked irritability, or attacks of inappropriate laughing or crying. Your parent may become paranoid or display bizarre behavior or strange ideas. A psychiatric evaluation is essential.

254. *Stroke—What You Face.* Nothing about a stroke is pleasant. Your parent may die, or he may emerge physically and emotionally crippled. You are likely to grieve along with your parent, since the person loved by you both has been unalterably changed. And yet you are not helpless—there is much you can do to improve your parent's life. Vigorous care following a stroke needs to be lifelong. You can help see that it continues—that exercise and activities are maintained and that therapy appointments are kept. Perhaps the most common error made by family members concerned about their parent is to do too much for them—to be overprotective. You can see that an appropriate balance between helping them and encouraging them to help themselves is maintained. In some locations, additional sources of support and information for both you and your parent are available in the form of groups of people who are in the same boat. Your state's department of aging should be able to identify such groups for you (see Chapter 29).

Living with someone who has had a stroke may be acutely stressful at times, and is always wearing. The satisfaction of promoting his recovery may outweigh the cost, but finally you may have to conclude that you have neither the strength nor the resources to provide a place at home. That is all right. Many people before you have reached that conclusion. Nursing homes and other medical facilities are available which provide a high level of care—in fact, which provide a higher standard of life for people with the unique needs of the stroke victim than you ever could at home (for hints on selection, see Chapter 23). Only you will be able to decide when that time has come, if it ever does. Consult with a physician, choose your facility carefully, then try to be comfortable with an undesirable, but necessary, outcome.

MISCELLANEOUS NEUROLOGICAL PROBLEMS

A few neurological problems deserve special mention because they are particularly common in old age. Some are unpleasant but minor, while others are potentially life-threatening.

255. *Trigeminal Neuralgia.* Severe, lightning-like jolts of pain which usually last only a few seconds and which feel as if they shoot through the side of the face occur in a few older people. The pain is one of the most severe known. It may last, off and on, for weeks, and it may return, off and on, for years. This condition, known as trigeminal neuralgia, or tic douloureux, is considerably more common among older people than among the young. Its cause is unknown but it clearly involves the nerve that supplies the cheek. Treatment with medications like Tegretol or Dilantin is often successful, but occasionally it is necessary to destroy part of the nerve with surgery or injections of alcohol.

256. *Shingles.* Shingles, or herpes zoster infection, is an equally painful condition which is common in older people. Your parent will experience severe pain and skin sores over a small area of his body—usually along a horizontal stripe across one side of his chest, over the forehead and skin surrounding one eye, or around the back of the jaw and ear on one side. A sharp or burning pain and, occasionally, fever come first, followed by the rash several days later. The rash clears in about two weeks, but the pain may last an additional week or two, or it may last for months after all other symptoms have disappeared. The condition is caused by the infection of a branch of a nerve by the herpes zoster virus. The elderly, who appear to gradually lose their resistance to this virus, become infected easily. Your parent can expect to be thoroughly uncomfortable for several weeks, but in uncomplicated cases the symptoms disappear completely. A few older people develop complications, including scarring of the eye, deafness, or severe, long-lasting pain. Depression is also common. There is no completely effective treatment. Most people need pain medication while the pain is

DISEASES OF THE BRAIN

most intense. Steroid medication can reduce the severity and duration of symptoms, and is frequently used in older people. Certainly, if the eye is involved, an ophthalmologist should be consulted, because the risk of permanent damage to sight is great if the condition is insufficiently treated. Several new medications, like adenine arabinoside or a solution of idoxuridine, appear to be useful, but who is most likely to benefit and which of the symptoms are most likely to improve has not yet been determined. Ask your parent's physician about the latest information.

257. *Medication Reaction.* Medical and neurological problems due to prescribed medication are so common and so various that they are treated in a separate chapter (Chapter 22). Practically any neurological symptom can be produced as an unwanted, and often unsuspected, side effect of a medication your parent is taking for some other medical complaint. A partial list of symptoms includes confusion, depression, headache, tremor, loss of memory, seizures, strange movements, bizarre behavior, weakness, numbness, deafness, and dizziness. Ask your parent's doctor whether a medication reaction might be responsible for his problem. Often the physician is not aware of all the medications that your parent is taking, so try to have a list available.

258. *Subdural Hematoma.* The elderly, often unstable on their feet and suffering from poor eyesight, fall frequently. A blow to the head during a fall, even if minor, may sometimes produce a slow leak of blood from fragile veins into the space between the surface of the brain and the thick membrane which lines the inner surface of the skull. The slowly growing pool of blood (subdural hematoma) may take minutes, hours, days, or even weeks to produce symptoms. Eventually, as it begins to press on the brain, your parent may develop weakness of an arm or leg, become stuporous and confused, or show changes in personality and behavior. When the subdural hematoma progresses rapidly, it is frequently mistaken for a stroke. When it develops slowly, emotional changes often predominate and you may think your parent is becoming senile. If no one realizes the true cause of these symptoms, your parent may receive days or weeks of inappropriate treatment, occasionally with disastrous results. Fortunately, diagnosis (when the possibility of a subdural hematoma is considered) is usually easy, and treatment is generally successful. The diagnosis is made with near-certainty by a computerized X-ray of the brain, the CAT scan. The most effective treatment is usually to bore a small hole through the skull over the collection of blood and drain it. Often symptoms improve markedly within a day or two.

259. *Brain Tumors*. Even though they are not nearly as common in old age as stroke, brain tumors should always be thought of if your parent is showing signs of brain disease. The majority of brain tumors grow from cells of the brain that have become cancerous, but about one third come from tumors somewhere else in the body (particularly the lung) that have spread to the brain through the blood stream. The most common first symptoms are weakness or paralysis somewhere in the body, a seizure, increasing confusion, or personality changes—although almost any combination of symptoms may occur. Headache may be a sign of tumor, but it usually has some other cause. Most often, symptoms develop over weeks or months. However, a few brain tumors are very slow-growing, especially among the elderly, and they may be present for years before symptoms appear. Diagnosis is most easily made by CAT scan, but to know which kind of brain tumor is present requires microscopic evaluation of a sample of tissue from the tumor. Any decision about treatment must take into consideration the type of tumor, where it is located, how widespread it is, how ill your parent is, what kind of symptoms he has been experiencing, and how old he is. The choice of therapy depends upon your parent and the specifics of his illness. Surgery is often useful, can sometimes cure, and frequently removes many of the symptoms, but some symptoms, like paralysis and speech difficulties, may not improve. Radiation therapy, either alone or in combination with surgery, is sometimes a better choice, particularly if the tumor is widespread or is in a hard-to-reach location in the brain. Effects of treatment and prognosis are difficult to predict. Many people live for several months, some live a year or two, and a few live for years or are cured. Do not be too willing to allow your parent to forgo vigorous treatment just because of old age—even at 80 or 90, an additional year or two of meaningful life is worth the effort.

21.

Other Medical Problems

260. *Anemia.* Anemia is not a disease—it is a sign that something is wrong. It should never be thought of as normal in the elderly. A person suffering from anemia has too few red blood cells (RBCs) in his blood stream, or RBCs which contain too little hemoglobin. Normal RBCs are filled with a standard amount of the iron-containing, oxygen-grabbing protein hemoglobin. Their sole task is to pick up oxygen in the lungs and distribute it to cells throughout the body. RBCs are made in the central marrow of many of the larger bones in the body. They last for several months, become worn, and then are destroyed by the spleen. As long as the normal chain of construction, use, and destruction of RBCs is uninterrupted, the body maintains a constant number of red blood cells.

However, that chain breaks down frequently in the elderly. Anemia occurs at some time in one of three older people. Although anemia can be caused by a poor diet—particularly a diet deficient in iron, protein, or other vitamins—disease is more likely to be responsible. While many different diseases can produce anemia, those most likely to are chronic diseases such as rheumatoid arthritis, liver and kidney disease, cancer, and any long-lasting infection like tuberculosis. Blood loss is caused most frequently by ulcers or cancer of the stomach or intestine. Much of the physician's effort will be directed towards sorting through the various possible causes of anemia.

While anemia may produce symptoms like fatigue, weakness, dizziness, or shortness of breath, just as often it may cause no symptoms. The anemia is then discovered by a blood test during either a routine medical examination or an evaluation done because your parent has become ill. In this second case, your parent's symptoms are usually due to the underlying disease rather than to anemia. Whether the anemia is mild or severe, and whether it appears with or without symptoms, it must be explained. Even though it may be produced by an easily remedied condition like inadequate diet, a silent cancer or other life-threatening illness is responsible often enough to demand a thorough search for the anemia's cause.

Most routine laboratory examinations include a measure of the number of red blood cells (hematocrit) and the amount of hemoglobin. If either is low, expect the physician to examine the blood with a microscope. The size and shape of the RBCs tell a lot about what may be causing the anemia. Small, pale cells may be due to blood loss or lack of iron in the diet (iron-deficiency anemia). Abnormally large cells may be caused by liver disease or by lack of important vitamins like B_{12} or folic acid. At the very least, inspecting the blood microscopically allows the physician to decide what additional tests are needed: for example, measures of iron and vitamin levels in the blood, an examination for kidney disease, or tests for cancer. Since many diseases produce anemia by affecting the cells in the bone marrow from which RBCs grow, a common test when the diagnosis of the anemia is uncertain is bone marrow aspiration. In this test, a needle is pushed through the outer shell of one of the large bones (a procedure which is moderately uncomfortable), and some marrow is withdrawn. When this marrow is examined with a microscope, often enough is learned about what is causing the anemia to allow treatment to begin.

Most anemias in the elderly are treatable; usually this means treating the underlying disease. Although that disease is not always curable, its symptoms frequently can be lessened by treating the anemia. Often treatment also includes improving the diet and beginning several months of iron supplements. In any case, anemia must always be attended to, first with a medical evaluation, and then with treatment of its cause.

261. *Breast Cancer.* Breast cancer is the most common cancer among women: one of every twelve will develop it. And it is deadly, ultimately killing many of its sufferers. It can be cured, however, particularly if caught early. In fact, it is a perfect example of why cancer should be checked for regularly in the elderly, since the likelihood of survival decreases markedly if breast cancer goes unrecognized.

The cause of breast cancer is unknown, and thus prevention is difficult, although we do know that it is more likely to occur in women who have never had children or who have family members who have suffered from it. However, nowhere is your parent's ability to guard her own life more in evidence than with breast cancer. She is the person crucial to discovering a tumor, not the doctor. Ninety percent of breast cancers are noticed first by the patient, usually during routine breast checks. Your parent *must* inspect her breasts regularly (monthly is recommended), first checking her reflection in a mirror with her arms at her sides and then raised to look for any irregularities, and then feeling her breasts carefully with her fingers for lumps. Your parent should ask her physician for instruction. If she tends to forget or avoid such a routine, remind her—it is vital.

The other method of catching breast cancer early is to have regular screening by mammography. A mammogram is a specialized X-ray of the breast which can identify a tumor which is still too small to feel. Many physicians recommend that a woman over fifty should have one done yearly, in the hope of identifying breast cancer as early as possible.

A small, movable lump buried beneath the skin in one breast is the first evidence of breast cancer in most women. It may be tender but usually isn't. Occasionally there may also be a slight bloody discharge from the nipple. If the cancer is discovered a little later in its growth, the skin overlying it may be wrinkled, puckered, swollen, or even ulcerated. As the cancer spreads to other parts of the body, additional symptoms may occur, such as bone pain or pain on breathing.

Every new breast lump must be examined. No physician can say with certainty that a new, small, movable lump is not breast cancer by a physical examination alone. Some of the tissue must also be examined under a microscope. If the doctor is fairly certain that cancer is present, he may sample the lump in his office with a needle to confirm his impression. More commonly, he will remove the lump in an operating room for inspection (excisional biopsy). If it is cancer, he may operate to remove the cancer at the same time.

Knowledge about the best way to treat breast cancer has been changing in recent years. Removal of the breast is usually essential unless the cancer is so extensive as to make surgery a token effort. Which combination of several possible operations, chemotherapy, hormone treatment, and radiation is best depends upon a number of factors, the most important of which is how widespread the cancer has become. In general, cancer which is limited to a small area of the breast is best treated with removal of the breast and surrounding tissues. The debilitating radical mastectomy (removal of the breast and surrounding tissues, including the chest muscles) has gradually been replaced with the more moderate total mastectomy (removal of the breast and nearby tissues, but leaving the muscles). If the lymph nodes under the arm (the first place the cancer usually spreads) also are suspected of having cancer, they are removed at the same time as the breast, and cancer-killing chemicals are given (chemotherapy). With more widespread disease, surgery and chemotherapy are often combined with radiation. However, if the cancer is obvious throughout the body, radiation and chemotherapy may be the only treatments used. Finally, some breast tumors are sensitive to hormone treatment (tamoxifen, estrogens). It is possible to determine which tumors are likely to be sensitive to hormones by chemically testing the tissue originally removed to confirm the diagnosis.

The loss of a breast can be as traumatic to your parent as the realization that she has cancer. Recognize your parent's emotional stress (which might not become obvious for weeks or months). Provide support and help her to grieve (see Chapter 9). Moreover, see that she receives a well-fitted prosthesis, which may do wonders for her self-confidence.

In spite of the best medical efforts, cancer of the breast remains a serious disease which is usually fatal if recognized late. Make sure that your parent regularly checks her breasts and follows through with a yearly screening program that includes a physical examination and mammography.

262. *Cancer.* Cancer is both common and serious: it kills one out of four elderly. In spite of that fact, or perhaps because of it, cancer is surrounded by myth and misunderstanding. Because it is unpredictable and each type is different, it is difficult to make accurate general statements about cancer. The most common types of cancer in the elderly are described in other sections: lung cancer, 173; prostate cancer, 211; breast cancer, 261; cancer of the large intestine and rectum, 198; stomach cancer, 193; cancer of the uterus, 264. You should understand the nature of the particular kind of cancer your parent has developed, since the course of the illness and the likelihood of cure often differ dramatically from one type to another. Nevertheless, there are some features of cancer and its treatment which are common to most types.

1. Cancer is not invariably fatal. In fact, almost half of the people who develop a cancer are cured, or die of some other illness. Cancers of the rectum and prostate are increasingly curable, while cancers of the lung and pancreas remain difficult to treat successfully, although every type of cancer has been cured in someone.

2. The likelihood of cure depends not only on the type of cancer but on the microscopic appearance of the cells, how widespread it is, its exact location, what tissues and organs are involved, your parent's general health, and other important but poorly understood factors. Upon diagnosis, each person's cancer is classified or "staged": the factors important to prediction are evaluated and the severity, or stage, of the cancer is estimated. The higher the stage (I, II, III, IV), the more severe the illness. But no

matter what stage the cancer is in, the disease's complexity makes prediction difficult and always allows for hope.

3. Most types of cancer become more frequent in old age, but most of these cancers grow and spread less rapidly in the very old. It is as though the cancer has become less vigorous along with its host. As a result, some people may battle cancer for many years, only to die of some other illness, while other people with cancer may die without ever realizing that it has been present.

4. Cancer should be identified early in the elderly, and evaluation and treatment should be no less thorough than in a younger person, since cure is just as likely. The major goals of the evaluation include identifying the original site of the cancer (lung, breast, intestine) and determining how widely it has spread, since those are the two key factors upon which to base treatment. It is sometimes surprisingly difficult to locate the origin of the cancer if it has spread to involve many organs.

5. If there is hope for a cure or remission, treatment should be vigorous, regardless of age. However, if your parent's health is poor and if aggressive treatment is likely to produce more problems than it prevents, more limited treatment that concentrates on relieving symptoms is appropriate. You and your parent should discuss this openly with the physician, and your parent should understand what is being done and why.

6. Treatment of a tumor may include a combination of chemotherapy, radiation, and surgery. All these methods are problem-fraught, and all can be life-saving. Both you and your parent should understand the risks, complications, and possible benefits of each. Discuss any proposed treatment thoroughly with the physician. The treatment of cancer has become very complicated and usually requires referral to at least one specialist, usually an internist specializing in cancer (oncologist). However, because cancer is a chronic disease, your parent should try to arrange to have one physician supervise care throughout the course of the illness, rather than allowing care to become fragmented among several specialists.

7. Both cancer and its treatment can produce severe side effects such as nausea, weight loss, and pain. These can usually be treated effectively. Nausea and weight loss often are best treated by careful selection and preparation of food, high-calorie dietary supplements, and antinausea medication like Compazine (taken by mouth or suppository). Chronic pain occurs in approximately half of cancer patients, and is profound in one out of five. Strong pain medication (morphine, methadone, Dilaudid, Demerol, codeine) may need to be given in large doses several times each day. This may be the only way to make life endurable for a few people and should not be resisted, particularly if your parent is unlikely to live long.

8. Cancer may be fatal. Eventually the likelihood of a fatal outcome may need to be recognized. If it becomes evident that your parent is dying, medical care may be redirected to treat only symptoms (pain, nausea). Affairs should be put in order. Both you and your parent will need to grieve (see Chapter 9). Throughout this process, you should be available to your parent and should discuss events and understandings as honestly as possible. Deception (denying the diagnosis, minimizing the significance of new symptoms) is rarely of value and is usually destructive. Hope is always called for, since the outcome remains uncertain until the last, but support and open, honest communication are necessary as well. Your parent needs to come to terms with his illness and his life, and you can help or hinder this process (see Chapter 9).

Persons suffering from cancer should look for help first from the professionals caring for them: their physicians, the nursing staff, and the social work department of the hospital. However, if that course proves unsatisfactory, there are several organizations which provide information and emotional support to cancer sufferers. Some, like the American Cancer Society, are professionally staffed, while others, like Make Today Count, consist primarily of patients and their families. Many of the organizations have local chapters, which are listed in the telephone directory, but initial contact can be made through their national headquarters.

American Cancer Society (ACS)
777 Third Ave.
New York, NY 10017
(212) 371-2900

Leukemia Society of America
800 Second Ave.
New York, NY 10017
(212) 573-8484

United Ostomy Association, Inc.
2001 W. Beverly Blvd.
Los Angeles, CA 90057
(213) 413-5510

International Association of Laryngectomees
c/o The American Cancer Society

Make Today Count
P.O. Box 303
Burlington, IA 52601
(319) 753-6521

OTHER MEDICAL PROBLEMS

Reach to Recovery
c/o American Cancer Society
(This is a group for women who have had or are to undergo mastecto-my.)

In addition, the Cancer Information Service provides information free of charge to anyone calling its toll-free numbers. The national number of the CIS is (800) 638-6694, but more specific answers to your questions often can be obtained by calling a number within your state (not every state has its own number).

Alabama: (800) 292-6201
California: Area codes 213, 714, and 805: (805) 252-9066
         Rest of CA: (213) 226-2374
Colorado: (800) 332-1850
Connecticut: (800) 922-0824
Delaware: (800) 523-3586
District of Columbia and northern Virginia: (202) 636-5700
Florida: Dade County: (305) 547-6920
         Rest of FL: (800) 432-5953
Georgia: (800) 327-7332
Illinois: Chicago: (312) 226-2371
         Rest of IL: (800) 972-0586
Kentucky: (800) 432-9321
Maine: (800) 225-7034
Maryland: (800) 492-1444
Massachusetts: (800) 952-7420
Minnesota: (800) 582-5262
New Hampshire: (800) 225-7034
New Jersey: Northern: (800) 223-1000
         Southern: (800) 523-3586
New York: New York City: (212) 794-7982
         Rest of New York: (800) 462-7255
North Carolina: Durham County: (919) 684-2230
         Rest of NC: (800) 672-0943
North Dakota: (800) 328-5188
Ohio: (800) 282-6522
Pennsylvania: (800) 822-3963
South Dakota: (800) 328-5188
Texas: Houston: (713) 792-3245
         Rest of Texas: (800) 392-2040

Vermont: (800) 225-7034
Washington: (800) 552-7212
Wisconsin: (800) 362-8038

263. *Diabetes Mellitus (Sugar Diabetes)*. A severe form of diabetes often develops in childhood. A less severe form commonly develops in late middle age. If your parent has suffered from diabetes since youth, its ups and downs are familiar. If it has developed only recently, your parent has some adjustments to make. He or she must understand the disease, and accept that it is a chronic illness which must be tended carefully.

Although we eat a variety of different foods, much of what we eat is changed into the simple sugar, glucose, which then circulates in the blood and serves as the exclusive food of the brain and occasional food for most of the other cells in the body. The body operates best when a normal level of glucose is constantly present. Thus the body has elaborate biochemical controls designed to prevent the blood sugar level from falling too low (hypoglycemia) or rising too high (hyperglycemia). Key to this control system is the hormone insulin, a protein produced by small clusters of cells in the pancreas (a gland which lies deep alongside the lower border of the stomach). Insulin is secreted by the pancreas into the blood in carefully metered amounts to help cells use glucose. If too little insulin is present, glucose builds up in the blood; if too much is secreted, blood sugar falls below normal.

Diabetes mellitus results when this system breaks down. In a few people, the pancreas stops producing enough insulin, resulting in a more severe form of diabetes. In the majority of elderly diabetics, however, insulin is secreted in normal (or above normal) amounts, but is of poor quality and partially ineffective. In addition, some older people seem to develop a resistance to the effects of even normal insulin, thus compounding the problem. The result, in either case, is high blood sugar.

The elevation of blood glucose produced by insufficient or imperfect insulin is present in all diabetics, but is often free of symptoms in the elderly; your parent may suffer from diabetes for years without being aware of its presence. This is especially dangerous because serious, long-term complications begin developing early in the disease. The appearance of these chronic complications may be the first evidence your parent has of the existence of diabetes (see below). However, high blood sugar alone can create some symptoms, particularly if it reaches very high levels. Most frequently, it causes excessive thirst and urination. If your parent always seems to be thirsty, investigate. As the blood sugar climbs even higher, he or she may become weak, lethargic, disoriented, and may ultimately slip into a coma. Occasionally, coma may be the first evidence that your parent suffers from diabetes.

Some people are at greater risk for diabetes than others. If there is a family history of diabetes, particularly in your parent's parents or siblings, he is more likely to develop the disease. In addition, diabetes is more likely if your parent is obese and inactive. A recent weight loss in a formerly heavy person is another alerting sign.

Too often a late and possibly fatal complication signals the presence of diabetes: heart attack, stroke, kidney failure, failing vision, decreased sensation in the feet, impotence, or an antibiotic-resistant infection. If the diabetes is severe, of long standing, and poorly controlled, complications and early death are common. Diabetes promotes atherosclerosis and its two associated killers, heart disease (see Chapter 15) and stroke (see Chapter 20), and heart attack and heart failure are the most common causes of death among diabetics. Stroke occurs frequently, and other problems are common as well. The feet and lower legs may gradually become numb, and yet may simultaneously burn and be painful. These changes in the lower leg are caused in part by the damage high blood sugar does to the nerves and in part by the poor blood circulation caused by atherosclerosis. Decreased sensitivity in the feet may cause injury (blisters, cuts, ulcers) to go unnoticed until infection sets in. Infection is often difficult to control in the diabetic, for a variety of reasons. As a result, feet frequently become infected and ulcerated, heal poorly when treated, develop gangrene, and occasionally may need amputation. Kidney infections and other forms of kidney disease are major problems for the diabetic. They may signal their presence by pain in the small of the back, swelling of the arms or legs, puffiness of the face, nausea, or the sudden appearance of high blood pressure and headache. Unless treated vigorously, these conditions can be fatal. The muscles in the thighs and lower leg may weaken, making walking and climbing difficult. Generalized itching, particularly around the vagina of elderly women, is common. Finally, the light-sensitive retina at the back of the eye may gradually deteriorate: diabetes is the leading cause of blindness in the elderly. This distressingly long list of diabetes complications is by no means complete. It should be borne in mind, however, that these problems are less likely to be significant if the diabetes is mild and if it is carefully controlled. Unfortunately, only a few of the complications improve once the elevated blood sugar is finally recognized and treated: kidney disease, muscle weakness, leg numbness, and deteriorated vision may get better, but little change is seen in atherosclerosis.

Diabetes can be diagnosed only if the blood sugar is elevated. Since everyone's blood sugar changes throughout the day, and rises after a meal, only certain kinds of measurements are useful. Blood glucose is usually measured before your parent has eaten anything in the morning, or two hours after a meal. In either case, a blood sugar level above that which is normal for your parent's age suggests, but does not prove, that diabetes is present. The standard, and usually conclusive, test for the diagnosis of diabetes is the oral glucose tolerance test. A person drinks a precise amount of a sweet drink and then the blood sugar is sampled hourly for several hours. If the glucose level rises too high and takes too long to return to normal, that person probably has diabetes.

Treatment is usually simple. The goal is to keep the blood glucose within normal limits—neither too high nor too low. Most diabetes that develops in later years is mild and can be treated by diet alone. The diet must be balanced (approximately 50 percent carbohydrates, 20 percent protein, and 30 percent fats) and the body must be kept lean. Fiber (bran, raw or slightly cooked vegetables, etc.) also helps. Your parent should also begin a regular exercise program. By these simple methods he should be able to control his blood sugar. He should work out the details in consultation with his physician.

However, medicine may be necessary. Opinions differ about the best medication to use if diet and exercise don't lower blood sugar into the normal range. There are really only two choices: glucose-lowering pills and insulin shots. Oral medication (Orinase, Diabinese, etc.) can be taken once or twice each day, and will bring most elderly persons' blood sugar into the normal range. When first developed, these medications were felt to be the ideal treatment for mild to moderate diabetes. However, people taking these drugs *may* have an increased likelihood of heart attack or dangerous heart irregularities, and thus these medications must be used cautiously in people with heart disease. Still, these drugs make a major contribution to the successful control of diabetes. The alternative treatment is daily (or twice daily) insulin injections. An injection in the morning will lower the blood sugar throughout the day for most people. Severe diabetes usually must be controlled this way.

Whichever type of drug is chosen, either your parent must be able to manage his own medication (give himself shots, take his pills without error) or someone must be available to help him. This is important because, if he mistakenly takes a large amount of medication (particularly if he is not eating well), his blood sugar can fall to dangerously low levels. This hypoglycemia can be life-threatening. Initially, your parent may be mildly confused or have trouble speaking. His behavior may appear strange, he may be disoriented, or his mood may change suddenly. He may be nervous and sweaty. All these symptoms can progress rapidly to unconsciousness. Such a hypoglycemic crisis can be corrected immediately if your parent eats something sweet like hard candy or a sugar drink. Be alert to these symptoms, because if your parent becomes confused he may be unable to recognize that he is having trouble. If such an episode occurs, find out why (for example, his regular dose of medication may be too high, or he may have skipped a meal) in order to prevent a recurrence.

Diabetes in the elderly, though usually mild, is a serious illness. The most common reason for failure of treatment is lackadaisical follow-through with diet and exercise. Do what you can to strengthen your parent's resolve.

264. *Gynecological Problems.* Gynecological problems are common among elderly women. Most are minor and can be treated successfully with medication and altered habits. However, because a few problems with deceptively subtle symptoms are extremely serious, even mild gynecological complaints should be evaluated by a physician. Your parent should not neglect routine gynecological checkups.

Disorders can develop anywhere along the chain of reproductive organs: the tissue surrounding the entrance to the reproductive tract (vulva), the tube leading to those organs (vagina), the muscular ring at the end of the vagina that closes the womb (cervix), the womb itself (uterus), and the ovaries (which lie within the abdomen, each attached by a short cord to opposite sides of the inner end of the uterus). These organs are considerably different from what they were in youth, most of the change having occurred at menopause.

Menopause is one of the most significant events in the reproductive life of a woman, and is accompanied by numerous physical changes, most of which are tied to lowered production of estrogen, the primary female sex hormone. This crucial hormone is produced by the ovaries, which become exhausted in late midlife and gradually cease production. As the estrogen level falls, physical and psychological changes follow. The tissues of the vulva and vagina become thin and dry, while the cervix, uterus, and ovaries shrink to a fraction of their previous size. Many of the supporting muscular structures in the area (muscles which also support the bladder and rectum) also atrophy. The decrease in estrogen also produces a few widespread changes in the body, the two most significant of which are a gradual thinning and weakening of bone and a loss of the protection against atherosclerosis (hardening of the arteries) that women enjoy before menopause. Physiological and psychological changes include hot flushes, temperature instability, night sweats, irritability, anxiety, and depression. The emotional consequences of menopause vary markedly from one woman to another: some women notice little effect, while others are incapacitated. The physical changes of menopause usually are over by a person's early 50s, but the psychological effects may last for a few more years in some people. Regardless of whether menopause has been completed in a woman's 40s or a decade later, by the time she reaches her 60s, the gynecological problems she faces are those characteristic of the older years.

The dry, thin skin of the vulva and vagina may itch, feel uncomfortable, and produce a thin, watery discharge. It becomes easily infected with bacteria and yeast, particularly in someone with poorly controlled diabetes, and, in that state, the symptoms can include a strong-smelling discharge, the urgent need to urinate, and even bleeding. The skin is readily damaged by physical trauma (as during sexual intercourse), and can become painful and bleed. The cause of such symptoms always needs to be determined by a physical examination and laboratory tests. Infections should be treated with proper medication once the responsible organism has been identified. Because lack of estrogen plays a role in the development of many of these problems, severe cases usually respond to application of an estrogen cream directly to the affected area. Unfortunately, the problems may return after the cream is stopped, so repeated use may be necessary. Equally important in long-term care is cleanliness (but not compulsive scrubbing) and cool starch powder or starch baths. Your parent should consult her physician for details. Usually, probems originating in the vulva or vagina are not serious and can be relieved by simple treatments. However, similar symptoms can be produced by a more worrisome disease elsewhere in the reproductive system, and so should be evaluated early.

The cervix lies at the far end of the vagina and acts as the border between the vagina and the uterus. Like the vagina, it can become injured and bleed, or become infected and produce a malodorous discharge. It can also develop benign growths that may produce pain and discharge (or, possibly, no symptoms at all), but which can be cured by surgical removal. Much more dangerous than either of these conditions, however, is cancer of the cervix. Although cervical cancer is most frequent in middle-aged women, one of every eight cases occurs in a woman over 70. Your parent may experience bleeding or a watery vaginal discharge, but she is more likely to have no symptoms at all, and the cancer may be discovered during a routine physical examination. Pain is a late and very serious sign. Cervical cancer is the most important disease discovered by the Pap smear, and is the reason your parent should continue having an annual Pap smear and pelvic examination. If she develops any of these suggestive symptoms, she should have a physical examination, a pelvic examination, and a Pap smear. The cancer is usually readily detected, but requires a biopsy (sampling of a small piece of tissue) for absolute certainty. Treatment depends upon how widely the cancer has spread. If it is detected early (as is usually the case with this slow-starting cancer if your parent has annual Pap smears), a hysterectomy (removal of the cervix and uterus) may be all that is needed. If it has spread, the recommended treatment is usually radiation or, occasionally, radiation and surgery. Caught early, cancer of the cervix is usually curable. Your parent should be diligent in getting regular checkups and should not neglect unpleasant symptoms in the hope that they may go away.

Beyond the cervix lies the uterus, another possible site for cancer. Although the uterus is afflicted with a complex of other growths and disorders, some of which are forerunners to cancer, uterine cancer itself represents the major danger. Cancer of the uterus is more likely to develop if a woman is taking estrogen over an extended period. Uterine cancer may occasionally be detected by Pap smear or by a routine pelvic examination, but the key symptom is bleeding from the vagina. Such bleeding must not be ignored. Although the blood may be due to some other cause, or come from some other location, your parent should take no chances. The physician will want to perform a pelvic examination, make a Pap smear, and sample some tissue from the uterus either by biopsy or curettage (scraping the inside of the uterine cavity—usually done under anesthesia and then examining the tissue microscopically). The diagnosis is usually easily confirmed or excluded. As in cancer of the cervix, treatment depends upon the extent of the disease: a hysterectomy and removal of the ovaries if the disease is detected early; radiation, and possibly more extensive surgery, if it is more widespread. As in cervical cancer, the likelihood of survival is good if the disease is treated early, but decreases markedly in more developed cancer.

The remaining section of the reproductive tract, the ovaries, is the most dangerous in older women. The ovaries are prone to numerous different kinds of growths, many of which are easily cured by surgical removal. However, cancer of the ovaries is a most serious disease. More than half of the women who develop it eventually die. The reason lies less in the virulence of the cancer than in its silence. Cancers of the cervix and uterus usually produce symptoms (vaginal discharge, bleeding) or are easily tested for (Pap smear), but ovarian cancer grows and spreads without giving any evidence of its presence. Occasionally there is mild abdominal bloating or twinges of pain in the lower abdomen, but usually the only way to discover the cancer before it is widespread is by a careful pelvic examination—one more reason for having an annual gynecological evaluation. If the physician feels a mass in the region of the ovaries, he will probably immediately search further by means of X-rays, sound waves (ultrasonography), or even by taking a look directly into the abdomen using a fiberoptic tube (peritoneoscopy). Ultimately, however, the safest route may be to examine the mass during surgery, for only then can benign lumps be differentiated from malignant ones. Treatment for small ovarian cancers usually consists of removing the ovaries and uterus. Radiation may be added if the disease is more widespread. If the cancer is extensive, cancer-killing medication (chemotherapy) is generally used.

With menopause, the muscles supporting the reproductive organs relax. This produces a variety of common problems, particularly in those elderly women whose muscles and ligaments have been previously stressed by difficult deliveries or by giving birth to numerous children. Several of the organs in the lower abdomen become less firmly tied down, and thus have a tendency to protrude from below. The vagina and uterus, bladder, or rectum (or any combination of these) may sag or even extend out from between the legs. Most often the condition is mild and your parent experiences symptoms such as a feeling of protrusion and heaviness in the area, leaking of urine with coughing or sneezing, and difficulty having a bowel movement. If the prolapse is more extensive, she may actually be able to feel the protruding mass with her hand. Treatments depend upon the structures involved and the severity of the condition. Mild cases may need no treatment, while surgery may be required to strengthen and realign structures in more serious cases. Occasionally, a hysterectomy helps. The placement of a supportive ring (pessary) which helps keep the vagina and uterus in place is a common, nonsurgical treatment. A decision about treatment depends upon a careful physical examination and discussion of the options with your parent's physician.

One of the most common, and controversial, medications used by older women is estrogen. As mentioned earlier, the body's natural production of estrogen decreases at menopause. Many of the unpleasant symptoms older women may experience are due partly to that decrease: hot flushes, sweating, dry tissue, emotional irritability, thinning of bones. Most of these problems can be reversed if estrogen is taken by mouth: flushes disappear, tissues become firmer, depression lifts, and bones decrease their calcium loss. But such estrogen treatment increases the risk of uterine cancer, and the likelihood of heart attack and stroke may also be increased. Estrogen is valuable, but must be used cautiously. It is generally not used for more than a few months or a year for conditions like flushes, dry tissue, or emotional distress—then the dosage is tapered and finally stopped. It may be used for long periods of time if a person is at risk to develop worrisomely thin bones (osteoporosis; see Section 240). It should not be used if a person suffers from serious heart disease, atherosclerosis (Section 158), liver disease, or cancer of the breast or uterus. Estrogens should never be taken without the careful supervision of a physician, and an annual gynecological examination (with Pap smear and uterine biopsy) is imperative. Recent research suggests that a combination of estrogen and progesterone (another female hormone), taken at different times during the month, is safer than estrogen alone. In any case, if your parent is using estrogen regularly, be certain that she is being supervised closely by her physician.

265. *Low Temperature (Hypothermia).* Thousands of elderly people die from cold every year in the United States. How can this be? It certainly isn't a phenomenon which attracts public attention, and, in fact, it is little recognized even among physicians. However, your intervention can be life-saving.

Victims of hypothermia don't freeze to death. Rather, their body slowly cools, over several days or several weeks, until life is threatened. The older body's thermostat often regulates temperature poorly. It may allow body temperature to fall unnoticed. This most commonly occurs in a person who lives in a home that is slightly too cool, e.g., 55–65 degrees. Initially the person may shiver and feel cold, but that often passes quickly, and the hypothermia victim enters a period of diminished awareness of his surroundings. He may still move around and take care of himself but appears drowsy and unalert. As his body temperature continues to fall, he may become pale, cool to the touch, tremulous, and confused. He may have slurred speech and difficulty walking. The more confused he becomes, the less likely he is to recognize and correct the situation. If your parent begins to develop drowsiness, confused speech, and slowed movements, particularly if his house feels cool, think of hypothermia and consult a physician immediately.

Hypothermia is a dangerous condition which should be treated in a hospital. If your parent is profoundly cold, admission to an intensive care unit (ICU) for rapid warming may be required. If his body temperature is closer to normal, slower warming with blankets, heating pads, and warm water is often sufficient. In either case, the risk of dying is considerable: almost half of those requiring rapid warming die. The greatest safeguard is for you to recognize hypothermia early in its course and to seek treatment for your parent before his body temperature falls too low.

266. *Skin Disease.* The elderly experience the same complex variety of skin disorders as do younger people, but suffer from most of them more frequently. Skin normally becomes thin, cracked, and dried with age. This is particularly true of those areas of the skin exposed to the sun and in those people who have had outdoor occupations, who take hot baths using strong soap, or who otherwise mistreat their skin. As a result, the skin in the elderly is prone to itching and scaling conditions, bacterial and fungal infec-

tions, and spots and discolorations of all types. Most of these conditions are irritating or unsightly and require the aid of a physician to correct, but they can be treated successfully. More worrisome is cancer of the skin.

Skin cancer is the most common of all cancers in old age. Some elderly people have a tendency to overlook or neglect sores that develop on their skin, even those on their face or hands. That is a mistake. New sores, even if without pain, should not be neglected, since the likelihood of their being cancerous is significant. There are three common types of skin cancer, each having a different degree of aggressiveness but each requiring immediate treatment. Basal cell carcinoma usually grows on the face, in areas of skin damaged by the sun. It usually begins as a small, raised nodule with rounded edges; grows slowly and painlessly; and ultimately can become a large, irregular, discolored, ulcerated sore. It is the most common of all skin cancers and the least likely to spread. However, if neglected, it will grow deeply and destructively into surrounding tissue. Unless it is let go too long, it can be very successfully treated by surgical removal. Squamous cell carcinoma is more worrisome because, unlike basal cell cancer, it is capable of spreading widely throughout the body if proper treatment is not obtained early. Squamous cell cancer can take almost any appearance, but most commonly is a flesh-colored or reddish-brown patch which slowly enlarges, bleeds easily, and may become ulcerated in the center. It also occurs most often in sun-damaged areas like the lips, the edge of the ear, or the back of the neck. Any such new sore should be called promptly to the attention of your parent's physician. A specimen will need to be removed for microscopic examination. Treatment is surgical removal of the sore and the skin around it. Fortunately, caught early, most squamous cell carcinomas are curable. The most dangerous of the skin cancers is malignant melanoma. It can take on many appearances, but usually it is flat or only slightly raised and is colored (brown, dark brown, black, or dark blue). It often spreads quickly throughout the body and can be fatal. Any malignant melanoma should be removed immediately, since it needs to be treated before it begins to spread.

267. *Thyroid Disease.* The thyroid gland, which surrounds the front half of the windpipe just above the collar bones, produces a hormone the body requires for health. Too much or too little thyroid hormone creates a variety of symptoms. In young people, too much hormone (hyperthyroidism) often results in nervousness, tremors, diarrhea, loss of appetite, weight loss, heart palpitations, emotional outbursts, and muscle weakness, while too little hormone (hypothyroidism) produces lethargy, weakness, constipation, sensitivity to cold, dry skin, hair loss, slowed heartbeat, and hoarseness. Both conditions occur frequently among the elderly (particularly

among women), and may look identical to the disease in a younger person, but just as frequently the symptoms may be very different. In fact, either disease may develop so quietly and in such an uncharacteristic fashion that the presence of thyroid disease may go long unrecognized, robbing your parent of years of good health.

Hyperthyroidism may appear as an unexplained loss of appetite and a weight loss extending over months. Your parent may be weak, tired, or depressed. She may have heart symptoms like chest pain, shortness of breath, or heart palpitations. In short, her symptoms may be completely unlike the picture usually associated with too much thyroid hormone, and thus her physician may not search for hyperthyroidism.

Hypothyroidism may be equally misleading. Your parent may complain only of lethargy or depression. On the other hand, she may become agitated and suspicious, or she may be bothered only by physical symptoms like stiffness, "arthritis," deafness, or constipation. Moreover, hypothyroidism may develop so slowly and last so long that it becomes thought of as part of her personality as she ages.

Both hyperthyroidism and hypothyroidism are easily diagnosed by laboratory tests. Since the laboratory tests must be specially ordered, failure to diagnose either condition usually lies with a failure to think of them. The presence of a goiter (swelling of the gland) may be an additional hint that thyroid disease is present, although often no neck enlargement is noticeable. If your parent is clearly not herself and is not improving, ask the physician if thyroid disease could be responsible.

Treatment is usually successful. The hypothyroid patient usually takes thyroid pills (Levothroid, Synthroid) once daily. The hyperthyroid patient usually has the overactive part of the gland destroyed by treatment with radioactive iodide or, less frequently, by surgery. Occasionally such treatment slows the production of thyroid hormone so much that thyroid pills must then be taken.

22.

Problems of Medical Care

Problems of medical care for the elderly center around the availability of physical and human resources, their cost, and the age of the patient. The elderly are likely to suffer more than one illness, to have complications surrounding surgery, and to experience problems arising from multiple medications.

268. *The Breakdown in Medical Care.* The majority of physicians, nurses, and other professional medical personnel are well trained and well meaning. The majority of families are willing to extend themselves to help their aging parents. The majority of older people desire good care. Yet ideal care for an ill, elderly person is often hard to come by. Why? Some of the biggest problems are social.

The resources for such care don't exist. It is true that most older persons need hospital care only for acute illnesses, and then only briefly. But what they really need is a spectrum of medical care that includes hospitals, skilled nursing homes (SNFs), intermediate care facilities (ICFs), day-care centers that provide nursing care, day hospitals, after-care programs, and extensive home-care services. We also know that we should provide just enough medical care for the elderly to meet their needs, but not so much that they become dependent. More is not better—a person who can get along at home with regular visits to a day-care center generally should not remain in a skilled nursing home. Unfortunately, although we know the types and levels of medical care that should be available to the elderly, and we have a general idea of who will do best with what kind of care, the full spectrum of treatment facilities and programs exists in very few places and even then they are not present in adequate numbers.

Medical care is expensive, and the means to pay for it are inadequate. Medicare pays for (and thus encourages) hospital care, but provides limited reimbursement for care in nursing homes or at home. Too often the result is that the elderly receive more care in the hospital than needed, and too little care elsewhere. Private health-insurance programs usually have the same limitations. Thus home care can be the most expensive for the elderly, since most of the money comes directly out of their pockets.

Too few health personnel are trained to work with the elderly. Many doctors and other professionals share the same set of biases against them as does the general public. They may view the elderly as excessively fragile, unmotivated, dependent, or unlikely to improve. They may underestimate the tenacity of the elderly. This can lead to improper decisions about what level of care is called for. If you disagree strongly with the physician's recommendations, don't automatically assume that you are probably wrong. Try to get a sense of the doctor's preconceptions about the elderly. He might be right, but then so might you. Most professionals are willing to modify their recommendations if your dissenting argument is convincing.

Investigate every medical alternative in your community—you may be surprised by what you uncover. Contact local senior citizens groups (such as Senior Power, Gray Panthers) and your State Division of Aging for information about nearby day-care programs, home health-care agencies, and skilled nursing homes. Visit facilities and talk to people. Don't rely solely on your parent's physician or the hospital's social worker for reliable information about medical alternatives. They may have fallen into the habit of utilizing only a few places, and thus you might inadvertently overlook more suitable possibilities.

269. *Illness in Old Age.* The elderly's body defenses are weakened and their organs are flawed. Six out of seven have at least one chronic disease—many have several. Even in the best of circumstances and with the best of care, the outcome of medical treatment may be unsatisfactory.

We must change our expectations. Although acute diseases occur and must be treated, the majority of the elderly's medical problems are diseases of deterioration, and will be with them for life. We should feel satisfied if many of the processes that afflict our parents are slowed, rather than stopped or reversed. Thus what seems like a failure of medical care actually may reflect our inappropriate expectations. Treatment should reflect a realistic perspective. It should be neither too vigorous nor too casual. Unfortunately, professionals often have difficulty deciding where to draw the line. If they view old age as irreversible decline, they may do too little and deprive your parent of years of satisfactory functioning. If they view the diseases of the elderly as an affront to their therapeutic skills, their treatment efforts may sap your parent's remaining resources. A middle course is usually best: treatment which recognizes that most illnesses can be stabilized and most elderly can continue to function, but which appreciates that decline is inevitable.

270. *Surgery in Old Age.* Surgery is a medical procedure with risks for people of any age, but especially for the elderly. However, a person shouldn't avoid important surgery simply because he is old.

Minor surgery is almost as safe for the elderly as for younger people. Major surgery is another matter. Any surgery that requires prolonged anesthesia during the operation or prolonged bedrest afterwards places an older person at a significantly increased risk. Complications, possibly death, are more likely. The reason lies in the fragile health of many older people, their lack of physical reserves, and the likelihood that they suffer from one or more chronic diseases. Thus their problems in recovering from an operation more often stem from underlying poor health than from the disease which prompted the surgery.

What conditions put your parent at greatest risk? The worst offenders are chronic heart disease, recent heart attack, chronic lung disease, liver disease, and kidney disease. Regardless of what kind of major surgery is attempted, the presence of one of these underlying conditions demands the most careful evaluation and care. Discuss the pros and cons of the matter with your parent's surgeon.

Modern nursing techniques have made surgery much safer in older people. For example, in contrast to the earlier idea that an elderly person needed extensive bedrest to recover from surgery, physicians now believe that a patient should be active as quickly as possible. Thus you may find the nursing staff getting your parent out of bed for a walk or to go to the toilet within hours of major surgery. Don't be outraged—some of the most serious complications of surgery, such as blood clots in the legs or pneumonia, can be prevented by such activity.

271. *Medication in Old Age.* No area of medical care for the elderly is as problem-fraught as the use of medication. One out of five older persons has suffered from a problem caused by a drug he was taking. The reasons are well known.

(1) The elderly take more drugs than any other group. This is in part because they have multiple diseases which require multiple therapies. Often this medication is essential; occasionally it is not. The elderly (and their doctors) often may feel that a visit isn't complete without a drug being pre-

scribed. (2) The aging body is less well equipped to deal with medication. Small doses reach high levels in the blood because the liver has difficulty destroying the drugs and the kidneys have difficulty eliminating them. (3) For reasons that are not understood completely, older people are more likely than younger people to experience side effects from medication. (4) The elderly often have trouble taking prescribed medication correctly. They may become confused by having to take numerous drugs on a variety of different schedules. Poor memory, confusion, poor sight, and poor hearing—all make correct use of medication difficult. Childproof containers are also often elderproof as well. Moreover, medication side effects like confusion and lethargy make older persons less able to follow directions carefully and thus more likely to take medication at the wrong time and in the wrong amounts.

Certain medications are particularly likely to produce problems: blood-pressure medication, heart medication (particularly digoxin), sedatives, sleeping pills, antidepressants, pain medication, and medication for Parkinson's disease. The more medications involved, the more likely they are to interfere with one another's actions. Since certain drugs are at particular risk to interact with others, be sure to have your parent's physician review any new combinations of medication.

You can be of significant help to your parent in preventing drug-related problems. Become familiar with the medications he or she is taking; find out the reason for taking each. If your parent is taking many different drugs (for example, six or more), is there a way to reduce that number? It is often best to have one physician who oversees all your parent's medication, to avoid conflicting prescriptions from different doctors. Have the physician periodically review the drugs with an eye to simplifying the regimen. If the number can't be reduced, can all the medications be taken at the same time, two or three times each day? Be sure your parent understands the schedule, and follows it. If you and your parent are active and diligent in reviewing his medication periodically, unanticipated problems are much less likely to develop.

Daily Realities

23.

Housing

Suppose you reach age 80 and have no place to live. Suppose the money runs out and you must give up your house, or you become too frail to climb the steps to your apartment, or your children feel that you can no longer care for yourself safely and insist that you enter a nursing home. What then? What do you do when unsatisfactory housing disrupts the patterns of a lifetime?

These worries and realities confront many elderly. The changing financial, physical, and emotional conditions of the later years frequently alter where a person lives, and with whom. These changes are usually undesired, and may be unanticipated. An illness may force your parent out of his or her home and into a sheltered setting. Make no mistake, however—the problem is just as poignant for the children of the elderly. Often it is the children who have to push for a change in housing: insist that the time for moving has arrived, involve the physician or social worker, or search for a nursing home. And yet new housing in old age need not be undesirable, but making a correct choice is frequently difficult.

Where should your parents live as they get older? Should they move to "retirement housing" before they have to, in anticipation of problems to come? If one of your parents has deteriorated, should he be separated from the other one? How long should your lone parent live by himself? Is it best for him to live in his own home, or with you, or in a nursing home? What are nursing homes like? How do you choose one? What are the alternatives? Answers to these and other questions are essential if you and your parents are to make sensible decisions about where they should live.

272. *Where Should Your Parent Live?* On the face of it, this is a silly question. Situations are too individualized to allow a single, specific answer. And yet, I will venture an answer—at home. Whatever "home" means to your parent, that is where he should live.

For most people, home is a place where they can make their own decisions. Although home has other qualities, like the presence of old friends and comfortable memories, most of all it is the place where your parent is in control of his own life. It is the place where he can create his own schedule and live by it. He can rise when he wishes and sleep when he wants. He can choose his own meals and eat if he feels like it. He can go out for a walk without having to explain his absence. He can make his own mistakes. Such freedom is as desirable at 80 as it was at 20. Anything you can do to prolong your parent's independence is worthwhile.

We tend to think of home as a house or an apartment of our own. Usually that is correct, but not always. Your parent may feel most comfortable surrounded by friends in a group residential facility, or living in a nursing home located in the community of his youth. Talk to each of your parents about where he and she would like to live. Don't assume that they wish to remain in the family home simply because you have fond memories of your years there and can't picture them anywhere else. Perhaps staying in the old neighborhood is not important to them now that their friends have moved or died. Perhaps the family home has slipped into disrepair with the years and is now a decidedly unpleasant place to live. Perhaps a manageable small apartment on one level suits their needs better now.

As you help your parents evaluate their future needs for housing, consider their current strengths and how they are likely to change with time. Can they get around, and for how much longer? Can they drive? Can they climb stairs? Do they live close enough to walk easily to important places: the bank, shopping, restaurants, friends' homes, the pharmacy, a medical center, places of entertainment, a library, a bus stop, church? Their ease of getting to these critical locations will decrease with time. How close do they live to you? Is the community safe, crime-free, and home to people with whom they like to associate? There are no firm rules about who are proper companions and neighbors for the elderly. Some older people like the diversity of a community composed of all ages, while others prefer to be surrounded by people of their own age. Once again, make no assumptions; allow your parents to correct your preconceptions. It might be best for them to move to a more ideal location early enough to settle in, make new friends, and develop new habits. The goal, of course, is to see that they live in a house or apartment and a community which encourages their independence indefinitely.

Other problems may limit where your parents can live comfortably. If either of their physical failings are severe, they may have difficulty living anywhere unaided. The nicest home or apartment can become a prison and health hazard if a person is bed- or wheelchair-bound, can't cook or feed himself, is incontinent, or is unable to clean or dress himself. Additional hurdles arise if either parent is confused, if his or her judgment is impaired, or if behavior has become unruly and unpredictable. It is in these situations, common among the very old, that the choice of the best action to take becomes cloudy.

Don't fool yourself into believing that as your parents' physical or mental capacities decline so does their desire to be in command of their life. On the contrary, as the number of things done well or even adequately decreases, the desire for final say about remaining functions increases. Because your parent needs to be cooked for or bathed, he is likely to resist being told when to go to bed. Often what passes for orneriness among the very old and debilitated is a determined effort to have *some* say in what happens to them; when personal control is lost, so is a large measure of human dignity.

Thus the answer to the question of where your parents should live is anywhere that permits them all the independence of action of which they are capable. One bit less is too little. One decision made for them that they could have made for themselves is one too many.

273. *Keeping Your Parent Independent.* Staying independent usually means staying out of an institution. Institutions, whether chronic care hospitals or nursing homes, and regardless of the commitment and sensitivity of the staff, need to control their residents. "Managing" their residents efficiently is essential for any institution to accomplish its many goals. The staff may mean well, but meals have to be served on time and activities must be planned that interest the greatest number of people. Individual habits and interests are thus undermined. Only when a person can determine the particulars of his life is he able to follow his own light, and that usually occurs in full measure only when he lives at home—alone, with his spouse or family, or with a friend.

Since keeping an aging parent at home as long as possible usually is important to his happiness, it is comforting to know that many services exist to help you accomplish this. However, since such services may be associated with a variety of different agencies (for example, fee-for-service, home-care units in hospitals, departments of social services, private non-profit community agencies), you may need to be diligent in tracking them down and in piecing them together to meet all his needs. Ultimately, however, a very old parent's needs may become greater than you can provide for. Don't conclude that institutionalization is the only alternative. Some of the most tenacious problems often can be provided for at home. If you have neither the time, the will, nor the expertise to take care of these problems yourself, home-care services of one kind or another are available in most communities to provide people to clean the house, fix meals, visit him, give shots, do the shopping, relieve his infirmities with therapeutic exercise, and much more. Some elderly people can be kept in their homes for several additional years by utilizing these services. Of course, they are not appropriate for everyone and for every situation, but always consider them when it appears that your parent can no longer stay at home.

Find out about such services by looking in the telephone directory under Home Health Services, Homemaker Services, Nursing Services, Community Health Services, Social Services, or some other similar title. Ask your parent's physician for sources, talk to his or her minister, or call the local Division of Aging. Write to the National Council for Homemaker–Home Health Aide Services (67 Irving Pl., New York, NY 10003), the AARP, or the NCSC (see Chapter 25). With persistence, most people can weave together a useful pattern of help for their parent.

Unfortunately, home care is not cheap. Some of it can be prohibitively expensive if regularly relied upon—for example, physician house-call services or special-duty nurses. Others are more reasonable (and at times free), such as homemaker–home health aides and visiting services. However, even these aids ultimately become expensive if your parent is chronically ill or has a long-term disability. In any case, paying for services which are successful in keeping your parent at home is invariably less expensive than the cost of a nursing home. One of our public embarrassments is that there are so few ways to pay for home care except directly from your (or your parent's) pocket. Medicare and some private insurance plans will pay for a limited number and only a few types of home-care visits (usually care for acute illnesses). A few public programs will provide home care at reduced rates, particularly for financially distressed elderly (such as Title XX of the Social Security Act and Title III of the Older Americans Act). Otherwise, you are on your own. You might consider a live-in companion such as another older person or a college student who would receive room and board and a small monthly salary.

There are other supports which aid in keeping your parent at home, beyond having someone come to the house periodically. Anything that keeps your parent active and interested in life helps to keep him independent. (See the chapters on socializing, recreation, and education which follow.) If your parent is able to get out, he may be able to receive much of the regular care he needs (and give you a rest) through regular visits to senior citizen centers, day-care centers, day hospitals, or outpatient medical clinics associated with hospitals. Contact these facilities and talk with their staff to determine what services they offer. The opportunity to get out of the house and be around other people can do much to lift your parent's spirit.

274. *Other Kinds of Independent Living.* Not every older person has a house or wants to live in one. Many prefer apartments or condominiums, often for very sound reasons such as low maintenance and central location. Although the majority of apartment-dwelling elderly individuals live in normal community facilities, a few are housed in low-cost, publicly-subsidized apartment complexes. Unfortunately, several bad apples have come close to spoiling this particular barrel—a few inadequate public-housing developments for the elderly have given all of them an undeservedly bad name. This is regrettable, since many public projects are of high quality. In fact, most of the good ones are so successful that they have waiting lists extending well into the future. Are any public projects near your parent a possibility?

Good, inexpensive housing for the elderly is at a premium. Besides subsidized apartments, a few locations have housing available specifically for older people. Most often, these take the form of apartments located in a facility that also houses a medical or nursing clinic, a place that provides meals (such as a federal nutrition site), a pharmacy, and other useful services. Such places may be safer than the community at large, and the rents are frequently kept within reasonable limits. Other low-cost housing, although often of doubtful quality, are boarding or rooming homes and single-room-occupancy hotels. These do have the advantage of giving an independent elderly person an inexpensive place to live where he can be completely on his own, but they can also be very isolating.

A few novel solutions to the lack of good housing have been tried in recent years. Many communities, through the local Division of Aging, have established foster-care programs. Frail or disabled elderly who don't need hospitalization or a nursing home, but who need help with daily activities, move in with a family in their community. The family receives a modest monthly payment and, in turn, provides a place to live, meals, and help with the older person's daily needs. Foster care can work very well, but it can be disastrous if the families (or the elderly) are poorly selected. Some older people are taking matters into their own hands and are developing a variety of unique living arrangements. In some neighborhoods that contain a large number of older people, the elderly have banded together in an effort to secure the necessary services and safety. Unrelated, elderly individuals are sharing homes (often six to twelve persons per home share the costs and the work as well)—they have even established a nonprofit organization to facilitate their efforts (Share-A-Home of America, Inc., begun by James Gillies of Winter Park, Florida), but the spread of the concept around the country has been facilitated primarily by civic groups or churches.

Finally, a major option for those people who have adequate financial resources is the retirement community. Many people find these facilities to be an ideal solution to their housing needs. The communities are usually well planned and regulated, with high-quality housing (individual homes, apartments, condominiums), a variety of services on the grounds or nearby, strict entrance requirements (both age and financial), and well-developed recreational/educational programs. They meet the vigorous elderly person's need for independence, social activity and stimulation, dignity, safety, privacy, and a sense of community. When they work, they can work very well. However, there are problems in paradise. First, there is the expense. Entrance costs may include buying a home and/or turning over some or most of the resident's estate to the facility. And maintenance fees in many facilities have shown a tendency to spiral upwards, regardless of promises made at the time of entrance. An equally severe problem in some retirement communities is lack of facilities to treat chronic medical conditions—the communities are for the "young old," and the frail or disabled fit in poorly. A few retirement communities offer a range of living options, from free-standing houses to apartments to on-grounds nursing homes. Thus a person whose abilities are flagging may move from an open location to one more structured and still stay within the same community, enjoying the same friends and pursuing familiar activities and interests. As with anything else, retirement communities should be approached warily—ask tough questions and look around, since although some are good, others are not. Examine the financial stability of the development carefully. In addition, your parent should attempt to live in his preferred retirement community for a week or two before buying, since some older people are surprised to find that they are put off by the lack of young people, the prevalence of rules, or one of the other characteristics of such a living arrangement.

275. *Should Your Parent Live with You?* The answer to this question is neither yes nor no—it is maybe. People have peculiar reactions when it becomes evident that their parent will not be able to live independently much longer. Some people, often driven by a sense of responsibility or guilt, reflexly insist that he move in with them. Others search for any solution *except* having him live with them. Neither reaction is likely to do justice either to you or to your parent. The only way to make a reasonable decision about whether your parent should live with you is to examine the pros and cons openly and realistically.

First of all, your parent may have no interest in living with you. Don't be surprised if closeness to you is not the most important factor in his choice of a place to live. Of course, older people often have "automatic" reactions to the idea of life with their children: "they wouldn't consider it," "they don't want to be a burden." These reactions generally are of no more value than your first reactions. What is of greater importance is your parent's careful consideration of those elements in his life that are most significant to him: for example, nearness to friends, familiar neighbors or neighborhood, or access to a particular church. It may be that the sum of these factors outweighs the benefits of living with his children. Pleasant as your home may be for you and your children, it may seem a prison to an elderly person with interests different from yours. Try to help your parent with this decision, since he may give unrealistic weight to certain factors.

Equally, you must take a realistic look at the pros and cons of such a move from your own perspective. Do you *want* your parent to live with you, or are you going along with the idea only out of a sense of duty? What will be the impact of the move on your family—can you get along with your parent and can he get along with your spouse or children for long periods of time? Your parent's personality is unlikely to change, nor is yours. The conflicts within the family will be the same as they always have been, only worse, since physical closeness is a powerful catalyst. Does your daughter's loud music clash with your parent's need for quiet? Will his tendency to criticize inflame your husband's (or wife's) sense of insecurity? Who will shoulder the major part of the day-to-day burden of taking care of your parent? Usually the daughter or daughter-in-law will have primary responsibility. If that is to be the case, it should be understood ahead of time so no one suffers any unpleasant surprises. What are the financial considerations? Is living with you cheaper than any of the other alternatives? It may not be, particularly if one of the alternatives is to create a home-care network involving outside agencies that enables your parent to live at home. In all these considerations, remember that conditions change. What made sense when your parent was active and able to care for the children when you were at work may no longer be feasible now that he is incapacitated with a stroke that has forced you to give up your job to care for him.

Having a parent live in the home often works out well. It is unlikely to succeed, however, unless the decision is made carefully and realistically. Discuss the potential problems and benefits openly with your spouse, your parent, and your children. Have a family conference. Set aside for the moment your feelings of guilt, since the move ultimately will be destructive if the reasons for it are not sound. It usually is better not to attempt such a move than to try it and have it fail. The answer to all your uncertainty is often to test out the arrangement by having your parent visit you, perhaps several times, and for increasingly longer visits. Such a trial will frequently give you the information you need to make a decision in everyone's best interest.

276. *Losing Independence—Preparing for a Move.* When we think of loss of independence in old age, we automatically think about a move to a nursing home. However, almost any move brings some loss and requires preparation. After the age of 65, a relocation usually involves a decrease in expectations. Our parents move from a large house to a small one on one level. Or they move to an apartment or some sort of group living. They may have to give up possessions and lose contact with friends. Moreover, the move has often been precipitated by a loss of health or a financial reversal. Even though done for the most understandable and realistic of reasons, moving is rarely pleasantly anticipated by the elderly, since the future after a move is usually more limited than beforehand.

The situation is worse if the move is to a nursing home or other institution. Both you and your parent are likely to see such a relocation in the blackest terms. The move is seen as an abrupt break from the life that had gone before. Evidence of the enormous impact on the elderly of transfer to an institution is found in the markedly increased death rate among people newly admitted to such facilities, regardless of how clean or new the homes. The best safeguard against a troubled or disastrous relocation is to prepare your parent thoroughly for the change.

Your parent must be made to understand the need for a move to an institution, if he is at all capable of such understanding. Without emphasizing his disabilities, try to help him realize why he can no longer continue at home (for example, he is too forgetful, he has fallen twice in the last month, his eyesight doesn't permit him to leave the house safely, he has been leaving the stove on, and/or he dangerously confuses his medication). Relocation will progress much more smoothly if your parent appreciates its necessity.

Discuss alternatives with your parent and with the rest of the family. Openly measure the pros and cons. Look at facilities closely and well in advance. Let your parent tour them and talk to staff. Perhaps he can stay in each for a day or two. Allow him time to adjust to the idea of a move—it represents a major change in his life. With such preparation, moves can go smoothly—but not always. Sometimes moves must occur in a hurry following hospitalization or after a sudden illness. Even then, encourage maximum participation from your parent—don't just drive to a facility and say "here we are."

277. *Nursing Homes.* Nursing homes are not the only institutions that house elderly individuals for long periods of time. Mental hospitals and certain medical hospitals provide long-term care to people who have serious problems. In general, however, the nursing home is "home" to many more elderly than all other types of institutions combined. Although it is not true that most people end up in a nursing home, at any one time five percent of people over 65 live in one, as do 20 percent of people 85 years or older. Moreover, 25 percent of all people will die in a nursing home, and about 30 percent will spend some time in one. Clearly, nursing homes are an important part of life for many elderly.

Nursing homes are not the nicest of places to live. This is not to say that they don't try their best to do a difficult job well. Certainly, some are clean and new and staffed by well-meaning, committed professionals. But they are not places where one would choose to live unless obliged to. They are institutions: long hallways, group dining rooms, single rooms or roommates, mealtime hours and bedtime hours, rules and regulations. Even at their best, nursing homes are more regimented, impersonal, public, and unfamiliar than home. At their worst, they are everything the rumors have them to be: dirty, unhealthy, emotionally sterile, cheerless places staffed by mercenary individuals without love or concern. Even though public disclosures and tightened state regulations have improved most nursing homes, they still vary widely in quality.

Most of us feel guilty when we begin to consider a nursing home for our parent. However, if we let guilt influence our thinking, we may very well make a poor decision. We should put our parent in a nursing home because it is the best place for him, and for no other reason. We carefully review all the options and conclude, sadly, that there are no others that work. We include our parent in the decision as much as possible. Even when all the evidence points to placement in a home, it may be hard to take the step. This is understandable—the situation is unwanted and the emotional pain real. Remember, however, that your parent is entering a nursing home because it is necessary: his life actually may improve after the move. In choosing nursing-home placement, there is room for sadness but little room for guilt.

By no means do I want to imply that nursing homes have no value. Many severely disabled older people fare better in a nursing home and live a higher-quality life there than in any other setting. Many nursing homes provide twenty-four-hour care by professionals (particularly by, or under the supervision of, nurses), ongoing medical treatment (physical therapy, tube feeding, oxygen and respirator therapy), and a structured, safe environment. Nursing homes are particularly useful if your parent requires continual supervision due to severe dementia or profound medical deterioration caused by conditions like stroke, arthritis, or heart disease. Equally troublesome problems to manage (or live with) outside a structured setting are wandering, irresponsible behavior, aggressiveness, sleep disturbances, incontinence, and inability to communicate. If these conditions or behaviors complicate your parent's later years, nursing-home placement may be called for, but only after you have explored other possibilities and consulted the appropriate experts (physician, geriatric social worker). Other avenues to investigate include homemaker services, home-care aides, day-care centers, and a live-in helper (Section 273).

Once you and your parent have determined that a nursing home is the best option, you have to find one that is suitable. This may be no easy task. Seek recommendations from physicians, nurses, geriatric social workers, friends who have used nearby facilities, or personnel of local organizations for the elderly. Make a list of homes with a good reputation. Pay particular attention to those located close to family members, since a satisfactory nursing home usually means one close enough to key relatives to allow frequent visits.

Part of the problem is that there are too many mediocre or poor nursing homes and too few good ones. How can you tell them apart? Once you have several homes in mind, investigate them. It is a buyer's market, so don't pull your punches. Visit them and look closely. Look underneath the surface.

1. Are the nursing home and its administrator licensed by the state? Be extremely wary of unaccredited homes, almost to the point of eliminating them from consideration.

2. Is the home clean and neat? It must be, but that is finally of secondary significance: a nursing home should be much more than just new and sparkling. In any case, look in every room, and begin to wonder if some areas are "off limits" to your inspection.

3. Check the kitchen and eating areas. Taste the food and look at the menu for a week, and a month. Is there a dietitian? Are snacks available? Are there rigid dining hours?

4. How many staff are there, and of what types? How well trained are the aides (the people having the most contact with your parent)? Is there a physician on the staff? Does he visit frequently and is he available at irregular hours? May your parent use his own physician? Are there a physical therapist, dentist, psychologist, pharmacist, and other professional people on the staff? How many nurses are there, and when do they work? Be sure that you learn who your parent will see regularly and who he will have access to if needed.

5. What equipment does the facility make available for resident use?

This includes recreational equipment used by your parent directly (pool table, stereo, etc.) as well as medical equipment used by nursing-home personnel (X-ray, laboratory, respirator). It also includes anything which makes the facility safer: railings, ramps, call boxes.

6. Most important, without which all of the other features are meaningless, what does the home feel like to you? Is it friendly and personal, or cold and institutional? Do the residents look bored and listless or active and alert? Are they sitting in silence watching the TV, or talking with the staff and other residents? Do the staff like their work? Don't just talk with the administrator: talk at length with staff and residents. Watch them. Are staff members friendly and concerned as they work with the residents? Are they patronizing, or do they treat the elderly people like individuals? Do they help the residents find something significant to do: make friends, join a group, help other residents? Is the resident's privacy respected? Are his wishes? Is there a mix of programs and activities available? Ask to see a schedule and examine it critically. Spend the major part of your time assessing the atmosphere of the home, for that is the level on which the facility will succeed or fail as a desirable place for your parent to live.

Expense is, of course, an important factor. Nursing homes may cost in excess of $20,000 annually. Many people who enter homes as private-pay patients ultimately have to rely upon Medicaid after their financial resources become depleted. Some couples even divorce so that the healthy member escapes responsibility for the nursing-home bills of the ill spouse. Is the nursing home you and your parent are considering approved for Medicare and Medicaid coverage? Is it a skilled nursing facility (SNF) or an intermediate care facility (ICF)? SNFs provide the most intensive treatment, have the highest concentration of staff, and are generally approved for Medicare (and Medicaid) reimbursement. Most nursing homes are ICFs: they provide twenty-four-hour supportive care supervised by licensed nurses, and are eligible for Medicaid reimbursement. Get these financial questions straight (Chapter 24) before your parent begins a nursing-home stay, since it would be a shame to make a change simply because they had not been thought through.

The move to a nursing home is such an important step for an older person that it is imperative to investigate the realities thoroughly. Several resources exist:

S. G. Burger and M. D'Erasmo, *Living in a Nursing Home* (New York: Ballantine Books, 1976, paperback).

J. B. Nassau, *Choosing a Nursing Home* (New York: Funk & Wagnalls, 1975).

How to Choose a Nursing Home (from the Institute of Gerontology, University of Michigan, 543 Church St., Ann Arbor, MI 84104).

How to Select a Nursing Home (from the American Health Care Association, 1200 15th St., N.W., Washington, DC 20005).

Or write several of the organizations listed under Political Advocacy Groups in Section 293.

Once your parent has entered a nursing home, he has entered a new society composed primarily of staff and other patients. You and your visits provide leavening to that rather concentrated mix. Every visit may raise new feelings of guilt and sorrow within you, and this may discourage you from making frequent visits. Try not to let that happen. Stay familiar with the care your parent receives. Expect him to be dissatisfied from time to time. Act as a sounding board for complaints, a problem-solver when those complaints appear justified, and a mediator when he becomes involved in counterproductive struggles with the staff or other patients. Although you should investigate repeated complaints, don't choose sides until you know the facts. Trust to the staff's professionalism until the evidence of unsatisfactory care is undeniable.

24.

Finances

Sound finances and good health are the two most critical elements of a successful old age. Limited finances may be the most common barrier to old-age happiness. Unfortunately, unless your parents have years until they retire, many of the important decisions which result in long-lasting financial security will have been made (or not made) long ago.

This chapter will touch only briefly on the elements of financial well-being. The topic is complicated and deserves a thorough review by you and your parent, preferably with the help of a financial counselor. However, one critical area that the two of you must understand and plan for, health-care financing, is discussed at length.

278. *Financial Planning.* Your parents *must* plan for their financial future. They must identify future income and spending accurately, and do it early enough to make meaningful alterations if necessary. Otherwise, they stand a good chance of facing a bleak future. Interviews with elderly Americans consistently find that at least half of them wish, often bitterly, that they had attended to their coming financial needs more carefully. Planning and saving should begin in earnest at about age 40. If your parents are retirement age or older, the die is already cast in many important ways, yet you and they should still take a hard look at finances to be certain that no important source of income is being overlooked. Involve a professional financial advisor (particularly those with specialized training, such as CPAs) if possible. Books on general financial planning may be useful, such as:

Sylvia Porter, *Sylvia Porter's New Money Book* (New York: Doubleday & Co., 1979).

J. B. Quinn, *Everyone's Money Book* (New York: Delacorte Press, 1979).

Books about old age which contain helpful sections on finances include:

H. Downs and R. J. Roll, *The Best Years Book* (New York: Delacorte Press, 1981).

J. Michaels, *Prime of Your Life* (Boston: Little, Brown & Co., 1983).

279. *Where the Money Comes from.* For most older people, income stems from three primary sources: Social Security, private pensions, and savings. Many young elderly supplement their income by working. The proportions of each of these sources of income for the older population as a whole are:

SOURCE OF FUNDS	PERCENTAGE OF TOTAL INCOME
Social Security	33
Pensions	13
Savings	18
Wages	33
Other	3

In recent years older individuals have tended to rely upon their Social Security and pension checks to provide spending money, while their savings have consisted of a house without a mortgage. Frequently, the money has not been enough. In general, the elderly require 70–75 percent of their former income to live comfortably. It is *not* true that a person needs far less income after retirement than before. Encourage your parents to carefully review their financial situation, including Social Security payments, pension income, assets of all kinds, estate planning, health-care provisions, and financial desires and expectations. Have they done their homework? Are their plans and expectations realistic?

Over 90 percent of older Americans receive Social Security; two thirds depend upon it for at least half their income. A person is eligible to receive a Social Security check if he or she is age 65 (62 for reduced benefits) and has contributed to the Social Security fund for an adequate number of years, or is a dependent of someone who is eligible. There is no substitute for knowing the rules. Your parent should make contact with the local Social Security office months or years before he or she plans to retire. They have many free pamphlets which describe various parts of the program, including eligibility rules, how to estimate the size of the retirement check, survivor's benefits, disability benefits, the late-retirement bonus, the reduction in benefits caused by part-time work, and much more. (In particular, your parent can ask for the comprehensive "Social Security Handbook," SSA Publication No. 05-10135). It is wise for your parent to learn years in advance of retirement what contributions the government's records show him as having made, so that any discrepancy can be corrected early.

Social Security is vital to your parents' financial well-being, and yet there is concern that the whole program will be bankrupt within the next few years. Such a conviction appears to be ill founded. In the spring of 1983, Congress took steps to assure the viability of the system by: (1) gradually increasing the contributions into the program; (2) permitting Social Security benefits to be taxed if an older person's income plus one half of his pension exceeds $25,000 per year; (3) decreasing the amount of early-retirement benefits; (4) increasing the age required for full benefits (age 67 by year 2027); and (5) increasing the bonus workers receive for delaying retirement. These changes will become effective gradually over the next twenty to forty years. The government finally appears convinced that Social Security is essential for the well-being of older individuals.

When your parent is learning about Social Security, he should also explore SSI (Supplemental Security Income). SSI provides small monthly checks to people of any age who have limited income and resources. Your parents may not qualify at first, but if their financial status worsens with time they may become eligible to receive SSI benefits.

Private pensions, another cornerstone in many persons' retirement plans, are frequently disappointments. If your parent is involved in a pension plan, he or she should take time to learn its ins and outs while there is still enough time left on the job to extract significant benefit from the program. Your parent should not assume that he will receive pension payments upon retirement, even though he has contributed to the pension program for years. There are tricks of which he should be aware. First, he should recognize that, unlike Social Security, most pension payments are not adjusted for the increase in the cost of living, so inflation eventually will deflate the value of the check. Long before he retires, he should determine (1) whether his job is covered by the company's pension plan, (2) how long he must work before he becomes *vested* (that is, eligible to receive benefits—often this means working ten years without interruption), (3) the effects of a leave of absence or prolonged medical illness on benefits, and (4) the impact of early retirement on benefits. Your parent should find out if the pension plan is *integrated* with Social Security (that is, if his pension check is first reduced by some factor which reflects the amount he has paid into Social Security). He should learn what happens to the benefits available to his spouse if he dies. There was a time when this information was hard to get, but in 1974 the federal government passed the Employee Retirement Income Security Act (ERISA), which, among other things, requires that employers with a pension plan provide employees with a "Summary Plan Description." All of these essential questions about pensions should be answered by your parent's company's description. Your parent should review this document carefully. Unanswered questions can be put to the plan's administrator, or to the local office of the Labor-Management Services Administration (under Department of Labor in the telephone directory).

The third key to old-age financial security is savings. Savings can take many forms (bank savings accounts, stocks and bonds, real estate, annuities, life insurance, money market funds, etc.). Any type of saving must be started early—a last-minute rush to put something aside usually doesn't work. It is in the matter of long-term savings that the advice of a professional financial planner should be sought, at least in initially establishing a sensible savings plan. Such a person can guide your parent into investments that make sense, as well as point out the undeniable benefits of establishing and making regular contributions to an IRA or Keogh plan. New ways of saving or of making better use of assets appear frequently. For example, the "reverse mortgage" allows an older person who is house-rich but cash-poor to sell his or her home, continue to live in it, and receive a monthly check. (This plan, however, carries the risk of depleting the home equity completely if the older person lives for many years.) Many elderly people find that if they review their financial position and arrangements carefully, they can find some areas for improvement. If you wish to help your parents directly, you can provide them with funds most economically by utilizing devices set up for that purpose, such as Crown loans and Clifford trusts. Consult your advisor.

All too often, older women are losers in the struggle for financial security. Their Social Security benefits are lower than, or dependent upon, their husband's. They may receive only a fraction of their husband's company pension after his death. Their savings may become depleted as the years pass. Older widows (or divorcees) are probably the most deprived sector of our population.

An elderly person living on retirement income can reduce money loss through a careful evaluation of expenses. Here again, professional advice is useful. Your parent should create a blueprint of necessary expenses (including a few "necessary luxuries") and follow it. Unexpected savings are everywhere, but may require persistence to find (stores which give discounts to senior citizens, reduced bus fares, etc.). Your parent should become aware of the tax breaks available to those over 65 (obtain the pamphlet "Tax Benefits for Older Americans" from the local IRS office).

One expense common in old age, health care, needs to be planned for particularly carefully to prevent it from demolishing the best of financial designs.

Financing Health Care

Medical care is one of the major expenses of old age. Financing medical care is one of its major worries. Steadily increasing costs have created a challenge that you and your parent need to address well before his or her sixty-fifth birthday. With a knowledge of what's available and with careful planning, the costs of health care can usually be met.

The options for financial protection are few, but substantial. (1) The centerpiece of any plan is the government health insurance for the elderly, Medicare. Before exploring any other health-insurance possibilities, you should become familiar with what it offers and how to use it. The related government program, Medicaid, can offer additional help with health costs if your parent's income is low enough. (2) Private insurance companies (Blue Cross and Blue Shield, among many others) offer programs which supplement Medicare coverage in a variety of ways. Such insurance can be valuable but must be chosen carefully. (3) Certain areas of the country have health maintenance organizations (HMOs) which provide their own medical care to subscribers. These can offer excellent value for the dollar, but they have their drawbacks and must be reviewed with care.

A variety of health-related expenses, such as regular nursing homecare, hearing aids, and eyeglasses, will need to be paid for out of your parent's pocket, since no readily accessible program provides for them.

MEDICARE

Medicare (and Medicaid) is part of the federal government's Social Security Act, amended in 1965. Obtain information about Medicare from your local Social Security office. Start by reading thoroughly their free booklet, "Your Medicare Handbook." Only when you understand what Medicare does and doesn't provide (and how to get it) will you be able to decide whether or not to obtain further coverage. Recognize that Medicare can be changed at any time by Congress and that pressures to modify it are mounting. Thus the description below may not be accurate for long—always check with the Medicare office for the most recent changes.

280. *Who Is Eligible and How to Get It.* Medicare is divided into Parts A (hospital insurance) and B (medical insurance). Medicare Part A is currently provided to anyone who reaches 65, *if* they are entitled to Social Security or railroad retirement benefits. Anyone entitled to Part A may *purchase* Part B coverage. Several other groups of people are also eligible, such as people under 65 who have been entitled to Social Security disability benefits for twenty-four consecutive months or those people insured under Social Security who need kidney dialysis or a kidney transplant. Moreover, your parent can continue working and still be covered. People who have not worked long enough to be entitled to Social Security may purchase Medicare coverage, as can people who already are eligible but want Medicare to start before they reach 65.

Your parent will not be enrolled automatically in Medicare at age 65—he or she should visit the local Social Security office at least three months beforehand to apply for it. A person's goal should be to become fully covered by the time he turns 65. He may cancel Part B coverage if he wishes, although that is usually unwise since Part B is an excellent dollar value. At the time of becoming covered, your parent will receive his Medicare card and claim number. He must use that card whenever visiting a physician or hospital.

281. *Medicare, Part A.* Part A covers hospital inpatient care. For a few, carefully selected people it covers care in a skilled nursing home (SNF) or specialized care at home. However, it doesn't pay all the bills in any of these situations, it doesn't pay the bills forever, and it excludes some things.

Care in the Hospital: For the first 60 days of each hospital stay, a patient pays only $304 (the "hospital insurance deductible," as of 1983). From day 61 to day 90, he pays $76 per day (the "copayment"). After day 90, he must pay full costs, except that he has available during his lifetime 60 "reserve days" (he pays $152 per day) which can help cover a long hospital stay. Moreover, after he has been out of the hospital (and not receiving specialized care) for 60 days, this whole sequence can begin again (minus the reserve days used). Since most hospital stays are much shorter than 60 days, most people find these benefits generous, unless they are cursed with a hospital stay lasting months. However, if things sound too good to be believed, there are some gaps—not all hospital charges are approved for payment.

Approved costs include a semiprivate room (two to four beds in a room), meals, medication and medical supplies, *regular* nursing care, lab tests, blood transfusions (after the first three pints), X-rays and radiation therapy, operating and recovery-room costs, special-care-unit costs (intensive care unit, coronary care unit, etc.), and rehabilitation services (physical therapy, occupational therapy, speech therapy, etc.).

Costs not approved include doctor's services (although Part B helps here), private duty nurses, the first three pints of blood, and any extra room charges not dictated by medical necessity (such as personal telephone, TV, radio, etc.). In addition, there is a lifetime limit of 190 days for care in a psychiatric hospital.

Several other problems may prevent payment. (1) The hospital must be one approved by Medicare. If possible, your parent should make certain in advance that any hospital he is likely to use is approved. (2) His treatment in the hospital must be necessary and must be prescribed by a licensed physician. (3) His hospital stay must not be disapproved (that is, found not to meet Medicare standards) by one of the hospital or professional review organizations that regularly look at the hospital charts of Medicare patients. He usually wouldn't find out about a disapproval until his hospitalization was over, at which time he would be presented with the whole hospital bill. This infrequent occurrence happens just often enough that your parent should be aware of it and be ready to appeal. As in problems with the rest of Part A coverage, he has 60 days in which to file an appeal. Usually hospitalization under Medicare goes smoothly, though, and there are no surprises if one is familiar with what to expect.

Your parent gives his Medicare claim number to the hospital at the time of admission. After his stay, he will receive a bill from the hospital for hospital costs minus Medicare payments (usually for the amount of the deductible, $304, unless he was in the hospital longer than 60 days). He will also receive a statement from an insurance company (not a bill) justifying the amount of his Medicare benefits. The statement does not come from Medicare, since they allow certain "intermediaries" (Blue Cross, Blue Shield, Travelers, Prudential, Aetna, etc.) to administer their accounts. The hospital bills the intermediary, which pays the hospital what Medicare allows, and then the hospital bills the patient for the rest.

Care in a skilled nursing home (SNF): Nursing-home care is provided by Medicare to a few elderly persons who need continuing treatment after a hospital stay. To be eligible for such coverage an elderly person must meet several requirements.

1. The patient must have been in a hospital for at least three consecutive days before transfer (not including the day of discharge).

2. The patient must be certified by a physician to need continuing skilled nursing or rehabilitative care for the condition which he was treated for in the hospital—just gaining admission to an approved skilled nursing home is not enough.

3. He must be admitted to the skilled nursing facility within two to four weeks after hospital discharge.

4. The facility's review organization must not disapprove the stay.

Once a person is approved for care in a SNF (a big hurdle), his first 20 days are completely covered. The next 80 days will cost him $38 per day (in 1983); all further days are at his own expense. However, during those 100 days of complete or partial coverage, Medicare will pay for the same sorts of services (drugs, nursing services, etc.) as it does during hospitalization. Your parent should therefore be certain that the nursing home he investigates is Medicare-approved.

Medicare is very strict about who receives approval. It must be clearly shown that your parent needs specialized care (care that only a specially trained person can provide) *every day*. If he needs anything less, the treatment is considered custodial care only, and that is not covered. If your parent is to be reimbursed, the care he receives must be expected to improve his condition rather than to maintain him at a plateau. Payment may be disallowed at any point during a nursing-home stay if it is felt that he no longer meets the criteria for needing skilled nursing care. As with hospital coverage, Part A does not cover doctors' services.

There is one protection against this risk of being disallowed: the courts often have not agreed with such Medicare rulings. If you feel that your parent is clearly in need of skilled nursing care and can't function without such help, and if Medicare disagrees, appeal. This first involves an internal review within Medicare, with your parent's participation, but later can progress to an independent decision by a federal court judge. The appeal must be initiated within 60 days.

Care at home ("home health care"): The final section of Part A coverage pays for skilled nursing and rehabilitative care at home. As with nursing-home care, there are stiff qualifications that must be met before Medicare will pay for such help.

1. Your parent's physician must determine that he needs part-time skilled nursing care, physical therapy, or speech therapy, and the doctor must set up a home health plan for him.

2. Your parent must be confined to home (that is, the medical condition must prevent him from getting around).

3. A Medicare-approved home health agency (such as a local visiting-nurse association) must provide the service.

Once your parent is approved for home care, he may receive an unlimited number of visits from any of these professionals at no cost (no deductibles or co-insurance) as long as he continues to need such help. He may also receive occupational therapy, medical social services, and certain medical supplies in his home. Services and supplies *not* paid for include a full-time nurse, medication or blood transfusions, meals, and homemaker services. Thus any help your parent may need in shopping, cooking, cleaning, or keeping the house in order will not be covered.

This section of Medicare offers good coverage for those confined to home, but there are significant gaps. Medications are not covered, and they can be very expensive. Many people with significant disabilities struggle to stay at home, not just because they prefer being there, but because it is too expensive to stay in a skilled nursing home after their 100 days of coverage has been used up. These individuals frequently have major difficulties handling the day-to-day responsibilities of living, yet homemaker services are not covered under Medicare. Finally, home health care may be hard to find. Many small towns and rural areas do not have an approved home health agency.

Hospice care: Medicare has begun, on a trial basis, a new Part A program for people whose life expectancy is six months or less: hospice care (Section 305). Beneficiaries receive a wide range of services, including short-term inpatient care, skilled nursing help, and home health care not provided under previous Part A provisions.

282. *Medicare, Part B.* Part B is designed to cover some outpatient medical expenses. It is provided to those people eligible for Part A, but at a regular monthly cost ($13.50 per month beginning July, 1983). Even though it is not free, it remains an exceptionally good value and should not be discontinued unless your parent is certain that his private insurance provides better coverage at less expense, which is unlikely.

Part B covers part of most inpatient and outpatient doctor bills, other services and supplies furnished in the doctor's office, services provided under a physician's orders in an emergency room or a hospital outpatient clinic, outpatient physical therapy and speech therapy, necessary ambulance transportation, certain prosthetic devices, and certain permanent pieces of medical equipment such as wheelchairs, canes, hospital beds, and oxygen equipment. Other services and material may also be provided. The regulations governing what is and is not approved are very specific, and are worth reviewing in detail in the "Medicare Handbook" and through talks with Medicare representatives.

Even though coverage by Part B is extensive, so are the gaps. Examine your parent's Medicare outpatient provisions carefully so that neither of you is surprised when the medical bills begin appearing.

1. A person must pay the first $75 worth of outpatient medical expenses incurred each year. He must also pay 20 percent of all "approved

charges" (that is, of all medical bills Medicare decides are covered by its policy and are reasonable).

2. Many people are confused by this issue of "reasonable" charges and waste their time being angry at Medicare or its doctors. This concept is important to understand because it is a frequent source of unexpectedly large medical bills. Medicare, through a complicated procedure, decides what it feels the charge should be for each service by a doctor or other supplier. That is the "approved charge," and Medicare will pay 80 percent of it. If the physician charges more than the approved charge (and this is very common), your parent will have to pay the difference in addition to paying 20 percent of the approved charge. In practice, it works this way: the physician charges your parent, who then pays him; your parent then sends a copy of his bills and a completed Medicare Form 1490S to his state's Medicare carrier; finally, the carrier sends your parent a check for 80 percent of the approved charge. A desirable alternative to this complicated and often expensive system is to use a physician who accepts "assignment." Such a doctor agrees to accept, as full payment, whatever Medicare decides is the approved charge. The physician then bills Medicare directly, and all your parent sees is a bill for the outstanding 20 percent. Neither you nor your parent should be shy about asking if a physician will accept assignment for whatever services he is going to provide.

3. The second and fourth largest medical expenses of the elderly—custodial nursing-home care and outpatient medications—are not covered at all. Only those medications received in the hospital or in a skilled nursing home or those that can't be self-administered are paid for—the minority of drugs. Nor are several other kinds of common medical expenses covered, including regular physical examinations, most immunizations, regular eye or ear examinations, eyeglasses, hearing aids, routine foot care, orthopedic shoes, false teeth, and routine dental care. In addition, the "Medicare Handbook" lists many other types of less common care which are not paid for, including acupuncture, most chiropractic services, naturopaths, and private duty nurses. If your parent uses these services, he will have to pay for them.

4. Outpatient psychiatric care is limited to $250 worth of care each year. This embarrassingly small upper limit has caused some people who could have been treated as outpatients to be treated in psychiatric inpatient units.

As with other Medicare rulings, your parent has the right of appeal. Some appeals must be initiated within 60 days and others within 6 months. Unlike appeals under Part A, the law does not permit a final review of the dispute by the court. The ultimate resolution is made "internally."

MEDICAID

When investigating ways of helping your parent finance health care, always check for possible Medicaid eligibility. Most elderly people do not qualify, but 5 million of them do; and out-of-pocket medical expenses are markedly reduced for those who meet the eligibility requirements.

283. *Medicaid—What Is It and Who Gets It?* Medicaid is a supplementary health-insurance program for low-income persons. About 20 percent of the people who qualify for it are over 65. Each state runs its own Medicaid program and thus eligibility requirements and services provided vary widely from state to state, but since part of the funding comes from the federal government, the states must follow federal guidelines. Explore coverage in your own state by visiting the local Social Security office or the state's social services office.

In most states, people who qualify for Supplemental Security Income (SSI) also qualify for Medicaid. To meet the standard, they must have an income of only a couple hundred dollars each month and almost no other resources, although most states allow them to own the home in which they live and to have an inexpensive car. These profoundly poor individuals are known as the "categorically needy." Many states also provide Medicaid coverage for the "medically needy"—persons whose income isn't as low as that of the categorically needy but who have crushing medical bills which lower their effective income to that level. You can discover whether or not your parent qualifies by contacting one of your state's social service or welfare offices. Moreover, he has to apply to receive Medicaid, so your visit can serve two purposes. Don't avoid looking into this possibility out of fear that your parent may be viewed as a poverty or welfare case. Millions of people in their post-retirement years find themselves qualifying for Medicaid for the first time, and the savings can be substantial.

284. *Medicaid—What Does It Cover?* Medicaid usually operates as back-up coverage. It absorbs many of the bills (depending on the state) left by Medicare or private insurance. In practical terms, this usually means that it pays Medicare's deductibles, copayments, and co-insurance. Thus hospital and outpatient care may become almost cost-free for your parent. It often also pays for things like glasses, hearing aids, and medication. Finally, and perhaps most important, it may pay for long-term nursing-home care. It is well worth your while to investigate the benefits of the program in your state.

———

285. *Medicaid—The Problems.* Unfortunately, Medicaid protection is far from ideal. Some states' coverage is only minimally better than Medicare; others have idiosyncratic limitations. Some services may require prior approval while others have a deductible expense or require a copayment. Coverage may fluctuate, frequently in rhythm with the state's budget deficits. Medicaid may be hard to qualify for, even if it is obvious to you that your parent is financially strapped.

Your parent can receive treatment only from a certified Medicaid provider. Because of the paperwork, the "hassles," and the low fee schedule, some hospitals and many doctors refuse to participate in Medicaid. Thus to be covered under Medicaid your parent may have to go to a hospital outpatient clinic or to a doctor who is his second choice to receive care. In any case, be certain that the person or facility treating your parent is an approved Medicaid provider.

Perhaps the most serious problem with Medicaid coverage for the elderly is that a married couple (or an individual) must spend their life's savings down to the poverty level before either one of them will be protected by Medicaid. Thus a wife may be forced to spend almost all of the couple's collective savings seeing her husband through his final illness, and then be faced with years of poverty by herself. And this can undo any couple's diligent preparation for old age. Some elderly couples, faced with a lengthy and financially draining illness by one of the members, have been forced to divorce, simply to protect some savings for the partner. It pays to become familiar with the laws which govern Medicaid eligibility in your state; reality can be a stern teacher for the unprepared.

PRIVATE HEALTH INSURANCE

286. *Private Insurance—The Need.* As outlined in the previous section, Medicare, good as it is, has gaps significant enough to financially cripple an older person unlucky enough to become ill in the wrong way. Although some of the gaps in Medicare's coverage usually provide only minor irritations (lack of coverage for eyeglasses, hearing aids, or dental care), others constitute major risks for a person carefully conserving finite resources (limits on days allowed for hospital and skilled nursing-home care, limited outpatient coverage, no payment for medications, no homemaker services, no custodial nursing-home care). On the average, an elderly person spends almost $1,500 each year on medical care *not* covered by Medicare. Unless your parent qualifies for the additional benefits of Medicaid, he or she should seriously consider obtaining some form of additional medical coverage to avoid the possibility of being financially ruined by an unexpected or lengthy illness.

287. *Private Insurance—The Problems*. Buying insurance to back up Medicare (Medigap insurance) is problem-fraught. It should be approached with eyes open to avoid unnecessary expense or unsatisfactory coverage. A few unscrupulous insurance agents have bilked some elderly people of thousands and tens of thousands of dollars by selling them unnecessary or inadequate policies.

Although most insurance companies are reputable and most policies are designed to fill some need, private insurance companies are in business to make money. Shop carefully and consider the following recommendations when investigating private medical insurance for your parent—or for your own later years.

1. Buy only the coverage you feel you need. Become thoroughly familiar with the gaps in Medicare and try to fill them. Most private policies have a "coordination of benefits" clause which prohibits them from paying for an expense that is covered by some other policy. Check for it. Concentrate primarily on adding protection for long-lasting illness, rather than on providing coverage for deductibles and other minor expenses.

2. Work with an established agent or firm, if possible with someone you know personally or who comes soundly recommended. Evaluate many different policies. Comparison shop. Check each policy over yourself, item by item.

3. The younger you or your parents are when the policy is purchased, the more likely you are to get adequate coverage at a reasonable price. Thus medical insurance should be evaluated thoughtfully long before age 65. The coverage of many policies changes dramatically when you reach 65 (or retire), so be certain you understand the protection provided over your lifetime. Elderly people, particularly if they are in poor health, may find it extremely difficult to purchase any meaningful health insurance if they have waited until their late 60s or 70s to buy it.

4. Many companies, including the nonprofit Blue Cross and Blue Shield, have designed specific Medigap policies. Ask about them. Group policies often have the best rates, so investigate any coverage that may be available through your employment, professional organizations, fraternal groups, church, union, etc. But be certain that the company (or union) policy which provides such good coverage while you are employed doesn't cease at the time you retire.

5. Check any policy you are considering for a "preexisting condition" exclusion. Some companies can interpret such an exclusion broadly: the chest pain you suffered before taking out the policy could be considered an exclusion to paying for the heart attack you experienced several years later. If possible, get someone knowledgeable to help you evaluate this clause in the policy you are considering. Such a preexisting condition clause may

be reason enough to stick with your previous, although inadequate, insurance.

6. Check for any waiting period from the time of purchase to the time the benefits begin. Most policies have a mandatory gap of several months to one to two years—a period of time during which you could be dangerously unprotected.

7. Be certain that the policy is renewable regardless of how old you become or how many illnesses you have suffered.

8. Check for any limit to benefits. Is there a maximum number of dollars that will be covered during any one hospital stay, or a maximum number of illnesses covered during a certain period of time? Read the policies carefully, so you won't be surprised if problems develop.

9. Be wary of any policy that promises to pay for custodial or personal nursing-home care. Few do, and then only at a prohibitive monthly expense. Moreover, most do not cover routine checkups or physician charges above Medicare's rates.

288. *Private Insurance—What's Available.* A vast array of health-insurance policies is available. Most people don't need them. Most people can obtain adequate protection by a combination of a Medicare supplement (Medigap) and a Major Medical policy. The trick is to review competing policies carefully and select the one or two that best meet your needs.

Medigap insurance is a minor blessing. Most of these policies pay many of Medicare's deductibles and copayments, thus making your first two months in the hospital or skilled nursing home less expensive. However, few of them cover the many services not paid by Medicare.

On the other hand, Major Medical or Catastrophic coverage can be a major blessing. Although often expensive to maintain and hard to get at a reasonable price if your parent is quite elderly, major medical protection can make the difference between solvency and financial ruin. Policies differ widely but all offer some form of increased financial protection during long or serious illnesses. However, most have a significant deductible built into the coverage and stipulate that you are responsible for a copayment (20 percent is the norm) during the course of the illness. As with most other kinds of health insurance, it is best to obtain good major medical protection well before you turn 65, and to make certain that it is "guaranteed renewable for life" without a major change in benefits. A few companies have begun offering "wrap-around" policies designed specifically for the elderly which have most of the features of Medigap coverage and some elements of major medical. Investigate each one carefully.

Other kinds of health-insurance policies are available, such as those against a specific disease or those promising to cover nursing-home care. Be wary—only in unusual circumstances are these policies of any real benefit.

OTHER HEALTH PROTECTION

289. *Health Maintenance Organizations (HMOs)*. HMOs are a new concept in the provision of health care. A group of general physicians and specialists, in cooperation with one or more hospitals and outpatient facilities, provides almost all health care to a group of subscribers. For an annual premium, you will be treated as an outpatient or inpatient without additional cost. Medical care aimed at prevention is encouraged, as are other mechanisms that decrease hospital care and surgery. HMOs often provide the most comprehensive medical care available anywhere. Thus, they often provide ideal protection to the elderly who belong to them.

Unfortunately, HMOs are not without their drawbacks. They exist in only a few places (the Kaiser-Permanente hospitals in the western United States, the Health Insurance Plan of New York, an HMO system in the Seattle area). Like many private insurance programs, some do not allow the elderly to join, while others make such participation prohibitively expensive. A subscriber is covered only if treated in that HMO's facility and by one of its doctors, so freedom of choice is markedly restricted. In addition, the quality of care in a few HMOs is less than desirable. Some patients complain that the care in an HMO is often impersonal and that they have to endure excessive delays in receiving treatment.

Like any other means of obtaining health care, HMOs have their problems and need to be evaluated on an individual basis. In general, however, they work well where they are available.

290. *Retirement Homes*. The most expensive health-related cost for many people is the cost of staying in a nursing home when they have become frail and unable to care for themselves. No insurance plan (except for Medicaid) satisfactorily provides for that need. However, such protection does exist in a few specialized living facilities.

A few retirement communities provide a range of living arrangements varying from independent houses on the grounds of the facility, to apartments, to custodial nursing-home rooms, to skilled nursing-home beds. A person or couple may enter such a community shortly after retirement, when relatively healthy, and stay there throughout all the vicissitudes of the years to follow. As their health and ability to get around decreases, they may move from a more unrestricted part of the facility to one where more support is available. Many people find this a satisfactory way of providing for any nursing-home care they may need in the future—in a familiar place and around people they have grown to like. However, there are drawbacks here too. Often, the entrance fee is exceptionally stiff, and sometimes, individuals are required to turn over most of their savings to the facility. In addition, there is often a monthly charge which may increase over time and as a person progresses to the more comprehensive care sections of the community. Moreover, these retirement communities are not widely available, may closely constrict a person's potential circle of friends, often do not provide for medical care, and vary greatly in quality and terms of enrollment. However, if there are some in your area, investigate them.

291. *Gaps.* No matter how thoroughly you plan for health-care protection, you will not cover everything. A sensible program will cover most expected payments as well as the bulk of the expenses associated with a major illness. However, your parent will almost certainly need to pay for eyeglasses and vision care, hearing aids, most medication, most dental care, custodial nursing-home expenses, and some home health care. Be certain that each of these expenses is necessary. Since it usually is considerably cheaper for your parent to live at home, consider developing with his physician a schedule of home-based care. Such a plan may be carried out by you, your parent, or an outside professional, and may allow your parent to stay in his home much longer than expected.

25.

Socializing

It is vital that your parent stay involved with others. His health and sense of well-being depend on it. He may be involved with his spouse, you, neighbors, or friends—what is crucial is that he stay socially active. He must have other people to talk with and be with. He must be able to communicate his deepest thoughts, concerns, hopes, and fears to someone. He should have someone with whom he enjoys spending time. See that your parent is not isolated and alone.

292. *Friendship.* Until an elderly person becomes very old and frail, friends usually provide the most important day-to-day relationships. A full social life makes things more pleasant at any age. The happiest older people typically maintain numerous friendships: they visit other people, are visited themselves, and pass few days without doing something with an acquaintance. However, the number of friends is not the crucial factor. More important is that your parent have one or more persons with whom he is close, has values and interests in common, and spends time. Old friends are often the best friends: they have similar roots to your parents, and similar perceptions of the past. Notice whether or not your parent has valued friendships and encourage him to maintain them, helping if you can with transportation and other support.

Often an older person whose friends have died or drifted away will make no efforts to develop new relationships. It is almost as though he has concluded that old age is naturally friendless. See that he looks up old friends, joins organizations that interest him, travels with a group, spends time out of the house at the local library or the senior center, and otherwise remains active. Friends from work who drifted away after his retirement may be retired now themselves and be interested in reliving old times. If the composition of his neighborhood has changed over the years and now consists exclusively of younger families, it may be time for him to move. However, there is nothing wrong with younger friends: age is a small barrier between neighbors with similar interests. Many older people like the stimulation that a mix of young and old brings. Most communities have groups of elderly individuals organized around recreational and educational activities. Find them and encourage your parent to participate (see Chapters 26 and 27). Senior Centers, devoted exclusively to interests and needs of the elderly, are found in many areas. Locate yours through the telephone book, by contacting your state's Division of Aging, or by writing for a directory to:

National Institute of Senior Citizens
National Council on the Aging, Inc.
600 Maryland Ave., S.W.
West Wing 100, Suite 208
Washington, DC 20024
(202) 479-1200

Regardless of how active and social an older person has been, there is a tendency for him to want to draw closer to family during the last years of his life. In part this reflects a loss of friends over the years and in part it results from a lowering of his energies and a desire to pull into the smallest, most natural circle of relationships—the family. Expect this and be receptive to it.

293. *Volunteering*. To many, volunteering has a bad reputation. It is seen by some as "make work" for those who can't qualify for employment. Such perceptions couldn't be further from the truth—the most human aspects of our society depend upon the efforts of volunteers. Many of our finest public organizations would grind to a halt without them: the Red Cross, the Peace Corps, VISTA, the Boy Scouts, Big Brothers, Goodwill, as well as political campaigns. Associations of volunteers act as important pressure groups and provide critical information and services. The good volunteers do is incalculable.

Moreover, volunteering benefits those who volunteer as well. Volunteers are able to match their efforts to their interests. They remain active, facing new challenges and meeting new people. Most of all, they are vitalized by the knowledge that they are doing good for others—that their efforts are meaningful.

Encourage your parent to try volunteering. The range of possible activities is enormous. There are large national programs and small local ones. There are programs which demand a commitment in excess of twenty hours each week, and others which require only an hour or two. Some programs pay a small salary, others pay expenses only, still others pay nothing. Some programs use only elderly volunteers and provide services only to the elderly, while others use and help those of all ages. Finally, some volunteer opportunities are part of well-developed programs, while others represent opportunities your parent has created for himself. Your parent should determine his interests and strengths, estimate how much time he is willing to give, and begin to look around.

Opportunities are everywhere. Most are local: clubs, churches, business organizations and nonprofit companies, Neighborhood Watch groups, museums and libraries, hospitals, and charitable groups. Even if your parent is confined to a nursing home, there are important jobs for volunteers to do within the facility. Your parent can call the groups that interest him and inquire about their needs. Most local groups needing volunteers are listed in the telephone directory under social service organizations, associations, church organizations, clubs, or senior citizens' service organizations. The state Division of Aging or its local branches usually maintains a list of possibilities. There is no shortage of opportunities.

Important national and international programs also provide exciting opportunities. There are many possibilities, and your parent can pick and choose. The following is a very abbreviated list of sources and programs.

Sources for Information on Volunteer Programs:

Volunteer: The National Center for Citizen Involvement
P.O. Box 4179
Boulder, CO 80306
(303) 447-0492

The Commission on Voluntary Service and Action
475 Riverside Drive, Rm. 1126
New York, NY 10027
(212) 870-2801

Four-one-one
7304 Beverly St.
Annandale, VA 22003
(703) 354-6270

In addition to these general sources, specific programs are worth contacting if their goals and activities seem interesting. Although the national offices are listed here, many of these agencies have local branches that may be listed in the telephone directory.

Volunteer Programs:

ACTION. ACTION is a federal agency which encompasses several national volunteer programs such as Retired Senior Volunteer Program (RSVP) and Foster Grandparents Program (FGP).

ACTION
806 Connecticut Ave., N.W.
Washington, DC 20525
(800) 424-8580

Big Brothers. Big Brothers (and Big Sisters) volunteers provide personal support to troubled youths. The time spent varies, but the rewards can be substantial.

Big Brothers/Big Sisters of America
117 S. 17th St., Suite 1200
Philadelphia, PA 19103
(215) 567-2748

FGP. The Foster Grandparent Program pays a small salary to selected low-income elderly to help care for low-income or handicapped children. This is an extremely valuable program (part of ACTION).

Foster Grandparents Program
806 Connecticut Ave., N.W.
Washington, DC 20525
(800) 424-8580

Green Thumb. This is primarily a rural project which pays volunteers the minimum wage to work approximately half-time at a variety of socially useful tasks.

Green Thumb
1012 14th St., N.W., Suite 600
Washington, DC 20005
(703) 276-0750

Goodwill. A variety of local agencies is supported by Goodwill funds to provide help to the physically, mentally, and socially handicapped. Volunteers are needed.

Goodwill Industries of America, Inc.
9200 Wisconsin Ave., N.W.
Washington, DC 20014
(301) 530-6500

IESC. The International Executive Service Corps sends experienced businessmen to third-world countries to help struggling industries and businesses. Expenses are paid. Their needs are quite specific and change with time.

The International Executive Service Corps
622 Third Ave.
New York, NY 10017
(212) 490-6800

Peace Corps. Although not exclusively for the elderly, the Peace Corps does take older volunteers. It requires a substantial commitment of time and energy, but the rewards can be profound. Once part of ACTION, the Peace Corps is now independent but can be contacted through the ACTION national headquarters.

Peace Corps
806 Connecticut Ave., N.W.
Washington, DC 20525
(800) 424-8580

RSVP. The Retired Senior Volunteer Program is a branch of ACTION which attempts to fill crucial gaps in community resources. Projects are created locally, and the range of activities is wide.

Retired Senior Volunteer Program
806 Connecticut Ave., N.W.
Washington, DC 20525

SCORE. The Service Corps of Retired Executives (SCORE) allows experienced retired business people to help small, struggling businesses.

SCORE
1441 L St., N.W., Rm. 100
Washington, DC 20416
(202) 653-6279

SCP. The Senior Companion Program is similar to the Foster Grand-parent Program except that the elderly help care for the elderly. The volunteers make home visits and provide care to homebound elderly individuals, as well as to nursing home residents. It is a branch of ACTION.

Senior Companion Program
806 Connecticut Ave., N.W.
Washington, DC 20525

SEEP. The Senior Environmental Employment Program provides an opportunity for the elderly to receive a small amount of pay for working in local projects designed to protect the environment.

Senior Environmental Employment Program
1909 K St., N.W.
Washington, DC 22049

Senior AIDES. This federal program pays low-income elderly individuals to work on a variety of community projects.

Senior AIDES
National Council of Senior Citizens
1511 K St., N.W.
Washington, DC 20005

United Way. The United Way offers a variety of volunteer opportunities on a local level.

The United Way of America
801 N. Fairfax St.
Alexandria, VA 22314
(703) 836-7100

VISTA. The Volunteers in Service to America (VISTA) is a program similar to the Peace Corps, but concentrates its efforts in poorly developed areas in the United States. Older volunteers are accepted.

VISTA
806 Connecticut Ave., N.W.
Washington, DC 20525
(800) 424-8580

Volunteer Medical Programs. There are a number of organizations which use volunteers who have medical skills or interests. Among these are:

Direct Relief Foundation
P.O. Box 30820
Santa Barbara, CA 93105
(805) 687-3694

American National Red Cross
17th and D Sts., S.W.
Washington, DC 20006
(202) 737-8300

Care/Medico
660 First Ave.
New York, NY 10016
(212) 686-3110

Also contact the Director of Volunteer Services at your local Veterans Administration hospital.

Political Advocacy Groups. The Gray Panthers is perhaps the best known of several political action groups composed primarily of the elderly and devoted to issues important to older Americans. However, several other groups like the American Association of Retired Persons (AARP) and the National Council of Senior Citizens (NCSC), although not existing solely for political purposes, have even more political clout. Older persons interested in flexing their political muscle or those merely wanting to keep up to date with crucial issues would do well to join one or more of these organizations. Both the AARP and the NCSC also have worthwhile benefit packages associated with membership. Interested elderly people may also want to participate in advocacy groups affiliated with past or present employment, such as the National Association of Retired Federal Employees (NARFE). Your parents should investigate to see if such an organization is available to them. Moreover, almost any political campaign or cause will welcome participation of older individuals.

AARP/NRTA
1909 K St., N.W.
Washington, DC 20049
(202) 872-4700

Asociación Nacional pro Personas Mayores [Spanish-speaking]
1730 W. Olympic Blvd., Suite 401
Los Angeles, CA 90015
(213) 487-1922

Gray Panthers
3635 Chestnut St.
Philadelphia, PA 19104
(215) 382-3300

International Senior Citizens Association
11753 Wilshire Blvd.
Los Angeles, CA 90025
(213) 472-4704

National Action Forum for Older Women
School of Allied Health Professions
SUNY
Stony Brook, NY 11794
(516) 246-2989

National Association of Mature People
2000 Classen Center
P.O. Box 26792
Oklahoma City, OK 73126
(405) 523-5060

NARFE
1533 New Hampshire Ave., N.W.
Washington, DC 20036
(202) 234-0832

National Caucus and Center on Black Aged
1424 K St., N.W., Suite 500
Washington, DC 20005
(202) 637-8400

NCOA (National Council on the Aging)
600 Maryland Ave., S.W.
West Wing 100, Suite 208
Washington, DC 20024
(202) 479-1200

NCSC
925 15th St., N.W.
Washington, DC 20005
(202) 347-8800

National Indian Council on Aging
P.O. Box 2088
Albuquerque, NM 87103
(505) 766-2276

Older Women's League (OWL)
3800 Harrison St.
Oakland, CA 94611
(415) 658-8700

26.

Recreation

294. *Having Fun.* Your parents are old only once, so they'd better make the best of the opportunity. Older people have the same need to enjoy themselves as you do. If anything, retirement and the other events of aging make their need greater. They have to redefine themselves in light of their changed and limited capabilities, and also must look at the years ahead with an eye to how they would like to spend them. They should select activities that are both enjoyable and worthwhile. Older parents should seriously think about how they spend their time, rather than leaving it to chance— they should consider old age a process of self-exploration and should attempt activities that are not only fun but fulfilling.

Sit down with your parents and help them decide what their strengths and limits are and what interests they want to cultivate. Be realistic about such important variables as limited finances, poor health, availability of transportation and recreational facilities, and proximity to friends. Encourage them to explore every possibility: from long-forgotten fantasies to the interests of their closest friends. They should also consider activities that many people would think of as work: recreation is in the eye of the beholder, and one person's work is another's pleasure. For starters, they might consider:

Drawing and painting
Photography
Watching educational TV programs
Gardening

Walking
Volunteer work of all kinds (see Section 293)
Movies
Party giving and party going
Cooking
Music (making or enjoying)
Shopping
Self-education and serious scholarly activities (see Chapter 27)
Weaving
Dressmaking and embroidery
Sculpture
Nature study
Exercise and sports (watching or participating)
Games (checkers, chess, bingo, croquet, backgammon, Scrabble)
Dancing (ballroom or square)
Travel
Drama (watching or participating)
Discussion groups of all types
Ham radio
Handyman work
Woodworking
Ceramics and pottery
Attending museums and art galleries
Politics
Playing the stock market
Crafts of all types
Religious activities
Hobbies and collections
Reading
Writing (poetry, fiction, articles)

The list is practically endless. There is a complex, meaningful, and enjoyable world available for your parents to tap—all that is needed is for them to start exploring. And, rather than pinning their hopes for late-life enjoyment on only one or two activities, they should sample widely. Your parents should mix indoor and outdoor pursuits and sedentary and vigorous activities. They should develop as many new skills as they can handle, and grow in as many ways as possible. If they are reluctant at first, your encouragement may allow them to take the initial step: after that the going becomes easier.

Your parents are limited only by their curiosity and drive. They should seek out local groups of enthusiasts. Clubs of all types are there to be joined. If your parent can't find one, he can start one. One of your parents can enquire at the local senior citizens center about activities locally available, but they certainly should not feel restricted to groups of older individuals. They can develop ideas and make connections by contacting or joining one of the national organizations of older people: the American Association of Retired Persons (AARP) and the National Council of Senior Citizens (NCSC).

> AARP
> 1909 K St., N.W.
> Washington, DC 20049
> (202) 872-4700

> NCSC
> 925 15th St., N.W.
> Washington, DC 20005
> (202) 347-8800

If your parents' interests tend toward self-exploration, self-expression, and personal growth, they should consider getting in touch with groups devoted to such worthwhile goals—for example, the National Association for Humanistic Gerontology (a spin-off of SAGE, Senior Actualization and Growth Experiences).

> SAGE—NAHG
> Claremont Office Park
> 41 Tunnel Road
> Berkeley, CA 94705

If your parents are not enjoying old age, if they are not having fun, ask yourself why. Even the very elderly and those who are sedentary by necessity should be able to find many pleasant things to do: watching TV, going to movies, reading or being read to, listening to the radio, corresponding by letter (there is a pen-pal program through International Friendship League, 22 Batterymarch St., Boston, MA 02109), participating in call-in shows, taking correspondence courses by mail (why not for credit?), obtaining educational tapes from the library, pursuing a variety of crafts, operating a ham radio. Don't let your parents' lassitude or demoralization prevent you from generating ideas which may lift them out of a rut. The choices of what they want to do ultimately are (and should be) theirs, but that shouldn't prevent you from giving a friendly push if you see them stagnating.

27.

Education

295. *Learning Must Never Stop.* The elderly must learn new things; older persons are at their most human when they have the opportunity to exercise their interests and curiosity. The most satisfied elderly individuals are actively engaged in life-long learning. There is even evidence that better-educated people and those involved in continuing education live longer.

Education, in some form, is available to everyone. It can vary from formal classes in a university to a field workshop on birdwatching with the local Audubon Society. Even a homebound older person can participate: by means of classes on educational TV, audio and video tapes mailed from the library, correspondence courses, radio, telephone. Your parent can seek a degree from a local college or university. Or he finally can obtain that high school diploma by studying for and taking the GED (General Education Development) examination. More commonly, he may pursue an interest just for its own sake: by reading, going to lectures, browsing in bookstores, joining discussion groups, or assembling a few friends with similar interests. It doesn't matter how he continues to learn, as long as he does so.

Opportunities are everywhere. High schools offer a wide range of adult-education classes. Many community colleges have special programs for the elderly. Universities (particularly the public universities) often allow the elderly to take classes and pursue degrees at reduced fees. Senior centers usually have some educational programs, as do special-interest groups (environmental groups, craft guilds, churches, the YMCA and

YWCA, museums and art galleries, business organizations, flying schools, etc.). The better nursing homes and retirement communities provide learning opportunities as an essential part of their environment, and many colleges have outreach programs which provide classes and lectures in those residential settings. If your parent has developed a serious interest in a topic, he might consider subscribing to the appropriate professional journals, many of which can be read with profit by the intelligent layperson. Moreover, there are newly developed, successful programs such as the Elderhostel program and the Institute for Retired Professionals (IRP) program specifically aimed at the continued education of older people (see references below).

You or your parent should check with local high schools or the Director of Continuing Education in colleges nearby. Call the state Division of Aging or the local chapter of the American Association of Retired Persons (AARP) for help. What do churches in your area offer? Scan the bulletin board in the public library. Finally, your parent can create his own educational experience: start his own discussion group, encourage the public library to sponsor a lecture series, or find experts willing to teach a skill to an interested group of older people.

Your most important role may be to convince your parent to tackle these new learning opportunities. Encourage him to read widely in the hope of finding a topic of interest. He may be afraid that he can no longer learn and has no place in a classroom of any type. Not so (see Section 28)— an older person can learn as well as anyone else. He may be afraid, though, to go out at night in a high-crime area, or have trouble arranging transportation, particularly at night. Try to arrange transportation and assure safety, since the loss of mental stimulation and the associated companionship is a serious loss indeed.

296. *Educational Opportunities for the Elderly.* Every location has its unique educational experiences, and there is no substitute for your parent's becoming familiar with what is available in his area. One place to start is to contact national sources and organizations for information that may be of use.

1. Several books are available which detail educational possibilities.

J. Adler, *The Retirement Book* (New York: William Morrow & Co., 1975).

W. Cross and C. Florio, *You Are Never Too Old to Learn* (New York: McGraw-Hill Book Co., 1978).

H. Downs and R. Roll, *The Best Years Book* (New York: Delacorte Press, 1981).

R. Gross, *The Life Long Learner* (New York: Simon & Schuster, 1977).

J. Michaels, *Prime of Your Life* (Boston: Little, Brown & Co., 1983).

F. Tenenbaum, *Over 55 Is NOT Illegal* (Boston: Houghton Mifflin Co., 1979).

2. Information about a broad spectrum of educational opportunities is available from several sources.

Institute of Lifetime Learning
National Retired Teachers Association/American Association
  of Retired Persons
1909 K St., N.W.
Washington, DC 20049
(202) 872-4700

Old Americans Project
Adult Education Association of the U.S.A.
810 18th St., N.W.
Washington, DC 20006

3. Community colleges and universities across the country offer courses and programs of study, often at reduced fees for the elderly. Your parent may occasionally be able to receive academic credit for experience.

American Association of Community and Junior Colleges
1 Dupont Circle, No. 410
Washington, DC 20036
(202) 293-7050

College Level Examination Program (CLEP)
The College Board
888 Seventh Ave.
New York, NY 10106
(212) 582-6210

4. There are several exciting, newly developed programs that are worth checking out. The Elderhostel program provides one-week, inten-

sive, live-in courses of study for the elderly during the summer at over 300 colleges, both in the United States and abroad. It can be an inexpensive, very stimulating vacation. The Institute of Retired Professionals (IRP) provides high-level academic experiences for selected professionals and retired business people. Investigate to see if your area has a chapter. The Oliver Wendell Holmes Association offers short educational programs in scattered locations, primarily devoted to pre-retirement planning.

Elderhostel
100 Boylston St., Suite 200
Boston, MA 02116

Institute of Retired Professionals
New School for Social Research
66 West 12th St.
New York, NY 10011
(212) 741-5682

Oliver Wendell Holmes Association
221 E. 49th St.
New York, NY 10017
(212) 935-3880

5. Correspondence courses of various types are plentiful.

National University Continuing Education Association
1 Dupont Circle, Suite 360
Washington, DC 20036
(202) 659-3130

The National Home Study Council
1601 18th St., N.W.
Washington, DC 20009
(202) 234-5100

University Without Walls
Union for Experimenting Colleges and Universities
Provident Bank Building
P.O. Box 85315
Cincinnati, OH 45201
(513) 621-6444

28.

Other Realities

286. *Crime*. Danger is all around us, or so it seems. We are all concerned about the rising incidence of crime, and no one so much as the elderly. Do they have special reason to be concerned? Yes and no. Older people are victims of crime less frequently than most other groups in the population, probably because they get out less and have less to lose. However, when they are robbed, defrauded, or burglarized, the impact on them is usually greater.

Although the elderly are in general less likely to be victims of crime, there are exceptions. Robbery (particularly purse-snatching and "strong-arm" theft of wallets, food stamps, and Social Security checks) among the elderly is common in the poorer areas of big cities. Burglarizing the homes of the elderly is also common in some neighborhoods. Finally, con artists find many easy victims among the lonely, isolated, and mentally-bewildered elderly. The type of crime prevalent among the older population varies with the location, so you should check with local police to determine the risks to which your parent is exposed.

However, there is a bigger problem than your parent's likelihood of becoming a victim: his fear of crime. This fear may be more disabling than any real risk he runs if worries about burglars and muggers are allowed to dominate and direct his life. He may become a virtual shut-in, going out only during the "safe" daylight hours. That is no way to live.

What can you and your parent do to protect against crime and to allow his life to be as normal as possible? First, determine the extent of your parent's concerns. If his life is being controlled by his fear of crime, ascertain whether he is being realistic. Check with the police. What is the incidence of crime where your parent lives? What type is it? Check with the neighbors and local newspapers. Once you have the facts, you can proceed with prevention.

Without turning it into a fortress, your parent's home should be made as safe as possible. Install deadbolt locks and solid doors. See that all windows lock securely. Install exterior lights, particularly at entrances. Consider installing an electronic security system, or at least the appearance of one. Mark important household property with his Social Security number, so that it may be easily identified upon recovery if stolen. However, no home can be made completely burglar-proof; other steps must be taken.

Find out what Neighborhood Watch or Block Watch programs are available. These programs have been shown to be remarkably effective in preventing burglaries, and the police will probably help your parent and his neighbors develop one. Moreover, most police forces nowadays are willing to instruct groups of citizens in the art of self-protection: why he should lock the house and leave lights on; how to respond to a mugger; what areas of the neighborhood to avoid and at what times; what numbers to call in the case of an emergency; where he should travel in a group and where it is safe to go alone; how to recognize suspicious behavior in a stranger in the neighborhood. As your parent moves from waiting for something terrible to happen to taking active steps for self-protection, he will begin to feel more secure and the world will seem less forbidding.

In addition, be alert to any "exciting offers" your parent describes. Fraud of the elderly is a major problem. Older people, particularly those on limited or fixed incomes, are often drawn to get-rich-quick schemes or "special bargains," and thus are easy prey for con men. You can help protect your parent by investigating any of these suspicious people or deals.

In general, old age is a safe time, but only if approached cautiously and with eyes open.

298. *Transportation.* Few of the benefits of being old can be enjoyed if the elderly person can't get around. Lack of ready transportation can be an almost insurmountable problem for those elderly who do not drive, are handicapped, or are too frail or incapacitated to use public transportation easily. Your parent can be similarly disabled if he lives in a neighborhood too dangerous to move around in alone. One of the greatest services you can provide your parent is to help solve his transportation needs.

Of course, the obvious solution is for you to drive him about. However, this "solution" rarely works for very long. It becomes wearing on you and embarrassing for him. Your parent's schedule may not fit with yours. And although you may arrange necessary trips to the store and to the bank, you may not have time to cater to more meaningful needs such as visits to friends. You must help your parent find other ways to get around. One partial solution is to organize a network of "chauffeurs" composed of other family members and friends. This can become awkward at times, but works most smoothly if your parent is an accepted, participating, social member of the group doing the transporting. The closer the family and the more they like to do things together, the more likely it is that such a collective scheme will work.

There are other transportation alternatives in most communities. However, you and your parent may need to be persistent and aggressive if you are to uncover them and use them effectively. Obviously, public transportation is a major option. Unfortunately, it is usually well developed only in metropolitan areas. Bus and subway half-fares for the elderly exist in most places. Review thoroughly all public transportation in your area: obtain schedules, talk with local officials, compare the routes with the places your parent usually goes. Such diligence may produce new options.

Many communities have developed transportation which is solely for the elderly. Most commonly, this consists of mini-buses (the Elderbus, Dial-a-bus, etc.) that will respond to a phone call, pick up your parent at his home, and take him to his destination for a small fee. These programs are typically subsidized by federal or local governments; inquire about them at your local or state Division of Aging. Some communities have developed car pools for the elderly or have assembled lists of volunteer drivers. Certain groups with programs for the elderly (senior centers, churches, YMCA) provide transportation.

More expensive, but readily available, alternatives include taxis (paid by Medicaid in some states, and for some purposes), ambulances, and limousine services. Cost may prohibit routine use, but your parent should know what is available and how to use these services in case there is an occasional need for them.

Don't take your parent's transportation needs lightly. Those needs, unmet, can seriously impair the satisfaction he gains from his later years. Without adequate means of getting around, your parent may be forced into inactivity and a sedentary life style which will compromise both health and happiness. On the other hand, don't feel you must bear all the burden of seeing that your parent has mobility. Be inventive and persistent in developing alternatives. Find out what is available locally. If nothing exists, help your parent and his friends start something: a car pool, a volunteer-driver service, or an escort service. It is that important.

299. *Legal Matters.* As you might expect, the variety of legal concerns faced by the elderly are too complicated for a simple discussion. However, they are also too important to neglect. Late-age situations requiring the help of a lawyer go beyond routine litigation to include such matters as general estate planning, wills, trusts, general money management, pensions, complications of Social Security and Medicare, taxes, employment discrimination, landlord-tenant disputes, and disagreements concerning eligibility for public and private programs—to name only a few. This does not mean that your parent must keep a lawyer on hand at all times, but it does suggest that at some point he should review his legal and financial situation carefully, usually with the help of an attorney. Useful sources for the elderly about legal matters include:

R. N. Brown et al., *The Rights of Older Persons* (New York: Avon Books, 1979, paperback).

T. T. Dunn, *A Lawyer's Advice to Retirees* (New York: Doubleday & Co., 1981.

D. C. Larsen, *Who Gets It When You Go?* (New York: Random House, 1983).

Your Retirement Legal Guide (from AARP, 1909 K St., N.W., Washington, DC 20049).

Lawyers are expensive. Moreover, many are unfamiliar with the legal problems common among the elderly and are unwilling to take on the task of educating themselves, in part, because the fees they can collect for such work are usually small. Fortunately, there are alternatives. Low-cost legal clinics are now available in most metropolitan areas. Unfortunately, these are usually staffed by young, relatively inexperienced attorneys, many of whom have little specialized training in the problems of the elderly. Many of these lawyers are diligent, however, and such diligence can go far. In addition, the federal government helps fund the Legal Services Corporation to provide legal help to those near or below the poverty level. Many elderly qualify. The Legal Services Corporation maintains offices throughout the country. For the address of an office near you, check the telephone directory, contact your state's Division of Aging, or write to:

Legal Services Corporation
733 15th St., N.W.
Washington, DC 20005
(202) 272-4000

A federally supported organization concerned exclusively with the legal problems of older people is the National Senior Citizens Law Center (NSCLC). Information about its activities and answers to specific questions may be obtained by writing to the NSCLC at:

1302 18th St., N.W.
Washington, DC 20036

or:

1636 W. 8th St.
Los Angeles, CA 90017

Two legal problems which may raise profound and heart-rending problems for the family of an elderly person are guardianship and civil commitment. They are discussed below.

300. *Guardianship.* Most older people remain alert and competent until the end. Unfortunately, some don't, and therein lies a serious problem for both those individuals and their families. What do you do if your parent begins to squander his life's resources, resources needed to see him through the rest of his days? A formerly careful manager of the family's finances may begin to make ill-considered investments, fail to pay bills, lose track of his financial holdings, make unnecessary and expensive purchases, or give away family possessions. Other problems may develop: your parent may eat poorly, insist on living in unsanitary surroundings, refuse necessary medical treatment, drive a car when he is no longer capable of doing so, or act in other ways that are dangerous or self-destructive. Most often, these inadequacies develop gradually and you have ample time to consider your responses, and to worry. What can you do?

All states have laws which allow family members or other concerned persons to intercede if a person is no longer able to manage his or her affairs. Although the procedures differ significantly from state to state, the general outline is usually the same. An "interested party" (you, or someone else who knows the situation) makes application to the court (call the local courthouse for information, or ask a lawyer) to review the competency of your parent. A court hearing is held, during which family members, professionals (psychiatrist, physician, social worker), and other people familiar with the problems may testify. The court (and only the court) then decides whether your parent is incompetent. The court then usually appoints a guardian to administer your parent's affairs.

If all that sounds simple, it's not. First of all, it is extremely difficult for most people to take a parent to court and publicly declare him incompetent. People battle with themselves, their parent, other family members, and professionals brought in to help. They concoct innumerable temporary solutions to serious problems, and, occasionally, find permanent solutions without going to court. But when they finally decide that there is no alternative to initiating competency procedures, many times they find that their problems (and their parent's problems) have just begun.

A further difficulty lies in the uncertainty about who is incompetent, and even about what incompetency means. You may be convinced that your parent can no longer manage his affairs. The court may not be so sure, nor may a professional who examines him. For example, your parent may be of sound mind, but his stubbornness and need for independence may be causing him to make choices which appear unwise to you. Some people (and the law) may consider that his right. Be prepared for a difference of opinion. Part of the difficulty here is the question "incompetent for what?" If your parent is incompetent to handle the checkbook, is he also unable to make purchases or live where he wants? Is your parent, then, also incompetent to make out (or change) his will? Some states allow their courts to specify which activities the incompetency decision extends to and which it does not. Thus a person may be appointed as limited guardian or conservator (for example, guardian of property) but not total guardian (guardian of person).

In addition, competency hearings can be acrimonious affairs. Longstanding family disagreements may surface, and heated arguments may rage in the courtroom between brother and sister and parent and child. Usually hearings aren't that stormy (your parent may not even be present), but resentment and distrust may result.

Yet another problem may arise with the assignment of guardianship. Not only may a guardian be assigned less (or more) responsibility than anticipated, but a variety of people or institutions are eligible to become guardians. Most frequently, a close and concerned relative is appointed guardian, as long as that person is shown to have the elderly person's best interest at heart. However, the guardianship may be assigned to an interested friend, a bank, a social service agency, or a mental health professional. Of course, the assignment may come as no surprise to you, yet you should be involved in that decision beforehand, whether or not you were the person requesting the competency hearing.

Other problems and complications may crop up throughout the process of providing outside control over your parent's affairs. During it all, however, your overriding concern may well be: "Am I doing the right thing?" There is no easy answer. Such actions are always painful. If your parent's actions are compromising his health and financial well-being, a guardian may be the only acceptable option, yet to be declared incompetent makes your parent almost completely powerless. It may remove his ability to handle money, manage property, buy and sell, vote, decide where and with whom he lives, travel, choose medical treatment, and much more. It can take the heart out of an older person and make him depressed or excessively dependent. It thus should not be initiated unless it is absolutely necessary. Because these issues are complicated, it usually is best to consult an attorney.

However, foresight may be able to prevent a guardianship battle altogether. The time to alter legal responsibilities is early on, when an elderly parent is just beginning to show signs of failing but is still competent. Many elderly people are willing to take the precaution of sharing their financial and legal responsibility with their children. There are several ways to do this. (1) Your parent may assign you power of attorney—that is, he may legally allow you to manage his funds *and* (as a separate item) specifically state that you may continue to do so even if he becomes incompetent. (2) A living or inter vivos trust allows your parent to be trustee of the funds involved until he becomes incapacitated, at which time you become trustee. Such a trust also circumvents probate and may protect the assets involved from being used to pay your parent's medical expenses. (3) Joint tenancy allows you both to supervise the family funds, but permits you to take over sole control when your parent deteriorates. None of these plans is foolproof, but they do hold out the hope of sparing everyone unnecessary stress as conditions change. Obviously, an attorney should participate.

301. *Civil Commitment.* What is more abhorrent than the thought that you might have to commit your parent? What a terrible way to end one of your life's most intimate relationships. Yet it may be necessary. Your parent's behavior may have become so uncontrolled that you fear for his life and health. He may no longer be able to feed or clean himself or he may wander away from home and get lost. His behavior may have become bizarre and unpredictable, frightening you and his neighbors. You may constantly, and legitimately, be worried about his safety or the safety of those who live near him. If it is obvious to you that he needs treatment or needs to live in a more supervised environment like a nursing home, it may also be obvious to your parent. On the other hand, an elderly parent may not recognize his deficiencies, leaving you to force him against his will into some facility for treatment (involuntary civil commitment). How do you go about it?

Laws concerning commitment differ widely. If you are considering committing your parent, consult a psychiatrist, psychiatric social worker, or other person knowledgeable about both mental health problems and your state's commitment laws. Such professionals may even be able to suggest alternatives that make commitment unnecessary.

In spite of variations from state to state, most laws require that to be committed a person have a mental illness that causes him either to be an immediate danger to himself or to others, or to be substantially unable to care for himself. Also stated or implied in most laws is that he be committed to a facility that can offer him treatment. The laws of most states differ depending upon whether your parent's condition is acute and likely to improve markedly with treatment or chronic and unlikely to get better. Thus if a person has suddenly begun acting bizarrely unlike himself, it is often fairly simple to place him in a hospital for a week or two against his will for diagnosis or treatment. It may be considerably more difficult to extend that commitment for months or years. Commitments are court procedures, and the court must be convinced that your parent meets the standards of the law and is unlikely to improve soon, or at all, before it issues a long-term commitment. Moreover, most states have definite requirements for reviewing all commitments at regular intervals. Although this may force you to go through unpleasant court procedures several times, it does help ensure that older people are not unfairly committed, and that people who improve after commitment are recognized and released.

In most states, being committed is quite different from being declared incompetent (Section 300). Thus a person may be hospitalized against his will, but still be legally able to manage his affairs. However, if a person is legally incompetent, it usually is easier to see that he gets proper supervision, since many states allow a guardian to sign him into a hospital as a "voluntary" patient, whether or not he is willing.

Never take commitment lightly. Whether it is short-term to a general hospital and meant primarily for evaluation and rapid treatment, or long-term to a nursing home or state psychiatric hospital, it makes your parent feel that he is no longer in control of his life. Although your parent's behavior may leave you little choice but commitment, work closely with a mental health professional to see if some other option can be arranged (for example, treatment as an outpatient or voluntary inpatient).

29.

Other Sources of Help

You may have little idea of where to turn for help with the problems of your aging parent; such problems have long been of low priority in our culture. Help is available, but you may have to hunt for it.

First, of course, you can turn to those old standbys, the neighbor, the doctor, and the minister or priest. A physician may be the person to check with first, particularly if the problem that concerns you is medical or psychological. Unfortunately, all too often a doctor's familiarity with resources for the elderly may be little greater than yours, and you may have to do your own research to obtain help for your parent.

Far and away your greatest aid sits in your own home: the telephone. Just about all the help locally available can be found by a diligent scrutiny of the telephone directory. Look in the sections devoted to city, county, state, and federal governments, particularly under such headings as "aging," "social services," and "senior citizens." Local information sources such as the Community Chest, churches, and the United Way may be able to direct you to the right people. Look in the Yellow Pages under the services you feel you need: for example, homemakers, nursing homes, or senior citizen service organizations. If you are persistent and use your imagination, the chances are that you will track down what you need, or find a knowledgeable person to answer your questions.

If a session with the local telephone directory doesn't suffice, consider contacting one of the agencies or organizations devoted solely to the elderly.

GENERAL INFORMATION

Every state has a public agency designed to serve the needs of older citizens. The agency may not provide services directly, but it should be familiar with almost everything within the state (and throughout the nation) which could be of use to you. These agencies have names like the Division of Aging, Commission on Aging, or Department of Aging. Call or write to the one in your state.

Alabama
Commission on Aging
740 Madison Ave.
Montgomery, AL 36104
(205) 832-6640

Alaska
Office on Aging
Department of Health and Social Services
Pouch H
Juneau, AK 99811
(907) 586-6153

Arizona
Bureau on Aging
Department of Economic Security
543 E. McDowall, Rm. 217
Phoenix, AZ 85004
(602) 271-4446

Arkansas
Office on Aging and Adult Services
Department of Human Services
7107 W. 12th
P.O. Box 2179
Little Rock, AR 72203
(501) 371-2441

California
Department of Aging
Health and Welfare Agency
918 J St.

Sacramento, CA 95814
(916) 322-3887

Colorado
Division of Services for the Aging
Department of Social Services
1575 Sherman St.
Denver, CO 80203
(303) 892-2651

Connecticut
Department on Aging
90 Washington St., Rm. 312
Hartford, CT 06115
(203) 566-7725

Delaware
Division of Aging
Department of Health and Social Services
2413 Lancaster Ave.
Wilmington, DE 19805
(302) 571-3481

District of Columbia
Office of Aging
Office of the Mayor, Suite 1106
1012 14th St., N.W.
Washington, DC 20005
(202) 724-5623

Florida
Program Office of Aging and Adult Services
Department of Health and Rehabilitation Services
1323 Winewood Blvd.
Tallahassee, FL 32301
(904) 488-2650

Georgia
Office of Aging
Department of Human Resources
681 Ponce de Leon Ave., N.E.

Atlanta, GA 30308
(404) 894-5333

Hawaii
Executive Office on Aging
1149 Bethel St., Rm. 311
Honolulu, HI 96813
(808) 548-2593

Idaho
Idaho Office on Aging
Statehouse
Boise, ID 83720
(208) 384-3833

Illinois
Department on Aging
2401 W. Jefferson
Springfield, IL 62706
(217) 782-5773

Indiana
Commission on Aging and Aged
Graphic Arts Building
215 N. Senate Ave.
Indianapolis, IN 46202
(317) 633-5948

Iowa
Commission on Aging
415 W. 10th St.
Jewett Building
Des Moines, IA 50319
(515) 281-5187

Kansas
Department of Aging
Biddle Building
2700 W. 6th St.
Topeka, KS 66606
(913) 296-4986

Kentucky
Center for Aging and Community Development
Department of Human Resources
403 Wapping St.
Frankfort, KY 40601
(502) 564-6930

Louisiana
Bureau of Aging Services
Division of Human Resources
Health and Human Resources Administration
P.O. Box 44282, Capitol St.
Baton Rouge, LA 70804
(504) 389-2171

Maine
Bureau of Maine's Elderly
Community Services Unit
Department of Human Services
State House
Augusta, ME 04333
(207) 289-2561

Maryland
Office on Aging
State Office Building
301 W. Preston St.
Baltimore, MD 21202
(301) 383-5064

Massachusetts
Department of Elder Affairs
110 Tremont St.
Boston, MA 02108
(617) 727-7750

Michigan
Office of Services to the Aging
300 E. Michigan
P.O. Box 30026
Lansing, MI 48909
(517) 373-8230

Minnesota
Governor's Citizens Council on Aging
Metro Square Building, Suite 204
7th and Robert Sts.
St. Paul, MN 55101
(612) 296-2544

Mississippi
Council on Aging
P.O. Box 5136, Fondren Station
510 George St.
Jackson, MS 39216
(601) 354-6590

Missouri
Office of Aging
Division of Special Services
Department of Social Services
Broadway State Office Building
P.O. Box 570
Jefferson City, MO 65101
(314) 751-2075

Montana
Aging Services Bureau
Department of Social and Rehabilitation Services
P.O. Box 1723
Helena, MT 59601
(406) 449-3124

Nebraska
Commission on Aging
State House Station 94784
P.O. Box 95044
Lincoln, NE 68509
(402) 471-2307

Nevada
Division for Aging Services
Department of Human Resources
Kinkead Building, Rm. 600

505 E. King St.
Carson City, NV 89710
(702) 885-4210

New Hampshire
Council on Aging
P.O. Box 786
14 Depot St.
Concord, NH 03301
(603) 271-2751

New Jersey
Division on Aging
Department of Community Affairs
P.O. Box 2763
363 W. State St.
Trenton, NJ 08625
(609) 292-4833

New Mexico
Commission on Aging
408 Galisteo—Villagra Building
Santa Fe,NM 87503
(505) 827-5258

New York
Office for the Aging
Agency Building No. 2
Empire State Plaza
Albany, NY 12223
(518) 474-5731

North Carolina
North Carolina Division for Aging
Department of Human Resources
213 Hillsborough St.
Raleigh, NC 27603
(919) 733-3983

North Dakota
Aging Services
Social Services Board of North Dakota

State Capitol Building
Bismarck, ND 58305
(701) 224-2577

Ohio
Commission of Aging
50 W. Broad St.
Columbus, OH 43216
(614) 466-5500

Oklahoma
Special Unit on Aging
Department of Institutions
Social and Rehabilitation Services
P.O. Box 25352
Oklahoma City, OK 73125
(405) 521-2281

Oregon
Program on Aging
Human Resources Department
772 Commercial St., S.E.
Salem, OR 97310
(503) 378-4728

Pennsylvania
Office for the Aging
Department of Public Welfare
Health and Welfare Building, Rm. 540
P.O. Box 2675
Seventh and Forster Sts.
Harrisburg, PA 17120
(717) 787-5350

Rhode Island
Division on Aging
Department of Community Affairs
150 Washington Court
Providence, RI 02903
(401) 277-2858

OTHER SOURCES OF HELP

South Carolina
Commission on Aging
915 Main St.
Columbia, SC 29201
(803) 758-2576

South Dakota
Office on Aging
Department of Social Services
State Office Building
Illinois St.
Pierre, SD 57501
(605) 224-3656

Tennessee
Commission on Aging
S & P Building, Rm. 102
306 Gay St.
Nashville, TN 37201
(615) 741-2056

Texas
Governor's Committee on Aging
Executive Office Building
411 W. 13th St., Floors 4 & 5
Austin, TX 78703
(512) 475-2717

Utah
Division of Aging
Department of Social Services
150 W. North Temple
Salt Lake City, UT 84102
(801) 533-6422

Vermont
Office on Aging
Agency of Human Services
81 River St. (Heritage 1)
Montpelier, VT 05602
(802) 828-3471

Virginia
Office on Aging
830 E. Main St., Suite 950
Richmond, VA 23219
(804) 786-7894

Washington
Office on Aging
Department of Social and Health Services
P.O. Box 1788—M.S. 45–2
Olympia, WA 98504
(206) 753-2502

West Virginia
Commission on Aging
State Capitol
Charleston, WV 25305
(304) 348-3317

Wisconsin
Division on Aging
Department of Health and Social Services
1 W. Wilson St., Rm. 686
Madison, WI 53703
(608) 266-2536

Wyoming
Aging Services
Department of Health and Social Services
Division of Public Assistance and Social Services
New State Office Building West, Rm. 288
Cheyenne, WY 82002
(307) 777-7561

Although these state agencies are probably the most reliable sources of useful information, you can also turn with profit to organizations such as those listed under Political Advocacy Groups in Chapter 25. For information about locally-based federal programs that may be of value to your parent, call the Federal Information Center in your area (listed in the telephone directory), or, if you can find no local listing, you can obtain a toll-free regional number by writing to:

FIC
General Services Administration, Room 6034
18th and F Sts., N.W.
Washington, DC 21415
(202) 566-1937

A comprehensive listing of programs for the elderly is available if you ask for the "Countrywide Information and Referral Resource List" (publication DHEW [SRS] 72-20907) from:

Administration on Aging
330 Independence Ave., S.W.
Washington, DC 20201

The Family Service Association, a nonprofit group composed of several hundred agencies, can help your parent make contact with numerous services available locally. Write to:

The Family Service Association
44 E. 23rd St.
New York, NY 10010

An additional general source on programs available of help to the older population is:

National Institute on Aging
National Institutes of Health
Bethesda, MD 20205

OTHER SOURCES

Food Stamps. Food stamps are available to people below a certain net income. To find out if your parent is eligible, contact the local (county) social service or public welfare office, or write to:

Nutrition Program for the Elderly
Administration on Aging (AoA)
Office of Human Development
U.S. Department of Health, Education, and Welfare
Washington, DC 20402
(202) 245-0213

Home-Care Agencies. Home-care services can be vital at times in allowing your parent to lead a fairly normal life at home. You can usually obtain information about what is locally available from the sources listed above (particularly the telephone directory). More general sources include:

National Homecaring Council
67 Irving Pl.
New York, NY 10003
(212) 674-4990

National Association of Home Health Agencies
205 C St., N.E.
Washington, DC 20002
(202) 547-7424

30.

The End of Life

What do you do when your parent is dying? You must attend to your parent's needs, your needs, and the matter-of-fact demands that hover around any death. It can be a turbulent time. Moreover, the way you deal with your parent during his last days, weeks, and months can determine whether or not his life concludes satisfactorily and with dignity.

302. *Your Parent's Needs.* The loss of life is the final loss. The emotional reactions your parent experiences when the nearness of death becomes evident are similar to those seen with losses of other kinds (Chapter 9). Expect numbness, a refusal to accept the idea of impending death, anger, depression, acceptance, or any combination of these (or other) strong emotions. Expect ups and downs. Most of all, the dying need to talk about death. All of this is part of the grieving process. A satisfactory adjustment to the idea of dying may take months, if it occurs at all. Of course, some people adjust quickly, particularly people who are very old, frail, and incapacitated, or those who are demoralized and "tired of it all." But most people will undergo the painful process of grieving in preparation for their own death.

One of your parent's needs at the end of his life is to anticipate his death early enough for him to grieve. Why? If grieving is so painful, why put your parent through it? Why not hide the diagnosis of a fatal illness or downplay an obvious deterioration? Isn't that more humane? No—for several reasons. (1) More often than not, it can't be done. Eventually, people facing death know it is approaching, whether or not you or the physician tells them. They find out the truth from the altered messages from their body, vague, evasive answers made to them, and the altered reactions of people close to them. By being less than truthful, you risk alienating your dying parent when he eventually discovers your duplicity. (2) Few lives are so tidy as to have no loose ends. Many people can profitably use the last weeks or months of life to make a will, help provide for the financial security of their family, make peace with estranged relatives, or seek religious consolation. Knowledge that time is short often provides the stimulus to do that. (3) Sad to say, the end of life is often the most productive time for your parent to get to know you, and you him. The intimacy of those last weeks and those last conversations may exceed anything that has gone before. You and your parent may develop a new appreciation and understanding of each other during the period of exceptional openness that often precedes death: a period when customary masks are discarded in favor of frankness and honesty. (4) Death is the last stage of growth. Your parent can use the pressure of time and the realization of mortality to review his life, reorder his priorities, and come to a more profound understanding of his life and values. The distinction between the superficial and the truly meaningful becomes clear.

Should we deny our parents the opportunity to put their affairs in order and make sense of their lives that so often accompanies the realization of impending death? Usually we shouldn't even though the temptation is strong to encourage them to minimize worrisome symptoms. However, a few elderly people are never ready to face death openly, and continue to deny its nearness until the end. Is your parent a person for whom the thought of death provokes intolerable anxiety? Would your parent's final days be made worse, rather than better, by learning that they were his last? It is frequently hard to tell. The rule of thumb is to allow your parent to be your guide as to how much to say. If he constantly redirects the conversation to more pleasant topics when you raise questions about his health, perhaps he is not ready to know more. On the other hand, you should introduce leading questions occasionally and be available when the barricades begin to crumble and he becomes ready to address his limited future realistically. For most people, that time will come. Encourage it.

The dying have other needs as well. Of course, there are the physical needs: to be kept free from pain, to be kept clean and comfortable, and to receive appropriate treatment. However, often the more important needs are social. The dying need companionship, support, and dignity. Yet too frequently it is there that we fail them; just when they require our support and our presence, we back off. We don't know what to say or how to act, and so are silent or absent. Those who are dying need meaningful conversation about topics important to them: you, their family, their lives, the futures of their loved ones. They need the dignity that comes with being taken seriously in their final hours.

What they don't need is our judgment about the way they choose to die. They don't need the spoken or unspoken expectation to be courageous, pleasant, silent and uncomplaining, or cooperative. Instead, they need the freedom to settle on their own final behavior, be it quiet or crabby, accepting or demanding. We should allow them, within limits, to meet their emotional requirements in their own way, without burdening them with our criticism. The impotence, discomfort, and desperation felt by some dying people can be relieved only by being unpleasant and demanding. Be patient, even though you find your parent's behavior trying and disappointing.

303. *The Right Time to Die.* Two horrors are associated with dying in the minds of some people: one real, one potential. The real horror is of living too long, of being kept alive by machines and intravenous feedings—and being incapacitated, dependent, impotent, in pain, and unable to communicate. In such a situation, we are not prolonging life, but death. The other—as yet unrealized—horror lies at the other pole: active euthanasia. A few people are worried that, sooner or later, the old, the frail, the debilitated will be "put out of their misery" by the injection of a lethal drug or by some other means. Of course, the expectation is that this would occur with the victim's permission, but some critics are concerned that such euthanasia decisions would ultimately be made by legal or political means. Between these extremes—life prolonged beyond all sense and life cut short artificially—lies a spectrum of times to die.

Is there any point in discussing the best time to die? Does your parent have any choice? Yes and no. Most people want to have some say about how their life ends. They don't want to hang on indefinitely, maintained by machines. Many critically ill individuals, those with little hope of recovery, reach a point where they prefer to die. In general, the sick fear death less than the healthy, and the elderly less than the young. Although some fight on to the last and never think of giving up, others no longer wish to endure the pain (though only a minority of those critically ill have serious pain), the lack of a future, or the indignity of being bathed and fed. Can your parent influence what happens next? Yes, even though this area is a legal morass. He can by developing an understanding with you and with his physician that when his time comes he be allowed to "slip away" without heroic measures. Such a tacit agreement is often more effective than any of the legal maneuvers often tried.

What is wrong with a legal approach? Simply, it usually doesn't work. The legal and legislative rules have not been worked out in most states in this country. Techniques like the "living will" (a declaration signed by your parent which states, in essence, that he or she wishes to die in a natural and timely way) have no legal validity in most places, and thus do not guarantee that your parent's wishes will be followed. And the legal questions raised are complicated. It is not just a matter of whether your parent should be allowed to die of natural causes. What if your parent is in serious pain? Is the doctor allowed to administer a lethal dose of medication at your parent's request? Can the physician leave by the bedside a similar dose which your parent can take himself? What if your parent is obviously uncomfortable but can no longer communicate or act on his own behalf? The list of possible situations goes on and on.

The legal complexity reflects even more complicated underlying ethical and moral dilemmas. There is no one easy answer to all situations, particularly an answer that can be arrived at beforehand. Of course, you first go to your parent to learn his wishes: does he want to be kept going until the last minute, or only if mentally clear; does he want antibiotics to fight infection but no heart and lung life supports; does he want to be fed artificially? But your parent may not know what he wants. What your parent wishes when healthy may not be what he wants when in severe pain or profoundly incapacitated. Coming to terms with his impending death may change your parent's wishes, or treatment of depression may change his perspective. In general, the best way for you to approach your parent's death is with flexibility. The physician should get to know your parent and his values so that he can better recommend alternative treatments as the final days wear on. Those final days proceed most smoothly and humanely if they are shared between you, your parent, and sensitive and concerned medical personnel. One of the greatest boons to this complicated and emotional issue has been the recent development of hospices (Section 305).

304. *Your Needs.* You, too, have emotional needs. The death of your parent signals the end of your oldest relationship and you will need to grieve. If your parent has been seriously ill for a long time it may be that much of your grieving has been accomplished already through anticipation of the loss. Even so, expect a reaction to the finality of his death. Only after a parent's death do many people realize all of the things left unsaid and issues left unresolved. Who doesn't carry a mental list of injustices committed and injustices endured, questions unanswered, angry accusations and angrier retorts, misunderstandings of all types? And who doesn't store memories of good times and shared intimacies? There are parts of your life, both good and bad, which belong to you and your parent alone, and which are available to and understood by no one else. That is what you are losing. Death erases any chance to make amends, to have a meeting of minds at

last, or to once again review the pleasures of the past together. It is this you grieve: not just your loss, but your lost chances.

So don't avoid the opportunity, often painful, to have final, close talks with your parent. It is striking that after a lifetime of living together the conversation best remembered is often the last one. Be available at the end, since the words you have with your parent at the end of his life are the words you will remember to the end of your life.

You have other needs, in addition to the need to grieve, which you should not neglect. During the time your parent is dying, and after, you need to continue living. Carry on with your normal activities and responsibilities, follow your interests, take breaks, and try not to become depleted. Get other family members and close friends involved with you and with your parent. You may find the support of people close to you to be the single greatest help during these difficult times. This passing of the torch from one generation to another is a unique opportunity to explore your deepest feelings and to grow. You are in a position to become more self-reliant and to redefine your values. Your exposure to death and to the profound (if fleeting) sense of being alone that it brings may force you to examine your life and actions in a most meaningful way. That such life-enhancing changes can occur during and because of your parent's death is not a desecration—it is the way life is.

Whatever changes you feel also may be experienced by other members of the family. Others will need to mourn as well. Be particularly aware of the problems that poorly handled sorrow may bring to your other parent (Chapter 9 and Section 38). There are support groups designed specifically to provide long-term help to those elderly people who have lost a partner. For information about groups in your area, write to:

National Association for Widowed People
P.O. Box 3564
Springfield, IL 62708
(217) 522-4300

Widowed Persons Service
AARP
1909 K St., N.W.
Washington, DC 20049
(202) 728-4370

Finally, make certain that financial and legal details are in order before your parent dies. Is the will finalized; are important papers and keys available; and are the funeral arrangements made? Problems are usually more easily resolved before your parent's death.

305. *Hospice*. The care of the dying has always been problematical. What is the kindest, most humane way to treat people during their final weeks and months? There is no general agreement. Clearly, it is best not to place them in an efficient but sterile hospital room, surround them with machines and strangers, and artificially keep their body functioning long beyond their wish or their need. It is equally harsh to provide no help or treatment, and to allow an older person to die in pain, poverty, and in isolation. However, between these extremes an alternative has developed which makes a lot of sense: the hospice.

The hospice is a facility, sometimes associated with a hospital and sometimes not, which provides care to people who have only a short period of time to live. Hospice is also a concept of care: a belief that most people would rather die naturally, without heroic medical efforts, in familiar surroundings, and cared for by family and friends rather than by strangers.

How does a hospice work? A person who appears to have fewer than six months to live makes application for care at a local hospice. The person must have decided not to pursue further curative medical care, although he may desire routine medical care for acute or chronic symptoms as well as treatment to control pain. From the time of entrance into the hospice program until death, he will usually be at home. There he will be cared for by family, friends, and visiting home-health-care professionals associated with the hospice. In the event that he needs more intensive care, he may enter the hospice for a few days (usually less than five), be stabilized, and return home. Each hospice provides a variety of services, including routine medical and nursing care, psychological counseling, nutritional advice, and, of course, numerous home-care services. Hospices emphasize family involvement, living at home, control of pain, confronting death meaningfully with the support of experienced counselors and family, and making dying a growing experience. The basic premise is that a dying person should be comfortable and talk about and understand what he is going through (grieve). Moreover, hospices generally attend to the psychological needs of family members during and for months after the death of the parent. Hospices were begun as a humanitarian response to the deplorable options for the dying, and so far they seem to be a marked improvement over most alternatives. Whether that will continue after hospices have become big business remains to be seen.

Over the last few years, hospices have developed throughout the United States. Moreover, Congress agreed to include hospice coverage under

Medicare, Part A, as of November 1, 1983 (inpatient care will be reimbursed at $271 per day and in-home care at $53 per day, with a ceiling of $6,500 during the last six months of life). Thus facilities are beginning to appear in most communities. If you have questions about the presence or future development of a hospice in your area, or about the hospice concept, write to:

National Hospice Organization
1901 N. Fort Meyer Dr., Suite 402
Arlington, VA 22209
(703) 243-5900

Hospice Office
Secretary of HEW
200 Independence Ave., S.W.
Washington, DC 20201

306. *Funerals.* I must admit to a bias here: I don't like the funeral industry. I see little value in expensive funerals, watertight and airtight aluminum caskets with costly interiors, $3,000 marble monuments, embalming, or any of the numerous other "necessities" foisted off on vulnerable, grieving families in the name of propriety and custom. Worse yet, some of these families can ill afford the expense. If, in the end, you opt for such a funeral, at least be aware that there is no need for it. No casket is perpetually airtight, and physical deterioration would not be prevented even if it were. Embalming will not preserve a body or prevent infection—nor is embalming usually required by law. Certainly think twice (or thrice) if the money to be spent is that of a surviving spouse who has years to live and limited funds. (Social Security Death Benefits, however, may help pay the cost of the funeral.) There are several less expensive alternatives to a traditional funeral.

Nonprofit memorial societies exist in most places to help arrange tasteful, inexpensive funerals. They recognize that the heart of a funeral lies in the memorial service that accompanies it: in the chance for the bereaved to assemble and commemorate the life of the person now gone. To locate a society near you, write to:

Continental Association of Funeral and Memorial Societies
1828 L St., N.W., Suite 1100
Washington, DC 20036
(202) 293-4821

Since the fate of the body is considered of lesser importance, memorial societies usually recommend cremation or very inexpensive coffins, but an alternative is the donation of the body to a medical school through the Uniform Anatomical Gift Act. Call the medical school for details. Organs may be donated to a specific hospital, medical school, or research institute by signing a Uniform Donor Card. Contact local facilities, or write to:

U.S. Public Health Service
National Institutes of Health
9000 Rockville Pike
Bethesda, MD 20014

Choice of funeral arrangements and disposal of the body are decisions your parent should make, if at all possible. On the other hand, memorial services are for the living, and should reflect not only what your parent would have wanted, but what you need.

INDEX